BEAUTY'S DAUGHTER

By Mollie Hardwick

Fiction

SARAH'S STORY
THE YEARS OF CHANGE
THE WAR TO END WARS
MRS. BRIDGES' STORY
BEAUTY'S DAUGHTER

Nonfiction

EMMA, LADY HAMILTON
MRS. DIZZY

In Collaboration with Michael Hardwick

CHARLES DICKENS ENCYCLOPEDIA
THE CHARLES DICKENS COMPANION
THE SHERLOCK HOLMES COMPANION
THE MAN WHO WAS SHERLOCK HOLMES
THE PRIVATE LIFE OF SHERLOCK HOLMES

Beauty's Daughter

Mollie Hardwick

Coward, McCann, & Geoghegan, Inc., New York

First American Edition 1977

SBN: 698-10805-1

Library of Congress Cataloging in Publication Data
Hardwick, Mollie.
  Beauty's daughter.

    1. Hart, Emily, 1782–1877?—Fiction.   I.   Title.
PZ4.H266Be3   [PR6058.A673]   823'.9'14   76-28761
Printed in the United States of America

Second Impression

ACKNOWLEDGMENTS

My grateful thanks are due to, among others, the following people : the Hon. Lady Meade-Fetherstonhaugh, Mrs Margaret Ross Freeman, Mr and Mrs William Lamb, Mrs Lily McCarthy, the late James George Hartshorn, former British Vice Consul at Calais, the Convent of the Holy Family, Balham, Mr Frank R. Argent, and Mrs Philippa Goodhart.

AUTHOR'S NOTE

This is a novel; but more than most novels it is based on fact –
fact that is to a large extent revealed here for the first time.

There have been countless books, both fact and fiction, based
on the life of Emma, Lady Hamilton. All have mentioned the
birth to her, in 1782, of a daughter christened Emily, by an unknown father for whom various identities have been suggested.
Correspondence recently discovered among the family papers by
Lady Meade-Fetherstonhaugh disclosed that Emily and her
mother were much attached, but parted in 1806. In 1811 Emily
wrote to Lady Hamilton pleading that she might be acknowledged. Thereafter she vanishes from history, as did that even
more shadowy child, 'Little Emma', whom Emma bore to Nelson
in 1804 and whose fate has hitherto been completely unknown.

Thanks to information kindly given to me by descendants and
relatives of Emma and her circle, following publication in 1969
of my biography, *Emma, Lady Hamilton*, I am able to recon-
struct the story of these two daughters for the first time. Where
facts are missing I have had to speculate and fill in, for this is, I
repeat, a novel; but the true story behind it is romantic and
dramatic enough to need no major invention.

MOLLIE HARDWICK

One

Beauty's Daughter

Suddenly summoned from a dreary boarding school to live with Lady Hamilton -
the belle of Regency society - Emily embarks on a series of adventures as she makes her way alone in London until her famous mother at last acknowledges her.

1

She scooped up a handful of pebbles and let them trickle through her fingers. There was a pretty pink one, and there a round white one, like an egg, and some dull grey ones; and at last a shell, a perfect one, that had been some tiny creature's house. Emily carefully laid it aside on her bonnet, which she had taken off when Mother was not looking. She was making a collection of shells. When she had enough, Mother had promised she would make her a necklace.

Guilty because she was bonnetless, she looked across the beach to see whether her sin had been detected. But Mother was still sitting on the breakwater, her hands in her lap, gazing out across the water of Dee to the mountains which Emily knew were Wales, where Great-grandmam lived, and where she had been staying herself until she and Mother and Grandma came to Parkgate.

She had been happy in Great-grandmam's cottage, playing with the black cat, Twm, who had infinite patience and never scratched the small hands that treated him so roughly. 'Knows you're only a baby, that he does,' Great-grandmam had said. 'But don't you try him too far, bach.' Then she let Twm out, and gave Emily the bull to play with, the china bull with the little dog snarling at its feet. It was one of her greatest treasures. Emily had had to be kept occupied, for she was so restless and fretful, waiting for Mother to come for her.

And at last Mother had come, by coach from London to Chester, and then by the carrier's cart to the village of Hawarden, where Great-grandmam lived in Swan Cottage; and Emily had been snatched up and hugged close to someone who smelt sweeter even than Great-grandmam's lavender bush, and had been kissed and cried over.

Emily had never seen anyone as beautiful as Mother. There

was an angel in a picture at Swan Cottage, a lovely lady carrying a baby off to heaven, but Mother was much prettier; Emily had never seen anyone like her. She had on a beautiful straw hat with a blue ribbon round it that tied under her chin, and a white dress of nice soft stuff, and her long hair was the colour of shiny chestnut-conkers. Emily was very interested in colour. She associated Mother's blue eyes with the lavender-smell of her dress, because they were almost the same shade, and she saw that Mother's face was quite different from anybody else's.

After they had all had a good hug and Mother had eaten some supper, Emily was lifted on to Mother's lap, and they sat in the only good chair, by the fireplace. She could remember some of what had been said.

'She's very well grown for only two,' Mother had said to Great-Grandmam.

'Indeed, yes. Grown out of all her clothes, she is.'

'I'll make her some pretty ones. I'm very handy with my needle, Grandmam!'

'There's a change, now, from my wild girl!' Great-grandmam was smiling.

'Oh, I'm that domestic you wouldn't believe. I can cook and give orders and do accounts and write beautiful.'

'There's clever.'

Mother's face became even more like an angel's. 'Oh, 'tis not my doing; 'tis all his, Greville's. Oh, Grandmam, how I love him! How I worship him, that has took me from poverty and distress, and made a lady of me!'

Great-grandmam shook her head slowly, in wonder. Emily put up a fat hand and stroked Mother's cheek.

'Pretty,' she said. 'Like the bull.'

Mother's eyes opened wide. 'What bull, my little treasure?' She laughed. 'I've been compared to a good many things, but never a bull before.'

'She means that, Emma,' and Great-grandmam pointed to the china group. 'She loves to play with it. Likely your cheek feels smooth to her, much the same as that.'

Emily nodded. 'Got no holes in, not like Aunt Connor's.'

'She means the smallpox marks,' Great-grandmam explained. 'Sarah Connor's badly marked, and most of her girls. Most of us round here's spoiled with it. I mind when I was a little thing my Mam sent me out to play with a raw onion in my hand that she said would keep me free of the pox, but I got it just the same.' She touched her face, where the soft wrinkles had long ago covered up the ugly pockmarks.

Mother held Emily at arm's length. 'Sharp eyes you have, little Emy, to notice that. Shall I tell you why my face is pretty? Because when I was quite small I was put to service as a nursery-maid with a clever doctor, not far from here. And he knew how to stop people from catching the smallpox.'

'How?' Emily asked.

'Oh, 'tis an ugly performance, with a needle they stick in your arm.' She pushed up her sleeve and showed Emily a lumpy blue scar at the top of a round white arm. 'Never mind, 'tis worth anything to keep one's looks.' She scrutinised Emily's wondering face. 'You've my eyes, baby, and goodish lashes, and I dare say your hair will curl with training. But you've missed my mouth. A very great painter says 'tis the eighth wonder of the world.' She smiled at her reflection in the dim blackened mirror on the wall, and Great-grandmam shook her head again, as if she were sad about something. Emily lay back against Mother's breast, and heard them talking and talking, about a coach and guineas and Greville, until the voices got fainter and she fell asleep.

Emily's mother shifted uneasily on the breakwater until her back was against a tallish spar. She was uncomfortable, her feet cold in the smart town shoes with the high front and the buckle, stained now with sea-water. It was a grey, dull day, English summer without sunshine, only an oppressive feeling in the air, neither one thing nor the other. She was uncomfortably aware of the symptoms she had come to the seaside to cure, a painful, irritating rash on her arms and legs: nests of weeping, itching spots that kept her awake at night and made her feel contaminated by day. Salt water was the cure, Greville's doctor had said: sea-water baths and a tumbler of the nasty stuff every twelve hours. Indeed, it seemed not so bad as it had been.

She found a piece of wood lying by her hand, a fragment of jetsam once part of a ship, and began to draw idly with it on a patch of pale sand. A heart pierced by an arrow. Herself, Emma Hart, transfixed with love for Charles Francis Greville, the aristocrat who had made a lady out of a poor country girl from Cheshire, once called Emily Lyon. She had not quite understood why, when Greville took her under his protection, he had made her change her name. She believed vaguely that it was something to do with putting a barrier between herself as she now was, respectable mistress-in-keeping to him, the second son of the Earl of Warwick, and herself as she had been, daughter of a long-dead Cheshire blacksmith, Henry Lyon, brought up by a mother who took in sewing and a grandmother who had carried coals to Chester until rheumatism attacked her, namely Dame Kidd of Hawarden, Flintshire.

What a parade of animals we are, she thought wryly: Hart, Lyon, Kidd. Like a child's primer, the sort of primer from which she had learned to read and write at the age of seventeen, when Greville had rescued her from disgrace.

She looked across the beach at small Emily, who was now frowning with temper because she had not found a shell recently – Emily with her own blue eyes and with the fox-fair hair of Sir Harry Fetherstonhaugh.

It had seemed like a dream when Sir Harry, that elegant young sporting fop, had taken her up and transported her to Uppark, his mansion in Sussex. She had known it was wrong to give herself to a man and go into keeping. Her Mam had said it was wrong, had always brought her up proper. But Mam had been a long way off at the time, living in as sewing-woman at a noble house, and she, sixteen and far too beautiful, had been kicked from pillar to post as servant, shopgirl, artist's model, and

general skivvy in a house which nobody could mistake for anything but a brothel.

Ah, well – a dream, not a year long. Wild and silly and only
sixteen, intoxicated by borrowed dresses and fast horses and
gentlemen's admiration, how could she not go wrong? But she
had been silly, never truly wicked. She closed her eyes, and was
again in the bedroom at Uppark, kneeling, clinging about Sir
Harry's silk-stockinged legs, partly consumed by distress while
another part of her (O vain Emma!) watched her performance,
interestedly, as a Fair Suppliant.

'The child is yours and no one else's, Sir Harry, indeed, indeed
it is! Though you caught me kissing with Mr Payne it meant
nothing, truly.'

He had pulled himself free and moved away to the window.

'And with Greville also, I suppose?'

She sobbed. 'He was only being kind.'

He turned and stared contemptuously at her thickening body.
'Very kind, it seems. *Très gentil, ma belle.*' (It was Sir Harry's
way to lard his conversation with bits of French which Emma
vainly tried to understand.) 'Well, be it Greville's or whose, I
am sick of you and your loose ways with my money. Twelve
guineas in Petersfield for a hoop skirt, *par foi*!'

'You told me—'

'Never mind what I told you. I am not accountable to trulls.
Go to the housekeeper and she will give you the coach-fare to
London.'

'To *London*?'

'I found you there, did I not?'

'But I've no home there. Nobody.'

'You've a mother, have you not?' He sneered. 'Of a sort . . .'

'Mam's at Stansted. I won't have her told!'

Sir Harry was tired of the conversation. He turned and strode
out, leaving her on the floor, feeling foolish and wretched. Already she saw on her elbow the rash which always followed upon
her nervous upsets, losing her nights of sleep and causing her
bitter humiliation when she saw strangers' eyes stray to her blis-

15

tered, itching hands. She looked round the darkening, bare room, a man's room, hunting clothes flung on a chair, an ancestral portrait hanging askew, a riding-crop in the fender beside the poker, and a dirty cartoon about the Prince of Wales displayed on the mantelshelf.

In this room she knew, she was sure, her baby had been conceived. It was a Fetherstonhaugh if everybody had their rights, Sir Harry being a bachelor as he was. And instead it would be – what? Another bundle on the orphanage steps, another little bloated body floating in the Thames among dead cats and dogs? Emma threw herself flat on the carpet and wept until her eyes were swollen up like plums and her throat was hoarse from sobbing.

And after all the baby had been born decorously, like any legitimate offspring, in the back bedroom of a villa in the hamlet of Paddington Green, the country retreat of Charles Greville. Little Emily's blue eyes had opened upon pretty sprigged wallpaper, the bough of an apple-tree tapping gently on the window-pane. Her modest christening had taken place at St Mary's Church, just round the corner, and when the christening party had returned home Mr Greville had put a fine silver pap-boat into the baby's curling hands as a baptismal gift.

Two years ago. Now it was June 1784 and the baby had become a lively moppet of two. She was running across the beach, holding out her hand and shouting. Emma tore her thoughts away from the beloved image of Greville, the dark, melancholy face, the full proud lips that had kissed her into blind adoration of him.

'Quietly, quietly! What have you there?'

Emily stammered incoherently, trying to say that she had found one of the creatures that lived in the shell-houses. She opened her fist to show Mother a small crab, battered from her clutch, still feebly moving.

'You horrid, cruel child!' Emma took the crab tenderly in her long fingers and hurried down the beach to lay it in a pool by the water's edge. Submerged, it began to stir, moved away and hid itself beneath a stone. Emily had come to watch. 'Alive,' she said.

'No thanks to you, little wretch!' Emma spun round and gave her daughter a resounding slap on the arm, bringing an angry colour up. The baby's eyes brimmed and she broke into loud sobs, tears rolling down her fat cheeks and splashing on to her faded pinafore, while Emma watched, helpless to comfort, hating the child and herself, not understanding why she had struck the blow so heavily, yet knowing she would strike it again if occasion served.

Little Emily was drawing the backs of her hands across her eyes, sniffing and gulping. She clutched at Emma's skirts and looked up beseechingly.

'Mother!' she said.

In a flash Emma was on her knees, her arms around her daughter.

'My poor baby, my little one! How could I be so cruel? There, give Mother a kiss.' As her lips found the wet cheek she saw herself and the child exactly as Greville's friend George Romney would see them if he were here; dear, brilliant, mad Romney who adored her so, who had put her on to canvas as a nymph, a praying nun, a Bacchante, a spinstress, each an unsurpassably lovely image of divine beauty. What Romney wished her to be, Emma became: sad, happy, noble, humble or wild. Now she was ideal motherhood, so young that she would have seemed the child's elder sister but for the maternal swell of her bosom, the tender curve of her arm about the baby shoulders, the fall of her hair above the upturned face. It was a pose she must remember. She picked up the heavy child and ran with her back to their lodging.

Mrs Darnwood's house, almost the middle one of the terrace facing the Dee, was comfortable, clean and decent. A sailor's wife, Mrs Darnwood had no fondness for her own company. She liked to keep a full house – 'no lodging without board' to discourage fly-by-nights – and did so with the help of her mother and her sister Polly, a young lady of whom Emma was a little in awe because she spoke so very correctly, pleasant though her manner was.

After supper, which was a general meal taken in Mrs Darnwood's basement room, Emma lingered. The prospect of sitting upstairs in the room she and the child shared was not entertaining, although its window looked out over the silver waters of the estuary, which turned at low tide to an expanse of shining sand. In parts it was quicksand: there were horrid stories of donkeys and children having sunk in it.

Mrs Darnwood was looking through a copy of the *Gentleman's Magazine* which Emma had brought from London.

'Only fancy, a tax on ribbons now!' she exclaimed. 'What will they think of next to persecute us poor women with?'

'What, indeed?' Emma sighed. 'With hair-powder such a price already . . .'

Polly's eyes were bright with interest. 'La, Mrs Hart, do you wear powder in London? How vastly smart.'

'Oh, now and then.' Emma waved airily. 'At Ranelagh 'tis considered the thing, or at a ton-ish private assembly.'

The sisters took it in eagerly. 'What high circles your husband must move in, Mrs Hart,' said Mrs Darnwood.

Emma felt herself blushing. 'My – Mr Hart has a good many fashionable acquaintances. But we live quiet enough at home.'

'And I can see you long to get back there, for all the pleasures of Parkgate. Oh, Polly and I have noted you looking every day for the post – haven't we, sister?'

Emma's blush deepened. 'Mr – Mr Hart is away at present, in Wales, with a relative who has estates there. I've no doubt he's much taken up with business, or he'd have written by now.' (If only, if only he would! she thought. Only one letter in a month. Did that really mean preoccupation with his uncle's Pembrokeshire lands, or something ominous – such as a Welsh heiress? Greville was very fond of money, and Emma had overheard one or two disquieting remarks.)

'Indeed,' she went on quickly, 'ours is a neat quiet house, but

18

home is home though 'tis ever so homely, I always say.'

The others nodded.

'Every Sunday we go to church, and sometimes there is one or two friends comes from London, but we keep little company and are quite content.' Emma raised her teacup (tea was only served to favoured lodgers) and sipped it, crooking her little finger as she had seen fine ladies do.

'One would never think,' said Polly, 'that your little girl came from London. She's more like one of our country children.'

Silently Emma cursed the Flintshire accent her grandmother had allowed Emily to acquire.

'Why, she has spent the last year with – with relatives across the river, and speaks a little rough, I must confess. But being in company with such well-spoken ladies as yourself, ma'am, must sure improve her.'

'Oh,' Polly was quick to conciliate, 'I meant no wrong of the child. She's so quick and noticing, and so fond of you, one can see.'

'Yes.' Emma smiled and sighed. 'We have many a little quarrel, but always kiss and make up. I fear my own temper's at fault, for I've not been much used to the society of children.'

'You may leave her with me when you go, ma'am.' Mrs Darnwood's suggestion was only half jocular. 'An empty cradle makes an empty heart, they say, and with my man so long at sea I fear 'twill stay empty this year and more.' Polly patted her sister's hand sympathetically.

'Is he far from England, ma'am?' Emma enquired.

'In the Leeward Islands or thereabouts, sailing in the *Latona* under Captain Sandys. An amiable commander, Will tells me, but too much given to—' Mrs Darnwood sketched an elbow-raising gesture. 'Sherry, of all things. Sometimes four bottles a night. It seems he has some young lady on his mind and takes this way to drown his sorrows. Will says there's a friend of his, Captain Nelson of the *Boreas*, bound for the same station, has reasoned and reasoned with him but all to no use.'

'Ah.' Emma shook her head. 'Gentlemen.'

They fell to talking happily about gentlemen and their strange yet endearing ways, Emma emboldened to describe some of Mr Hart's. Three charming heads close together over the teacups, they might have chattered all the evening but that Mrs Burton, Mrs Darnwood's mother, put her head round the door.

'Mrs Hart, I don't wish to disturb you, but the little girl's crying for you. I think you'd best go up.'

For a moment a shadow of annoyance lay over Emma's lovely face. Then she summoned up one of her sunshine smiles.

'My poor baby! The time has gone so pleasant, ladies, I'd forgot she'd been alone so long.' She made them a pretty curtsey and started off up the two flights of stairs.

In the second-floor front room Emily was shrieking, short regular shrieks of extreme horror. She had fallen asleep soon after Mother had left her, in the pale sunset light of the July evening. When she wakened it was dark, the furniture muffled in shadows. She had forgotten where this room was, and a moment before waking she had seemed to be in another room, one she had never seen : a big, cheerless room, with little tables and chairs in the middle of the floor, and no carpet or wallpaper. She had felt very cold and dreadfully frightened, for outside this room she knew there were only the shining sands of Dee, the sands that swallowed little donkeys and disobedient children; and if she strayed outside it she would sink into them, till they closed right over her head.

Now the room had gone, but she was in the dark and still frightened to death. She continued to shriek.

The door opened. Mother stood there, holding a candle high and looking extremely cross.

'Now then! Whatever's the matter?' She went over to the disordered cot and extracted Emily from a tangle of bedclothes.

'Oh, you naughty, wicked girl – wet again! Twopence that costs me for every sheet Mrs Darnwood has to wash, and what will she think of you? Get up this instant!'

Emily's automatic shrieks dwindled into gasps. She clambered out of bed and stood, chilled, while Mother impatiently dragged the undersheet off and folded back the blanket underneath to make a dry place. Then she pulled off Emily's nightdress.

'Soaking too. Well, you've no more clean. You must make do with one of my shifts. And a fresh diaper.'

The clumsy diaper, which Emily hated wearing, was adjusted, and the linen petticoat tied under her arms with tapes. She made a very curious sight, a short figure standing in a great spread of linen, like a very small candle in a pool of its own wax. Suddenly Emma began to laugh and laugh.

'Bless me, child, if you don't look the very image of Mrs Kelly, the Irish dwarf!' She rocked with laughter, and Emily joined in, her high babyish laugh still with the last of her tears in it. Emma put her back into bed and retrieved from the floor the much-loved rag-doll Great-grandmam had made.

'Here's Gwynydd, see, and all your shells are on the table where you can touch them if you want. Now be a good girl and go to sleep.'

'Sing.'

'Oh, fudge! Oh, if I must – if 'twill quiet you.' She was only reluctant in show, for she loved to sing. Greville praised her voice and was having it trained by a lady who came three times a week to teach her.

Sitting in the bedside chair, one hand clasping her daughter's, she fixed her eyes on the distant dark outlines of the mountains. There came from nowhere a song to her mind, not one of the elegant drawing-room songs that Greville liked, 'Fair Phillis', or 'My Mother Bids Me Bind My Hair', but an old sad ballad of love and death.

' "O where have ye been, Lord Randal, my son?
O where have ye been, my handsome young man?"
"I've been with my sweetheart – Mother, make my bed soon.
For I'm sick to the heart, and I fain would lie down." '

Long years afterwards, alone in the dreary room of her nightmare, Emily would still vaguely remember the warmth of the shift around her, the comforting feel of the doll in her arms, and the clear voice singing.

That same week the postman called at last. Emily saw her mother open a letter, read it, and run off with it, crying. Emily knew that she spent a long time answering it, up in their room, crouching over the table, the paper aslant under her hand as she covered it with her big scrawly writing, her pink tongue showing, a frown between her brows. Emily kept pulling at her skirt, begging her to come and bathe, but Mother always shooed her away, and at last she went sadly off by herself to collect shells.

Then another letter came. This time there were no tears, but another long letter was written. After this Mother was very kind, fonder then usual, playing with her for hours and taking her bathing every day from the van that the horse pulled into the sea. At first they would romp about at the edge, splashing each other, Emily squealing with delight; then Mother would swim away and far out till all Emily could see of her was a dark auburn head bobbing out of the water like a seal's, and Emily would begin to shriek for fear of losing her.

The bathing-woman and the other ladies disporting themselves in the sea crowded round Emily to comfort her, and she became quite friendly with them. But when Mother returned, she was always whisked away from them and taken back to be dressed.

'Best keep ourselves to ourselves,' she was told.

Mother was usually impatient when Emily walked beside her, staggering after that swift stride on short plump legs, but now she slackened her pace to match the child's. Together they strolled as far as the Boat House Inn, because it was entertaining to hear the noise of singing and a fiddle merrily played. At other times they walked by the sea-wall, sitting down when Emily's legs were tired to watch the packet-boat sail for Ireland, and Mother would tell Emily about her own childhood.

'I wasn't a lady then, Emy, but a wild giddy romp, just like you, and I knew neither my letters nor my twice-times. You will be much cleverer than that when you go to school.'

'What's school?'

'A place where – oh, where you learn all sorts of things.'

'Is school nice?'

'Why . . . yes.'

'Will you be there?'

Mother's arm came round in a hug. 'I shan't be allowed there. But we shall see each other . . .' Her voice died away and her eyes were troubled.

'When will I go?'

'Oh – one day. Not yet. First we shall go home, to London, and live in a pretty house with Greville.'

'Who's Gevel?'

'Oh, Emy, Mr Greville is a most kind gentleman. He has been an angel to me – so he will be to you. We shall be so very happy.'

'Who?'

'You, and I, and Mr Greville, and Grandmam, my mother – don't you remember little Grandmam?'

Emily could just remember a small lady who had come to Swan Cottage a long time ago and brought her a present. She thought it curious that if Mother was so happy about their going to London she should look so sad.

Emma was writing over and over again in her mind the words she had penned laboriously to Greville – Greville who was to play Fate and guide her daughter's future.

. . . I will give her up to you intirely. Do what you will with her . . . you shall take her, put her there where you propose. . . . You don't know, my dearest Greville, what a pleasure I have to think that she will be comfortable and happy . . . I come in to your way a-thinking hollidays spoils children. It takes there attention of from there school, it gives them a bad habbit. When they have been a month and goes back this does not pleas then, and that is not right, and they do nothing

23

but think wen they shall go back again. Now Emily will never expect what she never had.

At the end of that week they said goodbye to the Darnwood family and to Parkgate, and joined the coach for the long journey to London.

2

Emily was too young to be able to analyse the great superiority of the villa in Edgware Row, Paddington Green, to anything she had seen before. Great-grandmam's cottage had been a comfortably untidy place for a child to romp in, with a ladder instead of a staircase leading to the tiny loft where the old lady slept. Emily had a turn-up bedstead downstairs, and frequently enjoyed the company of Livvy, a brown hen who preferred to roost on the end of the mantelpiece rather than in the fowl-house at the bottom of the garden. Sometimes an adventurous pig would wander in on a winter day, hoping for the solace of the rag rug in front of the fire, to be ejected firmly when Great-grandmam discovered its presence. It was the way most country-folk lived, though luxurious compared with some cottages.

After Grandmam's, Mrs Darnwood's house had seemed to Emily awesomely large and grand, but lacking in the things which made Swan Cottage interesting: pigs and hens, and Grandmam's spinning-wheel which had whirred Emily to sleep after her dinner, and the box of 'treasurers' she was given to play with when she had been good. The stairs were steep for small legs, the windows high. Only in the basement, where they ate, was it homely, smelling deliciously of new bread and cooking.

But Edgware Row was a paradise. The rooms were not too vast for a person who was not three feet high herself, and they were full of the most beautiful furniture, some of it covered with silk and velvet woven with flowers, the wood, like the floorboards, polished like glass. The pretty wallpapers were hardly to be seen for the amount of pictures on them, some of Mother and other ladies, some of buildings and country places. There were carpets of rich red on the staircase, and of many colours in the rooms, on which no pig would have dared to set trotter.

Emily's room, her very own, was at the back, next to the one in which, Mother said, she had been born. It was as fine and dainty as a lady's. There was a dressing-table with a valanced dimity skirt on, a bed draped with curtains of white net, a cupboard on each side of the fireplace, a little gilt clock with a cupid sitting on it. Through the low window Emily could see the long garden which ended in an ivy bower containing a seat. There were two statues, one of a white lady and the other of a shepherd-boy with a dog.

Emily's delighted exploration of her premises was cut short by Mother. With her was a little girl of no more than thirteen, a tiny creature with a sharp pinched face, wearing a plain brown stuff dress and a white apron and mob-cap.

'This is Sally, Emily, who's to be your little maid as well as mine. Now see you're good and make no trouble for her.'

Sally and Emily exchanged timid smiles.

'Look after her now, there's a dear girl,' said Mother to Sally. 'I declare this pesky rash is on me again, and I've a running cold. I'll take to my bed and be miserable in comfort. Bring me a posset of hot buttered rum, will you, to bring out the fever?' With her hand to her head she vanished, like a beautiful distracted spirit.

'Can I wash you now, Miss Emily, and put you on a clean frock?' asked Sally. With a wide, gap-toothed smile, Emily stretched out her arms above her head to have her travelling-dress removed. She was going to enjoy having a lady's maid.

It was fortunate that Emily and Sally got on well, for the little maid was almost Emily's only company for the next week. Emma's ailment was not the nervous rash she had gone to Parkgate to cure, but a sharp attack of measles. When Sally took Emily to her mother's bedroom next morning they found her sitting up in bed examining with horror her reflection. From hair to breast she was one mass of red spots. She flung out a hand dramatically.

'Keep away! 'tis the plague! Don't touch me, don't come

26

near! Sally, send the child into the garden and run yourself for the doctor!'

For a week Emily was shut out from the room where her mother lay feverish and wretched. She would have nobody nurse her for fear they should catch the infection, but Sally was allowed to bring in such food and medicines as she needed. Emily, lurking behind Sally's skirts to get a glimpse of the beloved face, heard: 'I feel like a lost sheep, Sally, alone like this all day with not a soul near me. Thank God Greville is not here to see me such a hideous fright! But if only Mam would come . . .'

On the Friday Emily's grandmother arrived. Mrs Cadogan, as she was called, though her right to the name was sketchy, appeared at the kitchen door as Sally, Emily and Molly, the other maid, were eating their supper. It was a tribute to her authority that both maids rushed to help her off with her pelisse and fetch her a chair, nearly colliding in their zeal. She was short, neat, fair-skinned, with traces of the pretty girl she had been in her blue eyes and the soft dark hair, fast greying, which escaped from her massive cap.

'Well, Emily,' she said. 'My, how you've grown! Come and give me a kiss.' She surveyed the kitchen. 'Not much cleaning been done in here since I went away, has there? Oh, yes, I know Sally's got two ladies to look after now, but there'll have to be more elbow-grease put into it than this. Now you can brew some fresh tea, for I can see from here that's not fit to drink, and then I'll go up to Mrs Hart.'

'If you please, ma'am,' Sally ventured, 'madam said no one wasn't to go near her.'

Mrs Cadogan surveyed her loftily. 'If you think I'm going to catch anything from my own daughter that I've nursed these twenty years you're sadly mistaken.' And having drunk two cups of tea, with a nip of her special cordial, she departed upstairs.

Under her expert care Emma was up and about again in a few days, her skin unmarked and interestingly pale. Emily was disappointed to find that her mother was disinclined to play games with her or take her for walks, but would sit for hours in the morning-room at her *bonheur du jour*, writing long, long letters and staring out at the church across the green and the elegant houses that neighboured it. When Emily pulled at her skirt for attention she was rewarded only with an absent smile.

'Am I to tell Greville you send him your duty, Emily?'

Emily considered this question, but being able to make neither head nor tail of it, nodded. She had grown used to hearing Greville's name with no clear idea of who he was, but the servants spoke of him most respectfully, and Mother's face became rapt with happiness at his very name. Emily thought hard.

'Have I seen him?'

'Yes, when you were a baby. But you don't remember that.'

'Will he come soon?'

'Yes, oh yes, please God! It has been nine long weeks since I saw him. I think I shall die with the pleasure of it.'

Emily's mouth turned down, and her mother caught her to her breast.

'Not die truly, silly baby. 'Tis only a form of words. How you will love him, as I do, for he has been all father to you.'

'*Is* he my father?' Emily enquired.

'No, child, no. Your father was – a country gentleman. We'll not talk about him.'

'Is he bad?'

Emma laughed. 'No, indeed. It is just that – we had a little quarrel, and after that he had no wish to live with me.'

Emily hugged her mother's knees. She could not imagine anyone not wishing to live with someone so lovely and kind.

August passed into September, and one evening at dusk Greville came home.

Emily was in bed, almost asleep, hearing very far off the hoot of the white owl which lived in an oak-tree beyond the garden. She was barely aware of the arrival, the rumble of coach-wheels, the slam of a door, Emma's happy voice in the hall. Then her bedroom door was flung open and her mother stood there, flushed and smiling.

'Emily – he is come at last! Quick, get up and you shall come downstairs.' Still half asleep, Emily was bundled out of bed and into her wrapper, the ribbons that fastened it down the front tied hurriedly by her mother's trembling fingers. Downstairs they went, to be met on the next landing by Mrs Cadogan.

'Emma, what's got into you, bringing the child down at this hour? She's half dead with sleep.'

'No, she's not – are you, my poppet? Besides, Greville expects her.'

Mrs Cadogan shook her head and went off to order preparations for a meal.

Instead of descending to the hall, as Emily had expected, her mother approached the door of the drawing-room on the first floor, a room Emily had glimpsed but never entered. Its glories, enhanced by the light from the hanging crystal chandelier, dazzled her heavy eyes as she stumbled after her mother.

'Greville, see, here is my girl.'

The gentleman sitting in the wing-chair by the fire turned his powdered head languidly in Emily's direction. He wore a fine but sombre suit of dark grey, and a mulberry waistcoat richly embroidered with silken flowers. His elegant legs were encased in white silk stockings, high-arched feet resting on the fender, showing off the twinkle of cut-steel buckles. Emily could not have said what she expected, but it was not this nobly aristocratic face, dark-eyed and dark-complexioned, the aquiline nose of the Earls of Warwick, the full mouth, almost cupid's-bow in shape, which now drooped with displeasure. His first words echoed Mrs Cadogan's.

'Surely the child ought to be in bed, Emma?'

'She was all agog to see you,' said Emma untruthfully, 'and I could not refuse. There, Emily, greet Mr Greville, our dear benefactor.'

Emily's idea of a greeting was to run forward and lift her face for a kiss. Mr Greville recoiled in his chair as though a serpent had approached him, shaking off the small hands which clutched his immaculate coat.

'For Heaven's sake keep the child off, Emma! I don't wish my clothes ruined.'

Emma threw herself down at his feet, one arm round her daughter, a pleading, roguish smile on her lips; a touchingly beautiful group of Mother and Child. 'You have a thousand kisses for me, I know. Can you not spare one for her?'

With a sigh of resignation Greville bent his head stiffly and imprinted a chilly kiss on Emily's brow. She burst into loud tears, her face scarlet and her fists clenched, her feelings thoroughly outraged. Why should this horrid gentleman not wish to kiss her? Everybody kissed her: Mother, Grandmam, the maids, even Mr Miles at the livery stables when they travelled by coach. She howled louder and Greville clapped his hands over his ears.

'For God's sake take that brat away! Do you want me deafened? You know how I hate a din.'

Hurriedly, making a prettily apologetic face at him, Emma took Emily's hand and all but ran out of the room with her. Out of Greville's hearing, she stopped and asked, 'What possessed you to make that terrible noise? I was ashamed of you.'

'I don't like him! I don't like him!' Emily scrubbed at the spouting tears with the backs of her hands. Emma gave her a sharp slap, and as further punishment returned her to bed unkissed. There, still sobbing at intervals, she eventually cried herself to sleep. If she had been able to overhear the conversation in the drawing-room that night, and to understand it, she might have thought more kindly of her mother's anger.

'The child is utterly spoiled,' said Greville.

'No, not at all. She behaves very good and obedient as a rule.'

'You wrote to me from Parkgate that she was wild and giddy.'

'Only a little, and at first, being used only to Gran's company—'

He frowned. 'I wish you would not use these low, common expressions, Emma. How often have I told you that I dislike hearing you call Mrs Cadogan "Mam"? If you refer to your grandmother, say so.'

'Oh, Greville, I'm sorry. I will try to please you in all things, indeed, indeed I will.'

'Then please me by consenting to have that child dispatched to school as soon as arrangements can be made.'

She planted herself on his knees and curled an arm seductively round his neck. But neither the fragrance of her hair nor the exciting warmth of her body could melt his displeasure.

'You did promise it, may I remind you.'

'I know, but – I'm grown so fond of her, and she is so bright and clever. 'Tis precious dull when you're not here, Greville; only the maids for M— my mother and me to talk to, and little to do but learn lessons and work on silk. She keeps us all cheerful.'

'A squawling brat about the house don't contribute to *my* cheerfulness, as well you know, Emma.'

'I tell you, it was only a tantrum. And it may well be that *you* will father children one day – please God, by me. Will you call them squawling brats?'

'I shall make sure they are confined to the nursery, where they belong. Drawing-rooms are not for children.'

Emma fired up. 'You speak as though they was pigs! My Emily's as clean and good a child as you could find in a month of Sundays, and with good blood in her too.'

Greville turned a sardonic gaze on her. 'I presume you refer to Sir Harry Fetherstonhaugh's blood? In that case, and always supposing she *is* his daughter, may we expect her to grow up addicted to cock-fighting, dice and whoring? A charming prospect.'

Emma dissolved in a passion of tears. Greville sighed, and applied himself to comforting her with kisses. In bed that night it was at though they had never quarrelled. In the room across the landing, the subject of their dispute lay sucking her thumb for comfort, a frown crossing her baby brow as bad dreams nagged at her.

After this bad beginning a mutual avoidance programme was

31

the only possible sequel. Emily's childish intuition was aware of Greville's unfriendliness, and she took to playing where he was not likely to be; the house was fortunately large enough to allow of this. Soon she had forgotten their first disastrous meeting. Emma, longing to bring the man and child together, still confident that she would win Greville over, let the situation be as it would. But she noticed with pain that he was spending more time than usual at his town house in Portman Square and in the aristocratic company to which she was not admitted, or at Warwick Castle with his brother's family. Night after night, in his absence, she would sit in her little parlour, Mrs Cadogan on the other side of the fire, embroidering or drawing fancy portraits, her face sad and abstracted. Sometimes Emily was allowed to stay up late, listening to her grandmother's tales of Welsh wizards and fairies, or having her hair twisted into ringlets, strand upon strand, by her mother's fingers.

'I declare it will never *curl*!' Emma said. 'What am I to do with it?'

'Let it be,' advised Mrs Cadogan, finishing off a row of knitting in the shawl she was making for herself. 'The child's well enough looking, and I don't know that being a beauty's all that much catch.'

Emma sighed. 'It's done something for me – brought me Greville. Yet I want more, so much more. How do you think it will end, Mam?'

'How should I know? A girl in keeping can never be certain of anything. 'Tisn't likely Greville will marry you.'

'But he dotes on beauty, and where can he find a prettier woman than I am, though I say it? Why should he have taken trouble to make a lady of me if he didn't mean to keep me?'

Mrs Cadogan laid down her knitting. 'Mr Greville's a very faddy man, as you know, Emma. He'd not put up with ignorance and sluttish manners, even in a mistress. When he found you at Sir Harry's he saw you was naturally graceful and quick to learn, and thought it a chance to make a work of art out of you; something like one of his statues.'

'Oh, him and his statues and his vases and his bits of marble! I vow he thinks more of them than he does of me. He and his uncle are as bad as each other. And yet Sir Will'um did admire me greatly when he visited,' she said wistfully. 'He said I surpassed anything in art or nature. Sometimes I think his heart is kinder than Greville's, though he's so old and satirical.'

Mrs Cadogan suppressed a smile. She knew Sir William Hamilton's age to be fifty-four, which to a nineteen-year-old must appear ancient indeed.

Emma was determined on lowering her own spirits. 'I wonder Greville don't sell me to the British Museum along with his other precious discoveries. Well, let him do with me what he will.' She lay back in her chair, her head drooping on her hand, a picture of lovely dejection. Emily, who had been all ears during the conversation, broke in, agitated.

'Nobody going to sell Mother?' Emma hugged her.

'Silly girl, Mother was only in fun. Nobody shall sell me – or you. Greville is all heart, I know. Oh, Mam, you do think he will come round to keeping her, if he knows her to be quiet and good about the house? And perhaps we can get her a governess—'

Mrs Cadogan shook her head warningly, with a glance at the listening child. 'Time for bed, Emily,' she said briskly. 'I'll ring for Sally.'

Emily, sleepy and full of supper, had not taken in anything but the occasional word, hard though she had tried to understand. But something of her mother's fears had communicated themselves to her and she was fully aware of the all-powerfulness of Mr Greville in this household. The deep-seated feminine instinct which is born in girl-children led her, when Greville passed her in the hall, to attempt her new accomplishment of bobbing a curtsey. It was a one-sided and wobbling dip, but it drew the merest twitch of a smile from Greville. Thereafter she always curtseyed to him, and he sent Emma into the seventh heaven of delight by coolly praising the child's improved manners.

One wet winter day when Greville had gone into town Emily

wakened early from her afternoon sleep. Her room was cold and she knew she was not allowed to take toys downstairs. As she always lay on the bed fully dressed but without shoes there was no problem of awkward buttons and ribbons. Slipping on her shoes she went downstairs in search of amusement.

About to pass the drawing-room, she was charmed by the sound from within of her mother playing the spinet. A ghostly whisper of music, it breathed into the winter air of the house like an invitation. Giving a timid knock Emily went in.

Emma, pensively fingering out a Handel minuet, turned.

'Well, Emily, and what do you in here?'

Emily made her way to the instrument and looked affectionately up at the player.

'Emily play.'

'Emily play? Well, so she shall.' Emma pulled her daughter up into her lap and placed the baby hands across the keys. Instead of the expected dissonance there came a careful harmony, as Emily's fingers found two notes in accord, added a third, and proceeded to climb upwards, exploring a natural scale; then went backwards, sounding out notes pleasant to the child's ear. Emma listened, astonished. To her knowledge Emily had never touched an instrument before. She watched the plump unformed fingers strike the keys with natural force and authority, heard something like a tune emerge, and noted the serious, absorbed face.

'Here, Emily.' She lifted Emily's hands. 'I'll sing a song for you.' She began softly, one of the familiar nursery rhymes.

> 'Little Bo-peep – has lost her sheep,
>   And don't know where – to find 'em;
>   Leave them alone – and they'll come home,
>   Wagging their tails behind 'em.'

She sounded the first note, middle C, eight times repeated, before it led to the next line of the verse, and heard, with astonishment, Emily's finger repeat it exactly and go on with the tune.

34

She did the same with the following line, Emily copying her exactly, almost ahead, until the whole was played.

'Lord! We've a genius among us. I'll have you taught.'

Unheeding, Emily picked out one note after another, some sweet, some gay like birdsong, some dark and sad. She had always loved tunes and there had never been enough of them, Great-grandmam singing only rarely and in a cracked voice. Emma played another tune to her, and another, the child following her lips and her hands, rapt with attention.

When Emma's singing-teacher came next day Emily was allowed to sit on a stool in the corner and listen, which she did in utter silence. Afterwards Emma heard her singing snatches of melody, sometimes wrong, more often right, in her small true voice. By Christmas she knew four or five little songs, two of which she could accompany on the spinet with one finger.

'How I would love Greville to hear her,' Emma cried. Mrs Cadogan shook her head.

'Not at the spinet. She's not allowed the drawing-room, you remember. On this floor she don't exist. Or shouldn't.'

'Not even on Christmas morning?'

Her mother shrugged. 'Have it your own way.'

As it happened, Christmas came bright and sharp. Emma and Greville had spent a happy night, she at her most beguiling, he complacent at having won in a game of faro at his club, a rare indulgence for him. Looking down at him as he slept, by the light of her bedside candle, Emma felt a surge of power, a consciousness of her triumphant beauty that should overcome worldly considerations. She studied the noble profile, the fringed eyelids closed over the beloved melancholy eyes, the manly curve of the throat, a white stem rising from the calyx of the lace-trimmed nightshirt. He was her master and her slave tonight; some day she would be his equal.

After a spell of fog, Christmas Day dawned bright and cold. Emma and Mrs Cadogan had spared no effort to make the house spotlessly clean. Every piece of brass and silver twinkled with polishing, branches of holly decked window-sills, the maids were in their best, covered with voluminous aprons as they ran about the kitchen preparing the dinner.

Emily woke with a sense of excitement quite new to her. At Hawarden Christmas had meant that the church-bells rang for a long time to summon the villagers to church, after which there would be a mince-pudding for dinner and a great deal of drunken singing in the inns, as workers cast aside their daily cares. As for presents, children were lucky if they got even one; the rag doll Gwynydd had been a gift for Emily's second Christmas, made out of materials which cost nothing.

Scrubbed, dressed in her best frock and a new stuff cloak made by Mrs Cadogan, Emily set out with the others for the church across the Green. Everybody went but Molly, who was left behind to look after the dinner. Emma was radiantly beautiful in a dark green mantle against which her hair glowed like autumn fires, and her face was whipped into lovely colour by the cold as she walked proudly holding Greville's arm; and he was the very picture of richly-clad handsomeness. Mrs Cadogan had trimmed her bonnet up for the occasion with artificial flowers and fruit bestowed on her by the milliner, and even Sally's plain little face shone unusually clean and bright.

The village church was packed. Not only the Paddingtonians, but well-to-do people from grand houses round about were there, in the height of fashion, the ladies in hoops, their hair high-piled under the new style of hat, platter-shaped, tilting coquettishly towards the eyes. Emily wanted to look round at everybody, to see the Vicar, who was only a sonorous voice to her, hidden behind the high front of the pew. Her shiftings and peerings were not unnoticed by Emma, who gave her a sharp nip and a warning look.

'I-must-be-good-and-quiet, I-must-be-good-and-quiet,' she said to herself over and over again, and by a considerable effort managed to stand still and kneel without wriggling. It became easier when the singing began. She had never heard such beautiful music. The stirring within her which had began with Emma's song at the spinet started again, so strongly that she felt

36

rather like crying, but knew that it would be quite the wrong thing to do.

'Christians, awake, salute the happy Morn
Whereon the Saviour of mankind was born;
Rise to adore the Mystery of Love,
Which hosts of Angels chanted from above;
With them the joyful tidings first begun,
Of God Incarnate and the Virgin's Son.'

sang the congregation, and Emily ventured to join in with a very soft low humming which nobody heard.

The Vicar knew his flock better than to draw out the sermon, so that not long after noon everybody was free to go home to the anticipated dinner. As Emily, holding her mother's hand, passed him at the church door, he broke off his greetings to pat her on the head and say, 'Bless thee, little maid.'

Then they went home, to present-giving: something for everybody, distributed with good wishes, curtseyings and kisses. Emily had no notion of what anybody else received, having eyes only for her own present: a miraculously beautiful doll, dressed in the height of fashion, its silken hair powdered and its rosy cheeks adorned with beauty-spots. It was just like one of the ladies she had seen at church – more splendid even. She relapsed from chattering into wondering, wide-eyed silence as her mother put it into her arms.

Greville raised his eyebrows at the sight.

'What a needlessly expensive toy for a child so young,' he said loudly, as though Emily were deaf. 'I hope 'twas not bought out of the housekeeping money.'

'Indeed it wasn't,' Emma replied hotly. 'It was given me by Mrs Hackwood, very kindly, when I went for the fitting of my new dress – 'tis a fashion-doll from Paris. She knew of Emily and thought it would please her.'

Greville looked coldly on the fashion-doll. 'I hope it may not give her ideas above her station. I hope also, Emma, that you

37

don't chat to every tradesman of the child's history. Here, Emily,' and he awkwardly put in Emily's arms, still locked round the doll, an unwrapped book.

Mrs Cadogan followed him with her eyes as he sauntered out, and her lips moved in a Welsh phrase inaudible to the others. She took the volume from Emily's clasp and slowly read out its title.

'*Fables – in which the Morals are drawn incidentally in various ways Suited to children from five to seven years of age.* Duwch! How old does he think the babe is?'

' 'Twas very kind and will come in useful later,' Emma said hastily, leading Emily away for a tidy-up before dinner.

Such a dinner as that was: a Christmas celebration unsurpassed in Paddington Village. Emma had strained the housekeeping purse to its limits with joints of beef and pork, boiling fowls, and everything that went with them, followed by all sorts of sweet things and an orange apiece for Emily and the maids. Emily was allowed to have a little wine, which stupefied her utterly. All afternoon she slept, waking to find that Mr Greville had taken her mother with him to call upon Lord Abercorn, his relation, who was in town for a season. In the kitchen she helped Sally and Molly to finish up the scraps, and ate candy made by her grandmother to such an extent that she was suddenly and copiously sick.

Purified, once again sleepy, she retired with the new doll, Lady Anne, laid neatly by the shells on her bedside pot-cupboard, while Gwynydd occupied her usual place in her mistress's arms. Emily's heart was not inclined towards fickleness.

Happy, happy Christmas, thought Emily, drifting towards sleep. Next Christmas was a whole year away. If she wished hard perhaps it would come sooner.

But when Christmas 1785 came at last, Emily was gone from Paddington.

3

In the next months Emily changed noticeably. Good food and regular hours made her grow rapidly; constantly in Emma's company, she began to imitate her mother's graceful movements. Her speaking voice lost the singsong quality which had irritated Greville in early days, and it was evident that her natural talent for singing was combined with a remarkable memory for words and tune.

'I always say,' remarked Mrs Cadogan, 'that talking to children brings 'em on better than any horn-book. Look at you, Emma, brought up with me and Great-grandmam, as bright as a button, just like this one.' She pointed to Emily, who, flat on her stomach, was drawing a portrait of the cat. 'She might be all of five, compared with many that's still sucklings at her age.'

'Butter, four-and-ninepence. A nutmeg, three-ha'pence,' Emma muttered, deep in her household accounts. She put them aside and said in a hushed, anxious tone, 'Mam, do you really, truly think Greville is reconciled to her? Do you think he'll let me keep her?'

'Why, as to that . . .' Mrs Cadogan pursed her lips, pausing to glance at the absorbed child. 'There's been no talk of sending her away lately that I've heard. And she's a deal better behaved than when she came, no doubt of it.'

'But he seems so troubled these days, Mam. 'Tis not that I've crossed him, I'm sure, or he'd have scolded. I think 'tis part to do with money, for though the town house is sold there's many bills comes in, and he writes to Sir William very often. Maybe 'tis to ask for his portion in Sir William's lifetime.'

In fact that very matter came up in conversation the same evening, as Emma sat sewing by Greville's side in the library. A letter lay open beside him. Several times he glanced from it to her bent head before finding courage to broach the subject.

'Here's a strange rumour,' he said at last. 'Harry tells me my uncle is in love.'

Emma raised a bright face. 'In love? At his age? But such things happen. I'm glad for his sake. Who is the lady?'

Greville's expression was anything but glad. 'Harry gives no name, but my uncle has mentioned to me Lady Clarges, Sir Thomas's widow. He's enamoured of her music, it seems, and what he calls her gentle ways. He even made a joking proposal to her, it seems.'

'Of marriage?' Emma laughed. 'Well, if he must marry, let him. 'Tis no occasion for a long face.' A few stitches on she looked up again, troubled. 'Oh, but 'twould mean you'd no longer be his heir!'

'Just so.'

'And that would put you in difficulties?'

'My dear Emma, I should be ruined. I have more debts than you know. Some of my pictures must go to pay them, but for the rest . . .' He stared gloomily into the fire. 'The prospects are bad for business, with this war-talk and taxes continually increased. Soon 'twill be hard to live comfortably, let alone like a gentleman.'

Emma laid her hand tenderly on his knee. 'Let me help. You know I can make great economies. We could make do with only one maid, buy less meat and very little tea, for 'tis there the money goes.'

Greville patted the hand. 'You're very good, my Emma. Let us hope for the best. Perhaps we can find a way.'

After a day or two's thought, for he was not given to impulses, he wrote a long, carefully-worded letter to his uncle.

If you did not chuse a wife, I wish the tea-maker of Edgware Row was yours . . . I do not know how to part with what I am not tired with. I do not know how to contrive to go on, and I give her every merit of prudence and moderation and affection.

A catalogue of Emma's charms and virtues followed, and protestations of his own disinterestedness in offering her to Sir William. Since 'so beautiful a person cannot be without a protector', and since he was no longer able to fill that role, what more satisfactory than that Sir William should do so, thereby gaining a beautiful, submissive and prudent mistress rather than making himself slightly ridiculous by marrying at his advanced age? But Greville phrased it more subtly, he flattered himself:

At your age a clean and comfortable woman is not superfluous . . . your brother spoke openly to me, that he thought the wisest thing you could do would be to buy Love ready made.

He paused, to consider the end of the letter, nibbling his pen. A coal fell nosily into the grate without disturbing his reverie. In his mind's eye he saw the pretty face of Henrietta Willoughby, daughter of Lord Middleton, who had been his neighbour in Portman Square. She would grace his table-head, and was rumoured to carry a fortune of £30,000. She would not, of course, be Emma, the prettiest woman in London, his creation, his Galatea; but that could not be helped. He understood his uncle pretty well. It was not unlikely that persuasive words, added to Sir William's known fondness for Emma, might win the day.

But there was one outstanding obstacle: the child. If only bountiful Providence would give him some foolproof excuse for getting rid of it.

Emma loved a challenge. The thought of Greville worrying over debts and taxes drove her into a frenzy of economy which tried the rest of the household severely, and caused the tradesmen to murmur among themselves that Mrs Hart was becoming downright mean with her orders. Pease-pudding and water-gruel, that's what they're living on, complained the butcher, and the henwife at Manor Farm was displeased to learn that Mrs Hart had started keeping her own hens. This particular economy was a great trial to Mrs Cadogan and the maids, as Emma stoutly resisted the killing of any of the birds however poor a layer it might be. When overruled by the general opinion she would rush weeping out of the house and sit disconsolately on a tombstone in the churchyard until the slaughter was over.

Guilefully, she enlisted Emily as helper. Emily was clever and obedient and good with her hands. She took pride in gathering the eggs, digging up the pearly new potatoes, taking care of her own little plot of herbs. Armed with a basket rather too large for her she trotted willingly off to the baker's, or to the farm for butter. Greville could not help but see how useful she was thought Emma, and how she would pay for keeping as she grew older.

'And getting so pretty, too,' Emma said to her mother. 'She'll have my eyes, as near as anything, and though her lashes mayn't be so thick they're passable.'

Mrs Cadogan surveyed the rear view of her granddaughter, bending down to pick early strawberries. 'She'll be tall, like you and her granddad.'

'*And* her father.' Emily's shining marmalade-coloured hair was like Sir Harry's, too, and she had his high forehead. Every night the pretty hair was put into uncomfortable curlers, so that by day her head was glossy and straight at the front, tumbling at the back in a pretty cascade of ringlets. Just now the sun was on it, making it glint like guinea gold. Emma regarded it fondly.

'Don't you think, Mam, Greville will grow proud to have two pretty women about the house?'

'I dare say, my dear, I dare say.'

'And we won't have to pay a governess. I can teach her her letters. She can write a few pot-hooks already. What it is to have a bright child!'

Emily had indeed an enquiring mind. Her frequent questions sometimes produced no more satisfactory answer than 'Oh, go along, do!' from one of the overworked maids, or at times from her grandmother. She loved to touch things, arrange them this way and that, or to draw them. Particularly she enjoyed going with her mother to Mr George Romney's studio in Cavendish Square, for Mr Romney allowed her to run about as she wished, investigating the fascinating properties he kept for his paintings : models of heads, wooden bodies like great jointed dolls, stuffed birds, masks, a harp, a throne, gilded crowns and a pile of shawls and other draperies in which it was blissful to dress up.

'Do have a care, Emily!' Her mother, posed on the dais as a backward-smiling Bacchante, watched with alarm as Emily flitted about to the imminent peril of breakable objects or the canvases stacked against the wall.

But Romney said, 'Let her be. Do I not owe a debt to children?'

Emma gave him a look of heavenly sympathy. He confided in her as in no one else, this remote, melancholy man, and she knew about the midnight pangs of remorse he suffered for the wife and family he had left, long ago, to serve his art. If it pleased him to give Emily the run of his studio, let him, poor man.

And so it came about that Emily regarded the world as her plaything. She behaved so sensibly as a rule that she was not continually supervised unless Greville was at home. From this trust in her, and her own curiosity, came tragedy.

Off the library there was an anteroom, a small apartment crowded with shelves and showcases. Greville called it his 'Museum', for it held many of his treasures, objects dug from the buried cities of Pompeii and Herculaneum, rare fossils, the burial urns of Romans and the lamps which had lighted them, scent-bottles and hairpins, brooches and rings that had adorned beauties long dead, fine crystals, bronze and marble fragments. The famous Barberini Vase had stood there for a time; but Sir William Hamilton, who believed it had held the ashes of Alexander the Great, had sold it to the Duchess of Portland for eighteen hundred guineas.

Emily knew, of course, that the Museum was forbidden territory, along with the drawing-room, the bedroom shared by Greville and her mother, and the library. She had never meant to go in. But one wet June day, passing the door, she saw that it was open a little, disclosing a glimpse of wonderful things. Glancing round to make sure that she was not observed, she pushed the door a little more open; then, with sudden resolution, went inside and shut it behind her.

The Museum was like, and yet unlike, Romney's studio. There were the carved heads of bearded men and beautiful women, and the vases covered with strange scenes. In a niche stood a graceful, naked white figure, modestly veiling her charms. Above the fireplace a marble panel showed cherubs playing.

Emily longed to touch, to handle and examine. To her frustration the glass-topped showcases (she was just tall enough to see into them) were firmly locked; there was no getting at the interesting things inside. She wandered from one to another, vaguely aware that the objects were old and precious. They were strange too: a thing like a huge snail, and a mouse of stone who looked most lifelike, as well he might for he had died and been mummified in the boiling lava from Vesuvius seventeen centuries before.

Enviously Emily contemplated a pair of long earrings, with green stones in them, such as her mother wore. She would dearly have loved to try them on. In another case were beautiful coloured stones, uncut jewels, which reminded her of her shell collection. All sense of trespassing had left her. She was almost ready to stamp with temper when her eye caught a low shelf on which were a number of things within her reach. Some were bits of glass which she ignored; but one, a wooden box, looked worth the opening.

It was unlocked. She lifted the lid, and there, among the straw packing, lay what she supposed to be a doll. She took it out and examined it. It was not exactly pretty, being the figure of a creature half man and half goat, laughing fiendishly, half crouched as if to spring upon an unwary nymph. Emily thought he was a very curious shape, but perhaps that was because of his goat-half. Triumphant at having found something to play with she went down on all fours and began to walk him round the carpet, chanting one of her little tuneless songs. He was a tame goat, she pretended, the goat which her mother had wanted to keep for its milk, though Greville had shudderingly squashed the question.

She reached the fireplace, and decided that the goat-man would look well on the mantelshelf, by the clock.

'Up, up, up,' she told him, walking him up the marble colonnade that flanked the grate. But the mantelshelf was too high for her. To reach it, she stepped on to the edge of the fender, wavered, and let the goat-man slip through her small fingers, to be dashed to pieces on the fender's iron base.

For a moment she felt as though she too were lying there in fragments. Scarlet with shock, she looked at the ruin she had made. She thought of flight; but the evidence of her guilt would remain. Where to hide it? Hurriedly, sobbing under her breath, she gathered up the pieces by handfuls and piled them into her apron pocket, sweeping the bits that were too small to collect under the grate; then, looking feverishly round, she saw a stone vase standing in a corner. She dropped the fragments inside it, heard them clink as they fell, then, picking up her skirts, ran from the room.

Greville did not come to Edgware Row that evening, or the next. He was spending a lot of his time at the King's Mews, in a suite of rooms which the King had graciously granted to Sir William for his occupancy when he was in England. For two agonised days Emily waited, apprehensive of his coming.

'What ails the child?' her grandmother asked. 'Not a word to throw at the cat.' Questions produced no results. No, Emily didn't feel poorly. Nobody had been cross with her. Her flow of chatter had dried up, her little tasks were done with fumbling hands. Mrs Cadogan prescribed a good dose of calomel.

If Emily had cherished the slightest hope that Greville would overlook the absence of the figure, it was dashed within an hour of his arrival the following afternoon. He was in a good temper, kissing Emma heartily at the gate and commending her healthy looks. Emily, who had been in the garden with her mother, tried to escape, but for once he called her to him.

'Making yourself of use, child? That's good.' He chucked her under the chin, an attention never paid to her before. She lowered her eyes and flushed painfully, to his mild amusement. An arm round Emma's shoulders, he went into the house.

Emily was in bed that evening, sleepiness fighting with her fears, when the summons came. The new maid, Ann Murphy, was at her bedside, shaking her.

'You're wanted, Miss Emily. I'm to take you downstairs. Come on, I'll fasten your wrapper for you.'

Greville was waiting in the library, a pale-faced Emma beside him. His face was like a face of steel.

'I think you know why you're sent for, miss.'

Emily's lip trembled; she shook her head.

'A valuable object in my Museum has been destroyed. I have questioned the maids, and I am satisfied they know nothing. Perhaps you do?'

Emma touched his arm. 'She's only a babe, Greville,' she whispered. ' 'Tisn't a court of law.'

He shook off her hand, got to his feet, and moved towards the door. 'Follow me,' he said to Emily.

On a small table in the Museum the heap of fragments was laid out on a cloth.

'Do you know anything of this?' Greville asked. Emily's outburst of tears was sufficient answer. He turned to Emma.

'You see? As I told you – poking and prying; 'twas she did the mischief. Do you know what you have wrecked, child?'

'Doll,' stammered Emily, through her sobs.

'Your "doll" was a priceless figurine of a faun, from the ruined Temple of Apollo in Syracuse. It was sent to me only a week ago by my uncle, from Naples. You have done irreparable damage to a beautiful thing. No, come away from her, Emma. I wish her to recognise her crime.' He moved towards the cowering child, who shrank back against the wall.

'I have a nephew, Emily. Lork Brooke. He is much older than you, but a child still. If he had done this thing I should have had him beaten until he was unable to stand.'

46

Emma leapt in front of her daughter. 'No, Greville, you shan't touch her!'

Greville's smile was frosty. 'I had no intention of touching her. I merely tell her what sort of punishment she *should* receive. I hope it may never be said of Greville that he laid violent hands upon a female, of whatever age.' He pulled the bell-cord by the fireplace. 'You will go to bed now, Emily, and reflect on what you have done.'

Ann appeared in answer to his summons.

'Take Miss Emily upstairs and put her to bed. I don't wish any of the household to go near her until tomorrow.'

Ann dipped a curtsey. 'Yes, sir.' Emily, weeping loudly, was led away.

Through the long wretched evening, lying in her darkened room, she heard loud voices and sounds in the house: Mrs Cadogan saying 'Come and get your supper, Emma – 'twill do no good to starve,' and her mother, from behind a closed door, shouting tearfully that she wanted none. Then came Greville's knocking on the bedroom door, and sobs from within, until at last the door was unlocked, and silence fell.

They were not coming to her. Nobody was going to comfort her or bring her anything to eat. Cold, wet, exhausted with sobbing, she fell asleep.

In their bedroom Emma was shouting the same thing over and over again at Greville. 'She shan't be sent away! I won't have it.'

Patient and imperturbable, he said once more: 'You have no choice.'

'Then I'll go too!'

'My dear Emma, a moment's reflection will tell you that such an action would be very unwise. You are entirely without money, and I would certainly not settle any on you. Even without the child you would find it hard to live, and with her I fear there would be nothing for you but to return to your grandmother – or become a belle of St Giles's.'

She turned a flushed, tear-swollen face to him. Her hair

streamed about her shoulders, and in her distress she pulled at it as if to hurt herself.

'You'd put me on the streets? That's the measure of your love for me? Very well, I'll go, I'll practise every vice to excess, and as I die ruined I'll tell everyone "This I am, Greville made me!"'

'Indeed? And where will your daughter figure in this pretty scene?'

Emma was silent. She wound a handful of hair round her fingers, and stared at it unseeingly.

'You must realise, Emma,' he went on more kindly, 'that in your situation the mere existence of a child is an enormous handicap to you. How much more, then, its presence in the household.'

'We could say she was adopted,' Emma muttered.

'And do you think that would be believed? No, that way she would grow up with a shadow over her character, whereas among strangers she may pass for an orphan or a child whose parents have deserted her. There she may be educated, learn enough to earn her own living, quite innocent of any stain.'

Emma stared out of the window into the dusk wherein the lighted windows of cottages and houses looked like stars. The starry lights of homes in which children were being reared among their own people, smiled on by loving mothers and proud fathers; where every year or so a new baby would be born, welcomed with joy. Oh, had poor Emily but a father who loved her . . .

Greville read her mind.

'If you are thinking of appealing to Sir Harry, I should abandon the idea. After your wild conduct when you were in his keeping he would never own your child, and in any case he is now a bosom friend of the Prince of Wales, who spends much of his time at Uppark. No, you would find neither sentiment nor sensibility in him. Now *I* am all sensibility; I wish only the best for the child's future, and that must not be here. Must I reason with you all over again?'

Emma shook her head. Sighing, she pulled the silk cord that drew the curtains together, shutting out the lighted windows across the Green. Slowly she moved across to the bed and leant her forehead against the cool wood of one of the delicate posts at its foot. She closed her eyes, the miraculously long lashes lying dark and damp on her flushed cheeks. Greville, even in such a painful discussion, felt a stab of desire. Emma, he reflected, was the only woman of his acquaintance who could weep and rage simultaneously without losing a jot of her beauty. He would never get another like her: Henrietta Willoughby was plain in comparison, but one may forgive an heiress anything. He laid his hand on Emma's shoulder. She turned it aside.

'When must she go?' she asked tonelessly.

'I shall write to Mr Blackburn tonight for the address.'

'Blackburn?'

'He is a rising young Lancashire politician, a very sound man. It is his cousin in Manchester who takes in young children to educate. So you see, Emily will not be very far from her old home.'

Emma turned away and began languidly to undress. He watched her like a dog that has stolen something and fears punishment. When they were both in bed he caressed her cheeks, throat and breasts, his invariable prelude to love-making. But she turned her back on him for the first time since they had become lovers, and edged to the other side of the bed.

Emily was baffled. On the morning after her solitary confinement she was roused, washed and dressed as usual by Ann Murphy, taken downstairs and greeted unemotionally by her grandmother, the only person in the kitchen. Nothing was said about her crime, then or afterwards. Greville left for the King's Mews that morning and was not seen again at Edgware Row that week.

There was a strange atmosphere in the house, as though someone had died whose name must not be mentioned. Mrs Cadogan wore her tight-lipped face, Emma was silent and gloomy. Sometimes she caught Emily to her and squeezed her until she gasped for breath; at other times she would gaze at the child like the

Muse of Tragedy. Emily decided to find out from Ann Murphy (who was, after all, thirteen, really grown up) what the trouble was.

'Dunno,' said Ann. 'Lost sixpence and found a ha'penny, I shouldn't wonder?'

'Lost sixpence, Ann?' Emily's eyes were as round as that coin.

'It's a saying, Em. It don't mean a real sixpence.'

Emily gave up the riddle. 'Grandmam is making me a new cloak,' she said, 'and we are to buy stuff for a new frock today.'

'You'll be goin' for a holiday, then,' said Ann. 'Mr Greville shuts the house up in summer as a rule, I've heard. Saves money, leavin' the servants on board wages.' She snorted. 'If it weren't for Mrs C makin' things go a long way, Molly and me'd be livin' on the grass from the garden.'

The material for the new dress was disappointing. Emily had hoped for pink or blue, or even spotted muslin; she was just old enough to spend time in front of the cheval-glass admiring herself. But instead the stuff was a dull grey delaine, and Mrs Cadogan made it up from a plain pattern of which Emily did not at all approve. The cloak was grey, lined with dark red, and was reversible, with a deep hem. 'So it can be let down as you grow,' said Mrs Cadogan.

'Are we going away?' Emily asked.

'Maybe.' Her grandmother's eyes were fixed on her sewing.

'All of us?'

'Wait and see.'

She came and leant against Mrs Cadogan's knee, looking up with the same appealing gaze that her mother won hearts with. 'Are you cross with me, Grandmam?' she asked wistfully. Her grandmother laid the sewing aside.

'Cross with you, my little love? Of course not. Your Mam and I have got troubles, that's all.'

On Sunday there was a great treat. Her mother hired a coach from Mr Miles, a whole two-shillingsworth of coach; and the three of them were driven out to Hampstead. It was a fine day, cream clouds scudding across a forget-me-not sky. The Heath was in all its summer glory, the grass fresh and green, the ancient trees that had once been a Norman forest now sheltering Londoners who had made their way up on this their rest-day to enjoy Hampstead's pleasures. From the lane that ran across the Heath from the top of the steep cobbled street to Highgate, a mile away, Emily could see little farmsteads with animals which looked small enough to be toys grazing around them or gathered in the shade. Tethered donkeys cropped the grass, making the most of the time until their masters mounted them to ride down the hill to London again. Emily clapped her hands with pleasure at the pretty sights and happy faces.

'Here we are,' said their driver. The coach had halted under a patch of trees by an inn, from the grounds of which came chatter and music. 'The Spaniards' tea-gardens.' He lifted Emily down and lent a gallant hand to Emma and Mrs Cadogan, giving Emma's hand the least suspicion of an admiring squeeze.

Then they all went into the tea-gardens, which were enclosed by an old brick wall covered with climbing roses; and to eat they had shrimps and bread and butter, an apple-pie with a syllabub, and fresh milk to drink, brought from a farm not fifty yards away. 'And as different,' said Mrs Cadogan, 'as chalk from cheese to what they get in London.' It was slightly warm and tasted delicious. Emily drank three mugs of it, and had to be hurried to the privy at the back of the inn.

When they were replete she asked leave to go and play with one of the Spaniards' dogs, which was going the rounds of the tables and doing very well for itself in the way of scraps. Her mother and grandmother remained at the table, talking. As she came back, out of their line of sight, she heard Mrs Cadogan say '. . . ought to tell her tonight', and her mother reply 'No, let her have that, at least.' Emily wondered what she was to have, but sensed that she had better not ask.

The journey home was pleasant, as the coach travelled westward towards a glorious sunset. Emily fell asleep, and was ready for bed as soon as they arrived at Edgware Row. For a long time Emma sat by her bed, singing softly an old Welsh lullaby her grandmother had sung to her. Even after Emily was asleep she went on singing, holding the small hand in hers.

Next morning the first things Emily saw were the new dress and cloak on a chair. As Ann got her into the dress she wriggled impatiently at its stiffness, and Ann muttered a curse on the number of little fiddling buttons she had to fasten. Ann's eyes were red for some reason. Perhaps she had the toothache again.

After the splendours of Sunday, this Monday morning was disappointingly grey and cold. Emma was not down for breakfast, only Mrs Cadogan, who was not her usual cheerful self as she presided over the table. When Emily had eaten her porridge and drunk her milk, her grandmother went to sit in the big chair by the fire. 'Come here, Emily,' she said. Obediently Emily went and stood by her knee.

'I've something to tell you, child,' the old lady said after a pause. 'You're to go away this morning.'

'Away? A holiday?'

'No, love, no. You're going to school.'

'School?' Emily remembered her mother saying she would have to go to school some day. And one day when they had gone into London together they had passed a building which had the coloured figures of a small boy and a small girl set in niches above its door, and Mother had said this was a school.

'A school in London?' she asked now.

'Not London. A place – not very far from Parkgate.'

'Is it seaside?'

'No, a town.' Abruptly her grandmother rose, went over to the window, and stood looking out at the garden, drumming her fingers on the sill.

'My God, why was this left to me? How am I to do it?' she said aloud, then turned swiftly back to Emily. 'You'll learn all manner of things and be cleverer than any of us, I dare say. Very soon you'll have forgotten—' She broke off, shaking her head in angry frustration. 'Go out to play now, love, and Ann and I will pack your things, for we're to leave by eight o'clock.'

Dazed and apprehensive, Emily wandered outside and down the garden; but her beloved hens had no charm for her. 'School – away – forget'. The words buzzed in her head like the echoes of a crash.

Long before eight a weeping Ann was fastening the new cloak.

'Have done snivelling, girl!' snapped Mrs Cadogan. 'That'll mend nothing. Come, Emily, you're to say goodbye to your mother. She's in bed, too ill to come downstairs. Some find it convenient to be ill,' she added bitterly.

Emma was lying among pillows, her hair streaming wildly over them, a wet handkerchief clutched in her hand. She stretched out her arms and Mrs Cadogan put Emily into them. At the sight of her mother's tears Emily began to cry. Mrs Cadogan caught sight of a bottle of cherry brandy beside the bed, snatched it up and put it in her apron pocket.

'*That's* no sort of consolation, Emma! You'd best get up and do something useful to take your mind off. Now, the hackney-coach'll be here in five minutes to take us to the Saracen's Head, so be quick. And try not to upset that child any more.'

Emma was clutching her daughter, kissing the wet cheeks and caressing the gold hair from which the cloak's hood had fallen back.

'I'd give the world for you not to go. If it weren't for – I can't explain – things that mean I *must* part with you . . . Oh, Emily, some day I pray you'll be glad of this and bless your mother!'

Silently Mrs Cadogan took Emily from the round white arms that held her so tightly. Emma rolled over and buried her face in the pillow, so that she could not hear Emily's choked 'Goodbye' or see the door close on her.

The journey to the Saracen's Head, the coaching inn near Smithfield, was long and agonising to both: Emily asking questions to which there was no answer, her grandmother trying to keep up a flow of comment on the scenes through which they were passing. It was a relief when they came at last to the inn, a few doors from St Sepulchre's, the 'execution church'. Emily remembered it dimly from their arrival from Parkgate, the cobbled yard hemmed in by galleried rooms, the red coaches and bustling porters and coachmen, passengers and their luggage awaiting the signal to board the coach. She remembered most of all the savage-looking Saracen's Head sign, with its pointed mustachios and cruel eyes, frowning down at her. Mrs Cadogan made enquiries about the Manchester coach, which was pointed out, 'due to leave directly'. She sighed with relief. There would not be time to visit the coffee-room. The ordeal was almost over.

Arrived at the coach, holding Emily's hand and her pathetically small bag of possessions, she proffered her ticket to the guard.

'One inside? Right, ma'am.'

Emily stared. Her face had turned the colour of cheese.

'One, Grandmam? Only me?'

'Oh, my dear, how I wish I could come with you. I'd give my right hand for it. But he wouldn't give me the money, though I wrote him twice and told him 'twas a crying shame. Don't look at me so, child, for 'tisn't my fault, indeed. You're in charge of the guard and he'll see to all you want.'

Emily was now clinging round her knees, sobbing hysterically. 'Don't leave me, don't leave me!' The scene was causing comment among the other passengers, who were giving them curious looks. Mrs Cadogan heard someone say 'Shame! A little moppet like that.' She flushed miserably, trying to detach the clutching hands. A well-dressed woman approached them.

'If, indeed, you can't accompany the child, ma'am, I will be happy to do so. 'Tis not seemly a female child should be seen to only by the guard. Will you take my hand, little one?'

Mrs Cadogan murmured thanks. Emily's shrieks of 'No!' rent the air. The kindly passenger looked uncomfortable. The guard came to the rescue, picking up Emily with the adroitness of a practised family man and depositing her in the coach. Her protectress followed, and as the coach-horn sounded its signal the rest of the passengers got in or ascended to the roof. The doors were slammed. 'All right!' cried the guard from the box, and the coach began to move, with an elephantine sway, through the courtyard towards the archway at the end. A moment, and it was no more than a scarlet rear turning into the street. Then it was gone, on its hundred and eighty-six mile journey to Manchester.

Emily, perched on her bed, looked critically at her presents. It was her eighth birthday, not far from 'double figures'; not far from the age when she might be dignified as a 'Young Lady'. She sighed. It was kind of Mr and Mrs Blackburn to give her a hymnal, so that she need no longer share with Thetis or Maria at church; but she would so much rather have had – well, a bonnet, a nice high-crowned one that would have made her look taller.

As for the girls'. present, she knew it had taken Thetis painful hours to make the flannel needle-case – there were even specks of blood on one of its white leaves. She was very grateful to Thetis who hated sewing so much and got smacked for it when Mrs Blackburn's tenuous patience gave out.

From the high bedroom window of the house in Palace Street she could see the gardens in front of the Palace Inn at the end in Market Street Lane, with the young grass and the border of spring flowers stirring in the April breeze. It was a source of great interest to Emily that the inn took its name from the fact that Prince Charles Edward had stayed there in the '45 when he led his Highlanders south through Manchester. Dear, charming Prince! Emily kept a marker in her history book at the page showing his portrait with the fair flowing tie-wig and noble expression; but she was obliged to keep her partiality from the Blackburns, who prided themselves on their connection with Mr Blackburn's cousin, the Member of Parliament for Lancaster and a conspicuous Whig.

Emily doted on good looks. She had once horrified Mrs Blackburn by a suggestion that Judge Jeffreys, of Bloody Assize notoriety, could not have been as terrible as the books said because he was so handsome. Mrs Blackburn had made her write out 'Handsome is as handsome does' fifty times. No doubt her fondness for beauty was because of her own lack of it. She was quite glad the long mirror had been taken out of her room, because when it was there she had kept staring into it, in the hope that she might have gained a little height since the last time. But the image was always the same : four feet and a very few inches, fair hair scraped up into a topknot with two ringlets, one on either side of the pointed face with two enormous blue eyes in it. The doctor who had been called in last time she was ill had said that she ran about too much; she should curb her impetuosity and conduct herself more seemly. He had then said her smallness must be due to worms, of all the disgusting ideas, and had prescribed Evans' Worm Powders which tasted very nasty. But at least Dr Hardie had been kind enough to prescribe port wine as well.

'Are they not very expensive?' she had asked Mrs Blackburn when the box of a dozen bottles was brought down the area steps.

'They'll be paid for by your guardians, as usual,' Mrs Blackburn replied, opening one of the bottles and measuring out a dose of the pleasant ruby-coloured drink for which Emily felt she could develop quite a taste.

'Your guardians' – Who were they, these mysterious guardians? She was not encouraged to ask, and her own ideas were few. When she thought back into the past it was as if she were running down a passage, colliding suddenly with something ugly, terrifying, cruel; and then she had to turn back and run towards the present, looking back once to make sure the Thing had receded into the black cloud it lived in.

And so she could remember nothing clearly of her infancy. There was a time, she knew, when she had been very unhappy here in Palace Street. She had been small and terribly frightened, so frightened that she had been sick on the Blackburns' best carpet (or so Maria liked to tell her). Maria also said that Emily had cried for three days, until it was suggested that she might be best off in the Lunatic Hospital in Piccadilly, at the end of the Lane.

'How do you know?' Emily asked indignantly. 'You were a year younger than me – only a baby.'

'How could I forget?' Maria returned airily. 'You kept us all awake, and next-door as well. They thought you would die. Papa says 'twas the affliction of finding yourself an orphan that overcame you.'

'I am *not* an orphan!' The generally mild Emily stamped her foot. 'There are people who care about me and – and pay for my education.'

'Who are they, then? There, you don't know.' Maria spun round like a top and began to sing a song with the refrain 'O, list to the plaint of the poor Orphan Boy', which could rouse Emily to fury and had gained both of them a smacking on occasion.

Emily held her head in her hands as though to keep the hidden knowledge from flying away. What could she remember? A tree in blossom, a garden with something – a column, a statue? – in it. A dressing-stand draped with dimity. The delicious taste of a sort of gingerbread cake which someone very kind used to make for her. And when she looked at herself in the mirror there came to her a cloudy vision of another face, very, very beautiful, like the memory of a dream. Behind it rose a vista of silvery water and sand, followed, very oddly, by the picture of a pig walking in through a door. Beyond that, nothing.

Mrs Blackburn, that most sedate and correct of ladies, was not free from the vice of curiosity. Her Quaker forebears of York would have considered it idle and frivolous to spend even a moment in wondering what might be the background of her pupil. Not for the first time, she took an opportunity of probing her husband's knowledge as she sat with him in the parlour on the evening of Emily's birthday, a piece of sewing, as ever, in her hands.

'Mr Blackburn.'

Her husband's powdered head was almost invisible between the covers of his book. She gave a sharp, artificial cough, at which Mr Blackburn reluctantly gave her his attention, his spectacles half-way down his nose, as though anxious to return to *Remarks on the Text and Notes of the last Edition of Shakespeare.*

'Yes, my dear?'

'Is it not strange to reflect that two months hence Emily will have been with us for five years?'

Mr Blackburn did not consider it particularly strange, being more or less oblivious of the passage of time; but his wife continued, 'And yet we know no more of her early circumstances than on the first day she came to us. That is, *I* know no more. As to you, I can't say.'

He took off his spectacles, a gesture which somehow made it easier to hold his own in discussions with his wife – she appeared so much farther away, and surrounded by a pleasantly woolly outline.

'My knowledge of her is precisely the same as it has always been, Hester, and you know I am upon honour not to disclose it. Beside, it really amounts to very little. The arrangements were originally made by my cousin. I merely carry them out.'

This was as far as Mrs Blackburn had ever got with her enquiries; she knew that only guile would work upon him.

'One would think the child herself would prattle of her memories, yet she never utters one word of her friends and family. Such reticence is unnatural in a child.'

'I doubt that reticence is the cause. Emily is frank and open in her manners, conversing as well with adults as with children. My own view' – he began to fill his pipe – 'is that the shock she sustained in being parted from them has so outraged nature that she is mercifully prevented from recalling anything from before she arrived here.' He warmed to his theme as the tobacco took light. 'Much as when, in a carriage accident or a fall from a horse, a person suffers injury to the head, it may drive out the memory for a time – or for ever. Poor Emily was far too young to be torn from her home unprepared.'

'It was certainly very shocking,' agreed his wife, 'that she should arrive here in the care of a strange female, not even accompanied by an attendant. Perhaps whoever sent her would have been only too pleased if she had been lost on the journey.'

Mr Blackburn, summoning a mental picture of the person who had sent Emily, merely shook his head.

'It was, I take it, a gentleman? You can surely tell me that, Mr Blackburn.'

He sighed. 'Since you will have it, yes.'

'Emily's natural father, I take it. She must be a love-child, for sure. How is it possible for a father to banish his daughter so far? But he is generous, *that* I grant; twenty pounds a year for her board, and every penny besides paid, down to her pins and stay-laces. Well, it can never be said that we do not give her the best education to be had in Manchester – not only my own instruction and Miss Winder's, but extra French, music and dancing. She will be qualified to fill any station.'

Mr Blackburn refused to rise to this. 'Well, well,' he said, 'we must be glad of the money, since I can no longer teach regularly at the College.' After leaving Cambridge University he had become a teacher at Chetham's College, the Elizabethan foundation which was Manchester's pride. But the asthma which had made him a delicate child had followed him into manhood, and two severe illnesses had caused the Governors to tell him, regretfully, that his services were no longer required and that he must employ his scholarship as a private tutor. There were plenty of noble houses in the district with sons and heirs to be taught, but a married man with children was not what their owners required.

And so John Blackburn and Hester, his clever wife, had put up a plate advertising their readiness to educate young ladies and gentlemen in all the Arts and Sciences. They had at first done only moderately well. Then, in 1785, had come Emily, their first boarder, and with her twenty pounds a year, which was far more than she cost to keep.

They had been too absorbed in their discussion of Emily to hear the jangle of the door-bell below, and both turned in surprise as the servant-maid announced: 'The Reverend Thomas, sir.'

'Tom, dear fellow!' John Blackburn's book fell off his knee as he jumped up to greet his brother. There was little difference in age between them, but the clergyman looked to be the younger by several years, plump and rosy-complexioned, with the figure of a sportsman. The time he could spare from ministering to his small country parish was largely given to hunting with the pack of huge hounds for which Manchester was famous, and his enjoyment of the stirrup-cup was evident in his complexion.

'Well, John, how do you? And Hester?' He gave his sister-in-law a hearty kiss on her cool cheek. 'I called on you without warning, being here on business with the Dean. All's well with you?'

'Aye, we missed the fever that was about, I'm happy to say. And with you and yours?'

'Never better. Nance thinks to be brought to bed in a two-three week, and by the look of her belly 'twill be twins.'

Hester looked reprovingly on him. 'Five in family already, and now two more? How can you afford it, Thomas?'

'Why, we live cheap, grow all but our meat, and keep the childer employed about the buttery and the brewery. Work six days, praise and pray on the seventh, and nowt much can go wrong wi' you, so say I.'

Hester winced at the Northern expression. Thomas was regrettably given to such vulgarities.

'Will you take wine with us, Thomas?' she asked, in duty bound but hoping that he might refuse.

'Aye, I will that,' he replied. 'I'd hopes that the Dean would send down for a bottle, but my hints that the weather was uncommon dry were lost on him.'

His brother went to the corner cupboard where the decanter and glasses were kept; it was against his principles to trouble the maid, Bessy, with unnecessary journeys, for the girl had a shortened leg and limped painfully. He poured for Thomas and himself, Hester refusing, and raised his glass.

'To your forthcoming offspring, Tom.'

'Thank'ee. Not breeding again yourself, Hes?'

His sister-in-law flushed and bent her head over her sewing.

'No. I pray we may have no more additions to our family.

61

'Twould mean the end of my teaching for longer than we can afford.'

Thomas laughed. 'If you've found a way of throwing back Mother Nature's bounty in her face, what need to work? Take out a patent and live by selling your remedy.'

Hester's lips tightened, and the clergyman saw his brother glance quickly, furtively at her. She had indeed discovered how to prevent the fecundity Nature had twice forced on her; it took the form of depriving her husband of his marital rights. Hester Blackburn was an excellent teacher of the young, but her sensibilities were outraged by the bearing and tending of babies and small children.

Thomas might have offended further but that the sound of music and a young voice singing turned the current of the conversation. 'That's sweet,' he said. 'Who is the player?'

'Miss Hart,' replied Hester.

'Little Miss Emily? I must hear her better.' He rose, waving aside Hester's move to accompany him. 'No, sister, I can find the drawing-room for myself.'

The drawing-room, which was capable of being either one room or two, depending on its double doors, was papered in a modest dove-grey stripe and furnished with quiet good taste and a complete absence of luxury. Its only pictures were mezzo-tints of the four seasons, and above the mantelshelf a badly-painted portrait of Hester's mother, uncomfortable in the stiffly-corseted dress of George II's day. The brightest colour in the room came from Emily's dress of peacock-blue, throwing into relief the red-gold of her hair.

She turned as the door opened, her hands leaving the piano-forte keys. Seeing who it was, she rose and dipped a curtsey.

'Your servant, Miss Emily. Pray go on with your music.'

She shook her head, smiling shyly. He put his hand under her chin, tilting her face to the light. 'I was about to say "I hope I see thee well", child. But there's no need. Eh, but tha'rt a bonny lass!'

Emily blushed. A shrill giggle from the back drawing-room proclaimed that Maria had overheard.

'Law, Uncle Tom, don't let Mamma hear you talk so.'

'Peace, Maria.' Thetis Blackburn laid down the doll she was dressing and advanced to greet her uncle. Big and almost womanly for her ten years, she was all her father's daughter, gentle, thoughtful, wise. A born bearer, her uncle thought, big-hipped and breasted already, one created to suckle children and make their father a contented man.

She came sedately to her uncle and kissed him warmly.

'I'm happy to see you, Uncle Tom.'

'And I you. How's my Tetty, then?'

Eight-year-old Maria uncoiled herself from the floor, where she had been playing with a kitten. Like Thetis, she had mouse-brown hair, but it was always in a tangle. Her clothes seemed to get themselves wrongly buttoned and her apron was incapable of staying clean for longer than an hour. Thin, lively, spiteful, she was the only one of the three girls to get her own way consistently.

'You mustn't say Tetty, but Thetis, Uncle, though 'tis non-sensical.'

Tom Blackburn grimaced. Thetis had been born at a time when her father was going through a Miltonic phase. Captivated by the verbal music of *Comus*, he had insisted, against his wife's protests, upon calling their first-born after the silver-slippered nymph of Sabrina's invocation. But unfortunately for him she had been christened at the Collegiate Church by the Reverend Joshua Brookes, the arch-enemy of frippery and fal-lals, who, when handed the babe and requested to name her Thetis, scowled horribly. 'I baptise thee Jane, in the name of the Father, the Son, and the Holy Ghost,' he proclaimed for all the church to hear; and as Jane she was put down in the register. But Thetis she remained at home, calmly immune to the mockery of other children. She smiled at her sister.

'Uncle Tom may call me Tetty or what he likes, Maria. 'Tis all one to me.'

'There – you hear that, you little bizzom?' He directed a play-

ful cuff at Maria's ear, and turned to Emily, who sat dutifully
silent at the instrument again.

'That was a mighty pretty thing you were playing. How d'ye
call it?'

'A song by Josef Haydn, sir: "My Mother Bids Me Bind My
Hair".'

'Let me hear it again.'

Maria groaned and put her fingers in her ears as Emily played
the prelude.

> 'My Mother bids me bind my Hair
> With Bands of rosy hue,
> Tie up my Sleeves with Ribbons rare,
> And lace my Boddice blue.
> For Why, she cries, sit still and weep
> While others dance and play?
> Alas, I scarce can go, or creep,
> While Lubin is away.'

'Well done, little Saint Cecilia!' Her audience clapped his
hands, and Emily drooped her head modestly as she had been
taught to do. Something about her attitude disturbed him: a
quality of unnatural timidity, an air of being one to whom the
world might do what it would. The Reverend Thomas was not
an intellectual man, but he was a fatherly one. While acting as
temporary tutor in the household of Lord Ducie, at Strangeways
Hall, he had been filled with compassion by the appearance of a
young Negro boy, a servant of Lady Ducie's, a gentle youth who,
he was told, had been a slave in America until freed by the
Quakers. By the time he had gained his liberty both his parents
had died from the savage ill-treatment of their overlookers. Why
should this English child remind him of that melancholy-faced
boy?

Impulsively he held out his arms. 'Come here, Miss Emily.' As
she reached his side he lifted her on to his knee, just as he would
have done one of his own daughters. A look of surprise flashed

across her face. Her only acquaintance with the adult knee was being laid across Mrs Blackburn's for a spanking. She sat up straight and stiff, waiting for the usual lecture.

'You play and sing well,' he said.

'So do I,' said Maria.

'Don't be pert, Miss.'

Maria gave Emily a look that meant she would be well pinched when the visitor had gone.

'Do you like to sing hymns, Miss Emily?' he asked.

'Yes, sir.'

'Then you'll know our Manchester hymn, written by the great John Byrom, who was my grandfather's friend.'

Emily shook her head. Every Sunday she went to t'Owd Church, as the Collegiate Church by the river was affectionately nicknamed, but though she followed the service obediently nobody had ever spoken to her of the music which soared up to its glorious medieval roof, whose wall posts were held up by minstrel angels playing all kinds of instruments. Through the long sermons – dropping off to sleep during which was severely punished – her eyes would wander along the line of these heavenly players with their bagpipes, tabors, harps and recorders, and she would wish she could sit in the Choir and look at the grotesque carvings on the canons' stalls: the dragon, the hart, the jester, the fox teaching its children their letters. If she looked over her shoulder she could see the Lever tomb, with its interestingly sad memorial to six children dead between 1635 and 1647: "James in ye 1 yeare of his age."

They're now past hope, past feare or paine.
It were a sinne to wish them here again.

Perhaps they had died in Lady Lever's old house in Piccadilly, and had gone in tiny coffins, each with its own little procession down Market Street Lane, to the cold vault that was waiting for them. She was sure James and his sisters and brothers would like to have been alive again instead of lying there in the dark, mouldering, whatever that might mean. It sounded horrible.

The Reverend Thomas gave her a little shake.

'You're dreaming, miss.'

'She's always dreaming,' Maria said. 'Mamma makes her stand in the corner for it.'

Thomas ignored his niece. 'I was telling you that Mr John Byrom composed "Christians Awake".' He sang, in his pleasant port-mellowed baritone.

'Christians awake, salute the happy morn
Whereon the Saviour of Mankind was born . . .'

'I remember!' Emily's face was suddenly radiant.

'Remember what, child?'

A tiny church, as different from t'Owd Church as Hulme Hall from Mr Blackburn's house, and all hung with green boughs and garlands tied with scarlet ribbons – a beautiful, tall young lady who sang angelically, standing beside a smaller Emily, and a man in black with fine silver buttons on his coat, who stood on the other side of her, and was frightening. The picture flashed into her mind, and was gone.

She tried to recall it that night, lying awake in the room she was lucky enough not to have to share with Thetis and Maria. The Infirmary clock struck ten. Emily was far from sleepy. She wished she might have lit a candle and read a book, but that was impossible, for Mrs Blackburn removed the candle when bidding her goodnight. She thought longingly of the book she had read over and over again, *The Life and Perambulations of a Mouse*, and recited to herself the passage in which the mouse reflects on the folly of a human girl being afraid of it. ' "Here is a little girl now, thought I, in a nice clean room, and covered up warm in bed, with pretty green curtains drawn round her to keep the wind from her head, and the light in the morning from her eyes; and yet she is distressing herself, only because I, a poor little harmless mouse, with scarcely strength sufficient to gnaw a nutshell, happened to jump from the table . . ." '

66

The words slipped away from her mind. A dreadful feeling began to creep over her, the feeling of being nothing, in a great blank space that was also nothing. 'I should not be frightened by a little mouse,' she said to herself, 'if it were in my own room, and I were in my own bed, with my parents and my sisters and brothers nearby in case I should call. But I have nothing. This bed is not mine, this room is not mine. How wicked I must have been for them to have sent me away.'

It was no use crying. That merely caused one's nose to swell and one's eyes to look red and puffy at breakfast, calling down condemnation from Mrs Blackburn for the sin of moping. And most likely there would be another loathsome dose, after break-fast, of Evans' Worm Powders.

5

It was three weeks later, on a sultry morning in July, that the packing-cases came.

The first Emily knew of them was a thunderous rapping of the knocker, followed by Bessy's halting footsteps slowly making their way along the lobby. The three girls, toiling away in the hot, fly-ridden schoolroom, were only too glad of an excuse to look up from their books.

'Mercy me!' said Maria. 'Who can that be?'

Mrs Blackburn frowned. 'I have told you before that "Mercy me" is a profane expression. Think before you speak, child. Thetis, kindly give me the imperative of the verb *facere*.'

Thetis, who had been craning her neck to look out of the window, flushed guiltily and began to flounder through the conjugations. Her efforts were interrupted by the appearance of Bessy at the door.

'It's t'carrier, ma'am, wi' a couple of gurt boxes.'

'What can you mean, Bessy? I ordered no boxes. Tell the man he has come to the wrong house.'

Bessy waved a dirty piece of paper. 'I telled him that an' he said it were written here: Miss Hart, at Mr Blackburn's near t'Palace Inn.'

'For *me*?' Emily's gasp went unheard as Mrs Blackburn read the directions. 'It seems to be correct. Very well, Bessy, I will come down and see to it myself. Girls, I shall expect you to continue your Latin lesson as though I were with you.'

It said much for her discipline that they obeyed, very much against their inclinations. The schoolroom clock pointed to twelve before they closed their books and ventured downstairs. As they made for the two great wooden boxes standing by the front door, Mrs Blackburn appeared with the swiftness of a jack-in-the-box.

'If you imagine that we are going to spend the precious hours

68

of the day in the idle investigation of what I dare say will prove to be nothing of importance, you are quite wrong, young ladies. After lessons are over for the day the cases may be opened.'

'I wish Mamma would not talk so like a book,' Maria whispered to Thetis as they settled themselves at the dinner-table. 'It makes one quite hot trying to follow her.' Thetis gave her a warning look, and bowed her head for their father's saying of grace.

Emily got into grave trouble that afternoon. Usually a model pupil, she seemed unable to get anything right. In the history lesson she muddled up the Tudor kings with the Plantagenets and forgot the dates of both. Miss Winder, who came twice a week to teach English language and literature, complained to Mrs Blackburn that Miss Hart had stumbled disgracefully in reciting Thomson's *Seasons*, which had been the girls' study all that term. The final calamity came in the sewing lesson at the end of the afternoon, when the pupils sewed while Mr Blackburn read to them from some improving work. He read very well, and sometimes slipped in a work which was less improving than entertaining, so that it was no penance to work quietly, listening to him.

But on this day, when he was so kind as to choose 'John Gilpin', one of their favourite poems, Emily's mind was so distracted with curiosity that she stuck her needle right into the fleshy part of her left forefinger.

'Oh!' Her exclamation of pain brought cries from the others as they saw bright red blood spurt out, staining the white handkerchief she was bordering.

'Emily!' Thetis hastened to bind the wounded finger up with her own handkerchief, while Maria affectedly protested that she dare not look or she would swoon for certain. Mr Blackburn closed his book and came to examine the damage.

''Tis nothing, only a scratch, but the young bleed freely. I fear your work has suffered more than you.'

They all looked gravely at the ruined handkerchief.

'Perhaps we could hide it,' suggested Thetis. 'Mamma may not come to inspect our work—'

As if on cue, Mrs Blackburn sailed into the room. Her gaze slid past the sewing of her two daughters and lit implacably on the bloodied object on Emily's desk.

'So, Miss Hart,' she said, 'it seems that your carelessness extends to every branch of learning today.' Thetis began 'But she—' Her mother waved away the interruption. 'I have no intention of chastising your schoolfellow. For the remainder of the week she will use this – this gory rag as her only handkerchief.'

'Ugh!' said Maria. Mrs Blackburn quelled her with a glance.

'Perhaps, Miss Hart, this may teach you that clumsy habits of work lead to a filthy way of life.'

'Yes, ma'am.' Emily was determined not to show disgust; the thought of the unopened packing-cases sustained her. Mrs Blackburn appeared to read her mind.

'Now, I promised that at the conclusion of the working day we would investigate Miss Hart's mysterious packages. Follow me.' She led the way into the lobby, herself quite as curious as the girls. Here, perhaps, would be the answer to the questions her husband had always refused to answer. He, who had sat silent throughout the handkerchief incident, followed her with much the same thought in his mind, and a fear that the confidence he had kept so long might at last have to be broken.

As they went out Thetis whispered to Emily, 'Never mind, I'll give you a handkerchief of mine that you can use when she is not looking.' Emily squeezed her hand gratefully. Maria had already reached the packing-cases and was hopping round them gleefully. 'Perhaps there's a dreadful corpse inside. Half in one and half in the other.'

'Enough, Maria.' Her father tapped her on the head. While the others waited, in varying degrees of impatience, he brought in Will Clough, the handyman, from the garden, armed with a stout knife. A few minutes of energetic sawing of the ropes that tied the cases, and they fell away.

'They'll do now,' he said, and retreated, mopping his brow.

It was Mrs Blackburn's prerogative to step forward first and remove the loose lid of one case. The others gathered round to peer inside. An almost simultaneous gasp went up.

The case was full to the rim with dresses. Girlish dresses, each one cleverly cut for taking in or letting out, with an unstitched hem to be adjusted to the height of the wearer. Round gowns of lawn, full gowns of muslin, long-sleeved chintz and short-sleeved fine calico, shining sarsenet and watered tabby. Below them was a walking pelisse of soft merino in deep rose-pink, edged with swansdown, and a delicious muff to match, with a dove-grey satin bonnet frilled with lace inside the brim and topped with plumes dyed the same pink as the pelisse.

Mrs Blackburn unpacked the lot in silence, to the accompaniment of gasps and squeaks from the three girls and Bessy, who had come to watch. Piling the garments neatly on each other, she turned to the other case. It was packed with enchanting accessories. There were ribbons of all colours, little gloves of soft leather, lace scarves and fichus, an ivory fan and a sash embroidered with rosebuds, a tiny folding parasol; and beneath these a bewildering froth of underwear, chemises, petticoats, an embroidered lawn nightdress and a nightcap with a blue bow.

Mrs Blackburn stepped back and surveyed her lobby floor, almost submerged in clothing. Her daughters were excitedly examining this and that, exclaiming with pleasure. Bessy's eyes were round with awe, for they had never seen such garments before. Emily had scarcely moved during the unpacking; she was scarlet with excitement and joy. Somebody cared about her enough to send her these wonderful things, fit for a princess! Perhaps she *was* a princess, or a lady of title. It was the most glorious moment of her life.

'Well, well, well,' said Mr Blackburn. 'A most imposing array. Emily, you are a very fortunate girl – eh, my dear?'

Emily nodded, radiant.

'Oh my goodness!' cried Maria. 'Don't I just envy you, Miss Puss! Mamma, why have we no such beautiful things? 'Tisn't fair!'

Thetis beamed on Emily. 'I am so happy for you.'

Mrs Blackburn's dark eyebrows had been climbing higher and higher towards her severe cap, as she watched Emily's face.

'If you imagine for one moment, Emily,' she said loudly and deliberately, 'that you will be permitted to wear – or even keep – such preposterous items of clothing, you are sadly mistaken. Not one of these garments is fitted for a child in your situation; not a single plain stuff gown or calico article. You understand, I suppose, that when you are old enough you will have to work for your keep, perhaps at some employment little more exalted than Bessy here?'

Emily stared at her, aghast. 'Not – one thing ?'

'Not one. Even if your circumstances were other than they are, you know my views on plain clothing and simple living. These clothes are more fitted for a harlot than a Christian child.'

'Then what – what will become of them?'

'They will be sold, and the money put to some good use. The purchase of books, perhaps. And I shall of course make a donation to the poor.'

'Mamma, you cannot!' cried Thetis. 'They are Emily's, not yours.'

'Go to your room, miss!'

Mr Blackburn laid a hand on his wife's arm. 'My dear, can you not – some little finery for Sundays?'

She shook the hand off. 'I think I know best, Mr Blackburn.'

Maria had been standing on tiptoe peering into the cases. 'There's something else at the bottom, wrapped in cloth.'

Mrs Blackburn inserted a long arm and fished up the small package. In a moment she had unwrapped it. They all stared at the doll inside, the powdered and piled hair, hooped skirt, the beauty-spots on the sweetly simpering face. Before anyone could speak Emily had snatched it from Mrs Blackburn's hands. Shaking with rage and bitter disappointment, she shouted: 'She's mine and I *will* have her! She shan't be sold – no she shan't!' The doll clutched to her breast, she turned and ran upstairs, sobbing all the time. They heard her footsteps reach the top landing, and her bedroom door slam shut.

Before anyone else could take subversive action against her, Mrs Blackburn ordered Maria to go down and help Bessy prepare the supper. Mr Blackburn made a last attempt.

'Hester, are you sure this is wise? The child is alone in the world . . . some of the – ah – the undergarments might serve—'

His wife smiled pityingly upon him. 'I should have thought even a man could see how thoroughly unsuitable the things are. They show very clearly what kind of origin she has. I warrant her mother is a *Miss* Hart, as well.'

This was so true that Mr Blackburn wisely said no more.

Upstairs, Emily had stopped crying. Anger had dried her tears most effectively. Sitting on the bed she examined the doll from its tiny gold shoes to the miniature ship in full sail on the top of its coiffure. The dress was a little crushed, as though it had been lying in a drawer for a long time. She laid the doll against her face, stroking it, and whispering to it. 'Lady Anne. Lady Anne.'

Mrs Blackburn was not unaware that she had done a bad day's work for herself. Her husband – soft, feckless man – thought worse of her than he had done before; and only they knew what a silent bitterness lay between them in the wide bed which saw no embraces. Thetis's shocked eyes had told their own story, and even spiteful little Maria had been on Emily's side for once. It was very unjust, she told the conscience that nagged at her, for her reasonable action to have turned them all against her. Emily would have looked a figure of fun in such a rig among the sober-clad maids of Manchester. Only carriage-folk dressed so. Well, it would be best to let her keep the doll, rubbish as it was; it would soon fall to pieces.

She went into the lobby and took every scrap of packing-straw out of the cases, then examined the boxes' surfaces with a candle and tipped them up to see whether anything was written on the base. But they told her nothing, battered old things which had travelled on many a baggage-waggon between old house and new house. She scanned the directions, twice: 'Miss Hart, at Mr

73

Blackburn's near the Palace Inn.' The writing was a large slant-
ing scrawl, the writing of a generous, careless person, not at all
the delicate italic hand she herself taught.

A thought struck her as she gathered up an armful of the
clothes. Could they be harbingers of some friend or relation of
Emily's, who would suddenly arrive on the doorstep, demanding to see her in her finery?

She dismissed the thought. Whoever had sent the things anony-
mously meant to remain anonymous. Nobody would ever come
for Emily now.

In the stuffy parlour of a tall house in Somerset Street, London,
a lady was pacing swiftly to and fro like a graceful but impatient
tigress. The lovely girl Emma Hart, of the melting eyes and
dewy lips, had become a woman, in the pride and fullness of
beauty, twenty-six years old. The slender figure had filled out in
voluptuous curves. The simple dress had been changed to the rich
clothes of a fashionable lady in this summer of 1791, the satin
overgown revealing flowing skirts of her favourite pale blue.
Diamond earrings twinkled among the chestnut hair clustering
round cheeks which six Neapolitan summers had not robbed of
their English fairness. There was about her the unmistakable air
of a person used to having her commands obeyed; for the one-
time mistress of Charles Greville was now affianced to Sir
William Hamilton, His Britannic Majesty's Envoy Extraordinary
and Plenipotentiary at the Court of Naples.

She turned sharply and stamped her foot. 'You're being totally
unreasonable, Mam!' she snapped in a voice which had almost
lost its Cheshire accent.

Mrs Cadogan, too, had changed. The past few years had seen
her adjust from her former modest station as Greville's housekeeper to the position of Signora Madre, as respected a figure as
any at the British Embassy, able to speak fluent Italian and to
control a staff of servants virtually uncontrollable by anyone else.
Some of Emma's glory had reflected itself in her mother, and
yet in their new prosperity they were as close to each other as in

the hunger days. In a world in which people adored Emma, fawned on her, envied her, copied her, and in general did anything except treat her as an ordinary mortal, Mrs Cadogan was her conscience and stabiliser. Nobody admired more than she the skilled management by which Emma had brought Sir William round from being reluctant to take her in the first place to the immense step of offering to make her his wife. She had seen her daughter's heartbreak at the faithless trick played on her by Greville, and the dignified courage with which she at last accepted both the situation and the tender admiration offered to her by Sir William. There was greatness in Emma; but it needed leavening every now and then with good sense and disinterested advice.

'I'm being entirely reasonable,' Mrs Cadogan said, 'and I'm not having my granddaughter treated like a toy dog, given away one minute and snatched back the next. You've done nothing for her these six years—'

'Because I had no chance,' cried Emma. 'How could I, so far off in Naples? You said yourself 'twas best to let her settle once she was gone. And I thought that Greville would visit her—'

'That serpent wouldn't visit his own mother if she was on her death-bed next-door,' said Mrs Cadogan. 'He's not been near her, that I'll warrant. And now you want to go prancing off to Manchester and fold her in your arms like somebody on the stage. What then?'

Emma had not got beyond this affecting scene in her mind. 'I could return with her and introduce her to Sir William as a relative of ours, perhaps. Then we could take her back to Naples, to continue her education.'

'And you think he'll take it like a lamb, this child appearing from nowhere and as like as not looking like you? No, no, my girl, not he. He's no ninny, though you treat him like one sometimes. And "A bride's a bride, When the knot is tied", don't forget. You're not married yet.'

Emma brooded, her miraculous mouth drooping. 'She already has the clothes,' she said. 'She must guess—'

'I told you you were a fool to send them. All that finery! And not a word of writing to her. Do you want to send the child crazy? Bad enough growing up not knowing whose bastard she is, or whether she's one at all. How would *you* have liked it?'

Emma smiled dreamily. 'I should have had splendid visions that I was born in a castle – or even a palace. I should have told myself that one day a prince or a knight would come riding, riding to fetch me, and all my rags would be changed to gorgeous robes...'

'You might have done, but will she? Emma, I've made up my mind, and I'll not be gainsaid. I'll go to Manchester myself and see her. I'll tell her as much as I can safely – but no names. Then, when you're fast wedded, you can think what's best to do. If Sir William—'

She broke off as the door opened and Sir William entered with his brisk step.

'I hear my name,' he said. 'I hope you're speaking of me with charity, ladies?'

Emma flew to embrace him, clinging round his neck and dropping little kisses all over his face.

'As if we would speak otherwise of the dearest, kindest, sweetest man that ever walked the earth!'

He clasped her waist, smiling down into the beautiful face turned up to his.

' "Hang there like fruit, my soul, Till the tree die",' he said. Emma frequently put lines from his beloved Shakespeare into his mind. They made a handsome pair, thought Mrs Cadogan. At sixty-one Sir William was as upright and slender as when he had been a young soldier. His aristocrat's face, with the long nose and long humorous mouth, was burnt a deep brown by the Neapolitan sun, his hair under its powder still dark. He had known many women, had been adored by his first wife, plain, religious Catherine, until the day she died. Emma was an immeasurably lucky girl. What a blessing that she truly loved him, even though it was not the love she had given Greville.

'I have come to carry you off, my dear,' he said. ' 'Tis too hot a day to swelter here in town, do ye not think? Why should we

76

not summon the carriage and go on a rural excursion?'

'Oh yes,' Emma beamed with delight.

'Never mind about me,' Mrs Cadogan said. 'I shall be just as happy taking a nap.'

'But I insist. If I am to be a shepherd for the afternoon I'll have two nymphs or none – one for each arm.' Gallantly raising her from her chair, he kissed her hand and then Emma's, and sent them off to titivate for the excursion. The conversation would not be resumed today; but Mrs Cadogan's mind was still made up.

6

Some ten days later Mrs Blackburn was surprised by the arrival of an unexpected visitor. The surprise was literal, for she was still in her morning bedgown in which she dealt with the early work of the house, her cap was an old one, and she had on her feet the wooden chopines or clogs with which she navigated the kitchen floor when Bessy had allowed the washing-copper to boil over, or, as today, had dollied the laundry too enthusiastically. Hastily she kicked them off and put on slippers. Bessy was involved with suds and the mangle, and not presentable, so she answered the knocking herself.

The visitor was standing back in the road, surveying the frontage of the house with mild interest. She was a small woman, wearing what Mrs Blackburn could see at a glance was an expensive walking-dress of excellent cut, with a certain foreign air to it, and a plain chip bonnet suitable to the hot weather.

'Mrs Blackburn? Good day, ma'am,' she said. 'Do I take it you're at home to company?'

Mrs Blackburn was surprised by the almost rustic accent but, as the visitor was obviously respectable, bade her come in and waved her towards the parlour. The parent of a prospective pupil, perhaps, or more likely grandparent she judged on a swift summing-up of the lines on the small face and the droop left by a paralytic stroke on the right side of it.

'Indeed, ma'am, you'll think me not fit to receive. But the servant is – is much occupied, and I've had to turn a hand to help her. Pray take a chair, Mrs—'

'Cadogan,' said that lady, settling herself in the best chair. Leaning back, she produced a fan from her reticule and waved it gently. She had learned much in Naples beside the language.

'In what way can I help you, ma'am?' enquired Mrs Black-

78

burn. (Perhaps not low origins after all. Plenty of gentlewomen spoke with a country tongue, she'd heard.)

'My business is with Mr Blackburn, in fact,' was the surprising reply. 'Is he at home today?'

'He will be by dinner-time, or before. He was sent for early to go to Chetham's School; they've several boys staying over the holiday and the Master has asked him to tutor them. May I ask – if 'tis about a pupil?'

'In a manner of speaking,' replied Mrs Cadogan, managing to convey by her own manner and a social smile that she was giving no more information. 'So if I'm not in your way I'll wait for him. I must leave by the evening coach, but until then I'm not in haste.'

'Oh, you came by coach, ma'am? From London?'

'No, from Chester.'

'Ah, then you will not have a long journey.'

'Oh, I'm not going back there,' returned the maddening woman. 'I've many relatives in those parts. I left my luggage at the Swan and walked here, seeing 'twas such a fine day and only just round the corner.'

Mrs Blackburn struggled with her disinclination to squander money, and won. 'May I ask if you'll partake of a meal with us, Mrs Cadogan. 'Twill be simple enough, but—'

'Oh, anything will do for me. Hotpot or Irish stew, or a dish of nice tripe. I hear you're very fond of it in Lancashire.'

Shocked but relieved at this economical preference Mrs Blackburn hurried down to the kitchen and bade Bessy take her apron off and run down to the Old Shambles for a cut of cheap mutton, and herself began peeling potatoes and cutting up vegetables as though her life depended on it. There were the morning's lessons to get through yet, and how was she to entertain this mysterious visitor? As a start she made some chocolate and took it to the parlour on the best salver.

Left alone, Mrs Cadogan sipped her chocolate (she would much rather have had a cup of good ale or a really chilled white Vesuvio) and surveyed the room, noting its plainness. The furniture was scanty and old-fashioned, probably once owned by past

Blackburns, the decoration shabby – if decoration you could call it, the whole room showing no sign of feminine graces or masculine comforts. In the lobby a smell of washing-day had not escaped her sensitive nose, nor the horrible indefinable effluvia that came from imperfect drainage and were to be met with in most small town houses.

The place was clean enough, certainly. And the woman? Not very old, perhaps in the early thirties, might be pretty in a sharp-faced way if she liked; one of those who'd thrown away her own charms to spite herself or somebody else, most likely her husband.

Mrs Cadogan thought of the packing-cases and their contents, and shuddered. Poor Emily!

She had almost two hours to while away, but fortunately she had her spectacles in her reticule and was able to pass some of the time in looking at books, though they were far from entertaining. No nice novels, no *Monument de Costume* with pretty fashion-plates, only dull tomes with engravings of equally dull worthies. She paused for some time over a medical book in Latin with a remarkable frontispiece showing a gentleman in classical robes seated at his desk, surrounded by emblems of learning, confronted by a well-built young woman without a stitch on; the scene reminded her slightly of Emma and Sir William. Had the young woman called to complain? Or to consult her tutor upon some knotty point? Speculation kept Mrs Cadogan amused and prevented her from thinking of the object of her visit.

When John Blackburn returned and, after a few muttered words from his wife in the lobby, presented himself before the visitor, he knew who she was. In his first glimpse of her he saw a fleeting look of Emily, and instinct told him the rest. She took in at one glance his prematurely old face, his sweat-stained cheap cravat and rusty black coat and breeches, with here and there a button missing. Wife doesn't love him, she thought; downright starved he looks.

He made a nervous bow. 'You have come from Mr G, ma'am, I take it.'

'Not directly, sir, but in the same connection. Mr Greville don't know of my visit.'

She saw him glance round swiftly at the door as she spoke Greville's name. So there was a wifely ear pressed to the keyhole.

'I am glad to see you, ma'am. 'Tis not hard to tell you are a relative of Miss Hart.'

'A close relative, yes. No doubt you've wondered why she has not been visited before? Her family much regret it, but for many reasons 'twas impossible. I hope she has not been too fretted by it?'

'No. No. At first she – suffered from the parting. But she has settled well and is a model pupil. We are very fortunate to have one so obedient and so amiable. I—' he seemed to find it difficult to say – 'I am very glad you're come. I think she has needed someone of her own. No doubt you'll wish to see her?'

'If convenient. Mrs Blackburn has kindly invited me to dinner with you. I think 'twould be best if I met the child before we're all at table.'

'Of course, of course. I believe she is still in the schoolroom. I'll fetch her.' He paused at the door. 'Mrs Cadogan, I have kept faith strictly with Mr Greville. I have not mentioned his name to anyone, not even my wife. Will it now be possible to talk freely?'

'I fear it won't. There are still many things in the way. Thank you for your discretion, sir.'

It seemed a long ten minutes before he reappeared, saying quickly under his breath, 'I have only told her there is someone to see her.' Emily lingered outside the door. 'Come, Emily,' he said kindly. 'Here is a friend waiting for you.'

Like a frightened animal Emily crept in, her back to the wall, and stood with her eyes cast down. He gave her a little push into the room and went out, shutting the door.

'Come, Emily,' said her grandmother softly. She was not far from tears, but it wouldn't help to show emotion. The child looked up, with Emma's own great violet eyes. She moved a few paces towards the beckoning hand, her face as white as paper, unspeaking.

'Well, now,' said Mrs Cadogan briskly, 'if I haven't been sitting here all morning with my bonnet on. Seeing you look so cool made me remember it. Do you think Mrs Blackburn will be offended if I take it off?' She proceeded to do so, after Emily's shake of the head.

'There, that's better. I put my best pink ribbons in my cap today, for I thought you'd like them. I see Mrs Blackburn dresses you very sensible for your lessons. You had a grey dress like that when you were a little thing. Don't you remember?'

Another headshake. The head was bent floorwards again.

'And you don't remember me? Or anyone?'

Emily spoke for the first time. 'A few things, ma'am. But I don't know what they mean.'

'Why should you, indeed? You were little more than a baby. Let's not worry our heads about it. Well, and what a pretty girl you've made, my dear. Your mamma was always afraid you'd grow up snub-nosed, but it's quite straight, I'm glad to see.'

A flicker of awareness. 'Was she very pretty?'

'Not only was but is, very pretty indeed.'

'Like me?' The nervous tautness was going.

'No, not quite like you.'

But the questioning eyes were so much Emma's that Mrs Cadogan hesitated, with her hand on the fichu-brooch that held a miniature of a laughing Bacchante. No, it wouldn't do. She switched the conversation.

'And are you happy here, Emily?'

'Happy, ma'am?' The child had clearly never thought of happiness as a right.

'Are they kind to you? Do you feed well and play well?'

Emily looked puzzled. 'I learn my lessons, ma'am.'

Try as she would, Mrs Cadogan could get no more information, only a general impression that the child was naturally lively behind that front of meek shyness. During the meal that followed she was often aware of Emily's eyes upon her, of a faint tremor of the hands betraying inward excitement. She noted, too, the economical cut of meat, the small portions, the flavourless vegetables; good food ruined for lack of care. As Bessy passed in and out with the dishes Mrs Cadogan eyed her with disfavour. That the poor thing was crooked was no fault of hers, but that her hands were dirty and her nose inclined to drip was a matter for censure. Mrs Blackburn appeared not to notice it, steering the conversation towards matters supposed to impress the guest, such as the building of new streets in Manchester and the political activities of Mr Blackburn's cousin. Mrs Cadogan observed that her hostess spoke to her in one tone of voice and to the children in quite another, a cold and pompous voice left over from the schoolroom.

'Doesn't like children, she thought. Or her husband, much. Wants to be thought a great scholar. The bigger child's a poor biddable creature, the little wench a minx and Mamma's favourite. Emily treated well because I'm here. Such were Mrs Cadogan's reflections as she chewed with difficulty the last of the stringy meat on her plate and saw out of the corner of her eye a bread pudding, her great detestation, approaching. She decided to drop a bombshell into the meaningless chat.

'I hope you was pleased with the new clothes, Emily?'

Emily flushed, then paled, and looked at Mrs Blackburn, who tightened her lips and glanced round the table. Mr Blackburn pushed his chair back, saying, 'No pudding, Bessy. I must get back to my pupils. Excuse me, ma'am.' With a bow he left the room.

'As to the new clothes,' said Mrs Blackburn, 'we did not know 'twas you sent them, ma'am.'

'Oh, yes, 'twas I indeed,' Mrs Cadogan replied with cheerful mendacity. 'I should like to see Emily in one of the pretty dresses this afternoon, when we may take a walk, eh, Emily?'

There was a dreadful silence. Emily's eyes filled with tears.

'I fear that won't be possible.' Mrs Blackburn's eyes were not meeting her guest's. 'The clothes were – very unsuitable to our humble way of life. I – disposed of them.'

83

Mrs Cadogan put her knife and fork down with a decisive clatter.

'Wasn't that something of a liberty, ma'am? The clothes were Emily's, not yours.'

'I understood that Mr Blackburn and I were to use our discretion in all matters pertaining to Miss Hart. We could not have countenanced her wearing such things. Girls, leave the table and go to the schoolroom.' Reluctantly Thetis, Maria and Emily folded their napkins and left, Emily with a wistful backward look. Mrs Blackburn continued. 'We have been told that Emily will in time have to earn her own living. It is no kindness to fill her with notions of finery and puff her up with pride.'

'That's as may be. Times change and prospects with 'em.'

'You mean that Miss Hart's prospects have changed?'

'I can't say. Much depends on how I find her here. I thought to have seen at least a set of the clothes to be worn for best. Noll Cromwell's buried and dead, or so I've heard, and 'tis no sin for a child to look pretty. Her Mamma won't be pleased, that I can tell you.'

Mrs Blackburn saw vanishing all her extra income, the items charged to Emily's account and not incurred, the prestige of having a ladylike pupil to exhibit should any prospective parents come along. She began to speak, but Mrs Cadogan gently waved her aside.

'If it's all the same to you, ma'am, the heat's overpowering me and I'll put my feet up in the parlour for half an hour.' With profuse apologies for keeping her at the table, Mrs Blackburn bustled her out, dusted down the narrow day-bed and disposed her guest upon it. Mrs Cadogan produced a vinaigrette and took a refreshing sniff, before kicking off her shoes.

'I may take Emily for a walk, then?'

'Whenever you wish, ma'am.'

They walked side by side, the little ageing woman and the girl in the too-hot cloak and eclipsing bonnet. Mrs Cadogan was shown the Infirmary Gardens, and those beyond where some-

84

times the harmless poor lunatics might be seen to walk. She admired the great gun which hung outside Styan's Gun and Pistol Shop, the steps of the Palace Inn down which a tartan-clad Prince had once walked, the market-stalls at the New Cross where one might buy anything if one had the money. Emily grew more and more talkative, dropping the shy correct manner which she had been taught to use in adult company. Her hand slipped into the small gloved hand of her grandmother; as they paced along together, the likeness between them was plain. Emily tugged at the hand.

'Down there is t'Owd Church, ma'am, where we go every Sunday. I could show you very interesting things there if you would like to see them?'

Mrs Cadogan shook her head, smiling. 'Nay, little lass, my feet have come far enough for the moment. Let's sit down.' Outside an inn benches were empty and inviting. Emily's bonnet had fallen back and her red-gold head shone in the afternoon sun, brilliant against the grey brim. 'An apple of gold in a network of silver,' thought her grandmother. On her neat nose freckles were stealing out as they had on the classic nose of the young Emma, who had promptly banished them with lemon-juice. But this child turned her face up to the sun as though she could never have enough of it, her eyes half closed, veiled by the long lashes, her mouth smiling. Mrs Cadogan looked down at her and loved her.

The lashes lifted. 'I was almost asleep then, and I woke and saw you. I *used* to wake and see you – did I not?'

'Yes, my dear.'

'There is something – it troubles me . . .'

'What, Emily?'

'Did I do something wicked, to be sent away?'

'Oh, my dear child. No, no, whatever put such an idea into your head? If anyone was wicked, and I'm not saying they weren't, it was not you, innocent that you were.'

Emily's face cleared magically. 'Oh, I am so glad! I thought it was because of that. Then may I come home?'

Mrs Cadogan turned away. 'My dear, what can I say? There are things – it has all to do with changes, with your Mamma's life. Emily, you must know this. She is a great lady, so you must never think you come of bad stock. But, Emily, I can't tell some of it without telling all. This I promise you, I'll do all in my power for you. You're a sensible child, you'll not build too much on it?'

Emily shook her head. 'Please don't tell Mamma I am unhappy. Only that I would like to be with her – and you. It is not that I mind learning. I like to learn. Could Mamma teach me?'

'Some things, I expect. French and Italian, and music.'

'I should like that.' She subsided into a daydream. A sweep and his boy passed them, a group of women who looked curiously at the well-dressed lady, a farm-cart on its way from the countryside of Newton Heath. Above the low buildings around them the square medieval tower of the Collegiate Church rose serenely, a benevolent hen among its brood of dark chicks. Mrs Cadogan had never been much of a one for church-going and had small opinion of parsons, but she had a strong conviction that some powerful help would be needed from whomever they prayed to if Emily were to be restored to the life human power had stolen from her.

Emily was studying her with sleepy interest. She traced with a forefinger the line of her grandmother's eye and cheek, too polite to enquire why they drooped. 'A stroke of the palsy, my dear, brought on by a shock,' she was told. It had happened six years before, after she had seen Emily off to Manchester and had gone back home shaking, to fall heavily on the floor of her bedroom, lying there until the maid found her. It had been caused, the doctor said, by excess of feeling.

The church clock chimed four. 'Come,' she said, 'we'd best get back. Don't walk too fast for me, now.' Slowly they made their way round by the market-place into Market Street Lane, between old timber-framed and gabled houses and shops. 'Look,' said Mrs Cadogan, 'a pastry-cook's. I could fancy a cup of tea, and judging by that great pot in the window we can get one

86

there.' Up the steps, into Mr Hyde's shop, she led the wide-eyed Emily, and soon they were sitting by the wide chimney-place with a pot of tea and a plate of cakes between them: almond tarts, raisin-buns, jelly-cakes, iced sponges, a rich and bewildering array. Emily had never seen such a sight. She hardly dared to touch one, but with encouragement managed three before she was replete. Not had many treats, Mrs Cadogan reflected. Small because she's underfed. With satisfaction she watched her grandchild eat, waving away with her fan the flies which threatened to settle on the confectionery.

All too soon they were back in Palace Street. Mrs Cadogan sought out Mr Blackburn. 'A word alone, sir, if you please.'

He led her into the dark little study. 'I was hoping to speak to you, ma'am. I hope you're satisfied with Emily's progress?'

She temporised. 'I'm more than pleased with her.'

'And she will remain with us?'

'That I can't say. I'll not disguise from you that to my way of thinking a child's place is with its relatives, and it may be her guardians will wish that. 'Tis not in my power to say.'

'I see. And meanwhile, Mr Greville prefers her to know nothing of her circumstances?'

'It would be kindest. She remembers nothing of coming here, I could swear to that. Only a flash of memory here and there. She's a sensitive child, Mr Blackburn, and no mistake. I'd be pleased to think your good lady would put herself out a bit to make her feel at home.'

He shook his head. 'I can do nothing to influence Mrs Blackburn, ma'am. She has strong views on education and the bringing up of children. So far, I would say her methods have been successful, don't you concur?'

'As far as education goes, I do indeed. But there's more to it than that. Maybe I spared the rod a bit on my own daughter, but she's grown up with a loving heart and a quick laugh, and that's a great deal.' She stood up. 'The coach leaves in half an hour. Can I say goodbye to Emily?'

'Certainly. I believe she is in the schoolroom.'

Emily was sitting by the window, at an inky desk, weaving threads of gold and silver wire into a shape. A candle and a soldering-iron were beside her. Her eyes remained cast down as Mrs Cadogan entered the room, but her awareness and dread lay heavy on the air.

'That's pretty. Filigree work, isn't it, my dear?'

Emily nodded. Her eyes were hot and her throat full of tears.

'And what will it be when it's finished?'

The answer was almost inaudible. 'A basket. For Mamma.'

Mrs Cadogan put her arm round the bowed shoulders, and found herself clung to, pulled down, desperately held as she had been six years before, while Emily sobbed: 'Please don't go! I don't want you to go! Oh, please!'

'God help you, my dear. I must.'

7

Emma, Lady Hamilton, turned her left hand this way and that
in the autumn sunshine that streamed through the windows of
the lodging she shared with her husband of a day. Bright points
of light shot from the band of new gold on her finger, making
her laugh with delight.

'To think I am really Lady Hamilton! I shall never want to
wear another ring. Oh Mam, I'm so happy!'

She twirled round and seized her mother by the waist, dancing
her to and fro until Mrs Cadogan begged to be released. 'Have
done, Emma, do! You're like a wild thing.'

'No, no, no. I'm grave, sedate, respectable.' She broke into
song. '"I am frolicsome, I am easy, Good-temper'd and free, I
don't care a single pin, me boys, What the world thinks of me."
Don't you think I look fine, Mam? Poor Romney was overcome
to see me, laughing and crying at once, dear soul; he said I was
more glorious in my plain wedding-dress than in all the robes of
Attica, wasn't that kind? He's painted me sideways on, sitting in
a chair looking over my shoulder, wearing my highwayman hat,
and he's putting in Vesuvius behind and calling me "The Am-
bassadress".'

'You'll have to put that hair up now you're married,' said her
mother.

'Me, wear a dowdy cap like Mrs Bun the Baker's Wife? That I
won't. I'll set the fashion for Neapolitan ladies, you'll see. Wasn't
it a magnificent wedding-breakfast, though so quiet? I declare I
feel quite drunk, though I'd barely a thimbleful of wine. Poor
Sir William, he's still asleep after it.' She took off the high-
crowned hat with its waving plume and flung herself luxuriously
on to the day-bed, holding the ringed hand high above her head.

Mrs Cadogan went to the door and shut it.

'Emma, before he comes down – I think you should speak to him today. There's very little time left, with you returning to Naples the day after tomorrow.'

'About Emily?' Emma's face was all lovely gravity. 'I hadn't forgot. But I wanted to have my own little triumph first . . . Mam, *must* I say who she is?'

Mrs Cadogan sighed. 'I've told you before I think honesty's the best policy, then if things come out in the future you can't be called a liar. But please yourself.'

'And you'll help me persuade him?'

'If you think you'll need me.'

Her daughter swamped her in a warmly scented embrace. 'I'll always need you, dear little Mam.'

Sir William, whose liver was not his happiest possession, had wakened from sleep with a taste in his mouth like London fog, and a nagging headache. A draught of the gentian tisane Emma carried about with her helped to restore him slightly; enough, she judged, to be petitioned. Kneeling at his side, her smiling face turned up to his, she knew that she presented a most appealing portrait of a Fair Supplicant. Across the room Mrs Cadogan was engaged in a humdrum mending job which left her free to listen and take part.

Sir William tilted up his wife's chin. 'You've something to ask me. I know that look. What is it, my Venus? No more rings, mind, for I gave ye one this morning.'

She kissed the ring and the hand that had given it. 'What more could you give me than you've done already? No, 'tis for someone else. You recall Mam visiting in the North last month? Well, it happened she called on some relatives of ours – my Aunt Connor and her family. And on some others, called Moore, in Manchester. That is my uncle's name is Moore—'

Mrs Cadogan's cool voice broke in as she heard Emma beginning to flounder. 'The upshot is, Sir William, that these relatives have a little girl in their charge, an orphan child. Now,' she pretended to examine closely the stitching of a buttonhole, 'it struck me then, and I said to Emma when I got back, this child is uncommonly bright and of a very superior disposition.'

'Quite a lady, indeed,' said Emma. 'She learns music and painting and all sorts, and promises well, but, poor thing, she has no comforts, no pleasure out of life that a child should have – nowt but bed and work, as Mam would say, and dreadful dull clothes though she will be very pretty, favouring our colouring—'

Sir William's eyebrows rose. 'Oh, so she too is a relative?'

'Distant,' put in Mrs Cadogan hurriedly. 'The Moores are not her own people. She's nearer in blood to us.'

'Her mother was a poor betrayed girl,' improvised Emma, 'and her father a young spark with a stone for a heart. I've heard the mother was like to kill herself when she found she was breeding, and but for being taken up from the water in time she had been drowned.'

Sir William took a pinch of snuff, surveying his two ladies.

'A moving story. And who supports this orphan?'

They had not thought of this. 'A relative,' ventured Emma.

'*Another* relative? The child hardly seems to be alone in the world.'

'Emma feels,' said Mrs Cadogan, 'that she has been so blessed by fortune she would like to do something for one of her family that's been less lucky. The Connors are bright children too, but there are six of them, and this child is but one.'

Emma caught his dry hand in her own warm clasp. 'Pray, pray, dearest Sir William, can't I take her out with me as my companion and ward? 'Twould give her so much happiness and like as not bring her a good marriage.'

'Why, how old is she?'

'Almost nine.'

'*Nine?* The Court of Naples is hardly a nursery for sucklings, my dear. How would her education be continued?'

The two women looked at each other; neither of them had thought of that. 'There are my singing masters—' Emma began.

'And what use are the Arts alone to such a young child? To improve her it would be needful to cultivate her mind, educate

91

her in Latin so that she might become familiar with the Ancients—'

'Oh, but you could do that!' Emma burst out. ' 'Twould be the best way of teaching, to take her on expeditions with you, let her see tombs opened and statues dug up.'

'I have no intention of carrying a crèche about with me. What sort of a figure should I make, pray, trailing about Portici or Pompeii with a babe in arms—'

'Emily is *not* a babe in arms.'

'Emily?'

There was a silence in the room. 'She was called after me,' Emma said. ' 'Twas a compliment . . .'

He studied her downcast head, bent as gracefully as a lily on its stalk. The waves of rippling hair lay across his knees; he could feel the warmth and pressure of her breast. Even in the course of a silly argument she could arouse desire. Gently he made her look at him.

'Emma, my dear, I know your good heart, and that it would please you to raise up this young relative of yours in the world. But believe me, the odds are it would be but a bad life for such a girl. You and I know the Court, do we not? And besides, have you given thought to the way it would appear – you and I returning with a young child, as though we had to be wed before we showed her to the world?'

Emma looked at her mother, aghast. Mrs Cadogan nodded slowly.

'Sir William is right, Emma. It would look bad, indeed.'

'But—' Emma began. Sir William raised a hand.

'If you were going to say that I am incapable of begetting children, Emma, I would rather you did not. 'Tis true I have none, and my late wife and I were at last compelled to adopt a daughter, who died, poor thing. But I am not quite in the sere and yellow yet. Give me the benefit of the doubt. The scandal-mongers certainly will, if you and I are seen with a child between us.'

She still looked mutinous as he went on: 'I have purposely

92

arranged to go back to Naples so soon after our marriage that there'll be little gossip once the fact is known. Let us not attract more than we need.'

'I only want to help her,' Emma said.

'Help her to what? Is she a damsel to be rescued? Is she beaten? Tortured? Starved? Kept in vicious company?'

Mrs Cadogan answered. 'No, Sir William. But she deserves better than she has. I found my heart warm to her very much.'

'More than to these Connor children you mention?'

'Why, yes, if you must know.'

'Well, this I tell you, if you befriend her all the others will be after us too, expecting their brats to be educated at our expense and introduced at Court.' He grew heated, his Scots accent thicker. 'Have we nothing else to discuss, at this time when Europe is in ferment, our Queen's own sister in danger of her life from the Revolutionaries, but your relations? I'll have no more of it, Emma.' He rose and stalked out, leaving the two women staring ruefully at each other.

'It's of no use,' Mrs Cadogan said. 'God knows I tried, but his mind's made up. And he may very well be right. Don't forget that he stands to lose something from this marriage – the King has only given him permission as a private gentleman, not as his Ambassador to Naples.'

'And so I remain on sufferance,' said Emma bitterly. 'Oh, and I was so happy this morning.'

'And will be tomorrow, my dear. We must believe all's for the best where Emily is concerned, and try to forget. She is not meant for the life we lead, mayhap.'

Emma sighed. 'I must think so, I suppose, or 'twill break my heart.'

That night, their wedding-night, she was enchantment itself to Sir William, saying not a word of their argument; and he, who would have been very glad to sleep early on such a hot airless night, stayed awake to please his good-tempered, obedient wife, whose submission to his will that day had cost her something, and who had not deceived him for a moment.

The morning of their departure, a parcel was brought to Emma by her borrowed maid. 'Left by Mr Greville's servant, m'lady.'

'From Greville!' She turned it this way and that. 'So he's come out of his huff and sent me a wedding-gift. But this is addressed to *you*, Mam.'

'Me? What have I done to earn a gift, and from him of all people?' She took off the outer wrapping and they contemplated the packing of white fluff speckled with seeds and pods which protected the content and masked its shape.

'Raw cotton,' Mrs Cadogan said. 'Mind, or it'll be up our noses and all over the room.' Carefully she peeled it open, and took out a small basket of gold and silver filigree, simply made with flaws here and there as though the maker were unskilled. Emma stared.

'Who in God's name would send me this?' Underneath the packing inside the basket itself lay a folded paper. Mrs Cadogan opened it, adjusted her spectacles, and after a moment handed it silently to Emma. A childish copperplate hand had inscribed:

To Mamma, from her Loving and Obedient Daughter,
Emily Hart

When this you see
Remember me.

Two

Emily's Journal

8

July 28th, 1798

Just six years have passed since Mrs Cadogan's visit to me. Then I was a child; now I am a woman of sixteen years. I say 'a woman', though I am so young, because I feel that I put away childish things long ago. I never had a plaything but for the doll which was sent in the boxes of clothes, nor a playmate but Thetis and Maria, both now separated from me. Since there is nobody in whom I can confide, I have resolved to keep a journal in which I may perhaps be able to reason out my perplexities and set down my blessings. Besides, I take a little vain pleasure in writing – something I do well, I know.

Though I was so sad when Mrs Cadogan left me, I felt sure in my heart that soon I would be sent for. Day after day I waited for a letter or a knock on the door, growing dreamy in lesson-times and receiving many a slapped hand or a box on the ear for it. The knock would come, I knew, and there at the door would be a carriage, and Mrs Cadogan stepping out of it; or perhaps even my mother herself, the great lady in beautiful clothes, come to thank me for the filigree basket.

But nobody came for me, and nothing was sent. Mrs Blackburn observed my melancholy, and said to me: 'It seems you might have spared your trouble, making that piece of frippery for someone who no doubt has plenty of that sort of thing. At least I shall send them a bill for the materials – two and a half guineas it will cost them.'

'Oh no!' I said. 'It was meant as a gift.'

'And who are you to afford gifts? You have nothing but what they send you.'

It was true. I had nothing, and I was nobody. The time came

97

when no allowance for me had come for over half a year, to the alarm of both Mr and Mrs Blackburn. One night, as I was passing the drawing-room door on my way to bed, I heard them talking, and caught my own name. It was not vulgar curiosity, indeed, that made me stay and listen; there was a trembling in all my limbs that held me to the spot, ashamed to eavesdrop.

'Do you think we can afford to keep her for ever, without a penny?' Mrs Blackburn was saying. 'What with doctors' bills, stockings, petticoats, and everything else, she costs us a fortune.'

'My dear—'

'Oh, you see nothing of it, always from home or with your nose in your books. I tell you, those that are responsible for her have been hanged or transported or locked up in a debtors' prison. No good ever came of such people. One only had to look at that Madame Cadogan, with her low speech and fine clothes, to see what *she* had been.'

'You are quite wrong. I know these people, and they are most respectable. There is some natural delay—'

Mrs Blackburn's voice became impassioned. 'Don't think to talk me down with your excuses, Mr Blackburn. Either the child is paid for or she goes to the Charity, or into a cotton-mill. She's active enough and could earn good wages.'

I heard Mr Blackburn catch his breath as though he were going to cough. Then he said, gasping a little, 'Hester, I will not argue with you. I feel one of my attacks threatening. But this I will say, that tomorrow, unless I am taken ill, I intend to go to London to see Mr—'

'Mr G? I know,' said Mrs Blackburn with an air of triumph. 'Oh, you think I'm too stupid to learn our benefactor's name?'

His answer was almost a whisper. 'If you know it, you know it. It can mean nothing to you. And I beg you not to speak to Emily . . .'

Though still shaking, I managed to tiptoe past the door and up to my room. There I lay all night awake, with a terrible feeling on me of being a small dot in a great ocean of space, so that if I stirred even a little I would sink, down and down, until my eyes and mouth and nostrils were full of wet choking sand; and then I would be nobody indeed.

Mr Blackburn was spared the asthmatic attack he feared, but I fell ill myself, with a high fever which I think owed something to the shock I had received, for I remember crying out over and over again, 'Don't send me away! Oh, don't send me away!'

One day I awoke from a restless sleep, my bones aching and my head on fire, to see the doctor bending over me. I felt the sharpness of the knife in my arm as he bled me, and shut my eyes so as not to see the drip of blood into his cup. He murmured something about 'hysteric passions' and 'oppression in the mind' which was meaningless to me. Some time later I found Mr Blackburn standing by my bed, his expression kind and anxious.

'The doctor tells me your fever is caused by a troubled mind, Emily,' he said.

I tried to sit up. 'Indeed, sir,' I said, as well as I could speak, 'I think I have a violent cold.'

He sat on the edge of my bed and took my hot hand. 'So you may have, but there's more to it. Why do you call out to us so often? What distresses you?'

I turned away my face, afraid that in my weakness I might weep.

'Only that – I overheard you talking to Mrs Blackburn. Oh, sir, must I go to the Charity?' To my shame I was weeping already, and his kind hand was patting my shoulder.

'No, no, child, never. It was wrong to listen – you see, listeners never hear any good of themselves. But I promise you there shall be nothing like that. At the very worst, my brother Tom at Cheadle will house you. Would you like to go to him?'

'Y-yes,' I sobbed, remembering the jolly clergyman who sometimes called with his plump wife and children.

'But in any case I have business in London this week, and I will speak to your guardian then. Now you must get better, and trouble yourself no more.'

His frankness was so reassuring that I was almost better by the next morning, when he was to take coach to London. For the first time I was able to eat the porridge Thetis brought me for break-fast, and to wash my face and hands.

'Please fetch me a mirror, Thetis,' I asked her. 'I must look a great fright by now.' She flushed, and sought about the dressing-chest as though the mirror were not lying where it could hardly be missed.

'Emily, please don't mind—' she began. But even before I looked in the glass my hands had found the sharp stubble where my long smooth hair had been. The reflection showed me the worst. My face was as sharp and pointed as a starving cat's, my eyes ridiculously huge in it; and my hair, my poor hair, was all gone, my head shaven like the lunatics' in Piccadilly. Thetis was more distressed than I was myself.

'The doctor *would* have it cut off because you were in such a fever. Even Mamma tried to stop him. But it will grow again, Emily, truly it will, better than ever.'

When I was up and about again I wore a little cap tied under my chin, incurring much mockery from Maria. 'This is the priest all shaven and shorn Who killed the cow with the crumpled horn,' she would chant, dancing maddeningly round me, inciting Bessy to laugh at me with her, for Thetis never would.

When Mr Blackburn came back after three days I was sum-moned to the drawing-room, where he and Mrs Blackburn awaited me. I stood before them in my ridiculous cap and my everyday stuff dress, which now hung off me like a sack, to hear my fate.

'Sit down, child,' he said. 'I think you should hear what I have to report, since you know we have had trouble over your allow-ance. It seems the delay has been caused by Mr – by your principal guardian having fallen into straitened circumstances. Finding himself unable to pay the last half-year's account, he sent it on to – to another guardian now living abroad, suggesting that it might more easily be paid by him. Now, as you know, the Revolutionary troubles in France are likely to cause delays and even losses at sea. We may not know for some time whether your – your guardian at present abroad is willing to pay for you. But we will take it that he is, and meanwhile his bank is prepared to advance the money to me.'

'Thirty-two pounds eleven shillings,' said Mrs Blackburn ominously.

'I see, sir. I am glad,' I said, and curtseyed, prepared to leave the room. But Mrs Blackburn summoned me back.

'Not so fast. Your support seems uncertain, even so, and Mr Blackburn tells me your guardians have no plans for your future. You know you will have to earn your living as soon as possible?'

'Yes, ma'am. I have always known it.'

She smiled grimly. 'Then, as you are being instructed in the arts and sciences which will fit you for becoming a governess, you had better study the domestic arts as well.'

'Ma'am?'

'From tomorrow you will help Bessy in the kitchen, and wait at table.'

Our eyes met. Young as I was, I had the sensibility of one much older. I saw in her eyes that this new plan was not only to humiliate me, whom she disliked, but to displease her husband; and his cold glance at her confirmed my guess. I believe it disappointed her that I neither protested nor wept, but dipped my formal curtsey and said, 'If you wish it, ma'am.' When I had left the room I heard voices raised behind the closed door, but this time I did not listen.

I went to my room and stood by the window. What I saw was indelibly impressed on my mind. It was late January, the sky darkening towards dusk, the fallen snow on the cobbles of the horse-road already freezing; snow nestling on the roofs and gables of the old houses in the Lane. Few people were about; in the windows of shops and houses lamps were being lit. The sight should have been a melancholy one, but for some reason my heart was high with exaltation.

'This is the worst, then, that has so far happened to me,' I said to myself. 'My guardians, even Mrs Cadogan, have left England – they care nothing for me. Perhaps I am not worth caring for. I am not only to work hard at my studies but I am to do the work of a kitchen-maid. Very well. I will care for myself, and do the work expected of me. And I will forget all my dreams.'

It makes me laugh a little now, to think what a serious child I was; but I believe I had some spirit of resolution in me which helped me to fit into the new pattern of my life. I got little enough help from anyone else. Thetis, ashamed for my sake, got scolded when she tried furtively to give me a hand with the heavy work, while Maria never let an opportunity slip to call me 'our servant-girl' and drop things for me to pick up. Bessy, who might have been supposed to welcome my assistance, did just the opposite. On the first morning I appeared in the kitchen, ready to work there for an hour before lessons began, she turned roughly on me.

'What's tha want in my kitchen?'

'I'm sent to help you, Bessy.'

'Thee? A rattling nobbut as high as a flea? I want no childer smashing pots and getting me the blame, I tell thee. Get thee back upstairs.'

'But I must stay. I daren't go up before I'm told.'

'Eeh, dear. Well, theer's jobs to be done. Get started on t' washing-up.'

And, standing on an upturned box, I was set to scrape the leavings off the breakfast-plates and wash them in the stone-sink. Pipe-water from the conduit reached us for only two hours a day, and was, of course, stone-cold. I found later that Bessy went to the trouble of heating it in the fish-kettle for her own washing-up, but allowed me to wash the dishes in cold, so that they came out greasy and streaky and earned me a scolding. I got a second scolding when I presented myself in the schoolroom with hands red and raw from the hard water and coarse soap (which had sand in it for scouring off the grease).

I could do right for nobody, except Mr Blackburn, who dared not protest too much. But I remained calm, doing my work as well as I could and bearing my punishments unflinchingly. Often I was ill, but not ill enough to stay in bed; and strangely enough I began to grow taller and stronger with exercise, though I was hardly ever without a cold in the damp air of Manchester. What suits cotton-spinning is very unsuited to human lungs.

One thing I had to please me was that my hair grew again. Within six months of my shearing it covered my head in curls like a lamb's fleece, and was darker than before, almost auburn. I knew that it suited me, and cherished this, my only small vanity, in secret.

And so I became a woman in character before a change came to my body which shocked me dreadfully, for such things were not spoken of in our sort of household. One morning I awoke to find my nightgown and sheets all spotted with blood. Terrified, I rushed into the sisters' room. They were both sleeping, and I shook Thetis awake. At first I could not make her understand what had happened, and when she roused enough to see my plight she was as frightened as I.

I would not dwell on this episode except that I still remember Mrs Blackburn's impatient, brusque explanation of a very ordinary function; and I wonder now, as I did then, why a young girl should be instructed so carefully in music, deportment, needlework and the use of the globes, and yet be kept ignorant of what must happen to her body so that in time she may fulfil her destiny and bear children. Perhaps only the intellect is important.

Reading over what I have just written, I feel I have shown myself as a put-upon, melancholy drudge. I must be fairer to myself. Though I have not enjoyed the happiness of family life and play-fellows, I have within me a spring of joy always ready to well up when I am free of tasks and my time is my own. My music has been a delight to me, the hours I spend at the pianoforte passing like minutes. I love to walk in the busy streets, to wander round the market stalls at the Exchange and imagine myself a housewife able to buy spring flowers and bright stuffs to make children's clothes, round Cheshire cheeses and the chalky white cheese of Lancashire, smoked hams and brown eggs.

I like to walk in the fine fashionable streets round St Anne's Square, where sedan chairs stop before the new houses of pink brick with stone facings, and ladies in hoops and splendid hats come daintily down the steps to be carried to a rout or a breakfast. The Church of Saint Anne is new compared with my beloved Owd Church, but already the graves are clustering round it. One tombstone commemorates "An Honest Grocer of This Town", and I am pleasantly puzzled to wonder why his wife should describe him thus – had there been those at the graveside who accused him of giving short measure? How peaceful these scenes are, when one considers that bloodshed and terror reign across the seas! News has just come in (I write on August 10th) of a great victory over Bonaparte's naval forces at Aboukir Bay at the mouth of the Nile. The Commander of our British Fleet was Sir Horatio Nelson, who has gained great fame already.

I am resolved to record all the startling events of our time, so that although my life be insignificant my journal may interest those who chance to read it when my days are over.

9

September 1st, 1798
Why did I say that my life was uneventful? Today, after lessons,
I was called to the drawing-room. Mrs Blackburn appeared more
amiable than usual, and addressed me civilly, for her.

'Miss Hart, I feel the time has come when you must take some
employment. I can teach you nothing more, and I am sure you
would wish to experience a wider world than the schoolroom.'

'Yes, indeed, ma'am,' I said.

'We have found a situation for you which seems both convenient and suitable. Mrs Blomiley's finishing school is in need of
a junior instructor in music and the decorative arts. Her pupils
are young ladies, of your own age or younger, but in spite of
your youth she is impressed by my report of your skill, and is
prepared to take you.'

I was overcome by surprise and delight. 'I – I'm most grateful
to you, ma'am,' I stammered. 'And to Mrs Blomiley. Am I to
lodge with her?'

'No, you will live here, and what you earn will help us to keep
you; but you may keep some pocket-money for yourself. On
Monday morning you are to begin your employment.'

I knew myself dismissed, and was glad of such a brief interview for it left me free to rejoice alone. What a fortunate girl I
am!

September 5th
Nothing could be more delightful than my employment. Mrs
Blomiley's house lies between Smithy Door and Deansgate, a
most interesting and lively area of shops and inns. I presented
myself this morning promptly at nine o'clock, and was received
by Mrs Blomiley in her parlour.

I believe I had imagined her as a spectacled dragon of a bluestocking, starchy and severe. Imagine then my pleasure to find her a buxom lady in the early forties, comely and smiling. She received me with the utmost kindness.

'Sit down, Miss Hart. Why, what a delicate young lady you are!'

'Oh, not at all, ma'am,' I answered hurriedly. 'I used to be ill often, but now that I have stopped growing I feel very well.'

She laughed. 'I meant delicate in the sense of dainty. You are a perfect fairy compared with some of my strapping girls.'

I was startled into blushes to hear myself described as a fairy, after so many years of being ridiculed for my lack of inches as a dwarf, a pigmy, a little newt. Perhaps my best dress of watered black silk, never before worn on a weekday, helped to make me appear elegant. I hoped Mrs Blomiley had not noticed my work-roughened hands, but her bright grey eyes missed nothing. She asked me various questions about my accomplishments, and told me what I would be expected to teach : tambouring, chainstitch, embroidery with worsted, filigree work (alas for my little basket, vanished across what oceans?), and the making of artificial fruit and flowers.

'I am used to all those, ma'am,' I said, 'and to plain sewing as well.'

The sharp eyes twinkled. 'That will make a change indeed for our young ladies. Pray don't frighten them too much. Then, of course, you will assist Miss Piper in lessons on the harpsichord for beginners – they are mainly simple country tunes and dances. Mrs Blackburn tells me you play the pianoforte well.'

'I have played since I was a young child, ma'am. I am familiar with the works of the brothers Lawes, Purcell, Clementi – er – Coperario—'

Mrs Blomiley's laughter cut short my list. 'An earthly paragon! There sits your patron saint, Miss Hart, the blessed Cecilia herself.' She indicated the mantelshelf, over which hung a mezzo-tint showing a beautiful auburn-haired young woman in a gold robe, seated by an organ, hands clasped and eyes upturned to heaven. I was struck by a feeling that I had seen it somewhere before, though I visited few houses likely to have such a picture; and I felt a curious desire to look at it again and again, combined with a wish, almost as strong, to turn my back on it.

Mrs Blomiley had not noticed my reaction. 'I hope you have some skill in the household virtues as well as the arts, for you will be expected to turn a hand in my Culinary Academy, where my ladies learn to be good housewives able to roast a joint, kill a pig, or make a batch of mince-pies. Can you do any of these things?'

'I have had no experience in pig-killing, ma'am, but plenty in plain-cooking and the arrangement of a table.' I hope I made these sound the product of ordinary education and not of domestic slavery.

'Good, good. I shall train you myself in the higher cuisine. To tell you the truth, Miss Hart, I am hampered by having several gentlemen among my instructors, all excellent teachers but hardly qualified to teach the kitchen arts. And now, as to your wages.'

I heard that I was to get far more than I had hoped for, and my dinner into the bargain. My first day's work consisted of meeting my pupils, a pleasant enough assemblage of tradesmen's daughters, daughters of squires from the surrounding countryside, and some boarders whose families were abroad or temporarily travelling. I 'sat in' at a music lesson given by Miss Piper, a lady with a slightly deaf ear and a heavy hand on the keys. I believe I can bring some of her pupils on more quickly than she could. I hope this is not vain boastfulness. For I thank God humbly that He has brought me work for my hands and my brain, and I pray that I may do it well.

September 10th

This has been the happiest week of my life. My pupils have been biddable, my colleagues amiable to one so new among them. I am a different person from the Emily who holystoned floors and peeled potatoes such a little time ago. For Mrs Blomiley I have the greatest admiration. She is what I have so long wanted, one who takes the place of a mother. To all the pupils she is equally as kind, but I, in my orphaned state, treasure her kindness most.

Miss Parkinson teaches geography, Miss Riley history, Mrs Blomiley English and scripture, Mr Aston (brother of the printer) mathematics. Mr Bury Bridge teaches drawing. The singing-master is Mr Francis Carew.

I write the name with a trembling hand. Am I fool, a green raw ninny of a girl who must fall in love with the first man she sees? No, no. It is only the excitement of coming out into the world from my confinement here. Yet since I sat by Mr Carew at dinner on Thursday my life has been transformed. I sit here, in my small room, writing by the light of one candle; it is late, but I could no more sleep than grow wings and fly out over the roofs of Manchester. At supper I could not eat, for my heart seemed to be beating in my throat; yet now I am hungry. When I hear Mr and Mrs Blackburn have retired I shall creep down to the kitchen and help myself to some bread and cheese. Emily Hart, a thief in her benefactor's house! I am changed indeed. One face is before me, one voice in my ears, I long for one presence. Until I see him again – three long days and nights – I shall be no better than an automaton.

They have noticed, of course. When pouring the tea for us all after supper I absently filled up the slop-basin instead of Mrs Blackburn's cup, and decanted the sugar into the teapot.

'Emily's in love, Emily's in love!' chanted Maria. I blushed fiercely and scalded my hand in the steam from the kettle. Mrs Blackburn sharply told Maria to be quiet and me to take more care. I must watch myself in the future, since my wits seem to have taken leave of themselves.

Until Thursday I had had Mr Aston for my neighbour at table – a pleasant enough gentleman but more interested in his food than in conversation (as indeed I was myself, for Mrs Blomiley's cook feeds us royally, or so it seems to me after years of Bessy's food). When I saw that the chair next to mine was occupied no longer by Mr Aston but by a much younger gentleman,

I bent my head over my plate in a certain embarrassment, for I have never been used to the company of any male younger than Mr Blackburn. Only when addressed did I raise my eyes.

'Miss Hart, I believe.'

I looked up into a face of a curious delicate pallor which had no suggestion of sickliness, but rather the look of porcelain. The eyes, beneath thickly-marked dark brows, were a most remarkable shade which I can only liken to amber, between brown and gold; the lips full, sensuous but not sensual, beautiful altogether. From a fine square brow dark hair already flecked with grey swept back to fall long, loose and straight, over the collar of his black coat. I saw all this in a moment no longer than a heart-beat; yet it seemed I stared at him for hours before I answered.

'Yes, sir.'

'We are to be associates, are we not? I teach the young ladies singing.' His voice was light and pleasant, very faintly tinged with the Northern speech. 'My name is Francis Carew.'

I remember every word of our conversation, too much to set down. We talked of the fine weather, of the events in France, where the Revolutionary Party was said to be in chaos ('They have danced themselves to death with the *Ca ira*,' he said), of brave little Nelson being made a baron for his destruction of the French fleet; of a dozen more things. I, who would have called myself shy and awkward, talked as if I had been gagged for years and had only just been given leave to speak. The food grew cold on my plate. I saw that his also was hardly touched. When Mrs Blomiley rose at the end of the meal we parted, going to separate rooms to give our lessons, and to me it was as if the house had grown cold.

I know now that mine is not the only heart to be fluttered by Mr Carew. The young ladies who are not taught by him envy those who are, while those who are fight for his favours. With the cunning of passion I bring the conversation round to him as often as I can. Today one of our young misses bounded into my class waving her keepsake book.

'Look, look, he's written in it!' They crowded round her like wasps round a jam-jar, oohing and aahing.

' "When Music, Heavenly Maid, was young..." There, Annie Porter! Didn't you hope it would be "Will you come to the Bower?" '

Miss Porter tossed her curls. 'No, I didn't, so there, Mary Ann. And I don't care what it is, so long as *he* wrote it.'

Jane Kellet sighed. 'Oh, if I could only ask him to put in mine "Had I a Heart for Falsehood Fram'd!" ' There was a general unkind titter, for poor Jane is our only spectacled pupil, and suffers terribly from spots.

'Ladies, ladies!' I held up my hand. 'What a to-do you make about poor Mr Carew. Why not Mr Aston, or Mr Bury Bridge? I don't hear them being complimented by your attentions.'

Out of the general outcry came Jane's shrill voice. 'They're as old as our grandfathers, Miss Hart. And Mr Carew's only twenty-seven, because I asked him . . .' She subsided in giggles.

'I should have guessed him more,' I said with a casual air, 'with so many grey hairs.' The young ladies screamed like Maenads. 'But Miss Hart, grey hairs are so romantic!' And they babbled of the novels of Mrs Radcliffe and 'Monk' Lewis, books which would never be allowed in our house.

So it seems that Mr Carew is a general favourite, used to receiving female admiration, and that his manner to me is nothing out of the ordinary. Several of his pupils are almost as old as me, much better dressed, and a great deal more amusing and attractive. Most likely he is betrothed to some lady of whom none of us silly females has ever heard.

September 20th

I know now that Mr Carew is not betrothed. I have talked with him for more than an hour. After today's classes we chanced to leave the Academy at the same time. We bade good-day to each other before discovering that we were going in the same direction, at which we stopped and laughed.

'You look pale, Miss Hart,' he said. 'And I feel half **deafened** after trying to impress the genius of Arne on Sophy Clough – she seems to prefer her own version. Shall we stroll for half an hour, while the sunlight lasts, if you are not in a hurry?'

I would have agreed had Mrs Blackburn been waiting for me with a rack and thumbscrews. I took his arm and we set off in the direction of Hunt's Bank, past the tannery, into the pleasant lanes of Strangeways. Across the meadows we could see sails on the river, drifting peacefully in the red light of the sunset. Looking up at my escort, I was for the first time glad of my few inches, disdainful of the tall women I had always envied. I drew him to talk of himself, of his ancestors at Barlow Hall, and his father who owns a cotton-spinning mill in Cheshire.

'I was meant to follow him into the trade,' he said, 'but I was so crazed with music from my earliest age that he declared I would only be a nuisance to him, and I must do as I pleased. Happily for me, he was kind enough to pay my expenses on a musical grand tour, so that I could study in Rome and Vienna. Poor man, I can never repay him. I saw myself as a famous singer, mobbed in the opera houses of Europe – instead of which you see me a humble teacher of young persons who may be passable linnets but will never make nightingales. Like myself, come to think of it.'

'But you have a – a pleasing voice,' I said.

'Not pleasing enough for the opera patrons to pay to hear. I have no power, no volume, except for a chamber concert or a small assembly. And my tastes are unfashionably antique. Glorious Henry Purcell is my god – a god in eclipse at present. One day he'll rise again.'

As though the setting sun echoed him, it sank behind a line of dark trees, leaving the sky a streaked canvas of colour, gold and pink, purple and grey. A sharp wind from the river reminded me that I had only a light shawl round my shoulders. Whatever time could it be? The chimes of t'Owd Church answered me with six strokes.

'Mercy, I must go back, Mr Carew. I had no idea it was so late – they'll have the watch out after me.'

All apologies, as though it were not my fault as much as his, he turned back with me along the way we had come; but it was slower walking in the cart-ruts by the diminishing light. I was torn between happiness at being with him and fear of what Mrs Blackburn would say.

'If only my horse were stabled nearer,' he said. 'I leave him at a carrier's by the Exchange. I feel guilty to have kept you out late. Your family will be distraught.'

'They are not my family. But they will not be pleased.'

It was thick dusk when we reached the bridge again, and began the last stage of the journey, the uphill slope of Market Street Lane. By now I was angry with myself for not having noticed the time, and thereby letting my first happy walk with him come to such an ignominious end. When he asked whether he might come in with me and take the blame, I almost snapped at him that it was none of his fault and I would answer for my own misdeeds.

'You are so very young, Miss Hart,' he said. 'And yet so wise that one forgets it. Goodnight – and forgive me.'

But I saw him step into the shadows on the other side of the street to watch my safe entry into the house.

Mrs Blackburn was even angrier than I had expected. She marched me up to the schoolroom in front of her, and shut the door with a slam. I could see that she was enjoying her wrath.

'What do you mean, miss, coming home at this hour? Do you know I've had the streets policed for you?'

I suddenly decided to defy her. 'I saw no sign of it as I came through the town.'

'And where had you been, to be out of the town at all, pray?'

'I went for a walk,' I said, hoping that she did not notice my trembling.

'For a walk? So late? Alone?'

'No, with another teacher.'

Mercifully she took this to mean another female, or her anger would have been beyond all bounds. Even so, she was not going to let me off scot-free.

'You must be taught proper behaviour, Miss Hart, it seems. Hold out your hands.'

I put them behind my back. 'No.'

'Hold out your hands, I say.'

She had taken down the small crop which always hung on the wall. I backed away as she advanced towards me. 'I will not be beaten,' I said, more bravely than I felt. 'I am too old, and besides you have no right to touch me. I'm not your daughter – or your pupil, now.'

'I should like to know whose daughter you are, you insolent slut !' She stood over me, as I shrank against a chair, and when I began to answer she struck at me, the lash curling round my neck and across my breast. I screamed, and threw my arm up to protect my face, as the door opened and Mr Blackburn stood there.

'What is this noise? What are you doing, Hester?' I had never heard him sound so severe.

'Punishing this wilful child for frightening us out of our wits, thinking she was waylaid or murdered.'

He strode forward and took the crop from her hand, saying to me, 'Go to your room, Miss Hart.'

I am still in my room. It is very dark now, but I have a candle and tinder-box. There is a red throbbing weal on my neck where the lash caught it, and I am hungry and faint, but there is nothing but happiness in my heart; because of Francis, and because I have learned to stand up for myself. I am fearless, bold; I have youth and health and an education above the run of women. If I could win Francis's love (yes ! I dare to call him Francis in my mind) I should care no longer that I am a nameless girl without home or parents. Where he is, that is my home.

October 1st

Why did I tempt Fate? Why did I write so boastfully, as if there were only I and my selfish longings in the world?

A terrible thing has happened. I returned this afternoon to a household on which the worst of blows had fallen. There was nobody to be seen as I took off my cloak in the lobby, no sound of voices or pianoforte practice. Opening the door at the top of the kitchen stairs, I called 'Bessy!' A muffled, choking noise answered me. Swiftly I ran down, to find Bessy seated at the table, her head on her arms, sobbing and gasping.

'Why, Bessy, what's the matter? Are you hurt? Have you been scolded?' I cried. She shook her head without looking up; then, after a moment, gestured towards the ceiling. I hurried back upstairs. The parlour and dining-room were both empty, but for the cat, who, though he was never allowed in the living-rooms, was comfortably asleep in the best chair in the parlour.

The drawing-room too was empty. Only from the bedroom floor above came sounds which sent me hastening up towards the Blackburns' bedroom. I knocked and, as nobody answered, went in. Mrs Blackburn lay in bed, in her clothes with a coverlet over her; her eyes were shut and she appeared to be in a kind of stupor. Maria sat in a chair by the bed, her face almost unrecognisable with grief, tears running down her cheeks as though from a ceaseless fountain. On the other side of the bed sat our neighbour, Mrs Clegg, holding Mrs Blackburn's limp hand.

'Good God! What—' I began. Mrs Clegg shushed me with a finger to her lips, and, rising, motioned me to the door, following me out. As we passed the door of the smaller bedroom used by Mr Blackburn as a dressing-room, I heard the distressing sounds which meant one of his attacks of asthma.

Mrs Clegg led the way to the drawing-room, and shutting the door turned to me, her round sensible face grave.

'There's bad news, Miss Hart. I don't know as I can find words to tell you.'

My mind raced. 'Mrs Blackburn?' I thought of Mrs Cadogan's stroke. Perhaps this was another such. But Mrs Clegg shook her head.

'Sit down, lass. It seems – oh, dear. . . . Well; there was a bit of argument this morning between the girls. It was Maria's turn to go to market, but she'd a dress to finish and didn't fancy going. Flew into quite a fantod over it.'

I knew Maria's temper, a good second to her mother's.

'Neither did Tetty want to go, having a bad cold coming on and feeling thick in the head. But Mrs B took Maria's side, and between the two of them Tetty gave way. You know how biddable . . .' She stopped for a moment. 'She was a long time gone, so her mother sent Maria to look for her because some of the things were wanted for table, and Maria, the little slummock, seeing our Samuel in the street, wheedled him into going instead.'

I had a dreadful premonition of what was coming, and shut my eyes, as though that would soften the news.

'It was near on an hour before Samuel got back. He came and told me first. When he got down to the Market there was a great crowd collected on the corner by the Post Office. Samuel pushed his way in, and there she was, poor Tetty, laid on the cobbles with a coat over her and blood everywhere. Someone told him she started off to cross the road when a gig came pelting up from Exchange Street with her right in its path. She dithered and seemed not to know which way to go, and the next thing she was under the horse's hooves.'

I felt myself staring stupidly at Mrs Clegg.

'Samuel got a cart from the man in Travis Yard and brought her back. There was nowt anyone could do by then. I came in here with him and told them. They've taken it hard; you saw that. You're white as a sheet, lass. Do they keep brandy in?'

I pointed to the corner cupboard. Moments later I felt the sour taste of wine in my mouth, and drank because I must. When I could speak I asked, 'Where is she?'

'In the girls' bedroom. But don't go up now, love.'

I broke away from her and went upstairs, pausing for neither the monotonous sobs of Maria nor the choked breathing of her father.

It is night, and she lies there as I saw her, still, calm-faced, with a bandage round her wounded head and a white sheet covering the body a frightened horse had trampled. Poor Thetis, poor Tetty, gentle and willing to all. She had saved me from many a scolding, taken on my dull kitchen tasks when I went to the

Academy, comforted her father in his loveless marriage. We had talked much when alone together, and only I of all the household knew that in her Uncle Tom's parish there was a young farmer, Jabez Braithwaite, who was paying his attentions to her. She had spoken of him with quiet pleasure. 'If he can get round Mamma, Emily, I know Father will say yes to him, though he'll be sad to lose me. Oh, you don't know how I long to get away!'

She has got away, my only friend, the nearest to a sister I shall ever know in my nameless life.

I have not thought of Francis these last eight dreadful hours.

October 5th

Thetis was buried today. The Reverend Thomas Blackburn read the service beside her grave, in a corner of the churchyard that I passed with Francis on our walk. It was a cold, grey day, with wind in the rain. Her father looked ready to follow her, while her mother seemed struck with a kind of silent madness; Maria merely wept. There were many neighbours gathered round: the Cleggs, Mr and Mrs Blease from the Palace Inn, the Harrises and the Bramalls, old Mrs Kershaw, and Mrs Nancy Blackburn and the Cheadle cousins. I looked after the funeral breakfast myself, since no one else was capable.

The Reverend Thomas came with me to the stonemason in Cross Street to decide the matter of the tombstone. When I showed him what I had drafted out, he read it over twice, and pondered, then murmured it aloud:

> 'Here lies in hope of a glorious Resurrection
> Thetis Jane, dearly beloved daughter of John
> and Hester Blackburn of this parish.
>   Born February 12 1781, died October 1 1798.
>   Yet shall ye be as the wings of a dove;
> that is covered with silver wings, and her
> feathers like gold.'

He looked at me over his spectacles. 'Psalm 68. I never saw it used as an epitaph before. Why did you choose it, Miss Hart?'

'She has escaped,' I said.

It sounded bald, but he understood me. 'If her father wishes it, then it shall be.' He gave instructions to the stonemason, and we walked back together.

'You know they're most welcome with us,' he said. 'I've told my brother so. We've a big place, and Nance has done nursing, I think. We'd be happy to take them, and you too, if you can talk them into it.'

'I doubt it, sir. Mrs Blackburn seems to understand nothing, and Maria – well, you saw her.' Half-way through the service she had had to be taken away, weeping hysterically.

'She blames herself – it's the heaviest of crosses,' he agreed. 'But my brother would be best away, where he can get over the worst.'

I have tried to persuade Mr Blackburn into accepting his good brother's offer, but he will only smile and shake his head. So I must look after the three of them as well as I can, with Bessy's help. One thing is certain : I shall have to leave the Academy.

I don't know how to face the thought.

October 7th

I have been to the Academy to say goodbye.

The pupils stared in awe at me in my dyed black dress and bonnet, while the members of the staff pressed my hand and murmured condolences. Throughout all the past week, since the tragedy, I have been quite calm; my farewell to Mrs Blomiley nearly broke me down.

Sitting with her over tea and seed-cake, I said, 'I have been so happy here, Mrs Blomiley, even in so short a time. I had hoped to make teaching my profession, and I know it is what I was meant for; but as things are I must look after the household which has looked after me for so long.'

She patted my hand. 'And very creditable it is in you, Miss Hart, especially as they are not your own blood-kin. I needn't say how sorry I am to lose you so soon, and in such unhappy circumstances. It may be that you'll see your way to coming back, in time, and if so I shall more than welcome you.' She talked on in pleasant truisms, thinking no doubt that my unhappy face was caused by grief for Thetis. But I was savouring, for the last time, all that I loved about the house, my work, my pupils, and above all the one whose voice I strained to hear. Nothing – only the painful sound of Annie Porter's attempts to perform 'The White Cockade'. Then I remembered that it was not one of his days for teaching. I had had a kindly little note from him, just a few sympathetic words, signed 'Your Sincere Friend, Francis Carew'. Perhaps I would have the courage to answer it, suggesting that he might call on me in a little time. Mrs Blomiley was speaking—

'And to add to it all – troubles never come singly, you know – I am losing Mr Carew as well. He has been offered a teaching post in London, which will bring in far more than I can pay him, and so I must not stand in his way. Now why should my two youngest and brightest teachers be taken from me, almost at the same time? The ways of Providence are inscrutable and sometimes very irritating, Miss Hart.'

She clasped my hand in both of hers, and paid me what I was owed, and I made my way to the door. The flowery carpet was a daze before my eyes, the pink-striped wallpaper leapt out at me like prison bars. I wished I were with Thetis, buried near to where the little Lever children lay.

They're now past hope, past feare or paine.
It were a sinne to wish them here again.

Mrs Blomiley must have thought that my blurring gaze was directed towards the St Cecilia over the mantelshelf. 'I wish I could give you our beautiful little saint,' she said, 'but she belonged to my mother. If I can find a print of the picture, you shall have it. Surely no artist's model was ever such a favourite with painters.'

'Who is she?' I asked, not that I cared for that or anything.

'Why, don't you recognise her? She is Emma, Lady Hamilton.'

10

December 23rd, 1800

Why have I not taken up my pen before, in the year and more which has passed since Thetis died? There has been time enough in the long quiet evenings, with Mrs Blackburn sitting, hands in lap, or darning stockings, while Maria flicks over the pages of one of the novels she is always borrowing from Edge's Library, frowning as if the story displeased her. As for Mr Blackburn, he is very often out nowadays, except when suffering a bout of asthma. Just now he is visiting his cousin, the Member of Parliament for Lancaster, at Hale Hall.

To be honest with myself, there has been little worth recording. When I began my journal it was in the hopes that I might provide some useful information about our times for those who come after. A pious hope! What is there for the eyes of future generations in a life so obscure? The times are stirring enough, to be sure: the Czar of Russia turned Britain's enemy and become the friend of France, Bonaparte triumphant over the Austrian army at Marengo and Hohenlinden, Malta captured; while here at home the crops have been ruined by terrible storms and many poor people starve. I see them, begging in the streets, ragged dirty folk from town hovels, hollow-faced men and women who have trudged in from country districts to seek some pity and help. In places, the *Mercury* reports, there are 'bread riots', while our Manchester weavers grumble because the new machines are taking their living away. Are we to have civil war, then, as well as never-ending strife abroad? Poor England, sick and weary – has God turned His back upon her?

But these things will be read in the history books. What of my life, for any who care to know of it? When the time of our first mourning was over, I took matters into my own hands. Mrs Blackburn seemed sunk in a melancholy apathy from which I could not rouse her. She barely spoke, picked at her food, and sat for hours by the window, staring out. At last I tackled her, determined to break down the sullen .defence she had raised against the world. One day as she sat brooding in her usual place I marched in and addressed her roundly.

'Mrs Blackburn, I am disappointed in you.'

Startled to hear such words from me, she looked up sharply.

'I thought you a woman of good sense and understanding. It seems you are neither, or you would not keep up this idleness. That is the word for it – idleness.'

She turned her head away muttering something about 'my great grief'.

'What good will your grief do for Thetis now? You are supposed to be a devout woman. Don't you believe that God has her in His keeping? Would *she* sit and pine like this if you had been taken, or her father, or Maria? She would be looking after those who were alive, forgetting her grief by cheering others. What must she feel, looking down from Heaven to see her mother so useless?'

She raised her head, looking at me without expression, and said in a flat, dull voice the first words I had heard from her that day.

'You cannot understand. I never wanted her. I never wanted children at all. I kept my husband from his rights because I was afraid to bear more. And so I was unkind to her – to both the girls. And God took her from me, to punish me.'

Her words had shocked me. But I had a battle to win, and I pressed my advantage.

'Nonsense! God took her because the cold in her head made her giddy, and she slipped in front of a horse which was being driven much too fast on wet cobbles. It was her time to go, and who knows what future troubles she was spared? If you want to make amends to her spirit, which God knows must be a sweet and forgiving one, why not do some service for other children, children who are alive and need you?'

She stared at me. 'What children?'

'I will find some, never fear, if you will promise to teach them. I will give you all the help I can.'

I could see wonder in her eyes, the first emotion she had shown for a long time. 'Why should you help me?' she asked. 'You never liked me.'

'I was prepared to like you, ma'am, if you had chosen to treat me as a human child in need of love. But at least I owe you gratitude for your care for my body and mind. Perhaps you owe me something, too.'

She nodded slowly. 'And you'll stay with me?'

'I will stay.'

She rose, drew me to her, and taking my head between her hands planted a cold kiss on my forehead. The battle was won.

Near t'Owd Church, and within its precincts, stand some little old buildings which had once been the Black Boy Inn, but are now a charity school maintained by the benefit of a Mrs Bennion. The morning after my conquest of Mrs Blackburn I betook myself there, laying a posy of flowers from the Market on Thetis's grave as I passed. Outside the school I heard the rhythmic rise and fall of young voices. 'Nine ones are nine, nine twos are eighteen, nine threes are twenty-seven, nine fours are thirty-six . . .' I waited until the recital of tables, the last lesson of the morning, was over, and, freed by the clanging bell, a crowd of children in motley dress appeared in the yard, where they ran and skipped about me like lambs.

I went into the schoolroom, where a neat little elderly lady was piling up slates; she proved to be Mrs Bennion herself. I introduced myself and laid before her a plan I had devised, lying awake the night before. If she would allow me to take over three or four of her most promising pupils, I would undertake to have them educated privately in a small class. I explained the circumstances, watching her face brighten as I talked.

'But of course,' she said, 'both Mr and Mrs Blackburn are well known to me by name, and I have seen you all in church. I was most sorry to hear of your sad bereavement.' She went on to say that nothing would please her more than to let me have a few of her brighter pupils, both for their sake and that of the needy children for whom places would then be open. 'But I cannot say yes to you here and now, Miss Hart, for two clergymen from neighbouring parishes are also distributors of the charity, and I must consult with them. I feel sure they will agree.'

I thanked her, and arranged to call on her again within the week. At the door I said, with some hesitation, 'If I may ask one other thing, Mrs Bennion – would you be good enough to have a word with the parents of any who come to us? About – well . . .'

'Bugs,' said Mrs Bennion with startling forthrightness, 'and other inhabitants of Long Millbank, where so many of the chil-- dren come from. I will do my best, believe me, Miss Hart, but only a miracle would render them completely free.'

Or a bath, I thought as I left. I proceeded to Smithy Door, where I sought out Mrs Blomiley. It was strange and sad to go there again, to look up at the window of the music-room, to enter the familiar porch and be shown by the same maid to the dining-parlour where Mrs Blomiley took her dinner in solitary state.

She was pleased to see me, and promised willingly to send me any pupils too young for her classes whose parents would be pre-pared to pay fees; for, as I explained to her, without fees Mrs Blackburn would have difficulty in maintaining schoolroom supplies, candles and coal, books and slates and the like. I could not resist bringing into the conversation the name which through all our troubles has been ever in my mind.

'Yes, indeed,' she said, 'I have heard from Mr Carew. He is well situated in London, and enjoying the company of many dis-tinguished musicians. I believe we shall hear much of him one day.'

So he has written to her; and not to me. Very right and proper, of course. It was pretentious of me even to fancy that he had any warmer feeling for me than for poor old deaf Miss Piper. When did he say a word to me that suggested affection? When did he look into my eyes, press my hand, as I believe young men are supposed to do? His note of condolence was such as he would send to any bereaved acquaintance. By now he is a Londoner, meeting brilliant and famous people, mixing with the great; what should he want with an unknown, nameless girl in Manchester? No, Emily, put him out of your mind, my dear, and get on with your mission.

My scheme for the restoration of Mrs Blackburn worked like a dream. Three little girls were sent to me from the Charity School, all bright and promising but, alas, far from clean. Before Mrs Blackburn's eyes and nose could be offended I led them down to the kitchen, where I placed the slipper-bath in the middle of the stone floor and I filled it with three great kettles of hot water, and, much to their surprise, immersed each little girl in turn and scrubbed them thoroughly with kitchen soap, impervious to their cries. Fortunately it was Bessy's afternoon off. Then, having rubbed them dry, I washed their hair in turpentine, an infallible remedy against lice, and set them, wrapped in towels, by the fire, where with big eyes they watched me soak and scrub every stitch they had been wearing – which was very little, poor bairns. Then I draped the washed rags over the clothes-maiden, and gathered the children, pink and shining, round the deal table.

'Now,' I said, 'Mary, Dorcas and Sally, we will have our first lesson.'

I have done something which Mrs Blackburn must not find out. After Thetis's death, all her clothes and belongings had been tenderly put away in a chest with lavender, like sacred relics. I took them out, bundled them up, and early one morning took them down to the Market to the stall which does a flourishing trade in old clothes. The stall-keeper was delighted to have a quantity of garments in such good condition, and readily exchanged them for three small dresses and as many petticoats, smocks, stockings and shoes as she could find. In two evenings of sewing I made the garments fit each child as nearly as possible, and the next day presented them to their delighted wearers.

'You're a fool,' Maria said. 'Do you know what will happen?

Their parents will have every stitch off their backs and sell 'em for food.'

And some things may indeed have gone that way, but the frocks, mercifully, remained. Maria also pointed out to me spitefully that the three well-connected, well-spoken children sent by Mrs Blomiley would catch broad Lancashire accents within a week. I smiled and said nothing. If Mrs Blackburn could be said to have a passion in life, it is for the correct speaking of the King's English. I have always suspected that behind her own carefully refined voice there lay another, rougher one, the voice of her childhood, much despised by her. If anything could put her on her mettle it would be the voices of Mary, Dorcas and Sally.

So indeed it proved. With hidden amusement I heard her loudly mocking their broad vowel-sounds. ' "Mi feyther"! If you mean "my father", child, then say so. Watch my lips, now.' And she would mouth the consonants and vowels at them until they could produce a reasonable imitation. Such tuition was quite new to them, after the simple three R's of Mrs Bennion's classes, but they were bright little girls and took pleasure in learning to speak something like their well-bred schoolmates. It was noticeable that when they returned after the week-end their accents would have slipped considerably, and Maria, who objected to the presence of the children in the house as much as to my new influence over her mother, was quick to point it out.

'Really, Mamma, what *is* the point of teaching them one sort of speech when they'll go and talk quite another at home?'

'There are some, Maria,' her mother answered, 'who are able to speak with one voice among the peasantry and another among gentlefolk. If these children can learn to do so, their futures may well be brighter than if they had been left to talk in their own barbarous tongue.'

I reflected that such had been the case with me, and remembered how in the dim past Mrs Blackburn had dinned into me the dreadfulness of my infant accent, whatever that had been. She really has what Doctor Johnson called a bottom of good sense beneath her cold exterior. I have read this year a curious and striking work by a London blue-stocking, Mrs Mary Wollstonecraft, *A Vindication of the Rights of Women*, in which the author pleads for our sex to be educated equally as well as men, in order that they may become the intellectual companions of their husbands rather than mere playthings. I find this a sensible and attractive idea. What lies in store for a girl who fails to marry, other than a dreary round of governess-ship, or the thankless life of companion to some querulous old lady? Were it possible for us to become doctors, professors, politicians . . . the thought is laughable, and yet – if it were so, would the world be at war, as it has always been while men have ruled it?

January 5th, 1801

The school goes well. I have persuaded Mrs Blackburn to let me use the pianoforte to teach music to the children. Amelia and Charlotte are showing promise in French – or as much of it as I am qualified to teach them – and Mary is already a good little sempstress. Yesterday I was talking with Mr Blackburn on the very subject of my last journal entry: the lack of prospects open to women.

'I am glad,' I said, 'to have been fitted for a life at least above that of a servant. I am grateful above all things for my education – please remember that, sir, if you are ever downcast.' (Poor man, how often he seemed so.)

'Have you never thought that you might marry?' he asked me. I looked at him in surprise. To tell the truth, I had not. My feeling for Francis Carew I have long dismissed as a romantic fancy, no more concerned with the realities of life than with the solar system. 'No,' I said, 'in view of my state. What kind of husband would be willing to take me without name or patrimony?'

He hesitated. 'When I last saw your – your London guardian, he suggested that some clergyman might well be happy to marry such a well-educated young woman. And that a – a sum might be forthcoming for your dowry.'

I stared. 'To marry me out of Christian charity, you mean, sir – with the additional attraction of a kind of Easter offering? Thank you, I would rather be an independent old maid.'

He shook his head as though the whole question perplexed and tired him. 'Have you heard from my guardians recently, sir?' I asked.

'Not for some years – four, I believe it is. Your allowance still comes to me on a bank draft.'

A grim thought had struck me. 'Is it possible they might be dead? Now that the French are all over Europe many lives may have been lost. Have you thought of that, sir?'

He looked at me in a way which in a less dignified man might have been called furtive.

'I think you may dismiss that thought.'

'Then you know . . . more than you have told me.'

'Yes. But I am under oath not to say.'

'The man who pays my allowance – is he my father?'

'No.'

'And my mother – is she married?'

He was distressed at answering. 'Yes. Please leave questioning me, Emily. One day you may know, but it will be with their consent. I have enough to try me without betraying a trust.'

I watched him plod towards his parlour-study, head bent, a dusty shabby figure looking ten years more than his age. Ignored by his wife, bereaved of his favourite daughter, ill too often to earn a steady living: what gives him the will to live, I wonder, and why do I sometimes surprise on his face a look of – can it be pleasure, like one remembering a happy dream?

January 27th

I have found out Mr Blackburn's secret. I blush to write it, but I must, if only to convince myself that it was not imagination and that people do behave so.

It happened two nights since. Last November the Blackburns acquired a gig – a shabby enough little vehicle which had been advertised for sale, together with an old grey horse. This noble equipage was intended to save coach-hire on journeys to the home of the Reverend Thomas, and more ceremonious journeys to Hale Hall. Even on wet Sundays, we all went to church in it, although the horse would make it quite clear by a stiffening of his forelegs and a reproachful glance over his shoulder that he would prefer not to pull us all up the slope of the Lane. It was usually I who got out and walked beside him, enjoying the gentle clop-clop of his hooves and the fragrant smell of hay that came from him.

Two days ago I had driven out alone to Newton Heath, where a farmer friend of the Reverend Tom's had a side of bacon waiting for us. At the farm-house in the misty damp countryside I took tea with stout Mrs Fenton, admired her new baby, and collected the bacon for a very small sum, before driving back at a leisurely pace through the fallow, sleeping fields and arriving at Palace Street well before dusk. The flitch was heavy, almost as big as me, so I stopped at our door and took it inside before driving round to the mews where Simkin and the gig were kept. Then I led him to within a few yards of his stable, and went to open the door.

There are experiences which are spread over only a fraction of time, yet seem to last for years. In one of these flashing eternities I set my hand to the hasp of the stable half-door, and looked over the top (why, I don't know, unless to make sure the boy had not left a hay-rake or anything in the way) to see a sight I shall never forget. On the ground, couched on a stewing of fresh hay, were Mr Blackburn and Kezia, the barmaid from the Palace Inn. I had never seen any such thing, never read or heard of it, yet I knew in an instant what they were doing. Kezia's face was crimson, her eyes were shut, and Mr Blackburn, above her, half divested of his shabby blacks, was making strange noises like one in pain.

A sort of hot mist enveloped me. I stepped back as if from the edge of a precipice or a blazing fire, and leant against a wall until I had done shaking. There seemed to be no end to the ague of shock, until I pinched my own wrist hard and said to myself: 'Come, Emily, what you have seen is very ordinary indeed – only your ignorance makes it remarkable.' Then, finding myself able to breathe normally again, I went back to unharness Simkin, which I did with much clattering and talk, loudly asking the horse if he had not admired the turnips of Newton Heath, and whether he would prefer to work there or here, and other utter nonsense. Then, leaving him free, I walked to the door that led to the groom's home above the stables, some yards distant, humming as I went. In the short time that it took me to tell him the gig was empty, and to chat about the weather, the two in the stable escaped. I saw a movement out of the corner of my eye, and felt sure they had no idea I had seen them.

Poor Mr Blackburn; I should blame him, but I cannot. Every Sunday we pray to be delivered from such sins as fornication; yet I can see that for such a sad man it might well be more like salvation. What a strange time this is, with so many changes! I wonder what the astrologers say that Jupiter and Neptune are about.

April 4th

I am quite sure now that Mr Blackburn did not see me. He has been quite composed in his manner to me, and I hope I have in mine to him, after some early difficulty in meeting his eye. He spends a great deal of time at the Literary and Philosophical Society – at least that is where he is supposed to be. It is no business of mine, only it makes me strangely uncomfortable to know of such a secret in the house.

Is it selfish of me to wish that I lived among happy people? Bessy is growing older and lamer, and she grumbles about everything from our pupils' noise to the mice that invade the pantry from next-door. Mrs Blackburn has a smile for nobody, while her husband's pleasure, as I know now, is one to be taken in corners and behind doors, at the risk of his scholarly reputation. As for Maria, since her sister's death she has become lazy, slovenly and bad-tempered, living only for novels from the lending library about disinherited heirs, eloping young ladies and unfortunate nuns. I am twenty this coming month. Am I always to live in shadow, a kind of housekeeper to people who care nothing for me? Well, if it must be so, it must be.

April 20th

For the past week I have been assisting Mrs Blomiley with the suppers she and her cookery pupils provide for wealthy merchants who prefer to send out for the food when they have guests. I confess that I cannot, and never shall be able to, kill a sucking-pig or even a fowl. It is quite impossible to me. Mrs Blomiley thinks me very squeamish, I know, but I cannot help that. Some of the other girls feel as I do, but they cheer themselves by pretending that they have Frenchmen's necks beneath their knives. But I can make broth, roast, boil, and make an apple-pasty with the best of them. Today Abigail Thorpe and I went to the house of Alderman Shelmerdine in Deansgate, taking him a dish of Liverpool sole, a pair of fowls, and a Crown of Mutton, with a sweet of jellied apricots. We waited at table in the very handsome dining-room, decorated in the very latest fashion. The Alderman is a pleasant-spoken gentleman of about fifty, well set-up, a little after the fashion of John Bull in the caricature. He is a widower with one daughter, Cicely. They both treated Abigail and myself as though we were the guests, not the waitresses, and complimented us upon our cooking.

April 25th

I am astonished! Alderman Shelmerdine's servant called today with a note saying that he has orders for the Theatre Royal on Saturday night, and that Miss Cicely requests the pleasure of my company, her father to be our escort. Of course I shall attend.

April 30th

Tonight I have been through the door of a new world. To think that I, quiet-living Emily, should find myself on the arm of one of the most notable citizens of Manchester, like any fine lady, going to the play! We entered beneath a sign saying 'Boxes', and up a little stairway came into a little apartment, all red velvet and tapestry, with elegant gilt chairs, which commanded a view of the stage and the entire theatre, the audience being seated below us in a horseshoe-shaped half-circle and on benches. Another box beside us, and two opposite, contained well-dressed people compared with whom I felt a mere mouse. When we were seated, Mr Shelmerdine produced a pretty box of almond comfits and handed them to me.

'Sweets to the sweet, Miss Emily,' he said. I thought it a most charming and original compliment, and felt myself blushing.

'Yon's a pretty colour in those cheeks,' he said, with what I could not mistake for anything but an admiring glance. 'Our Cicely's like a snowdrop beside you.'

'I am so excited, sir,' I said. 'This is the first time I have ever entered the Theatre. It seems like a fairyland to me.'

Cicely laughed. 'Never been to the Theatre, and living only a stone's throw away? Why ever not?'

'Nay, don't mock, Cicely,' her father told her. 'Some folk don't hold with playhouses, and Miss Hart's people may be of them.'

'Mrs Blackburn was brought up a Quaker,' I said. 'She may have thought it wrong to bring me to the play when I was younger. But now I believe I may please myself.'

I saw looks of enquiry on both their faces, and knew they would have liked to ask me more of myself. But then the musicians began to take their places beneath the stage, one by one until all were seated; and at a sign from the conductor they began to play some airs by Purcell. I, who love music so much, had never heard orchestral playing before. I was stricken with wonder and delight. Then, as they ceased, the great red curtains began to part, until the whole scene was visible: a woodland glade, a blend of shade and sunshine, marvellously lit. There entered from the side a very personable young man, half leading, half carrying an old one, and saying, in a rich melodious voice:

'As I remember, Adam, it was upon this fashion . . .'

I shall never forget the moment, or any other moment of the play. Mrs Bellamy as Rosalind, bewitching as a rose-crowned girl, even more alluring as a gallant lad in leather breeches; Mr Bengough as her lover Orlando, slaying all hearts; the silver voice of Mr Bellamy singing the songs of Arden. I will say no more of the play, for my views on it, untrained as they are, cannot possibly be of interest to anybody. The evening passed like a dream. Tea and cakes were brought to us in our box by a waiter, and as I saw quizzing-glasses being directed at us from the opposite side of the theatre I felt ashamed for my plain dress and lack of ornaments. Cicely wore a pretty gown of gossamer satin, white with pink rouleaux and short sleeves slashed with pink.

When the play was over, and fair Rosalind had disappeared for the last time, blowing kisses as she went, I thought it was time to leave; but Mr Shelmerdine told me that the performance would conclude with a Harlequinade, *Harlequin Doctor Faustus*, an old favourite. I never laughed so much in all my life, and took much persuading that the amazing, dazzling Harlequin, with his leaps and dives and transformations, was not some kind of magic creature.

Mr Shelmerdine sent Cicely home in a chair and most courteously escorted me back to Palace Street. I thanked him for my treat more effusively, perhaps, than was polite, but he seemed to take it as natural and said I must accompany them again.

'Cicely's a lonely lass, with neither mother nor sister. She'll be glad of a friend, Miss Emily, if you can be spared to us sometimes.'

I assented gladly. I, too, am glad of a friend.

May 4th

Maria is bitterly jealous of me since the theatre excursion. She loses no opportunity of making me feel silly or of reporting some fault of mine to her mother. I have not cleaned the slates, or I have lost her best embroidery needle, or shut the cat in the drawing-room, or some other monstrous crime. Today she attacked my appearance.

'I wonder,' she said, looking me up and down, 'how grand

folk like the Shelmerdines liked to be seen out with such a fright as you, Emily.'

'Thank you,' I replied graciously. 'They seemed to tolerate it fairly well.'

'A dwarfish little thing like you ought to dress better.'

'Agreed, but how would you suggest I dress, when every penny spent on me must be accounted for to those who keep me?'

'Well, at least you might make more of yourself. That short hair makes you look like a boy.'

'You can't be aware, my dear, that the curly crop *à la guillotine* is all the rage in London. Besides, I like it.'

Maria tried a new tack. 'I suppose your elderly beau don't notice such things, as a young man would.'

I smiled amiably. 'Why not get yourself a beau, then you might know at first hand how men of any age feel?'

She glared at me with what even in my flippantly catty mood I recognised as real hate. 'Very well,' she said, 'just you see if I don't.'

Poor Maria, too thin, and cursed with a spotty skin even at nineteen. She has a loveless life and I must be charitable to her, knowing how the loss of her sister has poisoned her inmost soul. Thetis's grave is grown right over with grass, and ivy is creeping across the stone.

I am to go to Deansgate on Sunday.

May 21st

I have now visited the Shelmerdines once or twice a week since our jaunt to the theatre. Much as I enjoy myself there, I cannot help thinking that Cicely is not so devoid of friends that she really needs me for company. Already I have met her cousin Harriet, a very lively young lady known as Gussie, her brother George on leave from the Navy, and his betrothed, a Miss Charlotte Selby. Lieutenant Shelmerdine told us that Admiral Lord Nelson has been recalled from the Mediterranean and is on his way home, travelling by land through Europe. 'And,' he added, 'he is accompanied by his dear friends Sir William and Lady

Hamilton, Sir William having been replaced as Envoy Extraordinary at Naples. There is a good deal of talk about this in London, where they say it is felt at the Admiralty that His Lordship has spent too much time sporting in Armida's garden – in other words at the feet of the lovely Emma.'

'And is it true?' Cicely enquired.

'Not a bit of it, so say we. Our Nel is the most honourable man on this earth – and the greatest of commanders. He'd never let beauty stand in the way of duty.'

Cicely opened her eyes wide. 'Even ashore? I thought all you sailors were regular dogs in port.'

He aimed a mock slap at her. 'I'll thank you not to launch such broadsides at me in front of Charlotte, Miss Puss! What do you know of sailors?'

'Only you, George,' said Cicely meekly, causing Charlotte to giggle.

'Now, now,' interposed Mr Shelmerdine, 'I think we can allow that any man, sailor or not, may forget his duty for a pair of blue eyes.' He looked full at me. 'Especially a pair like Miss Emily's.'

'Good gracious, Pa, how complimentary you are today!' Cicely said, covering my embarrassment. And the conversation strayed to other topics, particularly the excitement caused by the great Mrs Siddons's forthcoming visit to our theatre.

I suppose Mr Shelmerdine compliments all ladies. He is a most kind and civil gentleman.

Tomorrow we all drive out to Cheadle, where the Reverend Tom's eldest daughter is to be confirmed. I am to wear my new straw hat with blue ribbons. I have thought since this afternoon more than once of Lieutenant Shelmerdine's mention of Lady Hamilton. Has she changed, I wonder, since she sat for the picture of Saint Cecilia? Mrs Blomiley never did find a print for me. *Surely* she has changed, for she appeared a mere child? I dislike to think of one so beautiful departing from the path of virtue; yet what has it to do with me, and what do I know of the different passions? More and more I realise how little I know of this world at all, I, who have never left Manchester, have hardly stirred away from the schoolroom.

I am looking forward so much to seeing Mrs Siddons.

July 17th

It has been almost two months since I wrote in my journal. Much of that time has been busy and happy, thanks to Mr. Shelmerdine and Cicely, who have introduced me to their pleasant circle of society. I have attended my first dance, only think of it! At the Assembly Rooms in June. Fortunately I learnt long ago several dance-steps which are still popular, so I did not disgrace myself on the floor. Cicely prevailed on me to wear a dress of hers, somewhat shortened and taken in; it is a dove-coloured silk with a flounce of blonde net and the same edging the bodice. I never wore anything half so pretty. Perhaps I should have refused it, but what is the use of pride for its own sake, when a gift is generously offered? I danced all the dances but one, including several with Mr Shelmerdine, who in spite of his age and heavy build is uncommonly light on his feet.

I begin to believe I was born with an inheritance of frivolity, since I take so easily to dancing, play-going and such light pleasures. Perhaps it would have been better if my guardians had left me with one of the weaver families by the river, to grow up as a loud-laughing, clog-dancing wench, free as air, with skirts above her ankles and a shawl on her head. I have seen them all my life with an emotion which I thought to be pity; I see now that it was envy.

11

July 31st

How could I write so thoughtlessly, or think so emptily, wrapped up in my own vanity, blind to what has been going on around me? I am punished by guilt and remorse – not for what has happened, but for failing to see it earlier.

Yesterday, late in the afternoon, I sat sewing by the open window in the schoolroom, from which I could look down into the garden and feel the sun on my face. Our pupils are on holiday; Mr and Mrs Blackburn had gone to some gathering at Chetham's College. Lost in my own thoughts, I was startled when the door behind me opened and Maria entered. She glanced round the room, and, shutting the door, leant against it and stared at me in silence.

'Do you want me, Maria?' I asked. 'If it is the accounts, do let us leave them until later. The sunshine is so delightful.'

She shook her head, and I noted that her hair, usually curled with care, looked as though it had not been brushed that day, and that her face was unheathily pale, the freckles she hated standing out like copper coins. She came slowly towards me, and sat on one of the pupils' benches. I began to feel uneasy, as though I would like to escape from what she was going to say. At last she spoke.

'I must talk to you.'

'Pray do.'

She looked down at her feet. 'I'm sorry I needle you so much. It's my nature, I suppose, to be spiteful.'

I could not help but laugh, though I was pleased and a little touched to receive an apology from one who had never had a kind word for me. 'A little needling between women is natural enough, surely,' I said. 'I hope I do not seem to bear you any grudge for it. What do you want to say to me?'

'Don't speak so loud! They will hear you in the next garden.'

She put her hand on my arm. 'Emily, I am not well. And there's nobody I can tell but you.'

'You look a little poorly, indeed. But why not your mother?'

'No! Not her, of all people. Oh, I must tell you before she returns.' But she seemed to find it hard to go on, twisting her hands and biting her lips as if in pain. I thought of the dreadful cancers which carry off so many, and wondered if her secret could be such a terrible one. At last she said:

'I am always in discomfort. Here.' She laid her hand on her stomach. 'I feel empty, and I eat, and then I have these hateful pains, and often I'm sick and giddy. Oh, Emily!'

She looked at me with a distress that made me long to be able to comfort her, but I knew nothing of medicine, no more than she, and I said so, urging her again to speak to her mother or to ask to see the surgeon. She shook her head violently.

'No, no, you don't understand. I . . .' A sudden flush swept up from her throat, suffusing her pale face. 'I – I have stopped – my courses.'

It was startling to hear Maria speak of a subject which her mother regarded as too low and distasteful to be mentioned. I still failed to understand her.

'Sometimes extreme cold will stop them,' I said. 'Have you had wet feet lately, or been very chilled? Not that there has been any rain lately, so that cannot be it. How long has it been like this with you?'

'Two months. And oh, Emily, Aunt Nance told me once that after two months one can be sure.'

I felt the blood draining away from my face as my ignorance gave way to understanding. Somehow, without reading or instruction, the facts of the beginning of life had become known to me; hints here and there, overheard gossip, possibly something Mrs Blackburn had tersely informed me of when I had had to confide in her, years before.

'How could I be so stupid?' I said. 'But Maria, surely there is no cause – such a thing could not be true?'

'It could,' she said flatly. 'It could and it is. It all came of that day you taunted me. About not having a beau.'

'*I* taunted you? Please tell me what you mean, Maria, at once.'

As though she were reciting some other's story, she told me how, miserable since Thetis's death, she had found her only pleasure in reading romances which she borrowed, one after another, from Edge's Circulating Library. This I had known; but not that the Library was also patronised by a young man of the name of Ezra Foxton, who had struck up an acquaintance there with Maria and suggested they should take walks together. I remembered then that I had once seen her with a young man, who was carrying an armful of books, in Market Street Lane, and had thought him, from a certain coarse look he had, to be some errand-lad she had paid to carry the weighty volumes.

He was in fact a clerk at Grant's, the drapers.

'I never liked him all that much,' she said, 'indeed very little, but I was so jealous of you having old Shelmerdine for a beau.'

I tried to interrupt, but she went on. 'I suppose it flattered me to be paid compliments, told I was pretty. We went for walks and when we reached a retired spot he would – take liberties.' She flushed deeply. 'After a time I began to like them, look forward to them. I made excuses to Mamma to go out in the evenings when he was free. Then one evening – it was hot and we'd walked a long way, as far as the woods near the Bason. He said we should lie down and rest under the trees. And – I tried not to let him, but it was too late.' She began to weep. 'And Emily, he hurt me so much, and I began to be frightened at once – of this happening.'

I drew her head to my shoulder. 'Don't, Maria, pray don't. He will have to marry you.'

She shook her head violently. 'He wants nothing to do with me. And he has no money, only a few shillings a week. Besides, I hate and loathe him. Oh, Emily, help me !'

'But what can *I* do, Maria? I stared at her helplessly. 'How can I help you, when I know less than you about it?'

'Help me to stop it,' she half whispered.

137

I hardly slept last night. Tossing from side to side, I selfishly wished she had not told me. Why should I bring trouble on myself – as trouble I knew there would be – for the sake of a girl who had been my lifelong enemy and had got into this plight through her own lust and folly? Yet her plight excited my pity, and she had appealed to me as a sister-woman. I have read in the romances Maria is so fond of about girls in her state who had been turned out of doors by their parents and murdered their babes. Indeed, the *Mercury* often contains gruesome stories of new-born infants found in the river or on dust-heaps, and of the young mothers who had killed them being hanged at the New Bailey. Maria hanged!

Ought I to appeal to her father? But he is no doctor; and the shock might bring on a fatal attack of asthma. As for telling Mrs Blackburn, the thought is almost ridiculous. And the Shelmerdines – no, no, I could not.

Suddenly an idea has come to me, as though a voice had whispered it in my ear. I will ask Bessy.

It is evening now, and something at least has been decided. I approached Bessy as I was helping her to prepare dinner.

'Bessy, a sad story has come to my ears.' My voice sounded as false to me as that of a stage villain. 'One of our young pupils – from Long Millgate – has a sister who . . . who is in great trouble.'

Bessy grunted. 'Doesn't surprise me, owt them folk get up to. Tha should never have browt 'em, in t' first place.'

'Oh, it is nothing criminal. Poor girl, she has been – betrayed.'

'What's that when it's a-whoam?'

'I – well, I mean she has been seduced by a wicked wretch.'

Bessy pummelled the dough mercilessly. 'Then she mun get wed to t'chap. She'll not be t'first to stand before parson wi' a great belly.'

I struggled on. 'The man cannot marry her – he has a wife already.' I began to be pleased at my inventiveness; perhaps I have more talent for deception than I thought.

'More fool she to meddle wi' him. Let her reap as she's sown. "In sorrow shalt thou bring forth childer", saith the Book.'

'But the poor thing is quite desperate, Bessy. Her – her father might beat her savagely if her condition were known. He is a very violent man.'

Bessy began to roll out the pastry. 'Then she'd get rid of it, choosehow.'

I nerved myself for what I must say. 'That is what she wants to do.' My voice must have trembled, for Bessy straightened up and looked at me sharply, raking my figure and taking note of my hot blush.

'It's noan thee, is it? Tha's not telling me a fairy-tale?'

'No, no, Bessy, of course not. How could you think such a thing? I – I am merely trying to help the girl.'

'I'm fain to hear it's noan thee,' Bessy said unexpectedly. It was the first time she had ever expressed any approval of me. 'Well, then,' she went on, somewhat more amiably, 'she'd best try four-pennorth of gin, taken hot, and another on top o' that, for as long as she can stand. Or some jump off a chair, time after time, to shake theirsen up; or take purges. I knew one lass as browt it on that way.'

I must have looked discouraged at these suggestions, for she added: 'Some goes to Mother Demdike – them that's noan feart of boggarts.'

'Of ghosts? What have they to do with it? And who is Mother Demdike?'

'Great-grandchild or summat of t' Lancashire Witches as were burned for sorcery time out o' mind sin'. There was the two Demdikes and a young lass, Jennet Device, all taken after they'd been proved to've thrown curses on neighbours and put a murrain on cattle when they'd a grudge toward t' farmer. Right wicked ways, they had. Of a neet they'd fly up to t' top of Pendle Hill on broomsticks and dance there naked wi' Owd Nick – or worse nor dance, more like. But they got caught at it. Burned to a cinder, every one, behind Lancaster Castle. Only folk say

Mother Demdike keeps a bone that was saved among t'ashes, to work spells with.'

'Spells that help women in trouble?'

She gave me a sly look, and turned to put the pie in the oven.

'That, and other things. Get along now. I've more to do nor prattle.'

I could see that I was going to get no more out of her, but said that at least I must know the address. It was Irk Street, she told me, at the back of the burying-ground, a part of the town we seldom visited.

My mind is made up. I am very much afraid of tampering with unholy arts, but for Maria's sake I must do it.

September 3rd

It was two days before the chance occurred to take Maria to consult the witch. I am afraid I invented an invitation from the Shelmerdines (who in fact are out of town) sent to both of us; and Mrs Blackburn seemed not to doubt it, though Maria's looks and bearing suggested anything but a pleasant social occasion.

The evening was dark and rainy, so that our best dresses got splashed with the sticky mud for which Manchester is known, and our best bonnets began to droop. Maria was utterly terri-fied, the arm I held shaking like a leaf in the wind. I had the greatest difficulty in getting her through the streets to our destination, and we got many a curious look from passers-by. But somehow we reached Irk Street, crossing the burying-ground of St Michael's which led to it. Then it occurred to me that we had no idea which house Mother Demdike lived in.

'Oh, Emily, let's go home,' Maria sobbed. 'We should never have come. Please take me back!'

'At least let us find her,' I said. 'She can do us no harm if she does no good.' I was far from convinced of this, but unless I had put a brave face on, Maria would have turned and run. As we stood in the unfamiliar, ugly street, on the edge of the New Town which was growing up to accommodate the factories and the workers, a woman opened a door to let in a barking dog. I darted across and asked if she could kindly direct us to Mrs Demdike's. She stared suspiciously at me, then pointed.

'Over t'cobbler's,' she said brusquely, shutting the door in my face.

The cobbler's sign of a large wooden shoe hung outside a cottage at the end of the street. The shutters were open, and there was no sign of life about. I gave a tug to the bell, and heard it clang inside. After a few moments, during which Maria tugged at my arm and pleaded piteously to be taken home, the door was unbolted and the dirty face of a little old man peered round it.

'Ah'm shut,' he said. 'What's tha want at this hour?'

'We are calling on Mrs Demdike, and were told she lived here.'

'Round t'back. Green door,' he said, and for the second time I found myself facing a shut door. Down the cobbled alley we went, into a mean yard where rabbits peered out at us from a ramshackle hutch. The green door yielded to a push. It led to a short flight of steps with another door at the top, at which I knocked with a firmness I was far from feeling. A voice called, 'Come in,' and we entered.

The room in which we found ourselves was the plainest imaginable, such as any cottage might contain; there was a truckle bed, an upright chair and a stool, a corner store-cupboard, and a rush mat in front of the empty fireplace. If I had expected stuffed crocodiles and human skulls I was agreeably disappointed; nor did Mrs Demdike herself look in the least like the popular impression of a witch. A small woman, neatly but shabbily dressed, she might have been of any age from fifty to seventy. I noticed that her woollen shawl was fastened with an unusual, beautiful brooch of antique design, containing a black shining stone surrounded with tiny pearls, and that the little window-sill behind her held pots of plants, some bright with flowers.

She came forward to meet us and addressed us in a voice

141

which was soft and pleasant, Lancashire enough but without the broad dialect of the Manchester streets.

'Come in, my young ladies. You've been sent to me?'

'Yes, ma'am,' I said, resolved to test her powers by saying as little as possible about our errand. Maria hid behind me, still shaking but, I thought, a little calmed by the reality of the 'witch' and her room after our wild imaginings. Mrs Demdike motioned us to take a seat on the bed, settling herself in the chair.

'I'm badly off for furniture, as you see. But it's enow, most times. Nay, don't talk, let me look at ye both. It's not often I get such a pretty pair of ladies to see me.'

I found my gaze irresistibly drawn to her eyes, which seemed of no particular colour, nor of any great expression, but which gave the impression of looking through my own eyes into my brain, like projected rays of light. The effect was uncomfortable and I felt my heart beating faster than usual. After a few moments' inspection she nodded.

'So one of ye's in trouble, and it's not thee, my curly-haired lass. Tell thy friend to lift her head up. I'll not bite her.' I nudged Maria, who obediently lifted her tear-stained, swollen-eyed face. Rather to my surprise, Mrs Demdike took less time inspecting her, and turned away quickly to address me.

'Ye've heard something of my family's story, I'll be bound.'

'A little, ma'am. They – I was told some of them suffered a very cruel fate.'

She smiled. 'You think 'twas cruel, not well deserved?'

'Yes, indeed. If they had done wrong to others they should have been punished, certainly, but not in such a terrible way. And I don't believe witches did commit—' I stopped, embarrassed, but Mrs Demdike looked amused.

'Nay, go on, I don't mind being called a witch. What do ye not believe, my clever young lady?'

'That they committed all those crimes they were tortured for in the reign of King James. I think they were the victims of ignorant and superstitious people, and of others who enjoyed inflicting pain.' I was surprised to hear myself uttering these sentiments, for I had never given much thought to the question at all; but I knew that what I was saying expressed my true feelings. There was wisdom in Mrs Demdike, and a mystery which alarmed me a little; but no malice, of that I was sure. And Maria had quite stopped trembling.

The strange eyes regarded me thoughtfully. 'Not many think that way, even now. I never walk down the street but I see the sign of the horns made at me. Ye looked round the floor for my cat just now, didn't ye?'

I had done so, indeed.

'There's no cat here, nor ever will be. Why should I keep an innocent beast to be stoned or drowned, as t'would be? Not a toad nor even a mouse shall suffer because 'tis Mother Demdike's; and may them as have murdered the innocents, these many hundred years, feel the pains of Hell for them! But ye've not come here, in fear and trembling, to talk of such things. My dear,' addressing Maria, 'how far are ye gone – two months or three?'

We both started with amazement, for the sharpest eye could not have seen any sign in Maria's figure of her condition – indeed, she was thinner than before, if anything.

'Two,' she answered. 'But how could you know?'

'Never mind that. I'll tell ye something more I know. Yon babe that's still asleep within ye was conceived of lust, not love, and 'twere better it were not born, for there's bad blood on both sides. Take care, next time, how ye go courting for spite.'

Maria, fiery red, gasped out: 'Oh yes, it's true, and I was wicked! But you *will* help me, please, please do!'

Mrs Demdike regarded her with an expression I could not fathom. 'I'll help thee, aye,' she said. 'But never blame me for what comes of it.'

'What – will I die?' cried Maria.

'Not you. Only your babe. Mark you, I do this because it has been only two months in the womb. More than that I wouldn't risk.' She went to the cupboard and came back bearing a stone

143

jar and a square of white paper, on to which she carefully poured from the jar a small quantity of dark-purplish grains, from which came up a very unpleasant smell, something like decaying fish. She folded and twisted the paper into a neat package, and put it into Maria's hand.

'Tonight, take a third part of this with boiling water poured on it, to half a cupful, before ye're in bed. Tomorrow night another third. By then ye may be past need of it, but if not take the last third. And mind you, this is not magic, but old medicine.'

Maria stammered something about thanks and payment.

'Aye, I'll not refuse. Show me thy purse.' From the coins Maria produced she selected two, both silver. 'If ye go without some bit of finery to pay me, let it remind ye not to go whoring.'

Ignoring Maria's outraged gasp, she laid a hand on my arm. 'I'd be fain to read your hand, young miss – and for nowt.'

I had risen, but she pushed me back to my seat on the bed, and sat beside me, holding both my palms before her. Yet I felt she was looking through rather than at them, as she spoke, in the voice of a dreamer.

'I see a loss, and a finding. I see a great house and a green garden, and blue ribbons, one on the breast, one in the hair. I see sickness, and death close by thy shoulder; and death for another, among great waters. There will be words that cannot be spoken, and a parting. I see thee with a ringless finger and a veiled face, and many a long mile between thee and home. But thou has a true heart and a brave spirit.'

Her voice ceased, and she seemed to come to herself. Looking directly into my eyes (and, I am sure, bidding me thus to remember every word she had just spoken) she said: 'When the worst of troubles come, call upon me, and I will answer and aid thee, living or dead.' She pushed me gently towards the door, where Maria waited. I shall never know whether I thanked her, or indeed said anything.

As I was half-way through the door, I heard her say: 'Luck go with thee, Beauty's daughter.'

12

I do not know what the date is, or the day, except that it is still August. I feel as though I were living in a dream, but I will try to set down clearly the events which have so changed my life.

Mrs Demdike's medicine worked all too well, on the third morning after our visit. Mrs Blackburn, entering Maria's bedroom to find out why she was so late in getting up, discovered her terrified, distraught, and bleeding so profusely that the doctor was immediately sent for. What Mrs Demdike had not told us was that a miscarriage can be almost as violent as a birth.

Maria was pronounced to be in no danger. Reassured of this, she told her mother the story in such a way as to deflect her anger from herself and direct it towards me. She had, it seemed, been brutally assaulted by a perfect stranger, and had begged me for advice when the consequences became certain; on which I had insisted on dragging her to an evil old woman who had given her a medicine which might very well have caused her death, and had muttered curses on her and strange spells over me.

The shock of the news brought on one of Mr Blackburn's attacks, and removed him mercifully from the scene. I was trying to eat my first morsel of food since all the excitement had begun when Mrs Blackburn entered the room and dealt me a box on the ear which sent me toppling over in my chair to fall painfully on the floor, where I lay, unable to rise, while she harangued me.

'I have always known you for a bad, wicked girl, Emily Hart! But for you my poor frail child would never have been led into such wickedness in the first place – you with your dressings-up and your playhouses and your rich lovers!'

'If you mean Mr Shelmerdine,' I said, trying to sound dignified from a very undignified position, 'he is not my lover, merely a kind old gentleman, and I should like to know what my visits to his house had to do with Maria's behaviour?'

'What, indeed! Seeing you so bold, the poor girl thought no wrong to answer a strange young man when he spoke to her in that lonely place—'

'He was not a strange man. He was Ezra Foxton who works at Grant's, and she knew him perfectly well and—' My words were drowned.

'And then to take her to a notorious witch, to have heaven knows what mischief worked on her, body and soul. Shame on you, vicious, abandoned girl! I knew no good would come of taking you into the house, nameless bastard that you were. I always said there was some shameful reason for my husband's silence about you, and I shall get it out of him, never fear. And now you can get up and pack your things, for not a minute longer shall you stay under my roof.'

I scrambled up. 'But where am I to go?'

'To the devil, if you please – you seem familiar enough with his sort. You'll earn a good enough living on the streets, I dare say.' She was ugly with anger, more ugly than I have ever seen her, or anyone. 'Get you gone, and never let me see you again.'

'I shall be glad to,' I said. 'But I must have time to find a place to stay, and to pack my clothes.'

'You can pack this with them,' she said with a kind of smile, and taking something from her pocket threw it at me.

It was a packet of letters, the seals broken. I opened one, and saw Francis Carew's signature at the bottom of the sheet. There were four altogether, the last dated months before. I took in the final words of it: 'I shall remember you ever with kindness and regret that you evidently do not wish us to continue friends.'

'You – kept – them,' I said, hardly recognising my own voice. 'You dared to stop my letters. Why, why?'

Mrs Blackburn shrugged. 'Partly to find out who was writing to a young woman in my care. And partly because you were useful to us at the time. That time has now passed. You may keep them.'

I must have rushed from the house, just as I was, though I have no memory of it, nor of running through the streets and arriving at the Shelmerdines' house. The first thing I recall is that I was lying on a sofa in Cicely's little parlour, and that she was holding a vinaigrette to my nose, looking anxiously at me. The powerful scent revived me, and I sat up and gratefully drank the tea her maid had brought in.

'But my poor Emily,' Cicely said, 'what can have happened to you? It must have been something quite dreadful, for you were half frantic when you arrived here. I thought you had run quite out of your mind.'

'I feel as though I had. But, dear Cicely, I would rather not speak of it yet. I am still too distressed. Please may I be alone for a little, to recover myself? You won't be offended?'

'Of course not, love. I'll put my afghan over you, there, so that you can be warm and snug, and here are some books. You shall stay here and read, or sleep, or what you like, and when you feel able to talk to me, pull the bell and Hannah will fetch me to you.' And the dear girl tiptoed out as though I had been dangerously ill.

The books she had brought me happened to be a pile of *Gentleman's Magazines*. I picked one up, because I did not want to think, and read, over and over again, a long and unexciting poem on the Beneficial Effects of Inoculation: I believe I shall be able to recite parts of it to my dying day. I must have fallen asleep over it; when I roused, the glow of the setting sun was reflected on the wall.

I could not bring myself to tell Cicely the whole disgraceful story, only that Mrs Blackburn and I had had a fearful scene and that she had turned me out of the house.

'But that's good!' Cicely cried. 'Yes, I mean good, and you needn't look so surprised, for now you can come and live here and, oh, how delightful it will be to have company always, and not to be so dull and slow by oneself. Now which room—'

'My dear Cicely, before you plan my boudoir, don't you think Mr Shelmerdine will have something to say about his house being turned into an hotel for wandering damsels?'

'Papa will be enchanted, and well you know it, sly creature!'

I had not known it. I had taken all his kindness for granted, as being a generous man's benevolence towards a girl less fortunate than his daughter. But when he returned home and, having heard Cicely's version of what had happened, came to me with such tender concern in his eyes, and such warmth in the clasp of his hand, I knew that I had been blind.

By this time I was quite calm, and told him something (though not all) of the truth, watching his face grow more and more grave.

'You should have left those people long ago, Emily,' he said. 'They are not fit to look after you. Nay, I've known John Blackburn many a year, since he tutored our George, but I'd never have thought that of him.'

'He had very little say in it, sir, and he is a sick man.'

'Aye. Aye.' He sat, looking at the fire, moving the glass of port in his hand round in small circles on the table. 'And these relations or guardians of yours – they've never written to you?'

'Not that I know of, unless more letters than – my friend's – – have been kept from me.' (Something had held me from telling him anything of Francis.) 'My allowance is still drawn from their bank. I suppose they are too rich to miss it. I wish I could have known them. It's strange to have no family of one's own – only a bank draft.'

Mr Shelmerdine drew his chair closer and laid his hand on mine. I noticed how strong it looked, and how well kept were the nails; it felt comforting above mine, which quite disappeared beneath it.

'My dear little Emily,' he said, 'I will give you a family, if you'll let me. A family of your own – of *our* own. Do you understand me? I'm a poor hand at saying pretty things. But I love you, and I want you for my wife.'

I must have looked at him strangely, for he went on hurriedly.

'I'm many years older than you. I've no right to ask it of

you. But you're a right clever lass, years ahead of your age, if I'm any judge, and it might be easier for you than for a feather-pated wench like our Cicely, bless her. Won't you – think about it, at least, Emily?'

My hand still in the clasp of his, I saw him as I had not done before; as a portly but not gross figure, of a height which dwarfed me, with comely white hair which had once been as dark as the kindly eyes. The expression of the face I can only describe as one of great goodness.

'I think we might agree very well, sir,' I said.

He lifted my hand and kissed it, and then, very gently, my cheek.

'I've been alone so many years, my dear,' he said. 'You've made me very happy, and with God's help I'll make you the same.'

I moved to his side and rested my head on his shoulder; and we sat there, in the firelight, until Cicely came in and discovered us.

I believe that she, the minx, had known her father's mind all along, but she was nonetheless surprised and joyful when he told her the news, kissing and embracing us both, and calling me her little Mamma.

'Now I suppose you'll grow very grand and scold me all the time, when you are an Aldermaness. Oh, do let me be your bridesmaid, dearest Emily, for we shall look so delightfully ridiculous walking up the aisle. What do you intend to wear? I think I shall choose pink. Shall you call Papa Edward, or Mr Shelmerdine? I must write to George at once to get leave from the Downs and we'll have a great rout and invite all the old pussycats from Church who want to marry you themselves, Papa.'

When she had given vent to her wildest spirits we sat and talked quietly, and they made me sing to the old-fashioned spinet on which Cicely never played anything more ambitious than 'God Save The King'. I don't know why an old song came into my mind, the song of a Jacobite soldier taking leave of our town

as the Prince's army began the northward march to Culloden,
defeat and death.

> 'Farewell, Manchester,
> Noble town, farewell;
> Here in loyalty
> Every breast shall swell,
> Wheresoe'er I roam,
> Here, as in a home,
> Ever dear, Lancashire,
> My heart shall dwell.'

'A sad song for a bride, my dear,' said Mr Shelmerdine (or Edward, as I must get used to calling him).

'I suppose it came to me because I have just come to realise
how much I love Manchester,' I replied. 'Dear, dirty old place, it
has brought me you.'

I am writing this in a fine handsome guest-room, where I stay
tonight; tomorrow I shall go to Palace Street for the last time, to
fetch my belongings. I am very, very happy.

Can it have been only last night that I wrote those words? I
could almost laugh now, to think of them.

When I returned to Palace Street an hour ago, the door was
opened by Mr Blackburn, looking grey and ill, but not angry as
I had expected.

'I am glad you have returned so soon, Emily,' he said. 'There
is someone to see you.'

He opened the parlour door and motioned me in. The visitor
turned her head and smiled as I entered.

'My dear Emily,' said Mrs Cadogan, 'I have come to take you
home.'

Three

A Great House

and a Green Garden

13

Emily sat up very straight on the delicate white-and-gold sofa, and deliberately gave her arm a sharp pinch. Yes, it was true, she was awake. Her hands were dirty with travelling, she was cold, had a headache and a keen appetite. She was nearly two hundred miles from Manchester, which seemed like another world. She was sitting in the most beautiful room she had ever seen in her life, the drawing-room of Number 23, Piccadilly, London. Long mirrors set into ivory panelling and flanked with gold sconces reflected the trees of Green Park opposite, rich in the colours of an early September morning. The carpet beneath her feet was a flowery spread of pale blues, pinks and greens, a treasure from China; on the marble mantelpiece a clock made of onyx was so heavily embraced by a gilt Venus and her troop of cupids that it was difficult to tell the time by it.

Time, in fact, had almost ceased to mean anything. It seemed centuries ago that she had stood staring at Mrs Cadogan in the Palace Street parlour and heard the explanation that her relatives were now returned from abroad and in a position to provide her, at last, with a home. For the first time in her conscious life she heard the name Greville used in connection with herself; he had arranged for the bank draft to be discontinued, he was in excellent health, so far as Mrs Cadogan knew, for he was not a frequent visitor to his uncle. Would Miss Hart be ready to accompany her to London by the next day's coach? asked Mrs Cadogan, and Mr Blackburn replied hurriedly that she would.

'But,' Emily broke in, 'I am to be married.'

'Married?' Mr Blackburn's face was a study in shock, and even Mrs Cadogan's calm was disturbed. 'What is this? We have heard nothing of it before.'

'I – only yesterday evening. Mr Shelmerdine asked for my hand, and I accepted.'

Mrs Cadogan was thoughtful. 'I see. This puts a different face on things, to be sure. Well, my dear, I am very happy to hear your news, but do you not feel that after so many years you would like to become acquainted with your own family, who long earnestly to see you? If only for your husband's sake,' she added delicately.

It was true, of course. Edward Shelmerdine, though he would have taken her nameless and penniless, could not but be pleased to find her well connected, befriended. And she felt an upsurge of eagerness to set eyes at last on the company of ghosts who had hovered in her mind since she first asked herself 'Who am I?' If Mrs Cadogan went away alone they might vanish again, never to return, leaving her once more a waif.

'I will be glad to come with you, ma'am,' she said, 'if I may first explain to my fiancé what has happened. Of course, it will be understood that I shall return to Manchester later.'

'Of course. Pray congratulate the bridegroom on my behalf.' She rose, and Emily saw that she was a little stiff in movement and more bowed in the shoulders than in her childish recollection. The droop on the right side of the face was more pronounced, the blue eyes faded, but the voice and manner as brisk and pleasant as ever.

'I had intended to come for you in the spring,' she said, 'but illness struck me down for a time and my daughter insisted that I stay at home. It was my second stroke, my dear, and they say that the third is often the last – so you see I must make the most of you while I can.' She kissed Emily warmly. 'I shall be staying at the Swan, and the coach leaves tomorrow at midday.'

When she had gone, ushered out by Mr Blackburn, he turned to Emily with a colder face than she had ever seen him wear. 'It is the best thing that could have occurred. My wife is indisposed and will prefer not to see you while you remain in our house. No doubt you will wish to visit your friends.'

The news she broke to Edward Shelmerdine was even more of a shock than she had feared. Looking suddenly older, he sat down and leaned his head on his hands as though it weighed heavily.

'You must go, of course. After so long, to be taken up by your own folk – it's a grand thing for you, lass. To my mind they're much to be blamed for leaving you all these years.' He essayed a smile. 'They don't know what they've missed, do they?'

Emily patted his shoulder. 'They have been abroad, Edward. There was nothing they could do about me. And if they are all like Mrs Cadogan I know I shall love them.'

'Mayhap you'll find a father to give you away at our wedding, and a mother to cry over the bride. I believe it's customary.' He looked ready to cry himself. Emily put her arms round him.

'Dear Edward, you are not to mind, for it won't be long, and I'm sure I shall come back to you happier. I shall write to you every day, just as I used to try to keep my stupid journal, and tell you all the wonders of London, and you are to keep very busy and cheerful, or I shall scold you very much when I come back.'

He stood up and took her in his arms, holding her close, searching her face. She knew in that moment, their first real embrace, that what lay between them was warmth rather than fire – the fire which had once been lit in her and gone out for lack of fuel – and that what she felt for him was a tender gratitude, the pent-up fondness she had never been able to give to a father. She stretched up and kissed him, boldly, on the mouth, feeling his closed lips pressing painfully hard on hers. Perhaps this was what love was like – how could she know?

He released her. 'You'll stay with us today, as long as you can? Cicely'll be beside herself when she hears.'

'I shall stay out of that house until the last possible moment,' said Emily grimly.

The farewells were over, her clothes packed, with her few books, in a shabby valise produced by Bessy from the attic and slammed down in front of Emily without a word. Mrs Blackburn remained invisible, except for a brief scurry past Emily in the passage, her face set in lines of violent disapproval. Emily hovered at Maria's door, then changed her mind. There was no more to say to anyone. When her last night was over, and she stood in the hall ready to leave, nobody appeared to carry the valise to the Swan for her, or even to say goodbye.

One should be sorry to leave a place where one's whole life up to the present moment has been spent, she thought, but I am only sorry not to be sorry. She shrugged and sighed, let herself out, and walked briskly over the rain-damp cobbles to the inn-yard of the Swan, feeling a pair of malevolent dark eyes boring into her back until she had turned the corner of the street.

The coach journey was a surprise, and far from a pleasant one. Her journey in infancy was now not even a memory to her, and she was not prepared for the jolting of the wheels over cobbles and ruts, or for the extreme stuffiness of the air. Mrs Cadogan had taken the more expensive inside seats, but Emily, in spite of the precarious position of those on top of the coach, felt after a few miles that she would almost have been prepared to risk it than to feel herself stifling in the atmosphere of old leather, straw with a strong flavour of the stable, and the various scents of their companions. She was wedged between Mrs Cadogan (who was a seasoned traveller and took all the literal ups and downs calmly) and an old man who could with advantage have patronised his laundress oftener. Emily found her sense of smell extraordinarily acute, not only with regard to him but to the staleness of the biscuits which were steadily eaten by the woman in the corner seat, and to a musky odour which might once have been perfume, wafting from the female half of a married couple.

But the worst annoyance was the impossibility of talking freely. Even over the noise of the wheels, the clatter of the horses' hooves and the conversations of the other passengers, Emily could not ask Mrs Cadogan all the things she longed to know, for they would certainly have been overheard. As it was, they chatted of the scenes through which they passed, the pretty villages of Didsbury and Cheadle, which were as far as Emily had travelled before, the rapidly growing industrial town of Stockport, and the beautiful country which opened out before them as they crossed into Derbyshire.

It was at Ashbourne, where they stopped for refreshment at the Green Man, that Emily tried to extract some information. But the rush for food and drink and even more necessary conveniences made it impossible to do more than ask a question or two as they gulped down coffee and cold meat and cheese.

'It's of no use, my dear,' said Mrs Cadogan, 'if the whole carriageful of 'em would be obliging enough to go to sleep, we might have a nice pleasant talk, but as they're not likely to we must wait until we stop for longer.'

But somehow as the twenty-hour journey went on, Emily began to feel incapable of asking a sensible question. She grew more and more tired, nodded off, and was startled awake by a jolt or some sudden noise, until her only wish was to reach London as soon as possible. Mrs Cadogan managed to doze. Stage after stage was reached, horses changed, passengers fed by inn-servants who would no doubt make the most themselves of the food which had to be left on the plates as the warning horn summoned the loiterers back to the coach. Evening came, the skies darkened; it became impossible to see anything but the lights of the villages and isolated houses they passed. When the coach stopped at Leicester, Emily made up her mind to a daring action. Approached by a waiter to take her order for refreshment she said boldly 'Brandy and water, hot, if you please,' and drank it back in two or three fiery gulps. The waiter made it no secret that he thought her a very fast young lady indeed, modifying his opinion only slightly when she coughed and choked and turned scarlet over the glass.

But it sent her into a blissful sleep, unaware of anything. The passengers might snore, the coachman shout to his guard; she knew nothing until Mrs Cadogan gently touched her arm.

'We're all but in London, my dear.'

Emily was awake in an instant, looking out at a little town which like her was awakening for the day. Mrs Cadogan told her it was Barnet, and scarcely had the horses been changed at the Salisbury Arms than the new ones were bearing them briskly into a long village in which every other building seemed to be an inn.

'Highgate,' said Mrs Cadogan. 'Down the hill and we're almost there.'

Quivering with excitement, and with the chill of the night which was still upon her, Emily looked excitedly from side to side as the buildings grew more frequent and they began to pass through town streets, until, with a flourish of the horn and even louder cries from the coachman and guard, they rattled into the yard of the Golden Cross, Piccadilly.

Barely were they out of the coach than a liveried servant was at their side, bowing.

'Ah, good morning, Harris,' said Mrs Cadogan. 'Thank God you're here. It's as cold as Christmas, and we've seen enough of inn parlours to last us a month of Sundays.'

'Her ladyship was particularly anxious you should not be kept waiting, madam. If you will enter the carriage, I will see to the baggage.'

'Baggage!' said Emily. 'Whatever will he think of my poor little valise?'

'I doubt if it'll prey on his mind,' Mrs Cadogan replied. 'Come along, my dear.' Emily followed her to an extremely handsome carriage, drawn up a few yards away, with a cockaded coachman on the box and a pair of sleek chestnuts standing in silent communion, their breath steaming on the cold air. The carriage door bore an armorial crest, chained unicorn-like creatures supporting some circular design and standing on the motto *Sola Virtus Nobilitat*. The coachman sprang down and handed them both into the carriage, where Emily subsided into a corner and stared helplessly at her companion.

'Pray, pray, ma'am, tell me something, or I shall go mad, I think. Whose is this carriage, and where are we going?'

'Indeed, I wish I could have told you before, but it was such an uncommonly crowded coach. This is Sir William Hamilton's carriage, and we are going to his house in Piccadilly.'

'Is he – my father, then?'

'No, no, child. Sir William is quite an old gentleman. But he is my daughter's husband, and you are our kin. I am, indeed, and how glad I am to tell you at last – I am your grandmother, my dear.' She put her arm round Emily's shoulders and kissed her fondly.

Emily hugged her, half laughing, half crying. 'Oh, dearest Grandmother! Why could you not have told me before? Oh, how happy I am! Then who is my mother?'

'My daughter will tell you all when we get home. See, we're going up the Haymarket. There is the Theatre Royal.'

Emily had a confused impression of hay-wains, carters, and a splendid porticoed building which looked as unlike the little Manchester theatre as the imposing Golden Cross to the Swan from which their coach had started. Then they turned left into a noble thoroughfare with great mansions on each side, such as Emily had never imagined, even in London; and in a few minutes there was beautiful parkland on the left of them.

'That is the Green Park,' her grandmother said, 'and here we are.' The carriage stopped at a large wrought-iron gate set in a high wall, which was at once opened by a man who touched his forelock as the chestnuts trotted up the drive and paused at the front door of a mansion smaller than some of its neighbours, but to Emily quite as imposing. A footman in powder admitted them.

'Her ladyship is not downstairs yet, madam,' he said to Mrs Cadogan, 'but she begs Miss Hart will make herself comfortable in the drawing-room for a few minutes.'

'I should have thought she'd have been a deal more comfortable in my parlour,' said Mrs Cadogan, as they went up a magnificent mahogany staircase. 'But if it's to be the drawing-room, then bring Miss Hart a nice hot cup of chocolate at once, Henry, for I'm sure the fire won't have got going.'

Nor had it. The great double drawing-room was chilly, the fire still a few sulky flames stirring beneath the logs. Mrs Cadogan vanished with a smile, like a fairy godmother in a

159

story, and Emily felt bereft in her absence. It seemed that she had sat there for hours, even after she had finished the chocolate, before the door burst open and with a musical cry an apparition in a cloud of white lace and swansdown ran lightly across the room and caught Emily to its breast. An ineffably sweet and expensive scent enveloped her, warm strong arms held her tight. Instinctively she returned the embrace as though she would never let the holder go. At last they drew apart, still clasping hands.

'Oh, my dear, my darling girl, you're here at last!' cried Emma, Lady Hamilton.

Emily knew her at once for the Saint Cecilia of the portrait, though many years had gone by since it was painted, and the slip of a girl had become a large woman, not so much fat as majestic of figure, full-bosomed, round-armed, the radiant complexion only a little marred by tiny broken veins hiding in the brilliance of her cheeks, the great sapphire eyes beaming with love and joy. Tears were streaming down them now, coursing down like mountain rills, without the slightest damage to her beauty. The long mirror opposite caught their images, the woman and the girl, unmistakably mother and daughter.

'Why, what a little thing you are!' Emma said with wondering delight, holding her at arm's length. 'No bigger than Mam. And bless me, your hair's done the same as mine, à la Titus.'

'Is it, my lady?' Emily looked with some surprise upon the dark-red ringlets which curled and twined merrily over her ladyship's perfect head. 'I didn't know it was so called. It merely grows this way.'

'Fancy! And it was as straight as a die when you were a baby, not a bend in it. Do you put it in papers?' She touched a curl lovingly.

'No, ma'am, I had a fever and it was cut off, since when it has grown like this. Did you – did you know me well, then?'

The unspoken question was in her eyes, yearning for the unspoken answer in Emma's. Once Emma would have told the truth, straight from her frank fond heart; but there had been deception upon deception, lie after lie, for Nelson's sake, until concealment and evasion became almost habit. She hesitated, and turned away from truth.

'Very well. And your mother too. She was a sister of mine – we were very close. I would have brought you up when she – she was obliged to leave England, but then I went to Italy myself, and so—' her dramatic gesture took in the Blackburns, the years of parting, the return, as professionally as Mrs Siddons would have done it. She saw the disappointment in Emily's face. Perhaps she would have to recant and tell, after all. 'Do you remember nothing of that time?' she asked.

Blue eyes met blue eyes, and the pair in which there was an enchanting spot of brown widened as Emily said, 'I think I remember you, my lady.'

'Yes,' said Emma, 'I believe you do.'

For a moment they looked at each other in silence. Enough had been said, and left unsaid, for the present. Suddenly Emma's laugh rang out. 'Why, you poor child, here you are freezing from that dreadful coach journey and starving, no doubt, while I keep you here chit-chatting. Come upstairs and we'll find a good warm robe of Mam's that will fit you, for you look blue with cold, and then we'll all have breakfast.'

Half an hour later, washed, warm, and fed, Emily sat by a roaring fire in the charming little parlour from which Mrs Cadogan ruled as housekeeper. They were all drinking coffee, Emma with her fluffy-slippered feet on the fender. Every now and then she would reach out to stroke or pat Emily, as though she had found a little animal in need of comfort and reassurance. Far from any such need, Emily was supremely happy, a lost soul suddenly admitted into heaven. The only drawback to her complete felicity was that her throat felt curiously sore, so that she accepted cup after cup of the steaming hot coffee ('Don't know where she puts it,' commented her grandmother) to ease the roughness; and a sharp pain had developed in her chest. Only a cold, but what a tiresome moment to catch one. She resolved to ignore it, and settled down to listen to Emma's story of her adventures since their last meeting. Mrs Cadogan, apparently oblivious, sat at her desk making out menus and doing accounts, occasionally ringing for a servant to give orders. What was news to Emily was an old tale to her.

'I left England, my dear Emy,' Emma began her chronicle of fact blended with romance, 'because Sir William' – she pronounced it Will'um – 'my dear husband that is, invited me to Naples so that I might further my music and study under Italian singing teachers. I was the most tremendous success you can imagine, my beauty and talents admired on all sides.' Emily opened her eyes wide, but to Emma there was nothing vain about such a statement. 'Those sweet, simple Italians had never seen anything like me. Do you know, my love, they actually took me at first for the Virgin Mary?'

Something like a suppressed snort came from Mrs Cadogan's desk.

'Well, I lived there happily for a time,' Emma went on, neatly omitting the real drama of her discovery of Greville's treachery to her and her own indignant fight against Sir William's strictly dishonourable intentions towards her, 'until it became quite plain to Sir William that we should be married. He was almost twice my age, but I was so fond of him and so grateful – you can't imagine how grateful! – that I was happy to say yes, and so in 1791 we came to England and were quietly married. The King (Sir William is his foster-brother, you know) was inclined to be difficult about giving consent, and indeed I was not received at Court even as Lady Hamilton—'

The date 1791 recalled something to Emily. 'Was that when you sent me some beautiful clothes, ma'am, and Mrs Cadogan came to see me?'

Emma beamed. 'Why, yes, and I hope you was as pleased to get them as I was to send them. Mam was not very struck by the place where you were, but Sir William would have us go straight back to Naples, so that I could do nothing about removing you.'

'Mr Greville—' Emily began.

'Oh, Greville?' Emma's tone was airy. 'Yes, it was Greville who made all arrangements for you, being Sir William's nephew and an old friend of mine. Later, of course, Sir William paid your allowance.'

Mrs Cadogan rattled her pen in the inkwell.

'But as I was saying, although the British Court chose to ignore me, I was most fondly received by their Majesties at Naples – indeed, my dearest beloved Queen made me her friend, her confidante, her adviser. Oh, I have been quite a politician in my time, Emy! Of course, those damned curs of Frenchmen were for ever baying at our gates – you know they had cut off Queen Marie Antoinette's head, that was my Queen's sister, and King Louis's? God knows what would have happened to us all if our great and glorious Lord Nelson had not come when he did.' Her face was dreaming, transfigured. 'He had visited us at Naples before, but it was not till after the Battle of the Nile that we received him as our hero, our Jove, the saviour of his country! And when the Bonapartist rebels stirred up Naples against their Majesties and all our lives were threatened, 'twas Nelson and I who saved them and carried them safe to Sicily, all but my poor dear little Prince Alberto who died in my arms. Oh, that voyage! Nothing, nothing could have been more terrible; a fierce storm raging, my Queen and her entourage sick and distressed, the waves flinging us from side to side so that even though we might escape drowning we risked having our heads cracked open and our bones snapped . . .' She rocked realistically, mimicking distraught tempest-tossed creatures. Emily thought she had seen something very like it on the stage, but not half so good as this.

'Later Nelson went back to Naples to exact justice, and I was beside him as his secretary and translator. 'Twas harrowing to the soul indeed. Executions and blood and—' She paused, then spoke earnestly. 'I hope you weren't told, Emy, that I had any part in it or that I rejoiced in some of those sights I was forced to see. The vile French put it about that I did such things as kiss Nelson's bloody sword, and cheer when they strung up the traitor Caracciolo at the masthead – and that I concurred in the hanging of Eleanor Pimentel who had just borne a child . . .' She shuddered. 'Nelson was under King Ferdinand's orders. What else could he do? And the King was blood-mad – the reek of slaughtered animals was like incense to him. I can't bear to be cruel, Emy. I don't think I could kill a Frenchman any more than I could a fly, though God knows I hate both.'

'I heard nothing of all this,' said Emily gently. 'And now that I know you I could never believe you would be unkind to anything.'

'Nor can he, our Nelson, only when his country calls, for loyalty is his ruling passion. In peace he's as gentle as a lamb.'

Emily clapped her hands together in delight. 'Oh, my lady, how I should love to see him!'

'You shall, child, you shall. At present the Downs Fleet claims him, and he lies off Deal, from which those beasts at the Admiralty won't grant him ever a day's leave to come home and see the new house I've found for him, ailing though he is and heart-broke after the death of our dear little Parker—'

Mrs Cadogan laid down her pen and turned round. 'Emma, this girl is fagged out after the journey, and coughing besides. You can tell her the rest of our adventures when she's rested, but now I think she should be put to bed and given a good hot draught.' Emily shot her a grateful look, for absorbing and entertaining as Emma's narrative was, she was beginning to feel quite unwell, and certainly very weary.

'Oh, how thoughtless I am,' Emma said cheerfully. 'But you know me when I get talking, Mam, and so will you, Emy, when you've lived with us a bit. Ring for Dame Francis, Mam, and get a warming-pan put in Emy's bed.'

'I did so half an hour ago, but you were too busy rattling on to notice. Come along, Emily, it's time you was resting.'

'And I shall write letters,' said Emma, 'for I must tell dear Sarah Nelson and Mrs Bolton and all of them that we have our dear sweet girl with us. I shall write for the rest of the morning.'

'What there is of it left,' her mother threw back from the

door. She led Emily up to a bedroom which looked to her tired, gritty eyes like a fairy's bower, all damask and lace. And in a few moments a neat smiling maid appeared, announcing herself as Nancy, and undressed Emily, who was too weary to find this unusual or embarrassing, before popping a hot woollen night-gown over her head and ushering her into a nest of warmed sheets. A steaming cup of something appeared from another hand at the door; Emily drank it, and was almost asleep before the last drop had gone.

Emma had begun her first letter when her mother reappeared, looking grim.

'Take care how you use that child, Emma.'

Emma raised a startled face. 'What do you mean, Mam? I love her, indeed I do. Didn't I show it?'

'Yes, yes, we'll take that for granted. But you must think of her wants before your own speechifying, poor creature that she is, brought up by those hard-hearted Puritans or whatever they are, worrying all her life about who she is and why she was left to grow up no more cared for than a farm cat. First I was to tell her nothing, either when she was a child or the other day – then I was to hint the truth; then you'd have me keep quiet and leave it to you. Leave it to you, indeed! A fine mess you made of it, for you needn't tell me that you told her that fairy-tale about your sister being her mother, and such rubbish. Oh, I know it's a delicate matter, what with my lord and Sir William and the others, but Emma, can you not be diplomatic to them and frank to her? It's cruelty to keep her in the dark any longer, and we've just heard about how kind you are to flies and Frenchmen. Well, little Emy's neither. She's your daughter and my granddaughter, which last I *have* told her with or without your leave, and I'll be glad if you'll remember it.'

Emma's beautiful mouth fell open with surprise. It was pos-sibly the longest speech her mother had made for years, and she was admiring and impressed; it was so nice to have someone she respected telling her what to do. But Mam's small face was quite red with temper and effort, and her mouth quivering ominously. Emma rose and put her gently into a chair.

'Mam, you're quite right, so don't exert yourself further or you'll bring your trouble on again. I know I've been weak and wavering about telling Emily. Mind you, there's no need to put it into words, for she knows it. I saw it in her face.'

'No fool,' murmured Mrs Cadogan.

'No fool indeed – a lot wiser than her poor mother, I'll be bound, in some ways. Now don't fret, Mam. As soon as she wakes I'll come out with it, and she'll have no more doubts.'

But when Emily woke it was with a raging temperature and a tearing cough. Either the cold journey, or her anxious state, or simply an infection picked up somewhere had struck at the delicate lungs; and the doctor hastily summoned by a frantic Emma pronounced her charge to be suffering from the dreaded, usually fatal, pneumonia.

14

Emily remembered very little of the ensuing days. She seemed to be neither asleep nor awake, but coughing, coughing, gasping for breath like a landed fish and unable to speak above a whisper to whoever was sitting with her – for she was never left alone, day or night. By the fire that burnt constantly sat one or another of the household : Mrs Cadogan, the old Welsh-woman Dame Francis, the maid Nancy, or Emma herself, who took her turn at nursing as competently as she had succoured the unhappy Neapolitans on the voyage to Sicily. She was almost run off her feet, for after weeks of legal wrangling she had almost got possession of the house whose purchase she had negotiated for Nelson, Merton Place in Surrey, and was constantly having to attend to matters of furnishing, staffing, and the preparation of the house itself.

'Thank God Sir William's away at Warwick,' she said to her mother. 'With him in a fuss and a fret about his books and his thises and thats I think I should have run mad, on top of everything else. And as to our dear Nelson, I never thought to see the day I should wish him delayed in coming home – but God forbid he should find us like this. Merton *must* be ready in time.'

'Unless it gets itself ready, I don't see much chance of that. One of us will have to be there to see that the privies work, at least, and there's a hole in the kitchen chimney that'll need mending before we can cook.'

'Well, *I* can't go, and there's an end,' Emma replied, frantically packing piece after piece of the dinner-set she had bought on Nelson's behalf and had had decorated with his arms. 'Drat it, there's the handle of the gravy-boat gone. How can I leave Emy, Mam, so ill?'

'I'm not that anxious to leave her myself, but I suppose I must if it comes to it. But Doctor Moseley says she must soon turn the corner – tomorrow, he thinks, or the day after.'

'God Almighty grant she does! Poor thing. Do you know, Mam, she said to me this morning, so faint that I had to put my ear to her mouth, "Don't let them cut my hair off." As though I would, her pretty hair. When she is well again I shall take her to Richmond and get Fawcett to coiffer it properly, the tips of the curls clipped at the back, and the front brushed forward as if the breezes ruffled it . . .'

The picture of her daughter thus beautified was enough to take her mind off the present troubles, and she continued her packing with a more cheerful face. Mrs Cadogan regarded her fondly; down one minute up the next was Emma, always doing something for somebody and without an atom of jealousy – though some mothers of thirty-eight would be jealous of a pretty young daughter. Look at her now, in an old bedgown with streaks of printer's ink on her face from the old papers with which she was packing the china, and yet more beautiful than any of your fine ladies that spend all morning painting their cheeks and sticking mouse-fur on their eyebrows. No wonder Nelson adored her and she him – dear, simple little man.

Mrs Cadogan sighed and went back to the sick-room.

That evening Emily appeared to take a turn for the worse; so much so that Emma, terrified, sent a servant for Doctor Moseley after eleven at night, and he, good man, turned sixty and worn out after a day of attendance at Chelsea Hospital, where two patients had died on his hands, got up and dressed and rode round to Piccadilly. Emily was delirious, muttering hoarsely words that could not be understood. She seemed to see nobody about her bed, and when medicine was put to her lips turned her head aside so that it spilt.

Emma sat by her bed, constantly bathing the dry burning forehead with eau-de-Cologne and sponging the cracked lips with water. She said very little, except to murmur endearments to the girl who could not hear her. In her heart she spoke to the God whose laws she had hardly thought of in the days when she was little more than a cheerful pagan who enjoyed singing hymns. 'Greville was my god then, You know, as Nelson is now; and because of Greville I sent my child away. It was very wrong, very wicked of me. I know that now – I've always known it, even when I pretended it was all for the best and tried to forget her. And, oh, God, if she dies now I shall know that You've done it to punish me. I pray You, on my knees I pray,' and she slipped from the chair to kneel by the bed with her wet face hidden in her hands. 'Spare her to me, and spare my Nelson, and I will be good for ever and ever more.'

Dr Moseley remarked with approval on Lady Hamilton's hitherto unsuspected piety. And God? In the old days at Naples, Lord Bristol, the Hamiltons' rakehelly friend who was most inaptly also Bishop of Derry, had remarked that God must have been in a glorious mood when He made Emma. He had certainly been extraordinarily kind to His beautiful creation throughout the years, and now perhaps He was inclined to listen to her. Within the next few minutes, while she still remained on her knees, Dr Moseley observed sweat breaking out on the patient's brow. Gently he raised Emma and put her in the chair he had been occupying, while he took her place and noted with relief symptoms that the crisis of the illness was over. Soon the sweating became general, until Emily's nightdress and bedclothes were soaked.

'Fresh linen, Nancy,' he ordered, and they lifted Emily and re-clothed her and the bed. Soon afterwards her restless tossing ceased altogether and she slipped into a normal sleep.

'Thank God, thank God!' cried Emma.

With the early morning post came two letters from Nelson. One was a string of eager instructions about Merton, ending:

. . . and I hope, Emma, you take care of your relative; when you can get her well married and settled we will try and give her something.

He had previously had a screed about the forthcoming arrival of Emily, with a strictly edited version of her origins which, good simple soul, he implicitly believed.

The second letter, sent by express, contained wonderful news: a peace treaty was to be signed between England and France. At last Nelson would be free to come home.

Resisting her mother's entreaties to take some rest, Emma flew about making lists and giving orders. Rest? What should she want with rest? Now that her mind was relieved about Emy she was off to Merton, only an hour's journey; and by late morning she was bargaining with a Surrey farmer over the price of sheep and ducks.

She had just returned, and was taking tea, when Sir William's coach was heard coming up the drive. She flew to meet him, covering his face with kisses and chattering welcome and news almost in one breath.

'Easy, easy, Emma! Let me have things one at a time.' He handed his cloak to old black James, the Negro butler. 'By Heaven, I've been talked to death enough at the Castle. Warwick's an amiable fellow, but the greatest bore alive – he don't give an echo fair play. 'Twas all I could do to get one or two good stories of my own in. All this, that and t'other about himself, how clever he was and how rich, enough to have paid all his father's debts and his own – except one to me, as it chanced. Come, where's the fire? I'm chilled to the bone.'

Over tea he heard how successful Emma had been with her farming negotiations, how it was going to be economical to keep pigs as well as fowls, and how that damned old bitch Mother Greaves had even taken the fish out of the stream when she left the place – 'just as I was going to surprise you with well-stocked waters. And Cribb the gardener's had to take on extra men to sweep up the leaves which are all over the garden, those Greaveses never having touched 'em in years, by the look of it. And Mr Dods is mending the roof, so at least we shan't be drowned in our beds.

Very much as an apparent afterthought, she announced the arrival of her 'relative' from the North, and that relative's sudden and dangerous illness. 'Poor girl. But she'll do very well now, Dr Moseley says, and you know how Nelson relies on his opinion.'

Sir William detected a certain limpid look in his wife's eyes which usually meant that she had something up her sleeve. He had heard the merest hint of some relative of hers coming for a visit, but no more.

'I hope, Emma' – his Scots origins always manifested themselves when he was annoyed – 'that we are not going to be burdened with a troop of your numerous Northern relations? You know that I love your mother, but I am not sure that I wish to extend my affections to her entire clan.'

'No, no,' said Emma hastily, 'this is a poor girl whose friends have deserted her. And you know my Aunt Connor has many mouths to feed, even though Nelson has taken Charles into the Navy, and one can't expect her to take on more, so I thought—'

Sir William eyed her speculatively. Just so irresistible had she looked when Romney painted her as Sensibility, Innocence, Kate, and other nymphs ignorant of the darker aspects of life. 'Would this,' he said carefully, 'be the same girl ye mentioned to me soon after our marriage? Greville's pensioner and mine, that ye wanted to take to Naples?'

'Why, yes! What a memory you have, dear Sir Will'um. The very same.'

Her husband made the Scottish sound sometimes written as *mphm*, and turned the conversation to the over-poached state of the Warwickshire Avon.

He visited Emily next day, when she was reported to be convalescent enough to receive. Chaperoned by Nancy – for Emma and Mrs Cadogan were both at Merton – Emily sat up in bed wearing Emma's prettiest peignoir of palest blue, in which she looked smaller than ever, her face pointed and pale, a lost kitten. She smiled tentatively and he bowed.

'Miss Hart.'

'Sir William. It is kind of you to visit me. Please sit down.'

She would have much preferred him not to sit down, for she

171

was very much frightened by his aristocratic mien, the fine features, the keen eyes which surveyed her critically from below bushy greying eyebrows. She had never even spoken to a titled person before Emma, who was after all only a Lady by marriage; and here was a Knight of the Garter, foster-brother to the King, cousin to the great Duke of Hamilton, scrutinising her as though she were a housemaid indisposed in suspicious circumstances.

Sir William, whose connoisseurship had trained him above all to observe, missed nothing of the resemblances between Emma and her 'relative'. The girl might indeed be one of Emma's apparently inexhaustible family tribe, but he guessed at a closer tie, especially in view of Emma's devious and prevaricatory story about her. Not Greville's child, certainly; there was a Warwick look of which she had not a trace. Harry Fetherstonhaugh's? Possibly. There was the foxy hair. At least she spoke like a lady, which was something if he was to be saddled with her as a member of the Merton household. He drew up a chair and began a guardedly pleasant conversation.

So smooth was his manner that Emily's nervousness ebbed away. He asked kindly about her health, about the present state of Manchester, about her education, and seemed delighted that she had been taught Latin. His delight grew when she mentioned hesitantly that she was to be married.

'Indeed? My felicitations. I was not told this. And to an Alderman of Manchester. I trust that with such a fair lady he will rise to Mayor.'

Hearing the growing weakness of Emily's voice, he cut the conversation short, having learned what he wanted.

'But I am tiring you. Pray take care, and I will send up a tonic that I assure you will cure anything short of death.'

The tonic, when it came, proved to be something in a bottle reclining on a bed of ice, borne by James the butler in stately procession with Nancy and a supper-tray laden with chicken breasts in aspic and a dish of hothouse strawberries. James placed his offering on a table and deftly drew the cork with an explosion which sent Emily's hands to her ears.

'Oh, what *is* it? What a dreadful noise!'

Deep reproach, as at a wounding remark, was on James's coal-black face. Even his white hair seemed to turn a shade whiter, as though about to be brought with sorrow to the grave.

'De finest champagne, Miss Hart. With Sir William's compliments.' He poured a glass of the stuff, palest gold tinged with pink, and presented it to Emily on a salver. One gulp of it sent the tears to her eyes and brought on an attack of coughing, but as soon as she had recovered she drank off the glass, watched by James with an air of melancholy.

'How very delicious!' She giggled without knowing why. 'Pray thank Sir William and say I am sure it will quite cure me.'

It was fortunate that Emma arrived back in time to stop Emily from overdoing her cure – by means of drinking a good part of the bottle herself.

After she and her husband had supped, and he had heard the latest news of Merton and was able to get a word in, he said, 'You did not tell me Miss Hart was to be married.'

'Why, I knew nothing of it myself till Mam told me the other night, we were so busy nursing. And to tell the truth I'm a little vexed, for I'd hoped to make a good match for her, and now she must go back and marry this Lancashire cit. So much education to be wasted.'

Sir William observed that education was never wasted, and turned to perusing an archaeological volume. Inoffensive as the girl was, he was not after all to be landed with her as a dependant. Emma's next words did not, consequently, disturb him.

'We must take her to Merton as soon as can be. Country air will be just the thing for her.'

Sir William put on his spectacles and studied most carefully a drawing of a burial urn from Herculaneum. 'If I might suggest it, Emma,' he said, 'would it not be a wise thing to address Miss Hart by some other name while she remains in his lordship's house? The name Hart, d'ye not see – it might carry an implication . . .' His gaze was still focused on the urn, and nothing in his mild tones conveyed the message Emma received

173

clearly: 'I have already allowed myself to be called an old cuckold for the sake of one of your bastards, and I prefer not to drag the name of Hamilton down any further.'

Emma clapped her hands. 'But óf course you're right, as ever! The world has such a wicked mind. Shall we call her Hartly? That will be like her own name without sounding like my old one. Oh, how clever!'

She dropped a kiss on the top of his bent head. It was the only kind of caress which passed between them nowadays.

My dear Mr Shelmerdine: I am afraid you will think me very remiss for not having written earlier to advise you of my address. But I have been ill ever since my arrival in London with an inflammation of the lungs, and am only now re-covering...

Emily put down her pen. The sun was in her eyes, quite strong sun for mid-October. She was sitting in a garden-chair on a little terrace at the front of Merton Place, wrapped up to the ears in shawls and blankets. The lawns before her were cleared of the offending leaves, but gardeners still scurried about with wheelbarrows, and the sweet smell of a bonfire came from one corner. Relays of removal men were carrying furniture up from the lodge gates; through the open door Emily could hear the two Italian servants, Julia the maid and Mariana the cook, arguing shrilly, while from the grounds which were to be Lord Nelson's 'farm' came the quack and cluck of poultry and the clamour of young pigs, accompanied by steady hammering.

On the little bridge that spanned the stream, a branch of the river Wandle, stood Sir William, leaning gracefully on its balustrade and watching with amusement the broad back view of his wife driving a post into the ground with a force which would have done credit to her blacksmith father. She wore one of the gardener's baize aprons, her skirt was kilted up to her knees like a fisherwoman's, her sleeves rolled up to her elbows. Mrs Cadogan, similarly attired, was holding the pigsty door in position. A handsome cockerel, his feathers iridescent in the sun, strolled past them at the head of a train of admiring hens. Sir William noted all these things to retail to Nelson in a letter, that the poor man might at least smile once or twice while he languished fretfully in the Downs.

Emily tried to resume her letter.

Sir William and Lady Hamilton are kindness itself to me. Lord Nelson is expected daily; I am all anxiety to see him, as you may guess.

I trust that you and Cicely are in good health; you are often in my thoughts . . .

She stopped again and sighed. It was not true. Dear, kind Edward and Cicely, she could scarcely even visualise their faces. It was as though, like the girl in the French tale of 'La Belle au Bois Dormant', she had slept for a hundred years since last she had seen them. This new world was so strange, so beautiful, and so comical, and she had become so fond of this 'family' of hers that it was a pain even to think of leaving it and returning to Manchester, where Mrs Blackburn might be lurking round a corner when one went marketing, where Thetis's grave grew ever greener with moss and ivy. Sweet Merton! So far she had only glimpsed on the journey the little agricultural village set in meadows, the woods of Domesday beyond them, the dimpling Wandle running clear past the walls of the old Abbey where the calico mills now were.

It was all quite unlike a Northern village, though it had the same features, an old church, inns and a pump, a tollgate near which the villagers were now busily putting up a triumphal archway to welcome the Hero of the Nile. How curious, reflected Emily, to feel so much at home in this South country about which she had heard so many disparaging remarks. Southern housewives, for instance, had been rated by Bessy as mere sluts. But Lady Hamilton, a housewife on a rather grand scale, was far from being a slut; while Mrs Cadogan's ordering of household affairs was impeccable.

Emily lay back, lazily watching through her lashes as Sir William began to throw pieces of bread to the ducks on the stream. Emma appeared, her hammer in her apron pocket, conferred with him, and dashed down to the lodge where she saw the carter's horses standing patiently in the shafts of the great covered van.

'They have no water!' she shrieked. 'Water for them, John!' And young John the footman was off to fill a couple of buckets. People passed into and out of the house. One was Gaetano, Sir William's valet, a Neapolitan of elegant, even effeminate appearance, but all too masculine in other ways according to Nancy. 'Black and blue with pinches, I was, miss, before he found out he got a slapped face every time. You want to watch out for him, if you'll pardon me.' Gaetano was carrying a pile of sheets which had been unceremoniously bundled into his arms by Dame Francis, and looked very put out at it. The Dame herself, singing shrilly in Welsh, was cleaning the french window nearest to Emily. It was like a sort of pantomime, wanting only the Clown, the Dog and the string of sausages. Sir William, with all respect, might stand for Pantaloon, Lady Hamilton for a statuesque Columbine. But Harlequin, where was he?

Emily fell asleep; the letter to Edward blew away and lodged in a thicket.

She slept heavily at night since her illness, and sometimes long into the morning. At dawn on the morning of 23 October she heard nothing of the commotion outside the house : the sound of the arrival of a chaise-and-four drowned by the cheers of most of those eight hundred people who made up the population of Merton parish. A combination of musical instruments played alternately 'See The Conqu'ring Hero' and 'Rule Britannia', dogs barked, and prematurely awakened birds added their chirps to the general rejoicing; for Nelson had come home.

176

Emily was still fast asleep when Nancy appeared with a tray of hot chocolate and rolls, and a face rosy with excitement.

'Miss! Miss! Oh, do wake up, his lordship's here! At last, just fancy, and such carryings-on you never did see, every other minute someone coming to the door with a greeting-letter for him, and milady half out of her mind with joy. Oh, hurry and get up!'

After that Emily could not get through her breakfast fast enough, and into her best morning-gown with the dark blue stripes, to which she added a white net fichu and threaded a red ribbon through her hair. And if that's not a fitting costume I don't know what is, she thought.

The hall seemed to be full of people rushing about and bumping into each other, to the imminent danger of the marble bust of Nelson which stood on a flimsy table. Gaetano saw her and said, 'Miledi look for you, Miss Hartly – I tell her.' He vanished into the drawing-room. A moment later Emma appeared at the door, in the white négligé of lace and swansdown she had worn when Emily had first seen her in Piccadilly. Her face was transfigured, beautiful beyond belief. Seizing Emily's hand she pulled her into the room.

'Emy, Emy, child, come and greet my lord!'

Lord Nelson was reclining on the sofa, propped up with cushions. Emily's first sight of him was one of disappointment – almost. She saw a little, thin man who appeared not much taller than herself, his face grey with fatigue and marked with deep lines. The blind eye was filmy grey; when he stirred one saw the empty right sleeve, pinned across the chest of his black civilian coat. Sir William was bending over him, talking, Mrs Cadogan mixing hot punch by the fire, wearing her best cap with the pink ribbons and beaming with pleasure.

'See, Nelson,' cried Emma, 'here is my little relative, Miss Hartly, who has been longing for your arrival,' and she drew Emily towards the couch.

Nelson smiled. As he did so it was as though the sun had come out on the darkest and coldest of days, an out-raying of all the charm, fascination and tenderness that caused him to be loved by his men as no leader had been loved before, from his Band of Brothers, Hardy, Collingwood and the rest, to the roughest ex-criminal pressed into naval service, drawing people to him as the wild creatures came to Orpheus's music.

'Forgive me that I do not rise, Miss Hartly,' he said. 'I am somewhat overdone with travelling, and Lady Hamilton insists on my remaining prone.'

Emily ran forward and, kneeling, kissed the brown, wrinkled hand. 'My lord!' she said.

15

Nov.ʳ 10, 1801

My dear Emily; I was most pleased to get your letter if, sad for the reason for its delay. By now I trust you are completely recovered and in full health and beauty. Both Cicely and I rejoice that we are not wholly forgotten in the pleasures of the Metropolis and of Surrey.

Affairs in Manchester go on much as usual; I doubt not you will find little change when you return. I have some works in hand upon the house that I hope will make it more comfortable for you. Shall you be with us for Christmas? we earnestly hope so, I in particular, as you may guess.

I am eager to hear of the arrival of the great Admiral, pray don't be slow in letting us know of him. All here are glad of the Peace, tho' it is feared in quarters it may not be of great permanence . . .

Emily tried to concentrate upon her letter from Edward, but there seemed to be almost as much noise now as there had been when the household first moved into Merton Place. Workmen were everywhere, building on new rooms, improving the kitchen, installing privies so sophisticated as to be the wonder of the neighbourhood. Dark old panelling was ripped out or painted over, and mirrors inset so that the garden was reflected back into the house and lady guests might admire themselves under the brightest conditions. The house was pervaded by the peculiar odour of workmen, a blend of paint, plaster, sweat and plug tobacco, and continually pierced by a howling draught from the ever-open front door. Nelson usually remained sheltered from this in his new library, which Emma had made into the equivalent of a humbler man's 'den', comfortable and quiet, where he might sleep if the inclination to read or write or compose speeches (for he was to make his maiden speech in the House of Lords) did not rule him. Very often it did not. He was still recovering from the long neurosis of his vigil in the Downs, from perpetual colds and semi-imaginary illnesses; at times he seemed fragile enough to break at a touch.

But he was happy. Emily had not known such happiness existed. When he and Emma exchanged glances a flame from Love's own torch flared between them, as Emily poetically phrased it to herself. She had not been prepared for anything of the kind. There had been whispers in Manchester, George Shelmerdine's flippant remarks, an ocassional aside overheard from some tradesman or bystander in the street – that was all. The servants at Merton preserved utter silence about the relations between milady and his lordship, and seemed equally devoted to both. Mrs Cadogan was as likely to reveal her daughter's secret as to recite the tragedies of Racine in the original, and Sir William was quite clearly greatly fond of Lord Nelson and happy that they were all together.

Emily wondered and wondered. She remembered Mr Blackburn and the inn-girl in the stable, and blushed. Surely such things did not happen among these noble people, the Saviour of Europe and the beautiful lady who was his Muse of Fire, his Bellona, his Santa Emma. 'Lady Hamilton is an angel,' he said once to Emily; and she knew that to him it was so. What else should an angel be but heavenly beautiful, kind, desirous of making all about her happy, and superbly clever in transforming her surroundings into the nearest thing to perfection? And Nelson, so gentle and sweet-natured, yet with something of a godlike air about him: how could he ever be imagined to commit ordinary sins? Yet he had, she knew, a wife, who surely could not be pleased with the situation. Once, reading in a window-seat, Emily heard a snatch of conversation as Emma and Nelson entered the room. Emma was saying, 'My God, what else does that Ethiop bitch hope to get out of you? Two thousand and your name are not enough, I suppose? She and her filthy misbegotten spawn—' And then there was a whispered word from Nelson, and a pause before he said, 'Why, here is Miss

Hartly quite solitary. Why should we not all go and visit the farm this fine afternoon? The air will do us good.'

It was very puzzling. So was the arrival, early in November, of a chaise containing a respectable, soberly-clad matron, bearing with her a baby girl of perhaps a year old or less. Summoned by the black maid, Fatima, an amiable but feeble-minded creature, to see 'de bébé', Emily was astonished to see Emma seated with a lapful of girl child, round-eyed, plump and stolid. It was playing thoughtfully with a rattle of coral and silver as Emma jigged it up and down on her knee. Nelson stood behind her chair, looking down on them both with an expression such as Emily had never seen on any face; so might God have looked upon the world when He had created it and found it good.

Emma looked up brightly. 'What do you think of my god-daughter, Emy? Is she not a fine child?'

'Very fine, ma'am.' Emily had not really the remotest idea of what constituted a fine child, but the little creature looked healthy and content, and was very well dressed.

'Come, Miss Horatia,' said Emma, 'greet your relative nicely.' She took one chubby hand and waved it up and down in Emily's direction, and Emily wished, not for the first time, that people would stop calling her a relative and tell her exactly what relative she was to anybody. Something about the visit of the baby and its nurse (who both reappeared at intervals) drove her to Mrs Cadogan, as that lady sat placidly sewing in her parlour.

Emily flung herself in an unladylike manner on the rug at her grandmother's feet.

'Dear Grandmamma, won't you put my mind at rest? How did I come to be in the world?'

'Why, the usual way, my dear, I suppose.'

'No, no, don't tease! That infant upstairs – am I any relation to her?'

'Caution and care baffle many a snare,' quoted Mrs Cadogan, biting off a thread.

'You are a naughty little lady!' Emily gave the small hand a light smack. 'I am very exercised about this. It keeps me from sleeping. Is Miss Horatia really milady's godchild?'

'We are all the children of God,' was the calm reply.

'So you won't tell.' Emily stared into the fire, hugging her knees. 'But at least you have told me something. If she were, you would have said so, and therefore I must think otherwise. I saw my lord kiss her before the nurse got back into the chaise. Please, Grandmamma, I do beg you, tell me. Is she – my sister? You know I must go away soon. Will you let me go unknowing?'

Mrs Cadogan put down the skirt she was making and looked down at Emily with a graver face than the girl had ever seen her wear. 'My dear Emy, take my advice. I was wrong to have brought you here, though I thought it right at the time. Go back, marry your good Alderman, think of us always with kindness. But for God's sake, go!'

Emily knew, as though an oracle had spoken, that this was advice she should take. But Emma would not hear of it. 'What, with Nelson's father coming to visit, and Christmas almost on us? Besides, you're not fit to travel, child. Your bridegroom must spare you to us a little longer.'

'I am useless here. I do nothing but laze.'

'Then go into the kitchen and learn from that fat slut Mariana how to cook à la pizzaiola. Or practise the pianoforte, or anything but bother me with silly suggestions.'

Emily obeyed. It was easier to unravel the most difficult sonata of Mozart than to fathom the mysteries of Merton.

The Reverend Edmund Nelson proved to be a gentle, saintly-featured old man, snow-white of hair and seeming frail enough for a puff of November wind to blow him away. He had a look of his son, the look which could only be defined as 'goodness', combined with the long, slightly pendulous Nelson nose and the stoop of the scholar. Emily noted that in his presence evenings in the drawing-room seemed curiously inhibited. Emma was on her best behaviour, gracious and simple, the country squire's lady to perfection, chatting of crops and pickle-preserving and the importance of keeping warm in such a climate (she had presented the old man with a luxuriously thick woollen plaid, which he politely wore round his shoulders on all possible occasions). His son, on the other hand, was less than easy in manner, silent and abstracted, and making frequent excuses to retire to his library to write letters, leaving the old man to be entertained by Emma and the covertly yawning Sir William. Early bedtimes were unavoidable, even welcome. Every day questions were asked and answered about the Nelson family, about whom Emma seemed well primed.

'And the good Mrs Matcham? She is not breeding again, I hope? Enough is surely enough. You know that Mrs Bolton's twins are to be with us any day now, and my lord's little niece Charlotte, dear sweet creature that she is? How we hope you will stay to see them; young life about one is so cheering, is it not?'

Yes, the old man would nod, yes indeed, whatever you say, ma'am. His jowls sagged on his clerical bands, his head bowed under some weight unseen. Some three days after his arrival, when the sun came out, he meekly asked Emily if she would escort him round the gardens.

'I am a country parson, my dear, as you know, and the air of Surrey is very sweet to me. But I would be glad to have a young arm to lean upon, if you would lend me yours.'

'Gladly, sir.'

She tucked the plaid around him and tied her own scarf over his cap. Together they strolled slowly by the side of the stream, now christened by Emma the Little Nile, watching the ducks drift sedately between the reeds, making, now and then, dives to the bottom in search of food.

'A good church,' said Mr Nelson. 'I hear you have a very good church. Saint Mary the Virgin, if I remember.'

'Yes, sir. The incumbent is Mr Lancaster, who often visits my lord.'

'He takes the Sacrament?'

'Who, sir?'

183

'My son. His lordship.'

'Oh, indeed, sir. He is most devout. And so is milady.'

Perhaps the last statement was not strictly accurate, but Emily sensed a certain discomfort between the old man and his hostess, and hoped that she might help to lessen it. Mr Nelson did not comment; he was surveying the gardens.

'My good son has found himself a pleasant habitation. In the spring we shall be entertained, I have no doubt, with the rose and the hyacinth, and many a daffodil.'

'I expect so, sir.'

'You love gardens, no doubt, young lady?'

'Alas, sir, I was brought up in a town – I know very little about them.'

She was aware that he was hardly listening to her, but looking before him in mournful thought, his lips moving soundlessly. They had strolled some time in silence before he said suddenly, as though it had been wrung from him : 'My part in this is a very painful one.'

'In what, sir?'

'My gratitude to Lady Nelson is very great. She has been to me even as my own daughters, ever kind and considerate of my infirmities. Can I now leave her to live alone?'

Emily was taken aback; it was the first time she had heard Lady Nelson's name spoken at Merton Place. She decided to hedge.

'No doubt she would be very happy to have your company, sir.'

'Yet then I shall be reproached for disloyalty to my son.'

'Oh, surely not!'

He turned sad eyes on her, and she felt his arm tremble on hers.

'Yes, I fear so. I have had, you know, an anonymous letter, accusing me of bad conduct to Horace. It hurt my feelings very deeply.'

'Who could have sent such a cruel thing, sir? I am sure you could never deserve such a reproach.'

184

'No. No. No. I have but done my duty to one who merits it, and who stands in great need of comfort. Yet Lady Nelson, too, will reproach me for visiting my son. Would God that the breach could be healed! But I cannot see how.'

'Could you not speak to Sir William, sir? He is very wise and sees – matters – as an onlooker, I think.' She felt this must sound very impertinent, but Mr Nelson only shook his head sadly.

'Sir William is a good man; he has made me most welcome. Yet I think he can do nothing here. We are in the Almighty's hands . . .'

He peered down at Emily as though he had only just seen her. 'You are one of the family, I believe, young lady? Yes, yes, I see the resemblance. You have quite a look of my dear daughter Matcham.'

Emily thought this was a happy coincidence, considering that she was no relation to Mrs Matcham, but forbore to trouble his mind further by explanations. 'Mrs Matcham and her family will be visiting Merton soon, I dare say,' she said diplomatically.

'They have not yet been invited, I think. But my daughter Bolton's girls are to come.'

'Yes, very soon, tomorrow, I think – the twins, Jemima-Susanna and Catherine. And Miss Charlotte Nelson, too. That should cheer you up, sir.'

He smiled for the first time during their walk. 'Yes. I dearly love our young people. You will all have good sport together.'

Charlotte Nelson, daughter of Lord Nelson's clergyman brother, had visited Merton before, just after Nelson's arrival home, and Emily was pleased to see her again. She was a pretty schoolgirl of fourteen, dark-eyed and rose-cheeked, lively without boisterousness and a favourite with everyone. Emma seemed genuinely fond of her, and enjoyed playing the aunt she would have liked to be in fact. The Bolton twins, sturdy and talkative, had the same touch of Norfolk in their voices as Nelson had. Emily found them agreeable but tiring, and was glad of the days when Emma swept them up to town, with Charlotte, to introduce them to the pleasures of London.

Sir William spent much time in London, but for him its pleasures were the Royal Academy, the British Museum, the Society of Arts, and the conversation at his club, the Thatched House Tavern. Though he smiled amiably on the young people, and indeed on all Emma's guests, Emily sensed that he was extremely glad to be out of their company and in that of his learned friends. She felt for him; it was so peaceful at Merton when Emma and the others were up at Piccadilly. She had excused herself from the expeditions on the ground that she was still too weak from her illness for London excitements – and indeed she was still troubled by a genuine cough which she slightly exaggerated.

Peace, peace. Outside the drawing-room the gardens were under snow. A log fire burned in the grate while Emily played for hours at a time on the fine-toned Broadwood. She knew that the servants sometimes listened in the hall, and was glad to give them pleasure.

But suddenly it was Christmas, and solitude was at an end. The Boltons were gone, but the William Nelsons had come: Nelson's clergyman brother from Norfolk, his wife Sarah, and Horace their son, who was Charlotte's brother.

Emily disliked the Reverend William on sight. He was a large, thickset man without the least resemblance to his brother. His speech was thick Norfolk and his voice loud and coarse. He treated Emma with the utmost familiarity, giving her smacking kisses and cracking risqué jokes with her as he did with the maids; Emily thought he brought out her worst side. He flattered Nelson outrageously, and made no secret of the fact that he expected at least a bishopric through his brother's influence. Don't he wish he may get it! thought Emily uncharitably. On their first meeting he had leered appreciatively at her, and given her a kiss on the lips which she wiped off as soon as his back was turned. But she sensed that he always watched her, slyly summing up her place in the household and her likelihood as a rival to his daughter Charlotte, Emma's favourite 'niece'.

His wife Sarah was utterly in contrast to him. A brisk little bird of a woman, she was barely taller than Emily, with the dark hair and almost black eyes she had passed on to her daughter. She seemed a simple, amiable creature, devoted to Emma, and her close confidante. At night they would go off to Emma's bedroom to brush each other's hair and chatter about the events of the day – and, for all anybody knew, about what Emma considered her 'secrets'. Did she know, Emily wondered, the truth about her own parentage and that of the baby Horatia who was brought so often to Merton?

There was no time to wonder about such things this Christmas. Life was one long round of festivities, visits to the Half-hides, the Newtons, the Parrys, and the immensely rich Goldsmids at Morden Hall, where the food was exotic and the company loud and cheerful. Emma and the four Goldsmid sisters, Polly, Sarah, Goley and Esther, performed on the harp and the piano and sang duets and trios, while Nelson fondly watched his brilliant lady and applauded all she sang and played. Then at night some of the neighbours would be at Merton Place for dinner, with the best china and silver out and more music afterwards. Emily had her first experience of being drunk, on the rich claret with which the attendant footman, John, kept filling her glass. She felt very ill next day, with a head that seemed to have been split in half with a chopper, and a dreadful thirst. It made her feel guilty and abandoned, and she resolved to return to Manchester when Christmas and its excitements were over.

There had been a Christmas present from Edward Shelmerdine: a cotton shawl woven in bright colours, warm and light to wear. No letter accompanied it, only an affectionate greeting, and, below: 'When do you return?' She had not known what to send him – for I know him so little, she thought ruefully – and compromised with a handsome pair of steel buckles which could offend nobody.

Now it was time to keep her promise and go back. It would be a relief to get back to the staid comfort of Deansgate after the noisy jollities of Merton Place. She went downstairs very carefully, for her head jumped at every step, and joined the early risers in the dining-room. Charlotte and Horace had helped themselves lavishly from the silver-covered dishes on the metal hot-plate, which had a small stove burning beneath it. Horace was finishing his third egg while Charlotte spooned sugar over her porridge. The grown-up members of the household were not to be seen, Emily noted with relief. She poured herself some coffee with a shaking hand.

'I say, Emily, an't you quite the thing this morning?' enquired Horace. 'You look very queer, don't she, Charley?'

'Mmm,' responded his sister through a mouthful of hot porridge.

'I *feel* queer,' Emily said, dropping into a chair and resting her head on her hands. 'I took too much wine last night. Never again, never again.'

'Oh, you're foxed, are you? So is Papa, often. He says the only thing is a tot of brandy, first thing.'

Emily shuddered. 'Don't, Horace, or I really shall be ill.'

'No, it's true, 'pon rep! I've often seen him perk up remarkably. Stay there. I'll get it for you.' And the helpful youth seized a crystal decanter from the sideboard and poured a good half-cupful. 'Hold your nose while you drink it, then you won't catch the fumes,' he advised. Emily did so, shutting her eyes as well, and to her surprise the draught began to work almost as soon as she had swallowed it. She looked with respect at Horace, who was now raising each dish-lid in turn, pondering on his next choice.

Mrs Cadogan appeared at the door, slippered and shawled.

'Run down to the lodge, Horace, there's a good boy,' she said. 'I saw the mail stop there and her ladyship's expecting a letter.'

Horace banged down the lid on a meat-dish. 'Cut off directly, ma'am,' he said, stooping from his substantial height to kiss her as he dashed out. In a very short time he was back, waving the

188

post. 'Here's one for his lordship, and two for Lady Hamilton, and one for you, Emy. *That* ought to cheer you up.'

'*Horace!*' Mrs Cadogan had seen the black-edged letter, which was already in Emily's hand. Charlotte, too, was looking at it with awe. Emily turned it round and round, the fateful piece of paper bearing a Manchester postmark. Before she broke the seal she knew what it would say.

Decr. 26th 1801.

My dear Emily, how can I bring myself to write to you what I must write? I know it will break your Heart as mine is already broke. Yesterday, at about noon, as we were returning from the Christmas service, my dear, dear Father expired of an apoplexy, falling at my feet without warning.

I can only rejoice that he had no suffering, indeed he had been very happy just before, talking of your gifts and saying that next Christmas you would be with us. I have sent to George ...

Emily laid Cicely's letter down beside the brandy-glass. She felt nothing for the moment but shock, mingled with a sense that she had somehow known that she would never marry Edward.

'Is it very bad news, my dear?' Mrs Cadogan was by her side, ready for anything, used as she was to Emma's reactions to bad news.

Emily looked up and said, 'Very bad, ma'am. I think I will go and be by myself for a while.'

The awestruck young people watching her, she went from the room. Not to her own room, where she had lain awake for two hours before breakfast, feeling ill and ashamed of herself, but to the little conservatory Emma had had built, with its panes of pink and blue stained glass reflecting in them colours of the hothouse flowers they sheltered. There were wrought-iron chairs; Emily sat in one, wondering why she was not in transports of tears. Perhaps because the fumes of last night's wine were still dulling her brain; perhaps because she could now admit to herself that poor Edward had become as shadowy to her as the rest of her life in Manchester. 'Perhaps I am mad,' she thought. 'Perhaps I have forgotten him, as I forgot my childhood, because my brain is disordered. Or else I am some kind of monster with no heart. Yes, that must be it, for I am more aware at this moment of my own discomfort than of Edward's death or poor little Cicely's sorrow. Base, unfeeling creature that I am, after all Edward did for me.'

Emma paid her coach-fare to Manchester to attend the funeral, and produced a number of dresses of her own which could be dyed black and altered to fit her. 'Not,' she said, 'that I hold with ladies attending funerals, indeed it's not at all *comme il faut*, but I realise that you must go to support your poor friend.' Tears of sympathy stood in her lovely eyes, making Emily even more ashamed that she herself had shed so few.

In fact Emma was not a little relieved (though of course one must not profit by other people's tragedies) at the removal of Emily's somewhat unsuitable fiancé. Now she could keep the dear girl with her, and find someone really splendid for her. A title perhaps? Some nice young moneyed gentleman who wouldn't insist on an exact pedigree. 'After all, there were a few after me when I was in Greville's keeping,' she reminded herself, 'and I had no connections or anything. Nelson and I will put our heads together, and ten to one we'll find her just the right man. A sea officer? A Jew? All the Goldsmids' friends are rolling in money, and so handsome with those dark eyes . . .' In her mind she had Emily out of blacks and into a wedding-dress before one could say knife.

But Emily had other notions. When she arrived back from the funeral, having seen Cicely borne off by her brother and his wife, Emma had caught one of her heavy colds and had retired to bed with it. She was propped up on pillows, her hair, almost long again, loose about her shoulders. Her eyes watered with sneezing and her nose was red with the frequent application of handkerchieves; but she gave Emily her heavenly smile, and contrived to be still beautiful enough to paint.

'Thank God you're come, Emy. I'm sick of Nancy's face, and I daren't have my lord come near me for fear of catching the infection. What's that you've brought?'

'A dish of grapes from Mrs Halfhide, ma'am, with her love.'

'Oh, thank her for me, kind soul. But I can't eat all these – take some to Lord Nelson.' She pulled off a few and gave the rest of the bunch back to Emily. 'He needs sustaining, with so much business up at Westminster. Have you something to read to me?'

'*Castle Rackrent*, Miss Edgeworth's new novel.'

'That's nice. Is it Gothick or humorous?'

'A little of both, I think, my lady.'

'Good.' Emma lay back with the bedclothes pulled round her, while Emily began to read. She appeared to be asleep, but after half an hour or so opened her eyes and smiled.

'Highly entertaining, but your throat must be as raw as mine. Ring for tea, there's a dear girl.'

Emily obeyed, then seized the chance she had been waiting for.

'If I might speak to you about myself—'

'Of course, child. What is it?'

'Well – I feel – very useless, ma'am. I do nothing to earn my keep and take everything from you – food and clothing, everything. Without you I should have nothing but the poor things I wore when I came here. No, pray don't tell me I give you the pleasure of my society, for that's little enough. Is there nothing I can do?' She leaned forward earnestly. 'I told Mr Blackburn I would take any situation in which I could earn my living.'

Emma blew her nose musically. 'What a serious little thing you are. What do you expect me to suggest? That you help Mrs Cummins to do the washing, or Cribb to grow vegetables?'

'Yes, if needed. Anything. I can teach. I *did* teach in Manchester.'

'And who is there to teach here? Only Charlotte, and she is at school in Chelsea.'

'There are the neighbours' children . . .'

'And how do you think it would sound, Lady Hamilton's relative going into service as a governess?'

'Very well, to me. Better than saying Lady Hamilton's relative took everything from her and gave nothing, lived like a parasite. Oh, I beg your pardon, my lady – I didn't mean to sound rude, but I can no longer be idle.'

Emma raised her eyebrows. 'Don't tell me you are one of these New Women poor Mrs Godwin wrote of, for I can't bear 'em.'

'I don't think so, ma'am. I never heard of her. But it hurts my pride, living on your charity, when I am only – a distant relative.'

Their eyes met, Emily's pleading 'Tell me!', Emma's beautifully refusing. Suddenly Emma gave an explosive sneeze, and the moment was gone. When Emma had recovered from it she said : 'The Goldsmids. I'll see if one of them needs music lessons. Would that content you?'

'Anything, ma'am.'

In fact, Mrs Abraham Goldsmid was only too glad of the offer of a music-teacher for her daughter Rachel, and highly flattered to have any kin of Lady Hamilton's in her house. Emma had made it very clear that Miss Hartly's musical talents had not sufficient outlet, and that she felt it her duty to communicate them to the young. The money, of course, was no consideration at all.

And so every day Emily went down the road to Morden Hall, where she had been before as a Christmas guest, and was welcomed into that warm Jewish family with open arms. Fortunate little Rachel, to have a jolly Dutch mama and a papa who looked like a sane and cheerful George III, which image he cultivated, the English country squire to perfection, when not in the City engaged in financial transactions. Like the Goldsmids themselves, the house was large and bright-coloured. There was a lot of gilt everywhere. Emily felt like a very small Gulliver in that Brobdingnagian drawing-room, but Rachel was a willing, sweet-tempered pupil, and the money was generous. At last Emily was happy to travel up to Town with Emma, and shop in Bond Street for clothes for herself and presents for the people at Merton.

So began 1802, a year of peace for England and for Merton Place. In April, soon after Emma's birthday festivities and the damping news of old Dr Nelson's death in Bath, the Peace of Amiens was signed. 'Now at last I may enjoy Paradise Merton,' said Nelson; and from that day he seemed to grow better in health and to be free from the cloud of melancholy which had shadowed him for years. He loved to stroll by his Little Nile, hand in hand with the small Horatia, guiding her staggering steps; sometimes with Emma by his side, or Emily, or Charlotte. He and Sir William would go fishing, sitting solemnly on chairs by the bank of the Wandle, in almost silent companionship.

In the summer the Hamiltons and Nelson left for Sir William's estates in Pembrokeshire, after which they made a triumphal tour of Wales and the Midlands, accompanied by a flock of Nelsons and Matchams. Scarcely were they back, to a Merton Place where workmen had been busy all summer improving and enlarging, than it was winter: Christmas parties again, all Nelson's available relations in the guest-rooms, and dinners and dances. Emily wrote in the journal she had re-started: 'I am becoming quite a sophisticate.'

16

The world began to change at the end of March 1803. Sir William, who had been visibly growing older and frailer throughout the winter, was taken seriously ill. He insisted on being taken up to London. 'Let me die in my own house,' the weeping, protesting Emma was told. 'I would not be a burden to my dear friend.'

He died in April, at 23 Piccadilly, Emma and Nelson by his side. Emily was glad to be at Merton, away from the storms of emotion that must be breaking over the house of mourning. She sensed that with the rational, patient Sir William gone, the household would not be the same. Mrs Cadogan went up to see to various matters for Emma, and came back with a grave face.

'My lord is recalled,' she told Emily. 'There's to be war again, and he takes up the Mediterranean command any time now.'

'Poor Lady Hamilton! How does she take it?'

Mrs Cadogan shook her head. 'She wept for a week for Sir William. I doubt if she's any tears left. And to make matters worse, she's poorly left. Sir William's made that serpent Greville his heir, not her. All she's to have is the London furniture, an annuity, and three hundred miserable pounds. And Greville wants her out of the house in three weeks.'

Emily was shocked. 'But why? Surely she deserves better. What has she done?'

'Spent too much money, that's what, my dear. Give Emma a house to fit up and a purse with a tight string, and she'll be a model of economy. Give her the same and an open purse, like my lord's, and she'll bankrupt herself. Can you add up?'

'I think so.'

'Then help me tackle these bills. We might as well know the worst.'

Emily did not see Emma until the middle of May, when she

was sent for to attend a wedding. Young Kate Bolton was marrying her cousin, Captain Sir William Bolton, at the house in Clarges Street which Emma was renting. It was a cheerful family affair, helped by the still disordered state of the furniture and the general air of bustle Emma could not help generating round her, however saddened by recent events. She looked thinner, Emily thought, and more beautiful in the black which threw into relief her bright complexion and the soft auburn hair with a few threads of grey beginning to show in it. Emily asked after Nelson.

'He is gone. We said our farewells last night. By now he should be in his flagship *Victory* at Portsmouth.' Her mouth drooped. 'God knows when we shall meet again.'

When the first fever of settling into Clarges Street was over, Emma lacked occupation. She began an endless round of visits: to the Boltons in Norfolk; to the William Nelsons, now at Canterbury where William had procured a canon's stall; then off to Southend for the sea-bathing. Emily went with her to the seaside – for once without Charlotte or anybody else but Emma's coal-black maid Fatima, the quaint grinning creature who spoke only when spoken to. Emma seemed out of sorts and distrait, even snapping at people now and then. It was all very unlike her, Emily thought.

At last one bright morning came when it was warm enough to sit out on a balcony of their hotel, looking across the blue heat-hazed estuary to the Isle of Grain. Emily had brought out some embroidery, but Emma's hands were idle in her lap. It was the pose of Romney's wistful Miranda, even to the shady Leghorn hat. How strange to see a picture come to life, thought Emily, yet with such changes . . .

'Do you think there will be fish for luncheon?' Emma asked suddenly.

'Why, yes, my lady, there's always plenty of fresh fish here. Would you like me to speak to them about it?'

'Do, there's a dear girl. I used to despise fish, but somehow I can't seem to fancy meat at present.'

'That's the hot weather. There's such a stench about the butchers' shops, anybody would be put off.'

Emma shuddered. Emily, intent on shading a silk leaf, did not see the struggle that was going on within her companion, and was startled when Emma leaned forward and took her hand.

'No, it is not that,' she said. 'Emily, I must tell you. I can keep it secret no longer. I'm breeding again.'

Emily's embroidery-ring and its contents slipped from her lap. For a moment she felt her breathing stopped, and a hot blush sweeping up to flood her neck and cheeks. Emma saw it with pity.

'I'm ashamed to upset you so,' she said, 'but I have no one else to tell. Only my mother knows. It was our last night together, the night before Kitty's wedding. We were both desperate with grief, Nelson and I. That was why, I suppose . . . he never loved me so fiercely. He – I think he knew I had conceived. He'll be glad, happy to think of having another child by me – oh, I know *you* weren't deceived about Horatia. But Emily, what shall I do? Sir William's gone, dear blessed Sir William who would have protected me, and Nelson's hundreds of miles away. Where will my reputation be, with so many eyes watching, and I living alone?'

'Would it not be best,' said Emily, her blush fading, 'to let Clarges Street again and live very quietly at Merton, seeing nobody, until you are – recovered?'

Emma pouted. 'I think I should die of boredom. I must have company to keep me from melancholy. And then, it would look so strange if I dropped out of London society all at once.'

In other words, thought Emily, you won't give up parties, and pleasures, even to save your name and his lordship's. Well, we are as we are. Aloud she said, 'I'm sure all those who might safely visit you would do so.'

'Yes.' Emma sighed. 'Yes, I suppose so, and there are the works to see to, the new room and the kitchens. But afterwards? What shall I do with the child? To settle Horatia at Merton is difficult enough, for all Nelson goes on about it as if it were the easiest thing in the world. How then could I suddenly produce another child as an inmate?'

You could get rid of it as you did of me, thought Emily unkindly. Then, relenting: 'Why not wait and see, ma'am? Providence will surely looked after you. Perhaps you could seem to adopt it, as a companion for Horatia.'

Emma's face brightened. 'You clever, good girl! Of course there's a solution to everything. And if I'm clever with scarves and drapes nobody will notice beforehand. I crossed Europe with Horatia demanding to be born – surely I can manage as well now.'

But for all her brave words she became increasingly alarmed. As the year and her pregnancy grew she dashed from one place to another as if daring fate and the eyes that watched. At Canterbury Emily was pretty sure that Sarah Nelson knew; the hair-brushing talks were renewed, significant glances exchanged. O foolish Emma, to trust to more than one.

On a night in August she told Mrs Cadogan and Emily: 'I wrote to Nelson begging him to come home.'

The hearers gasped.

'Did I ever do such a thing before? Can he not think of me sometimes? No, it must be always the call of his country – duty, duty, duty! Has he no duty to me?'

'This is not like you, Emma,' said Mrs Cadogan. 'Did you happen to mention why you wanted him home?'

Emma hesitated. 'No . . . Not in so many words.'

'Then how should he know what you meant?' her mother asked placidly. 'A woman might read between the lines, a man never, especially with a cabinful of other correspondence to deal with, by the light of one eye.'

'Then I shall write again and say we will go out to him,' said Emma mutinously.

'We?'

'Yes. You and Emily and Charlotte and Horatia, and a few servants – Fatima and Nancy and Dame Francis and the Italians. We could join him at Malta or go out to his estates at Bronté, where the climate is delightful and Emily and I would suffer no more bad colds.'

'You must be mad,' said Mrs Cadogan.

In fact Nelson would have none of these suggestions, indeed paled when he read them; and received only at Christmas the news that his beloved had strong reasons for her requests. It was enough to send him into the depths of fear and worry; he was too distraught this time to care about the baby. They had, after all, Horatia, and his happy dreaming in his letters to Emma about 'our children' had had nothing to do with realities. Asked about the name of the coming child, he dashed off: 'Call him what you please – if a girl, Emma.'

Up to the last moment Merton was a hive of visitors, entertained by Emma with bright smiles and some very elaborate drapery. Emily wondered what she would have done in her predicament in a former age, say the Elizabethan, when women appeared to be bosomless and wore iron corsets down to the hips. 'But I suppose she'd have invented a new fashion.' When Emma grew too heavy to move about gracefully she caught a fortuitous chill and retired to bed, where she was only too glad to go after a round of social gaieties for which she was all too unfit.

'How ill my lady seems,' observed Charlotte to Emily. 'And how her girth has increased. I declare I'm quite concerned for her.'

'Oh, so are we all. I believe,' Emily said conspiratorially, 'it may be the dropsy. Dr Moseley has her case in hand, and as you know he is an excellent man. There are all sorts of cures nowadays, you know.'

'I suppose there are. But Mama seems so exercised about it. It is not like her to worry.'

On a bitter night in early February 1804, Emily woke suddenly. Footsteps were running up the corridor past her door, then up the attic stairs beyond where the servants slept. There was a sharp rapping on a door. It opened, and voices murmured indistinguishably. The footsteps descended, and hurried away out of hearing.

Emily sat up in bed and lit her bedside candle. The fire in the grate was almost burnt out; the room was full of menacing shadows. She pulled on a wrapper and went barefooted to the door. Outside there was nothing to see, only the dim light of the lantern which illuminated the corridor and staircase all night. On the attic floor a door opened and softly shut; someone was coming down. Emily shrank back, leaving her own door open only just enough to see that it was Nancy, in her nightcap and some flannel garment, trying to hurry without making a noise. Emily emerged, startling her, and asked, 'Is there anything I can do? Is someone ill?'

Nancy looked aghast. 'Lor, no, Miss! You go back to bed. I'll see to it.'

Emily obeyed. But sleep had left her. She poked up the fire into some semblance of brightness, wrapped her cold feet up in a shawl and got back into bed, where she struggled by the flickering candle-light through two or three dull numbers of *The Lady's Magazine*. From somewhere came noises, doors, whispers; once a long moaning cry that might have been an owl's. She fell into a half-doze full of alarming visions, mad thoughts, neither asleep nor awake. Something put Mother Demdike into her mind. What had she said when she read her palms? Only scraps of it came back. She got up and rooted at the bottom of her travelling-bag for the last volume of her old journal.

There it was. 'I see a loss, and a finding. I see a great house, and a green garden, and blue ribbons, one on the breast, one in the hair.'

Of course it was Merton Place – Nelson's blue Ribbon of the Garter, the blue ribbon Emma had worn in her curls until Sir William's death. 'I see sickness,' the prediction went on, 'and death close by thy shoulder; and death for another, among great waters . . .'

She shut the notebook hurriedly. Something made her reluctant to read any more. How close was death?

The cry came again. Emily snuffed the candle and got back into bed, huddling in her wrapper. She pulled the bedclothes over her and burrowed in the pillow. Warmth overcame her. She slept.

When she awoke the morning seemed unusually light for February. She looked at her watch. It was almost eleven, quite three hours later than her normal rising time. She washed, dressed and did her hair without taking in the curious fact that Fatima had not come to do her hair. How slothful to lie in bed till such an hour.

The house felt cold and empty, though that couldn't be, of course. A faint clinking came from the kitchen, as though dishes were being washed. Emily peeped into the drawing-room, where a fire had been only recently lit. Phillis Thorpe the parlour-maid, who was vigorously cleaning a window, bade Emily a cheerful good-morning. She proceeded to Mrs Cadogan's parlour, tapped and entered.

Her grandmother was sitting in the rocking-chair by the table, which bore traces of breakfast. She looked a very old woman.

'Oh, Grandmamma!' The forbidden form of address sprang to Emily's lips.

Mrs Cadogan turned her head wearily. 'Emy. Come in. Shut the door.'

'I heard noises in the night. Was it ... ?'

'Yes. It's all over. Oh, don't be alarmed. Emma will do very well now.'

'And – the baby? Not dead?'

'No. Better it were.'

'Why? What ...' Terrible images flashed across Emily's mind.

Mrs Cadogan rose stiffly. 'Come and see. Emma's fast asleep, but be quiet.'

Nothing of Emma was visible in the wide bed but her hair, dark with sweat, spread on the pillow. She was breathing heavily.

'I gave her a draught,' whispered Mrs Cadogan. 'Here is the child.'

In a corner, on a sofa, was a wooden box which at first sight looked very much like a coffin. At close quarters Emily recognised it as a drawer from the mahogany tallboy. Mrs Cadogan drew the covers away from the occupant. The baby looked impossibly tiny to Emily, like a swaddled doll; but in its temple, from which the angry flush of birth was beginning to recede, a blue vein throbbed. It lay partly on its side; Mrs Cadogan gently moved the little head sideways so that both cheeks were exposed. On the left cheek, covering it and extending to the eye and the chin, was a naevus, a purple 'port-wine' stain: a tangled mass of blood-vessels, hideously disfiguring the face.

Emily exclaimed in horror – to be quickly hushed. Mrs Cadogan replaced the covers and together they tiptoed out of the room.

In the corridor Emily turned to her, agitated. 'What is it? Why did it happen?'

Her grandmother shrugged. 'Nobody knows. Some old wives say it comes of port-wine in the blood, handed down from the father. Others tell you it's the Devil's Mark, a punishment for sin. My opinion is that this one's due to Emma's age. Thirty-nine, not the best of health, worried out of her mind – a babe often suffers from such things.'

'Is it a girl?'

Mrs Cadogan nodded. 'More's the pity. Women'll take a man whatever he looks like, but no maid with a face like that's going to catch a husband.'

They were back in the parlour. 'My dear, I'm dead for sleep and so is Nancy. Will you go and keep watch over them for an hour or two? There's no one else I can ask.'

'Oh, gladly, gladly! I'll do anything I can. Has – Lady Hamilton seen the poor little thing?'

'No. After the bad time she'd had I spared her that. Time enough when she wakes. As to what's to be done, we'll talk of that later. And remember, Emy, nobody in the house is to know anything of this, anything at all. Nancy's told the servants my lady's been took very ill in the night and mustn't be disturbed. There'll be some food brought on a tray, which you can take in,

201

and if Emma can sup any of it put the rest outside. Don't give the servant a chance to see in.'

For almost two hours Emily sat, hands twined together, praying that Emma would not wake while she kept watch. She was fortunate. At midday the promised tray arrived, and half an hour later Nancy, still heavy-eyed but able to take over.

It was late afternoon before Nancy came to Emily's room to summon her. For three hours Emily had walked, round every country lane in the district: down Pickle Path alongside the Wandle, over Terrier's Bridge, through Merton Rush with its weatherboarded cottages, past the remains of the Abbey and the printing works owned by their neighbours. The air was cold and fresh, the ground hard with frost. Towards dusk the sky took on vivid pinks and purple streaks, glowed and darkened until the footpaths could hardly be seen. There was a light in the church. Emily ventured in, to find Mr Lancaster's middle-aged bride arranging the communion table for the next morning.

Emily greeted her, but was grateful when she made her final curtsey to the altar and slipped away, leaving the candles still burning. Anybody from Merton Place could be trusted not to waste the church's money. Emily knelt and tried to pray, but her mind was too confused to form clear prayers. She seated herself in a pew and looked round the church, at the alabaster monument to Gregory Lovell, Queen Elizabeth's cofferer, and the memorial to great Captain Cook, killed by savages long before.

There was Sir William's wooden hatchment, displayed after his death both at Piccadilly and Merton Place, now given to the church as his only memorial, for his body lay far away in Wales, beside that of his first wife. On it was the Heart of Douglas, the ship with sails furled, the supporting twin-horned unicorns which brought back a sharp memory of the inn-yard where she had first seen those armorial bearings. She sat staring about her, wishing she could pray for the disfigured child and its mother, and all of them, but no form of words came. Outside, the sky was blue-black. She knelt briefly, and left, locking the church door, in which the new Mrs Lancaster had trustingly left the key.

On the way back to Merton Place ice was forming in the cart-tracks and over the cobbles, making her walk precarious. Black skeleton trees stood out against the last of the light, drifts of unmelted snow gleamed in the fields. It was a relief to see the light of the lodge-keeper's candles through the windows, and one or two isolated lights in the house itself.

When she had changed her shoes and dress she went to Emma's room and tapped. Mrs Cadogan's voice answered.

Emma was propped up on pillows; by the bedside her mother was knitting. The wooden box still lay on the sofa. Emma appeared supernaturally beautiful, her eyes enlarged by crying, not diminished by the great shadows round them. She held out her arms to Emily, who went into them, embracing her word-lessly. (Oh mother, mother! if I could but help you and my sister! her heart cried.)

Aloud she said, 'Is there anything I can get you, my lady?'

Emma shook her head. There was a dish of forced fruit on the commode by her bed, and a half-empty decanter of wine.

'Stay a little.'

Emily sat down. 'How are you now, my lady?'

'Empty.' Emma's smile was Tragedy itself. 'So much pain, for such an end.'

Something impelled Emily to ask, 'May I nurse the baby?'

Emma looked surprised, and Mrs Cadogan's head came up. 'I don't see why not, if you want to,' she said.

Emily picked up the small tightly-wrapped form from its pathetic improvised cot, and sat down with it in her arms. The baby's eyes opened, and it whimpered for a moment, before sleeping again.

'She's a quiet child,' said Emily, 'and her eyes are beautiful – as blue as yours, my lady.'

Emma surveyed her wonderingly. 'How good you are with children. I wish I were. I can't bring myself to touch her.'

'But she is my lord's,' Emily said gently.

Emma wailed. 'How cruelly disappointed he will be! He

longed so for a family, always talking of "our children". What would he say to this?'

'I expect he would love his child, whatever was wrong with it.'

'But how can I show it to him? How can I have it here, and let people see it? Having Horatia about is bad enough, God knows. Questions and hints all the time, and this story to remember, always calling her our godchild...'

'But that would have been the same, even had she been – perfect. Surely people will call you all the more charitable to befriend a child marked as she is. And then, do you not think my lord will be more inclined to pity and love her because of her disfigured face? He knows what it is to have one,' added Emily boldly.

'His glorious wounds!' Emma hid her face in her hands.

The baby began to cry thinly, turning its head to suck at a fold of the shawl that bound it.

'She's hungry,' said Mrs Cadogan. 'Give her the breast, Emma.'

A look of revulsion crossed Emma's face, but she held out her arms. Emily put the baby into them, and its cries ceased as it began to feed. The unmarked cheek was upwards; Emma looked down at it with the face of a compassionate angel. 'I haven't enough milk for her.'

'Not surprising, at your age,' said her mother. 'We must put her out to nurse as soon as may be. But where? Not in Merton, and my lord don't trust Mrs Gibson any more not to talk of our affairs.'

Emily looked from one to the other of them. It seemed incredible that they had not planned beforehand, with the inevitability of the child's birth. For the first time Mrs Cadogan looked wholly peasant, her native wit and her training obscured by grief. A sudden surge of anger swept over Emily. She took the child, now crying again, from Emma's breast, and rocked it in her arms. 'Damme,' she said to herself, echoing Nelson's favourite expression, 'if I will see my sister die for want of thought.' Aloud she said: 'I am going out, to Raynes's farm. The baby must have fresh milk.'

Mrs Cadogan was startled. 'Why, what will you say?'

'Never mind. I'll think of something.' Emily tucked the child up again in its drawer-crib, where it lay still crying. Emma began to shiver, turning her head from side to side on the pillow; her colour was unhealthily high.

'What is it, my lamb?' Her mother bent over her and sponged her brow. Lamb, thought Emily, yes, a lamb would do.

The Raynes family had a hay and cattle farm in West Barnes Lane, one of the biggest in the district; it had been a farm when there were monks at Merton Priory. Emily had chatted with young Mrs Raynes on one of her walks during the autumn, and had admired the neat farmhouse and unusually clean appearance of the farmyard. Even so, she was glad of her pattens to protect her feet as she cautiously crossed the slippery cobbles to the farmhouse door. Mooings came from the byre, and a sweet smell of hay.

Mrs Raynes herself answered the door, peering cautiously round the chain before loosing it. 'Who's that? Why, it's the young lady from Merton Place, isn't it? Pray come in, and excuse me keeping the chain up at first, but you never know these dark nights who might be prowling about.' She looked curiously at Emily, and her toddler, peering round her skirts, disappeared altogether when the stranger entered the kitchen.

'What can I do for you, miss? Not bad news of the war, I hope?'

'Oh, no, Mrs Raynes. Thank God, his lordship is well and hoping to be home in the summer or earlier. No, it is quite a small thing; one of our sheep dropped a lamb early and our shepherd found it almost dead. He said' – great heavens, what an accomplished liar I am, Emily thought – 'that you would know a way of making it feed.'

'Dearie me, yes, miss. How wise you was to come to me. Careless, silly things, they don't know how to take care of their own. I have the very thing here, ready for when one of our lambs falls out of season, though we've been lucky so far, touch wood.' She turned to a cupboard in the ingle-nook and brought out a curiously-shaped brownstone pot, something like a sausage with a teat-like end. 'Here, you see, here's what I feed the very young lambs with, warming it well first and scouring it out after. The cow's milk does 'em no harm, poor things, being better than none.'

Emily examined it. 'How very well designed! Why, it's almost small enough for a human baby to suck from.'

'That it is, miss, only you wouldn't use plain cow's milk for an infant.'

Emily looked innocent. 'No? What would you use?'

'Why, sugar of milk if you could get it – otherwise fresh cow's milk mixed with boiled water, half and half, the whole kept warm in a pipkin at night for when the child wants to feed. But it must be well scoured after, mind, lamb or child.'

'Might I borrow it, Mrs Raynes? The poor thing seems likely to die if it will not feed.'

'Why, a pleasure, indeed, only you won't mind if I send for it if need be.' She bustled about, wrapping the feeding-bottle in a clean cloth. 'Mind the hole don't get stopped up, and make sure the milk be fresh.'

'Oh yes. I really came for that. Could you spare us some? The milk in our kitchens has been there since yesterday morning.'

Mrs Raynes looked surprised; it must, she thought, be a valuable lamb. 'Take as much as you want, and welcome, miss.'

Emily left with a quart-beaker of milk under one arm and the feeding-bottle in her hand. She hurried back to Merton Place as though black ice were not forming beneath her feet, making the paths treacherous. Mrs Cadogan opened the door to her cautious tap, and pointed to the bed, where Emma lay moving restlessly, her eyes closed.

'Looks like childbed fever to me. I'll have to get Dr Moseley, whatever she may say. Better alive than dead, even with the chance of rumours getting round. But surely he'd never speak, when he stood at Sir William's deathbed and has been like one of the family to us.'

'No, no,' Emily said. 'My lady has made a particular favourite of Miss Moseley, and she is such a friend of Charlotte's. In any case, doctors are bound by their oath not to speak of whatever they know about their patients.'

'Aye, that's true. But 'twouldn't be safe to get Doctor Parrett – innocent that he is, the news would be all over the parish without him saying a word. I'll send John to town tonight.'

'Better wait till tomorrow. The roads are thick ice. He might finish up in a hedge.' She unwrapped the feeding-bottle with pride. 'See!'

'Mercy on us!' Mrs Cadogan put on her spectacles. 'A titty-bottle. I've not seen one of them since my sister Sarah's milk failed with her youngest. Wherever did you get it, Emy?'

Emily explained quickly. 'And now we need some boiled water.' Mrs Cadogan set about boiling the small copper spirit-kettle by the fire, while Emily examined the baby, who began to wail as soon as picked up. It looked puny, the unblemished side of its face a bad colour, like putty. A thought struck her.

'Ought she not to be baptised? In case—'

'Yes. That's a kind thought. My lord would have her called Emma.'

'Must it be Emma? Have we not had enough of Emmas and Emilys?'

'That's true. Change the name and change the luck, they say. But if my lord wants it, Emma it must be. Who's to christen her, though?'

'I am,' said Emily. 'It would never do to ask Mr Lancaster to come. If the intention is good there's no need for a priest. You must stand godmother. Can you remember the responses?'

Mrs Cadogan passed her hand over her face, as though a cobweb lay on it. All these confusions and alarms, and to think the young woman who was taking charge and ordering her about was that very little Emily of twenty years ago, and now here was another little Emma in an even sorer plight. 'I'll do the best I can,' she said.

Emily poured some water from the kettle into a small crystal bowl from Emma's dressing-stand and carried it over to the cot-side. Memories rushed in at her of christenings in the Reverend Blackburn's house of his numerous children, the form being slightly different because they were being baptised in a private house. Perhaps the extempore service would be out of order, but it would not matter, and if she could not remember it all that would not matter either to God.

Mrs Cadogan came and stood by her side. 'Shall we say the Lord's Prayer?' Emily suggested. Together they recited it. Then Emily said, alone, 'Almighty and everlasting God, heavenly Father, we give Thee humble thanks, that Thou has vouchsafed to call us to the knowledge of Thy grace, and faith in Thee. Give Thy Holy Spirit to this infant, that she, being born again, and being made an heir of everlasting salvation, through Our Lord Jesus Christ, may continue Thy servant, and attain Thy promise . . . Amen.'

She turned to the grandmother of them both. 'Dost thou, in the name of this child, renounce the Devil and all his works, the vain pomp and glory of this world, with all covetous desires of the same, and the carnal desires of the flesh, so that thou wilt not follow, nor be led by them?'

'I renounce them all,' said Mrs Cadogan firmly.

Emily dipped her finger in the water and signed the tiny brow with the Cross.

'Emma Charlotte Nelson, I baptise thee in the Name of the Father, and of the Son, and of the Holy Ghost. Amen.'

The child stopped crying; its limpid blue unseeing eyes looked up with what seemed like wonder.

'God bless her,' said Mrs Cadogan. 'And you, Emy. But why Charlotte?'

'She must have another name; best to have a Nelson one.'

Mrs Cadogan gave her an unexpected kiss. 'You're a rare girl, Emy. You should have been a priest.'

'A priest – me?' Emily laughed. 'Never. Nor a nun, either. Now the ceremony's over, give me the feeding-bottle.'

She lifted the baby and sat herself down comfortably in a low chair, directing the teat at the soft formless mouth. The baby groped frantically for a moment, then fastened on it and began to suck. Its eyes rolled up in ecstasy, one tiny claw-hand came up towards the bottle. Emily touched it, and it closed round her finger, clinging to it. An almost frightening surge of feeling encompassed her, as though she were only that minute become a full woman, and a great love for the little creature she held.

'Emma Charlotte is taking her food,' she said. 'Never fear for her. I shall take care of my sister. I shall take her to Aunt Sarah in Cheshire.'

Four

A Ringless Finger

17

The window-panes of Aunt Sarah Connor's tiny front room were filmed with the mist which hung in grey veils over the lane outside, growing thicker over the ferry landing and the waters of the Dee. Dampness dripped from the trees and glistened like a snail's trail on the cobbles. From the living-room at the back of the cottage came the sound of weeping, the combined weeping of the Connor girls who called Emily 'Cousin'. Never did bad news come to so apt a setting, Emily thought.

She picked up the newspaper again and mechanically re-read the date, 7 November 1805, and the opening words of the obituary notice which had plunged all England into grief. 'It is with indescribable regret that we have to inform our readers of the death of Viscount Nelson in battle.' Phrases she already knew too well sprang out of the column : a career of matchless glory prematurely ended by a Frenchman's bullet fired from the maintop of the enemy ship *Redoubtable*, our Isle mourning the fallen hero, the war-torn *Victory* bringing home the body of her Admiral for burial in St Paul's.

'My poor mother,' Emily said softly. 'Poor bereaved lady, what will she do now?'

The child playing on the floor looked up enquiringly, with the sweet, vacant smile that sat so oddly on the small face with its purple blemish, as though the masks of Comedy and Tragedy were joined in the middle. Little Charlotte – the name by which Emily let her half-sister be known – would soon be two years old, but she could neither speak clearly nor understand any but the simplest words. She had been born not only with her disfigurement but with brain damage also.

Emily talked to her long and gently, as one would talk to a pet animal, not in the hope of being fully understood but in an attempt to convey some meaning, however slight, by tone of voice and expression.

'Your father is dead, little Charley. He died fighting for our country, in great glory, and so he has gone to heaven to be with the angels, and his name will be written in the history books. But, oh, Charley, our poor mother, who loved him so much that she wouldn't distress him by telling him about you!'

The child crawled towards her and settled at her feet with the curious gracefulness she had inherited from Emma; a damaged cherub looking up at its god. Emily stroked the tangle of short hair, so like Nelson's own rough crop.

'It was not just your poor face, you see, Charley. We took you up to Mrs Gibson in London to be nursed, and it was she who told us that you were not as bright as you should be. And so she wrote to your father to tell him that you had died.'

Charley thoughtfully nibbled the mane of the wooden horse which was her favourite toy, so easily pulled round the floor on a string. Emily took it out of her mouth.

'I expect you would think that hard, Charley, if you understood. But our poor mother is a beauty; perhaps the most beautiful woman of her time. And she couldn't bear that her Nelson should see you. Indeed, Charley, it would have grieved him very, very much, for he had the kindest heart in the world. I think he would rather not have known, though he does not, God bless him. I went to Merton when he last came home, three months ago . . .'

She remembered how she had gone back, that bright August day, from her voluntary exile in the Wirral, to join the band of relations all rejoicing in Nelson's return from the sea after two and more weary years; Connors, Boltons, Matchams, Horace and Charlotte, the Reverend William, deafly blustering, and little Sarah Nelson chirping by his side. And above all Emma, large, bounteously beautiful, all her ills cured by seeing her lord home at last. Dear, funny, gentle little man, so beloved by all, down to the very gardener's boy whom he never saw but his hand went into his pocket for a shilling; nobody could have been less like a

214

conquering hero, and yet he had a magic about him which raised him above all others. He had asked especially to see her, Emily, and had folded her in his one arm and given her a tender kiss, as though he knew her nearer to Emma than the sharp clever Connors or the loud-voiced Boltons or any of them. She had had to leave before he was recalled to sea, to take on the enemy at last, and so had missed his heartbroken leave-taking of Emma and the four-year-old Horatia.

'I wish I had seen him again, Charley,' she said. 'I should like always to remember him more clearly than anyone I have known, your glorious father. But you were here with Aunt Sarah and I couldn't leave you for long, even though Aunt has borne so many children and brought up six.'

Ann, Sarah, Cecilia, Mary, Charles and Eliza. Charles was in the Navy, placed there by Nelson's influence, and a problem to all because of his attacks of madness, seeing phantoms on deck and startling his mates from their hammocks in the night with dreadful visions. There was something a little strange about Ann, too. The oldest of the girls, she had a powerful imagination, telling rambling stories of which she was the heroine, and more than believing in them, Emily suspected. Haughty and high-nosed, she despised the fairly humble cottage which was her widowed mother's home, and told fancy tales in Chester of the mansion they lived in. Emily she had suspected on sight as being a rival to her, and she questioned her incessantly about her life.

'Then if Cousin Emma is not your mother, who is? Not *our* mother. You shan't lay claim to her; she is far too grand for you. Did you know our grandfather was a rich man and owned Connah's Quay? And our father played the violin so marvellously that he was offered thousands of pounds to play in Liverpool itself? There!'

'Indeed, Cousin,' Emily would say meekly, hearing the story for the hundredth time. She knew perfectly well that Patrick Connor, Ann's grandfather, had been a warm man indeed, by way of the smuggling trade, and had left his son Michael enough of his ill-gotten gains to bring up and educate the six children. Michael's musical gifts had consisted of skilled if occasionally drunken performances on the flute at weddings, fairs and parties, and even at church, though the vicar of Hawarden was understandably nervous of a versatility of repertoire which could produce 'Heart Of Oak' or 'The Carman's Whistle' in the middle of a funeral service.

Sarah, the next daughter, was a Merton favourite; clever, witty, she kept everybody amused, flattered Emma to the top of her bent, out-talked the verbose Mr Lancaster and stopped the Reverend William in his tracks when he attempted an argument with her.

'Bloody bluestocking,' he boomed out, 'that's what you are, miss. Ought to have had your bottom tanned when you was no bigger than Horatia. Eh, Emma?' But Sarah had laughed and turned to someone more amusing. She and her sister Mary took turns in governessing Horatia, a willing if stolid pupil. They were 'The Girls', pensioners of Emma's bounty, as ready to take a hand at cards or distribute Merton-baked bread to the local poor as to flirt with Nelson's sea-officer friends. And Sarah, while staying at Clarges Street, had attracted the lecherous eye of 'Old Q', the senile Duke of Queensberry, Emma's cousin by marriage, whose octogenarian pleasure it was to sit on his balcony overlooking Piccadilly, mentally undressing any pretty woman who passed by, his quizzing-glass at his one useful eye. Young Sarah was no Venus, compared with her cousin Emma, but she had a bright eye and a satin skin, which the old man loved to stroke when he could lay fingers on smooth neck or arm.

Eliza, the youngest, in her teens, was the quiet one of the family. Domesticated, pudgy, she was her mother's right hand in the household economy, feeling no shame that the family living came mainly from the cockle business. It was no indignity to her to wade out in the shallows of the Dee, her skirts kilted indecently high and secured with string, in search of shellfish and shrimps, stared at and jocularly hailed by the youth of Ferry.

Eliza, of all the family, was truly fond of little Charley, taking over the child when Emily was tired or otherwise engaged. She had a natural, down-to-earth manner with children and animals; one day she would become just such a woman as her mother, shapeless with child-bearing, froglike of face, with just a fleeting look of her aunt, Mrs Cadogan.

A pull at her skirts from Charley recalled Emily to the present time. Tucking her sister under her arm she went into the kitchen, where the general mourning had subsided somewhat. Mrs Connor sat with her elbows on the table, Ann beside her; Mary rocked disconsolately by the fire; while Eliza (dry-eyed, for she had never known Nelson) boiled the kettle for tea. Charley crawled rapidly across the floor and settled on the hearthrug, beaming.

'Dear me, Emily,' said Aunt Connor. 'How do you suppose poor Lady Hamilton's left? Shall we ever see Merton or Clarges Street again?'

'I'm sure I don't know, Aunt. But Lord Nelson will have seen to it that she'll never want.'

'Yes, yes. Thank you, Eliza, and a drop of brandy in it, just for the once. Poor thing, poor thing, to lose Sir William and now him. All our lives will be changed now. Damn the cursed Frenchman, I say!'

'It won't change *my* life, Mamma.' Ann smoothed down her stuff dress complacently. 'I shall go and console her. She looks on me as a daughter, you know.' She shot a bright malignant glance at Emily, who stared expressionlessly back.

'Rubbish, Ann!' Her mother snorted. 'If anyone goes to her it'll be Sarah, when she gets the news in Bath. Mrs Matcham will let her go, for all she finds her so useful with so many children to manage. Sarah will be the one she'll turn to in her grief, poor lady.'

'She'll send for me, I tell you, Mamma. You'll see.'

But it was Emily who was summoned to Emma's side.

'My dearest Emy, by now you will have heard the dredful

217

news. O that I too had died in the fatal battle that took our great, our glorious Nelson who was my pride my joy my very life. Endead I have no care to live now He is gone and my health is so bad I do not expect to be parted from him long, I cannot leave my bed or see anyone but the good kind doctor who attends me and my dearest Horatia. Good God what a Father she has lost, and I what a Friend. Beleave me Emy those at Canterbury has never come near me since, and Doctor Nelson that was is now made Earl Nelson with a pension of five thousand a year by his greatfull Country. Greatfull endead to our departed Angel, but what has his Brother done to deserve reward, his Brother whose son I sent to Eton and brought up his Daughter by my own hand?

My heart is broke Emy, I entreat you if you love me come to me at Clarges Street.

Of course she would go. Some might desert Emma in her misfortune, as the William Nelsons had done, it seemed, but all Emily's heart longed to be with her mother. There was only the question of Charley, and that was soon solved.

'I'll look after her,' said Eliza. 'She's as happy with me as she is with you. I'll take her cockling and she can dig in the sands. And nobody,' she glared, 'nobody's going to laugh at her poor face while she's out with me. Any of those boys tries it, I'll knock his teeth in.'

Mrs Connor was perfectly happy with this solution. The allowance Emma had settled on the child would continue to come in, helping considerably towards household expenses, for Charley had a bird's appetite. What with that, and what Sarah sent from her situation with Mrs Matcham in Bath, and Mary's contribution as a governess in a house near Chester, the Connor home would stand for some time. Emily packed, conscious of a stir of excitement at the prospect of leaving the dull Northern scene and returning to the mother who, even under this blow of fate, would still create more wonder, more glamour about her than any other living creature.

So, of course, it proved. In the elegant drawing-room at Clarges Street Emma floated towards her, arms open, black gauzy draperies like drifting storm-clouds. The tender enfolding embrace seemed to be scented with funeral lilies instead of the old blend of rose and jessamine. An appealing little black net cap surrounded Emma's curls; her complexion against all the black was pure rose and cream, her eyes all the more lustrous for the tears they shed.

And yet, as she sank on to the daybed and began to tell Emily her woes, it was quite clear that there was not a scrap of affectation in her. Others felt grief, gave a certain amount of pained utterance to it and suppressed the rest. In Emma grief became lovely, noble; she gave it full rein, a goddess bereaved – Venus, widowed by the boar's tusk, mourning for Adonis.

'Do you know, his last words were of me, Emy? Even in his pain and with the battle raging around him and the wounded men in their blood, he thought of Emma. And that very morning he'd signed a codicil to his will saying "I leave Emma, Lady Hamilton, a Legacy to my King and Country, that they will give her an ample provision to maintain her rank in life". And then he wrote that Horatia too was to be provided for. Yet, would you believe it, the *Earl* and the *Countess* are as cold as Christmas to me – me that was their benefactor and taught Charlotte all my own accomplishments! And that Saracen' – Emily recognised this epithet for Lady Nelson – '*she* is to have two thousand a year for life, and his sisters fifteen thousand each, from the Government's pocket! Yet Emma and his child may starve for all those beasts care.' She mopped her eyes with a lawn handkerchief edged in black and embroidered with H.N. and a coronet. A smile like a rainbow brightened her face.

'But now my little Emy's come, and I shall no longer be alone.'

Emily pressed her hand. 'I am so happy to be with you again.'

She discovered before long that Emma had not been exactly alone before her coming. An hour never passed without the doorbell ringing, a message of sympathy, a bouquet, a request to call upon Lady Hamilton. Friends in London society who had been to her parties and entertained her, ladies whose reputation had suffered, like her own. The beautiful Duchess of Devonshire and that charming creature, Lady Betty Foster, with whom she shared her husband. The Duke of Queensberry, a grotesque caricature of Sir William, staggered in on shrunken legs almost every day to pay his respects, until Emma had to ask him to desist because the newspapers were making something of it. But Emily had never before seen in the flesh the personage who arrived one afternoon in a spanking turn-out bearing the royal arms and was shown in by Emma's butler, Mr White, as though he were God himself; the portly, corseted man who had left youth behind but gallantly kept up its likeness with dyed curls and a touch of darkening on the eyebrows. Florizel, he had called himself once, Prince of Hearts as well as Prince of Wales.

He bowed with astonishing grace over Emma's hand, then over Emily's.

'Delighted to encounter any relative of m'dear Emma's.'

As she rose from her curtsey he looked her full in the face, man to woman. He was fat, he wore cosmetics, he was known for a rake and a rip, but there was something so irresistibly good-humoured in his glance, and such sweetness in his smile, that Emily was instantly conquered. He had some quality of charm that redeemed all. Emma gave him a keepsake lock of Nelson's hair set in gold and pearls. He kissed it, and her hand, and unashamedly wept.

When his short visit was over, Emily stood staring out of the window at the carriage bowling along by the Park. Emma looked at her with amusement.

'Struck dumb by His Highness's charms, Emy?'

'I was thinking . . . nothing. Yes, he is indeed an enchanter. How curious, when the King and Queen are so very dull.'

Emma laughed. 'You don't stand a chance with him, my dear. He don't like women unless they're older than him – witness Mrs Fitz and Lady Jersey. Lor', what frumps he does pick!'

Emily sighed. She had not, in fact, been planning an assault upon the Prince's heart on her own account but on Emma's. How convenient and right it would be if only the Prince's unsuitable wife, whom he detested, could be divorced or otherwise disposed of. With Nelson gone and Emma free, what more delightful than that these two charming creatures, matched in their size, in their love of pleasure and their admiration for glory, should be united? There might be a little trouble with protocol and perhaps some difficulty over the Royal Marriage Act, but these things could be got round, and surely Emma might be forgiven for marrying a future king, however deep her heart might be buried with Nelson?

'I believe the girl *is* in love with him,' said Emma.

The visit of the Duke of Clarence did not raise any such matrimonial hares in her brain. Prince William had his father's pineapple head, popping blue eyes, and eccentric staccato manner. He was reputed to live with, and off, the actress Dolly Jordan – 'He gives her a child a year and takes her wages in return,' Emma said when he had gone. He had been Nelson's midshipmate and best man at his wedding, and his sorrow, though gruffly expressed, was sincere.

The third royal brother to call was the most breathtaking. They were large, but he was gigantic, a huge frame lavishly upholstered with flesh. As he loomed up in the door of the drawing-room Emily fought a desire to laugh; it was so like a play or a fairy-tale, three princes entering one after the other, each more extraordinary than the last. The Duke of Sussex was not only very big for his thirty-two years, but very solemn. Seated in a fragile chair whose spindle legs threatened to give way under him, he commiserated gravely with Emma, drew Emily gravely into the conversation (which was far above her head, being of politics, the inevitable rise of Liberalism, and the shortcomings of Lord Moira), gravely sent for his little Negro page, Mr Blackman, who awaited him in the hall, to fetch him his snuff-box.

Emily was astonished to hear Emma address him as Gussy and enquire whether there was any news of Goosy.

The Duke slowly shook his large elaborately-curled head. 'More obdurate than ever to call herself Duchess. An injunction must be brought, though I dislike litigation.'

'And the children? My dear little god-daughter and the boy?'

'Alas. Entirely given over to her. It was a condition of our separation, and I suppose I must not complain. I fear she will spoil them sadly, especially Augustus.'

Emma sighed. 'So sad, after such a sweetly romantic beginning, that you and Goosy should have been parted by the King. Oh, that wicked Royal Marriage Act!'

'My father may be proud of himself,' said the Duke bitterly. 'He has not only destroyed our perfectly legal marriage but our sentiments for one another. When lawyers fall to wrangling, love flies out of the window.' He rose. 'My dear Emma, I rejoice to see you sustaining your sorrow with such fortitude. I shall never forget your kindness to me. You deserve every good fortune. Pray remember me to my good friend Mrs Cadogan.' He bowed and made a stately exit, Mr Blackman trotting at his heels.

'Ah,' said Emma, 'poor Gussy, he has had such an unhappy life. You know he fell in love with Lady Augusta Murray and married her twice, once in Rome and again in England at St George's. The King found out and sent him abroad, and as soon as he was gone annulled the marriage. Well, Emy, I may not have become Lady Nelson, but I have had more happiness than any woman alive, though she'd been wed by the Archbishop of Canterbury himself. Let nobody tell you marriage is perpetual bliss. But what am I thinking of, croaking on like this? We must get you married, dear girl. I'm a selfish thing to keep you to myself.'

Emily kissed her. 'I shall never leave you.'

And indeed Emma's need for company was great, while decency prevented her from mixing yet in society. The grief which came over her in private could find no expression. Fits of melancholy oppressed her, driving her to eating between meals and idly flipping through novels which failed to amuse her. Her only relief came from visits: a call from Nelson's devoted secretary, Doctor Scott, or one of their other friends. Even Captain Hardy, who disliked and disapproved of her, paid duty calls for which she was grateful. For outings there were only discreet drives in a closed carriage, or excursions to Merton, where Mrs Cadogan presided over the servants and the building works which had now become meaningless but must be completed. Horatia was there, looked after by Sarah Connor, who had been relinquished by Kitty Matcham. Sometimes Emma would pick the child up and hug her warmly, calling her Nelson's own daughter, poor forsaken orphan, and at other times would almost ignore her presence – which treatment Horatia bore with her usual stolidity.

Mrs Cadogan took Emily aside. 'The other little one – how is she?'

'No brighter, I fear. She will never mend. But in her way she's happy. Eliza writes to me that she loves to play on the shore and build houses with stones.'

'And Emma never speaks of her?'

'Never. It's as though the child were really dead.'

'A nice Christmas we shall have, with my lord laying in state at Greenwich, and the funeral to come. As if January weren't bad enough without. And then there's all these debts, and that Earl sniffing round to see what he can get, canting on about his dear brother and shedding crocodile tears, the great fat hypocrite! Seems as if we'll never get back to normal. God knows what's to become of us.'

Sighing heavily, she took up the thick file of wages bills which Mr Cribb had brought in, and began to tot them up, her new steel-rimmed spectacles half-way down her nose.

Strange to say, the sad time they had feared so much, when the great bell of St Paul's tolled for the hero who was being laid to rest in the vaults below, passed like a bad dream. Emma's grief was real and bitter, but she could never resist seeing the people who came to offer their condolences, and Emily was constantly on duty at Clarges Street. Every day was charged with emotion combined with heavy hospitality; at night she would fall into bed with aching feet and a throat tired with talking. Yet it passed the time. January merged into February; the snowdrops were out at Merton and young lambs frisked in the meadows. The air was cold, crisp and exhilarating; Emma, walking by the Little Nile, took deep breaths of it. She would never cease to mourn for Nelson as long as she lived, but mourning was so exhausting. She returned to the house with a brisker step than of late.

'Life must go on,' she said to Mrs Cadogan with a beautiful, brave smile. '*He* would not wish us to live like nuns for ever. Of course, I could not possibly be seen entertaining in town – but do you think it would be wrong of me to hold a little musical party here, quietly, with only our friends? Of course, it would be very decorous, no frivolity. Braham could sing " 'Twas In Trafalgar Bay", which always moves me so much, and Betty Billington and I might give some Handel duets. Oratorio, I think. That would be quite proper.' She drew a sheet of paper towards her and began to make a list. 'Sussex *might* come, we could always ask him – and the Denyses. She has such a pretty voice though her face is quite dreadfully plain, poor woman – I mean Lady Charlotte, of course, not Elena, who squawks.' Without waiting for her mother's approval or otherwise, she gave her whole attention to planning the party.

They made a handsome gathering in the Nelson Room, which was also the music-room: John Braham the singer, with his huge Jewish nose and flashing dark eyes, and his singing partner, Nancy Storace, who was also his mistress – a fact which everybody knew and nobody mentioned; the buxom Mrs Billington, once a particular friend of the Prince of Wales; the Denyses, who lived in Hans Place, Chelsea, and had a country house in Yorkshire – Peter Denys shortsighted and Swiss-accented, his wife plain and snub-nosed, as Emma had said, but Emily thought she would have made a pretty pig with wonderful red hair and a skin of alabaster. She wore rich black velvet with pearls. Some of the other ladies had been relieved to hear Emma's dictum that purple or white dresses would be acceptable. Mrs Billington was splendid in violet with gold embroidery, one of her stage dresses, and the lively Nancy wore chaste white satin. Beneath pictures of Nelson and his battles, each garlanded with crape, a lively chatter of operatic voices grew louder every minute as new arrivals were ushered in – 'And a pretty penny it's all going to cost' said Mrs Cadogan grimly.

When everyone had had enough tea and talk, Emma sat down at her gilded harp and sang Tom Moore's 'She Is Far From The Land', bringing sympathetic tears to every eye. The sustained applause died down, and Braham rose to render the ballad at which all London had wept that winter. In the silence before he began the solemn recitative, one might have heard a pin drop. Emily did hear the distant jangle of the doorbell; another guest arriving.

'O'er Nelson's tomb, with silent grief oppress'd,
Britannia mourns her hero, now at rest.
But those bright laurels ne'er shall fade with years,
Whose leaves are water'd by a nation's tears.'

Emily saw the door open. The new arrival entered quietly, unnoticed by the company, and sat down on the nearest chair.

'Twas in Trafalgar's Bay,
We saw the Frenchmen lay,
Each heart was bounding then . . .'

Emily heard no more of Braham's stirring song – for she found herself looking into the eyes of Francis Carew.

18

There was no possibility of a mistake. No other man could possess those strange amber eyes, like clear river water above brown stones, or the high serious brow and full lips. But there were lines on the brow and about the mouth, and Emily fancied she saw a look of discontent or preoccupation. The premature streaks of grey in Francis's hair had spread, making him look far more than his years. Thirty-five he must be by now, she guessed.

He had recognised her. Wave after wave of shock went through her, leaving her face as pale as his. They stared at each other as though riveted, only coming out of their trance as Braham ended his song with a resounding 'England, Home, and Beauty!' and bowed to the weeping Emma as applause broke round him. When he sat down Mrs Billington rose, a majestic figure, to sing an aria from Handel's *Semele*; and after that somebody Emily had not met performed a complicated piece of Mozart on the pianoforte. Emily fidgeted, trying not to look towards Francis but unable to keep from glancing sideways through her lashes. What must he think of her, after that business of the letters? Would he even wish to speak to her? Passionately she hoped and prayed that he would, opening and shutting her fan, tracing the designs on its ivory stick with her finger.

After what seemed like hours the interval arrived. Fatima, in her best cap, distributed wine and cakes, and a storm of chatter broke out in which Francis left his chair and came hurriedly over to Emily.

'I must speak to you,' he said. 'Can we slip out without being noticed?'

Fortunately many of the company were standing about with their refreshments, so that the departure of two people went unnoticed. Emily beckoned him to follow her down a narrow passage leading to the conservatory. Inside, she shut the door and they confronted one another, silent. Yellow lamplight turned the conservatory flowers all one colour; the sweet stuffy scent of forced plants was all about them.

'So I've found you at last,' said Francis gravely. 'I can hardly believe it.'

'Nor I.'

'Why did you never write? I thought—'

She sat down on a basketwork seat, drawing him down beside her.

'There's so much to explain. Let's say as much as we can before they miss us.' She told him, leaving out some details, the story of the intercepted letters, read too late. 'I thought you would hate me. I had no idea where to find you, to tell you about it.'

'Mrs Blomiley knew.'

Emily looked down. 'I dared not ask her.'

Francis was frowning. 'You said *four* letters? But I wrote you five.'

'There were only four.'

'Ah. That would be because one came back to me, with a message written on the outside to say you were gone away leaving no address.'

Emily gasped. 'She was as wicked as that? Oh, how could she?'

'I shall never forgive that,' said Francis. 'When you and I both needed friends, to part us . . . but now I've found you again.' He smiled for the first time, and drew her to him. It seemed perfectly natural that she should rest her head on his shoulder and that their hands should be clasped. It was as though the gap of years had matured their relationship instead of arresting it, turned them into people who could communicate perfectly with few words. No longer was she missish, or he over polite. He bent his head and kissed her. It was a kiss that transformed the world into a magical place and herself into a woman deeply and passionately in love, conscious of every nerve

227

in her own body and his. She clung to him, prolonging the kiss, parting her lips under his, while his hand found her breast, exciting her almost unbearably. Then he gently released her, and rested his cheek against her hair.

'Your pretty curls. I've never forgotten them. Are your eyes still as blue, like the wood-violets of Italy?' He tilted her chin. 'Damnation, I can't tell in this light. How old are you now, Emily?'

'Twenty-four, sir.'

'Don't call me sir, pray. The time has gone for formalities between us.'

'Yes.'

'And what in the name of heaven are you doing here?'

'I am – a relation of Lady Hamilton. I live here partly as her companion.'

'Good God! And I have been tutoring the child of her husband's kinsman the Marquis of Abercorn, at Stanmore Priory. What a world of coincidence this is. Or Fate, let's call it. Do you believe in Fate, Emily?'

'I have never thought about it. But now I think I do.' She stroked back his hair. 'You've turned so grey. Has your life been so hard?'

He laughed, not mirthfully she thought. 'No harder than anybody else's, I suppose. I've been everywhere and done everything, travelled with my pupils, drudged in a school where they flogged and starved the boys, sung in an opera chorus. That's how I came here, through Elena Denis. We travelled down together. I imagine she's making a lengthy toilette.'

'How curious! There's another Denys here, only I think she spells it with a Y; and she's a Lady.'

'Unlike Elena. But I mustn't be waspish about the poor woman. After all, without her I should never have found you again.' He lifted her hand and kissed it. 'What a fool I was to let you go, before. If only that damned woman had not interfered – before it was too late.'

'Too late?' Emily echoed. 'But we're here, together, and no-body can stop us—'

Francis's voice and look were infinitely sad. 'My dear, I'm married.'

Before she could answer, or even take in what he had said, the door opened to admit Nancy.

'Oh, Miss Em'ly, thank goodness you're here, and do excuse me, but my lady noticed you was gone and sent me to look for you, in case you was took ill.'

'Thank you, Nancy,' Emily forced herself to say. 'I'm sorry my lady has been worried. I felt the heat and came out here with Mr Carew, an old friend of mine. Tell my lady I'll join her in a moment.'

They were alone together in the dusky corridor, Nancy speeding on ahead. Emily felt Francis's arms close round her and hold her tight.

'We'll talk tomorrow,' he said. 'Don't think of anything till then. God bless you.' He kissed her forehead, and they went decorously back to the music-room.

The rest of the evening was a daze to Emily. Francis was introduced to Emma by Elena Denis, who turned out to be an improbably blonde lively lady wearing rouge, and Emma greeted him with such charm that Emily felt a pang of jealousy. Then he was absorbed into the band of musicians, some of whom he knew already, and persuaded to sing, though he tried hard to escape. Emily noticed as he stood by the pianoforte that his velvet jacket was faded from its original sapphire, and shabby at the sleeves and elbows, and his stock, though smartly tied, looked old. She heard Emma comment on the music-score.

'I don't know this. Is it very ancient?'

'Elizabethan, my lady. Meant to be sung to the lute.'

'I haven't mastered the lute, but I'll do my best with the key-board.' She flashed him a brilliant smile, and played the prelude correctly at sight.

The silver tenor was a little tarnished since Emily had heard it

in Manchester, as though its owner had been made to sing too
often and too loudly.

'Since first I saw your face I resolved to honour and renown
   you;
If now I be disdained, I wish my heart had never known you.
What, I, that loved, and you, that liked, shall we begin to
   wrangle?
No, no, no, my heart is fast, and cannot disentangle.
The Sun, whose beams most glorious are, rejecteth no
   beholder;
And your sweet beauty past compare made my poor eyes the
   bolder.
Where Beauty moves, and Wit delights, and signs of kindness
   bind me,
There, oh there, where'er I go, I'll leave my heart behind
   me!'

She caught the glance he gave her above the heads of those
clustered round him, and at the same time saw her mother turn
her head to the singer, thanking him with her eyes for what she
took to be a compliment to her. 'Poor Mamma,' she thought. 'She
has lost her love, and I've found mine.'

She left the music-room early, while Emma was showing
pathetic relics of Nelson to the company. Francis was sitting on
a sofa between Mrs Denis and Mrs Billington, who had one
enormous arm round his neck.

It was not, after all, Francis who told her what he had not
been able to tell in the conservatory. When she came downstairs
after a night of wakefulness and wild dreams he was nowhere
to be found, though a few yawning guests were breakfasting in
the dining-room. Emily saw Elena Denis among them, and joined
her by the coffee-pot. Mrs Denis, looking several years older in
the morning light, greeted her cheerfully.

'I noticed you last night, dear – such a pretty child, and so very like dearest Emma's family.'

'I believe I am supposed to be, ma'am.'

'Have some coffee.' She poured with a heavy hand, then dived into the brocade bag which swung from her arm, producing a lacquered snuff-box which she offered to Emily. 'You don't? Nor these, I suppose?' Incredulously Emily recognised the cylindrical brown object as a segar. Mrs Denis saw her startled face and laughed. 'Never seen a lady smoke, child? Well, I suppose Emma don't think it feminine. But I find it soothes the nerves without irritating the throat.' She lit it from the fire and puffed contentedly, watched fascinatedly by Emily and the maids, who were clearing away. Emily had never seen anyone so raffish except on the streets, yet Mrs Denis spoke with a good accent and moved with natural grace. Nor was she a fool.

'I can see you think I'm a sad dog,' she said slyly.

'Oh, not at all, ma'am. I was just wondering how long you had known my lady.'

'Since you were in swaddling-bands, I'll bet. No, to tell the truth we met in Naples, when she was first there in keeping with Sir William, poor man. Not poor because of that, you understand me, for they were very happy and she misses him dreadfully, especially now.' She heaved a deep sigh, and blew out a cloud of smoke which Signora Storace, hovering near with a teacup, pointedly waved away before retreating to the window. 'Yes, there she was with him and there was I with Bristol – the Earl-Bishop of Derry, you know. What a rakehell he was, and what a comedian! You can have no idea, child, what a beauty Emma was in those days. Even Romney – no, he softened her down too much. Angie Kauffman saw her clearer. Well, four years after she married Sir William I got married myself, and we came over to England just before them.'

'Is your husband with you now, ma'am?'

'Simon?' She pronounced it the French way. 'Lord no, he's looking after our little inn on the Windsor Road. He can do that and his painting as well – did I tell you he was an artist, especially in the winter, when trade's poor? Now what did I set out to tell you? What an interminable rattle I am. Tell me, my love, do you come from that dreadful savage North, like the others of Emma's tribe?'

'From Manchester, ma'am.'

The statement produced just the result she had hoped.

'What a miraculous coincidence! So does the young friend I brought down last night, Mr Carew, who sang so sweetly, didn't you think?'

'I – we are slightly acquainted,' said Emily, hoping that the blaze-up of the fire under the attack of a poker wielded by the shivering Braham would account for her colour. But little escaped Mrs Denis's eye. She greeted Braham with a friendly kiss and returned to the conversation. There was a story, she felt, behind that blush.

'Really. Indeed. Well, I suppose it's a smaller place than London. And have you two foreigners kept in touch since you left that barbarous place?'

'Oh, no, ma'am. We had entirely lost sight of each other until yesterday.'

'Ah.' Mrs Denis heaved another great sigh. 'Then you'll not know what tribulations he has been through – for which, heaven forgive me, I blame myself. Yes, you may well look at me with great eyes, miss, and wonder who I am, at my age, to influence the fate of a young man. But to do me justice I had no idea what she was.'

'Who, ma'am?'

'Why, Kate, Kate Christofero – at least so she called herself, when I met her at Drury Lane, where we both sang in the opera. I must say I found her *très amusante*. She had such a sharp wit and a – *je ne sais quoi*. A kind of *belle sauvage* allure.'

'What was she like?' Emily asked, hoping she was not trembling as much as she felt herself to be.

'Like? Oh, middleish, with a bedpost waist and the blackest eyes and hair you ever set eyes on – blacker than that poor native's.' She nodded towards Fatima, who was collecting china on a tray. 'I believe her family came from Greece, though it's my belief her father kept a stall in Covent Garden. Well, we became very friendly – at least as friendly as women ever *do* become, which isn't saying much, my dear – and when I was invited to Abercorn's for a week-end I got an invitation for her as well. How I wish I'd cut my hand off before I gave it to her! There was to be a masked ball. I remember I went as Diana, with a dear little pearl bow and a diamanté crescent in my hair. I could have fallen to the floor when I saw the gear Kate had chosen. A houri, my child, if you can imagine it – with transparent trousers and no tights beneath, for she had sandals on her bare feet, and what even *she* daren't expose covered with a great cluster of false jewels, and two smaller ones stuck on her breasts. What with, I don't know – glue I suppose. She had a circlet of gold coins in her hair and a gold veil across her face, not so thick that one couldn't see her eyes and mouth.'

Inside Emily's brain something was crying: 'Hush! Go away! I don't want to know!' But of course she must go on listening.

'That was when I met our young friend Francis. Not dancing, I remember, but leaning against a wall talking to the Marchioness, who was *enceinte*. He was in ordinary dress and I thought him very charming. When the Marchioness presented him to me I saw his eyes light up, and, do you know, my dear, it was because he had seen me with that wretch Kate and knew I could tell him who she was. I saw him seek her out, and in the next dance there they were, moving like angels together and lost in each other's eyes.'

She threw away her segar, which had gone out long before.

'Of course she egged him on. After what she'd come up from, even a music-master was a catch, especially at the Priory, where everybody visits, including their Royal Highnesses. Before a fortnight was out he'd married her. He took rooms for her in Stanmore Village and there he lived with her, doting like an idiot, and going to the Priory less often than Abercorn liked. Then, in a few weeks, she ran away.'

'Ran away?' How could she, how could she? It was untimely

233

for Emily that at such a moment Emma should sweep in, bestowing embraces on all present and calling loudly for fresh coffee to be brewed. Then she clapped her hands and addressed the company.

'My neighbour Mr Goldsmid has very kindly invited us all to luncheon at Morden Hall, and of course I accepted, though I made it plain that I am officially seeing no one. But to visit almost next-door is not like going into society, is it?'

All agreed that it was not. Emily, to her great frustration, became separated from Mrs Denis as they gathered round their hostess. Francis was nowhere to be seen, nor did she set eyes on him until they were all seated at luncheon in the enormous dining-room of Morden Hall, before an imposing array of plate and a central épergne of monumental proportions, representing Venus and Mars with cupids, in silver-gilt. Francis had been placed far away from her, next to a Goldsmid sister. From time to time they exchanged glances, but the opportunity to meet only came when the meal was over and Abraham Goldsmid invited the company to stroll in his gardens, the afternoon being mild.

They met in one of the shubbery walks, both having detached themselves with difficulty from other chattering guests. Francis raised her hand to his lips, then took her arm, and they strolled slowly along the path.

'I missed you this morning,' she said.

'I went walking, for miles I suppose. I wanted to think.'

'Yes, I too, but there has been no time.'

'We are not mad, are we? To feel as we do for each other after a week's acquaintance, years ago, and only now another meeting?'

Emily shook her head. 'I have asked myself that a hundred times in the last few hours. Do you think me very unmaidenly to show that I love you?'

He shook his head emphatically. 'Not to have shown it would have been the way of a coquette, and I know my Emily better than that already. Besides—'

'Besides what?'

'I have been studying you and our hostess very intently during that excellent but lengthy lunch. A case of "*mater pulchra, filia pulchrior*"? Aren't I right?'

'I too was taught Latin from Virgil, Mr Carew. Yes, you are right, though I am not acknowledged as her daughter. And I am certainly *not* more beautiful.'

'Then you are the daughter of a woman who was born to love and be loved. Did she hide her love for Lord Nelson, do you suppose, and pretend coldness?'

'No. No more than I can. Francis – Mrs Denis has been talking to me.'

'Elena? About me?'

'Yes. Believe me, I didn't question her. You were mentioned, and she told me at great length about – your marriage. Up to the point when your wife ran away from Stanmore.'

'I see. Well, I'm spared having to tell you myself. What happened then was that I absented myself to go after her and find her; and when I returned, not having found her, the Marquis dismissed me. So I was back in London, homeless and workless, without Kate.' He smiled wryly. 'And also without my silver fob-watch and a few other valuables.'

'Oh, the wretch!'

'I fear she was. And is. When I finally traced her she was living in rooms provided by a young sprig of the nobility, and I was told smartly to take myself off. So I found a cheap room in Soho and advertised that I gave singing lessons, without much result. Elena saw me one day, staring into a pastrycook's window, and took me home with her for a solid meal. Then she found me a place at Covent Garden, in the chorus.'

'And your wife?'

'Oh, she returned to me from time to time, in between admirers.'

'And you let her?' Emily was indignant.

'It seems strange, I know. Perhaps I behaved like the poor cuckold I was. But she still had power to charm me, though she was growing fat and coarsening. Yet, Emily, I disliked her intensely.'

'So did Mrs Denis, apparently.'

'Yes, and with reason. She stole an admirer from her – one from whom Elena had high hopes.'

Emily looked startled. 'So Mrs Denis is—?'

'A demirep, like my clever Kate. Katina was her real name, by the way.'

'And where is she now?'

'Heaven knows. In keeping somewhere, or in gaol for stealing spoons. When I get back I may find her awaiting me – or gone again, with more of my belongings. I had a book of Dibdin's songs, signed by himself for me – that went. I can't think what she intended to do with it. Don't look so horrified, my Emily. Worse wives have happened to better men. What troubles me is ourselves. How can I claim you, fettered like this?'

'I would come with you – without marriage.'

He bent to kiss her. 'I believe you would – and to a sleazy two-pair back in Dean Street. How could I let you do that?'

'I would do it gladly. Only I cannot leave her, yet, my lady. She needs all of us about her till the grief heals a little. Oh, I know you think her shallow and frivolous – I could see it in your eyes today when she was so gay at table. But inside she is desolate. It's just that she must have company, talk, affection.'

'Yes, I know. But you must leave her sometime, if not now. And she doesn't even acknowledge you. Surely that would be a small price to pay for your devotion.'

Emily shrugged. 'No price is small if one is not prepared to pay it. Even Horatia is not acknowledged.' She shut out the memory of that third unacknowledged one staring at the reflection of her ruined face in the shallows of the Dee. From the direction of the ornamental lake she saw approaching the furred and shawled form of Emma, leaning on the arm of Abraham Goldsmid, and she swiftly moved away from Francis's side.

'Tonight,' he said. 'We must talk tonight. Tomorrow I go back.'

236

The evening was a repetition of the previous one, but for a change of programme. Emma and Betty Billington sang the anthem 'My Song Shall Be Of Mercy And Judgment', after which Emma rendered 'I Know That My Redeemer Liveth' so beautifully that even the preoccupied Emily was moved by it. The music went on so long that the evening ended long after midnight in a flurry of yawning, smiling good-nights, a roomful of people between Emily and Francis; and Mrs Cadogan, catching sight of Emily's strained anxious face, seized her and propelled her towards the door.

'That's enough. Off to bed with you if you don't want the doctor called again. I'm dropping for sleep myself. Upstairs now.' And taking a candle from the hall she made Emily precede her up the staircase.

When the sounds of retirement had died down, and the last door had been shut, Emily crept out, a cloak over her nightdress. She guessed where Francis would be, and there he was, in the dark passage that led to the conservatory. Silently they went in together and Emily turned the key in the door. They were in each other's arms at last, and Emily was lost in a storm of desire that drove out fear and caution. As she clung round Francis's neck her cloak fell off; she heard him gasp as he realised that she was only wearing a thin lawn robe.

'No!' he said. 'Emily, don't tempt me. Let me go!' and tried to free himself from the small tight-clinging hands. But already his body had responded to hers; every second it became more difficult to resist. The heady scent of fruits and blossoms was an aphrodisiac; tendrils of vine caught at Emily's hair, turning her into a young Bacchante. Francis drew her down with him to the rush-matted floor, and with trembling fingers began to unfasten the ribbons at her throat.

19

From the window of their second-floor room in Arundel Street, Strand, Emily could see the river only a few yards away, winking sleepily under the traffic of barges, wherries, private boats and colliers – like a lion superior to the teasing of insects. She pushed the window up as far as it would go to let the comparatively fresh river air come into the stuffy room. Then, as she often did, she looked at her surroundings with a quiet joy.

The room would not have passed as a dwelling for a scullery-maid at Clarges Street or Merton. It was small, with a low ceiling which in this hot weather provided a permanent ball-room for flies. The carpet, once a handsome red turkey pattern, was faded and darned, and the furniture was minimal. The centre of the room and of their lives was a large bed with four posts but no canopy. For the rest a table and two chairs, a washstand-commode and a long mirror supplied their needs. The walls, on which remnants of several layers of paper were to be seen in places, bore a few pictures: a print of Emma as a sibyl, a miniature of a young woman in a blue dress who was Francis's mother, and a glass representation of Abraham about to sacrifice Isaac, which belonged to their landlady.

To Emily everything in the room was beautiful, transfigured by first love. It was a setting for Francis, the jewel of her life.

It had been hard breaking away from Emma. For weeks after the wild, wonderful night at Merton, Emily had longed to tell her of the change that had transformed her from a girl to a woman. But Emma was low in spirits, bothered by Nelson's executors and the non-cooperation of the new Earl. She fled from Merton to Clarges Street, where she could be distracted from her melancholy by constant visitors, and seemed more than ever dependent on Emily's company. Sarah Connor was still at Merton, governessing Horatia, whom Emma emphatically did not want under her feet in London, and Sarah Reynolds, another cousin, joined her. Emma was going through all the permutations of her family and Nelson's – Boltons, Matchams, anyone who would pass the time for her. One wet day, when she was particularly low, another relative came to mind.

'I shall send for Ann Connor, Emy. I recall she is most amusing and does all kinds of imitations. There! Don't you think that a good idea?'

Emily did not. The thought of Ann, sharp of tongue, nose and eye, queening it in the household was a dismaying one.

'Do you not think Mary or Cecilia would be better? Ann can be spiteful at times.'

'And what is there to be spiteful about here? No, she shall come and amuse me.' She sat down at her escritoire and dashed off an invitation in her big scrawling writing. An acceptance came almost at once, followed by Ann herself, with the air of a very important person doing Clarges Street an honour by descending on it. She embarked immediately on a programme of belittling Emily and ingratiating herself with Emma. Distinguished visitors found themselves overwhelmed with attentions, not always welcome.

'That young woman means to rise in the world,' said Lady Betty Foster to Emma. 'Mark me, she looks for marriage in the nobility.'

'And why not? The Connors are close kin of mine. Her manners are impeccable.'

'She talks too much,' said Lady Betty thoughtfully. 'And some of her tales are very odd. Does she really dine regularly with the Dean of Chester, and has she truly been invited to launch a ship from Liverpool Docks?'

'If she says so, then of course she has. You're very hard on her, Lady Betty. Now I don't pick holes in a person till they've done me wrong.'

Francis called sometimes, and was graciously received by Emma, who thought his visits were a tribute to her own charms. Ann always put on her Sunday cap when he was announced, as she did for all gentlemen callers, but though she flashed many smiles at him she missed nothing of the glances that went between him and Emily, their closeness at the pianoforte, the chances seized by each to touch the other.

Elena Denis and Ann got along famously. Ann flattered the older woman to the top of her bent, encouraging her to talk of her admirers, of the Earl-Bishop and the Princes. Soon she was visiting the small inn near Staines for long hours of tea and delicious gossip with her dearest Elena, during which she gathered much priceless information about Emma, to be stored up and used when necessary.

By this means she easily extracted the story of Francis Carew and the Greek wife. It made her extremely thoughtful, for here might be a weapon to get rid of her rival, Emily. She felt her hand closing round its hilt when one morning, entering Emily's room without knocking, she found her leaning over her wash-basin being violently sick.

Emily turned a greenish face towards her. 'The supper – last night,' she managed to say. 'It must have disagreed . . .'

'Really? I thought it excellent. But then I can digest anything. The turtle soup was perhaps a little fatty, and the fowls may have hung rather long—'

Emily was sick again.

After this Ann watched Emily very closely: the newly let-out darts in her dresses, the moving of some buttons on her bodices, other details unmistakable to anyone with a mother as fertile as Sarah Connor. It was the sweetest moment of her life when she went to tell Emma of her discovery.

Emma stared at her uncomprehendingly. 'Pregnant? Little Emy? Quite impossible.'

'All too possible, dearest Lady Hamilton. Have you not noticed her manner with Mr Carew? They know each other very well indeed, believe me.'

Emma was pacing about in agitation. 'I don't believe you. Yet there's something about her face . . .'

'Send for her, then. Ask her yourself.'

'Yes, I will. But alone.' Ann's face fell. 'She must not be shamed if there's any truth in this story.'

Ann hovered round the shut door of the room in which Emily and her mother were talking; but the doors were stout and the keyhole blocked with a key on the inside. If only she could hear!

But within there were no accusations and denials, no slaps or screams; only Emily quietly weeping on the floor, her head on Emma's lap. Emma patted her hair mechanically. So it was true. The daughter she had planned to compensate by a splendid marriage had ruined herself, just as she, Emma, had once done.

Aloud she said, 'I was rescued by dearest Sir Will'um. But who will rescue you?'

Emily wiped her eyes and swallowed down tears. 'I shall manage.' She got up and sat by Emma's side. 'I won't stay here to disgrace you. Francis and I will live somewhere we're not known, and I shall say I am married.'

'But his wife? Oh God, these wives, how they torment us!'

'How can she find us? Francis will tell nobody where we are. And she may not even be in London.'

Emma sighed heavily. 'I don't like it. I wish Mr Carew had never come to Merton, or had had more – more discretion. I am very angry with him.'

'It was my fault,' Emily said hastily. 'I should never have put us both in danger.'

In Emma's mind rose a vision, all too clear, of a room in Palermo, a lamp left as a sign, Nelson fighting his conscience as he at last took what she offered so freely, and thereby betraying both his wife and his dear friend, Emma's husband. It is in our blood to be sirens, she thought, yet we are not wicked, Emy and I, no more than Mam was when she conceived my brother William three years before marriage. And we suffer for it, God knows. She would have loved to keep Emily under her roof and wage such a campaign of secrecy as had hidden the birth of Horatia and 'the other one'; but she was tired, so tired, now that Nelson was gone, and perhaps it had all been futile after

all, since she had to proclaim Horatia as Nelson's daughter before the nation if she was to win a pension.

'If you must go, Emy – and I can see nothing else for it –
then promise to stay near and send word to me in the slightest
need. I'll do all I can, you know that.'

They embraced and cried, and Emma pressed twenty guineas
she could ill afford into Emily's hand.

So it came about that Francis and Emily moved into the
room by the river, where no curiosity was displayed about him
and Mrs Carew, as Emily called herself; he off in the morning
to teach young ladies in Edgware to sing popular ballads, she
sometimes doing their modest shopping for the cheapest meat,
fish and vegetables, or exploring the London she knew so little :
the Round Church of the Templars, the pictures in the Royal
Academy at Somerset House, where young Emma had once
posed as a model and where the superstitious whispered that
Nelson's ghost already walked, for it had been the headquarters
of the Admiralty. But Emily was happiest in their dear room,
sewing delicate small garments for the one who was to come
before Christmas, her boy or girl; a boy, she hoped, to look like
Francis and avoid the ill luck which seemed to dog the women
of her family. Under her fingers a tiny coat was blossoming with
heartsease and rosebuds, violets and maybloom. Nothing in the
past seemed real. All her memories were clouded over, only the
present and the future mattering. She had no wish to visit
Merton, or even Clarges Street. Every week presents of food or
wine came by Nancy, the most trustworthy and inconspicuous
of Emma's servants. Emily would send back with Nancy a note
of thanks and reassurance in answer to the anxious scrawl sent
to her. Emma had been in Norfolk with Mrs Bolton. Horatia
was everybody's darling there, and they had all paid a return
visit to Merton. The Earl and Countess had unbent enough to
invite Emma to holiday with them at Cromer; 'but you know
my dear Emy I would not like to be away from London when
you was in the straw, tho' I know you are not due for some

months, I am almost affraid to go anywhere but that my heavy heart requires change and amusement. I hope you keep well and don't forget to take the Drops, they are excellent in this hot wether . . .'

'Why does she worry about me so?' Emily asked Francis. 'I was never better. There would be more sense if she worried about you, coming home so tired every night after that journey.'

'My love, it's far better for me to travel out to Edgware than to take a post in town, where I'm known. The air is good, and I don't mind the journey, truly.'

She stroked his hair. 'My lady sent a phial of rose-water to-day. Tomorrow you must take it with you. I do believe you have more white hairs. How bad I am for you !'

But at night, close in the hard, rough-sheeted bed, they were happy as neither had known happiness before, even though their lovemaking was gentle and incomplete for the sake of the coming child. Mice scuttled in the skirting-boards, flies and mosquitoes buzzed and bit; the open window let in smells of soap-works, breweries and boat-yards from the south bank of the river, and the noises of the traffic in the Strand which never ceased. And if Francis lay awake open-eyed in the darkness long after Emily had fallen peacefully asleep, he never allowed her to guess it.

Sitting at the window she stretched and yawned pleasurably. Almost five o'clock; he would be home soon. She had made a stew from an economical recipe of Mrs Cadogan's, and it simmered fragrantly on the hob of the little fire. Browsing round a bookshop she had found an old book of music which Francis would like, and had cleaned it and laid it on the table to await him.

The baby kicked sharply. It had begun to stir in the last few days, to Emily's awed delight. She laid her hand over it.

'Don't be impatient, my dear. This is no weather for you. Wait until the snows come, my little Winter King . . .'

Half dozing, she failed to hear the footsteps on the stairs. As the door opened she turned in surprise.

'Home so soon?'

But it was not Francis who stood in the doorway. She stared uncomprehendingly at the woman who confronted her, shutting the door behind her: a heavily-built woman wearing a yellow dress which made her skin look even sallower than it was. Her hair and her eyes were black, and the shadow of a moustache surrounded her full mouth. Emily had never seen her before.

'I think you have come to the wrong door,' she said, as the other remained silent. 'Are you looking for somebody?'

'Mrs Carew?'

'Yes. But—'

The woman strode forward and struck her across the mouth. 'Liar!' she said. 'Filth, whore, dirty thief!'

The chair went over backwards as Emily struggled out of it and tried to escape from the hands which were clawing at her clothes, striking at her face and body, tugging at her hair, while words she had never heard before came from the loose mouth. She tried to defend herself, but her attacker was strong and vicious. Turning her head towards the window, she screamed. There was nobody to hear her, only children playing and a dog lying in the sun. She was up against the wall now, the woman gripping her hands until she cried out.

'Who are you? What have I done? Oh, please let me go!'

The other's face was almost touching hers, the black eyes surrounded by yellowish whites glaring terrifyingly, the hot breath stinking of wine and onions and something else unfamiliar. Emily's wrists were jerked up until her arms were held against the wall in the position of crucifixion, while a strong knee pressed painfully against her stomach.

'Who am I? I am the wife of your fine "husband", madam, and I am going to kill you.'

'You're mad,' Emily gasped. The answer was a flood of words in a language she did not recognise, and one of her arms was released so that her assailant could strike her across the face. In spite of the pain she used the freed arm to hit back with, driving the woman back a few steps into the room. They struggled violently, Emily with the strength of desperation, but it was a losing fight. She reeled and fell to the ground, where the woman began kicking her.

'*That* and *that* and *that* for you! Bitch, trollop, hussy!' Emily tried to roll over so that the kicks would land on her back, but her movements were too clumsy. The woman was down on her knees, pummelling the twisting body with her fists.

'You thought – I had forgotten my husband – *Mrs Carew*. You see – you are wrong. Perhaps this – will teach you – to leave the married ones alone.' Another rain of blows beat about Emily's head and body. She felt a tooth loosen and a trickle of blood run from her lips. Then a savage banging of her head against the floor sent her into blessed unconsciousness.

When she came round she was lying where she had fallen. Aching from head to foot, she managed to struggle up on to one elbow, her head spinning with the effort. The terrible woman was gone. Gasping with pain, she felt in her skirt pocket for the little watch Mrs Cadogan had given her at Christmas. It was not there. She was aware of a great soreness in one of her fingers; it no longer wore the cheap wedding ring. The miniature of Francis's mother was gone from the wall, and a little figurine of a deer, the landlandy's property, from the mantelpiece.

There was no means of telling the time, but the sky had darkened and the air was cool; it felt like early evening. Then where was Francis? A cold shock went through her heart. Had the madwoman met and injured him, too? Frantically she tried to get up, supporting herself on the fallen chair, but her multiple bruises and strains dragged her down again. She picked up the only object she could reach, one of Francis's shoes, and beat on the floorboards. Surely somebody would hear. Then she remembered that the room below was empty; they would have taken it themselves but for its being dearer than the one a floor above. The landlady, then. But she would be down in the basement, and was elderly and deaf

'O God, what shall I do?' Tears of shock and fear began to trickle down her cheeks until she was weeping uncontrollably.

Then the pains began.

20

It was Nancy who found her the next morning. Emma had lain awake most of the night, visited by uneasy thoughts and half-dreams, all centring round her daughter. When Nancy brought her chocolate at eight o'clock, Emma said, 'I wish you'd step round to Arundel Street, Nan. I don't know how it is, but I feel something is wrong with – with Miss Emily.'

'Of course, my lady. But like as not nothing's wrong. You're a bit out of sorts, that's it. You know what you are for worriting about nothing.'

'Perhaps. But go just the same, there's a dear. Take some of the stuff Cribb sent up – there's a duck, and some spare ribs. I shan't feel happy till I know it's all fancy.'

But the sight which met Nancy's eyes at Arundel Street caused even her rosy Norfolk cheeks to pale. No answer coming to her knock, she opened the door with a cheerful greeting, then dropped her basket with a shriek. Someone she could barely recognise as her pretty Miss Emy lay on the floor in a pool of blood. She had been sick, and there was blood there too. At Nancy's cry her blackened eyes opened briefly, and some incoherent words came from her swollen mouth.

'Oh, my God!' said Nancy. 'Oh, Miss Emy, whatever's happened? No, don't try to say anything. I'll go and get help.' She hurtled down the stairs and into the street, where the staring eyes of step-washing housemaids and errand-boys followed her as she ran up towards the Strand. There she hailed a hackney-carriage, whose driver looked startled to be summoned by a young woman of the servant class with blood on her apron.

'Bottom of Arundel Street? Why, yer could walk there in a minute. You don't want no cab.'

'Never you mind that, young man,' said Nancy. 'There's a lady had a bad accident and I want help to take her home. You'll get well paid, don't fret about that.' And she scrambled in and slammed the door. The driver shrugged; it took all sorts.

When he followed her into the room where Emily lay he turned white at what he saw.

'Gaw! I've seen things, but that . . . is she dead, then?'

'No, but she soon will be if we stand here like dummies.' Pushing him aside she snatched a blanket from the bed and, with the cabman's help, raised the now unconscious Emily and wrapped her in it. Together they lifted her, but the cabman refused Nancy's help down the stairs.

'I can manage her, miss. Light as a feather, poor thing. Gaw!'

Had Dr Moseley been as much in favour of cupping as the majority of his profession, Emily's life would have been over within a few hours. But he was one of the few enlightened physicians who had begun to doubt that a patient who had lost quantities of blood could be benefited by losing more. 'The young lady has suffered a severe miscarriage, besides heavy battering,' he said to Emma. 'What blood she has left must be conserved.' He looked down with pity at the damaged body of the girl who had been one of his daughter's friends.

'But who can have done it?' cried Emma, wringing her hands. 'That wretch of a husband – or whatever we are to call him?'

'Well. The injuries could only have been inflicted by a strong man, I would judge. A woman might have used a knife, or her nails – and there are no scratch marks. Fists and feet have done this.'

Emma paced about. 'I can't understand it. He seemed such a mild young man, though he behaved wickedly. Why should he attack her like a St Giles's bully when she would have given him anything?'

The doctor shook his head. 'It seems that robbery was the motive, since her few valuables are missing. But the violence hardly suggests a musician – particularly an English one. Are you sure, my lady, that nobody else knew where to find Miss – er – Carew?'

'Indeed not!' Emma was vehement. 'That's to say – Nancy knew, of course, being our messenger. And my mother, who is as secret as the grave. Could I have rescued the entire royal family of Naples from the vile Bonapartists if I'd been given to gossip?'

'No, no, ma'am, of course not. But, Miss Connor, now. Would you say she might have mentioned it, casually, to a friend?'

Emma reluctantly consented to have Ann questioned. A flat denial was the result, and an affronted flouncing from the room. 'It's odd,' said Emma, looking after her cousin, 'how bad news takes people. When I saw Nancy and that cabman carry my poor Emily in, I dropped like a stone. But when Ann was told she burst into laughter until I had to slap her face. I suppose it was the hysterics. She wept afterwards, of course.'

'Ye-es . . .' Dr Moseley was thoughtful. 'Miss Connor strikes me as a little unbalanced. But the question is, how are we to find Miss – er – Carew's attacker? You are convinced it was not some random thief who knew she was alone at the top of the house? Her landlady denies having had any robberies before. Of course, there's Hungerford Market nearby, and the vagrants who scavenge in the river mud. Anyone could have slipped in on the chance of finding a lonely woman to rob. She used to sit by the window a great deal, I believe. Could she not have been seen by some villain or other?'

'The only villain is that Francis Carew, to my mind,' said Emma hotly. 'No doubt he wanted rid of the coming child and her too, having wormed his way into some other poor confiding female's confidence. Find him and you'll find the hand that struck my poor girl down.'

'The first step is surely to enquire of his employers. He may have met with some accident and been detained with them.'

'I wish I could think so. I got him the place myself, at Mr Hallet's of Edgware, through Dennis O'Kelly. I'll send to him today.'

But at Mr Hallet's the messenger was told that Mr Carew had

left there at the usual time on the afternoon of the attack, and had not been seen since. Bills were therefore posted and advertisements put in the newspapers for information concerning Francis Carew, with a full description; but nothing was heard of him. It was as though he had vanished from the face of the earth.

For two weeks Emily hovered between life and death, despaired of by those who watched over her. The bruises and swellings began to disappear, but she remained either insensible or delirious, and Dr Moseley diagnosed injury to the lung already weakened by pneumonia. Then, miraculously, youth took over. The haemorrhaging ceased and consciousness gradually came back. She was able to smile weakly at one or other of the familiar faces bending over her; and sometimes the faces were strange. One, large, oval and port-wine coloured, belonged to an equally large gentleman who seemed to be called Sir Harry. Emily woke from a doze one day to find him sitting at her bedside holding her hand and talking away to someone in a mixture of French and English. '*Elle ressemble beaucoup à ma mère, la pauvre petite,*' he was saying, '*mais les cheveux sont à toi, Emma.*' Emily wondered idly why she should look like his mother, and why he should converse in French, since he was without question English. He smelt very slightly and not unpleasantly of horses. When he had gone, Emma plumped up the pillows, and laughed and cried at once over the discovery of a bank-note underneath them.

Emily never asked for Francis; for she had no memory of him, or of what had happened to her. Only when she began to regain health she looked down at her body, and touched her slender waist with a look of puzzlement.

There was a night when she woke from a deep sleep to find a light shining in her eyes. Somebody was holding a candle, somebody with a sharp face and long wild black hair. 'Why didn't you die?' the person was saying. 'You were meant to die. I'd have done it better myself. I could do it now, as you lie there, and they'd never know, you dear little mamma's pet. Shall I? Shall I?'

The sharp face was getting nearer, and there was something between it and Emily: something round and patterned. She watched it helplessly as it approached, inch by inch. Suddenly it was withdrawn as the door opened.

'Oh, it's you, Ann,' said Mrs Cadogan. 'I thought I heard Emy call out.'

'Why, so did I, Aunt, and came at once to see to her.'

'Yes. Well, go back to bed now. I'll sit with her till she falls asleep again.' She sat down, and at once got up again. 'What a pesky hard chair. Where's the cushion gone?'

Next morning Emily remembered nothing of these happenings.

But a day came when, as the bed-curtains were drawn back and the sunlight flooded in, it was as though it also flooded into her mind, splintering the glass sphere in which she had existed since the attack. Suddenly she knew everybody and everything. Everything, that is, except what had happened that day in Arundel Street. Patiently they questioned her; but she could recall only details of the afternoon.

'I was sewing, I think. It was so hot I thought of letting the fire go out, but the cooking-pot was on the hob with our supper in it.'

Doctor Moseley tried again. 'Try to call back the moment when your assailant entered. Think of the door, and visualise the person. Was it a man or a woman?'

Emily passed her hand wearily over her brow. 'I'm sorry. I can see nothing. You know as much as I do.'

'There was no money to be found anywhere in the room. Do you think someone came to rob you?'

Mrs Cadogan said, 'Her watch that I gave her is missing, and her ring. And the landlady says there was a little ornament that's gone, too, and a miniature. Looks like the thief knew you was alone.'

'I am so tired,' Emily said. 'Please may I sleep a little now?'

Outside the room the three of them, Emma, Mrs Cadogan and the doctor, paused for conference.

'I fear there's little choice in the matter of the criminal,' said Dr Moseley. 'A man who would seduce a young lady in Miss – er—'

'Miss Carew,' said Emma quickly. 'We have decided to call her that in future. It is a kind of compromise between her past state and her present – not that we have any fondness for the name.'

'Exactly,' said the doctor. 'As I was saying, a man who would seduce a young lady in her situation is capable of anything, in my opinion. And we must remember that the musical temperament is – saving your presence, my lady – subject to sudden fluctuations and hysteric conditions. A brainstorm perhaps caused this young man to become temporarily deranged. When he saw the dreadful thing he had done, he fled in horror. His body may well be at the bottom of the river.'

'I hope it is!' cried Emma passionately. 'Or rather I hope it's not, so that I may get my hands on him one day, that wretch, that murderous deceiving villain! God help him if he crosses Emma Hamilton's path again!'

'I don't believe it,' said Mrs Cadogan, setting her mouth stubbornly. 'Francis Carew would never do such a thing. There's them that would, and them that wouldn't, and he's no more a murderer than I am.'

Alone, unable to sleep, Emily wept into her pillow. 'Francis, dearest Francis, come back to me! How could you leave me so?'

And three hundred miles away, on the high seas, Francis, filthy, unshaven and gaunt, was scrubbing the lower deck of His Majesty's ship *Culloden* – having been taken by the press gang on the information of Ann Connor.

21

Clouds like black pearls hung over the line of fells opposite Draycott Hall. The stones of the wall that barriered the drive from the lane were dark with the rain that had fallen that day. When the sun came out there would be a glow of autumn gold in the trees which were now sombre black sentinels in the valley.

Emily opened the window and breathed the strong sweet air. The doctors had been proved right in saying that her life could not be answered for unless she left London for a purer climate, so damaged was her health after the attack she had sustained and the loss of her coming child.

July 1806. She remembered back to the night she had left Clarges Street for the last time; weeping in her mother's arms, going back again and again for another farewell kiss. Emma's grief had been real and violent, all the more so because she could do nothing to help the daughter she loved. Merton had country air, to be sure, but in the troubled state of Emma's finances its future was uncertain. Perhaps she would give it up; she thought so sometimes, and went about seeking the approval of her friends. Then she recalled the happy days with Nelson and vowed, 'It shall be his shrine.' She would give up Clarges Street instead. So, rather than risk Emily's life, she must part with her.

As ever, when Emma made a decision she acted at once, and by her dynamic enthusiasm overpowered any objections other people might have. It took her no time at all to convince Lady Charlotte Denys that she needed a resident governess for her two young daughters, who spent most of their time at their home in Yorkshire. As soon as Emily was strong enough, she was whisked round to The Pavilion, Hans Place, that elegant house built by the great Henry Holland in the most fashionable quarter of Chelsea – Emma giving her during the drive a swift biography of the Denyses. Peter Denys, a shrewd young Swiss, had been employed as drawing-master at Lord Pomfret's country seat, Easton Neston in Northamptonshire, and had greatly impressed the Earl and Countess, so much so that he had actually been permitted to marry their daughter Lady Charlotte, after her father's death. 'And he, my dear, only a schoolmaster's son – his sister kept a boarding school across Blackfriars Bridge. Well, he got a fine fortune with her – the London house and land, some property in Bath and a country-house in Yorkshire. He manages the late Earl's lead-mines up there. Such a funny little man, but with a sound head on his shoulders.'

The sight of Lady Charlotte brought back with stinging sharpness the night of the musical soirée at Merton. Emily's pretty pig-lady was still in black, though now it was summer lace and gauze, setting off her dazzling white skin and the family pearls which looked dark against it. She greeted Emily kindly.

'I remember you so well from the musicale. My husband and I were so sorry to hear of your terrible experience. I hope you're quite better?'

'Almost, thank you, ma'am.'

'I have two small girls, as you know: Anna-Maria and little Charlotte. Emma tells me you are an excellent musician and are experienced in teaching children. Do you think you would do for them?'

Emma broke in with an impassioned eulogy of Emily's powers, which Lady Charlotte heard out with gentle patience.

'Yes, yes, I am sure you are right, dear Lady Hamilton. And it would relieve my mind to have someone responsible at Draycott Hall other than the servants when we are away, as we very often must be.

'Besides,' she went on, 'it would be such a pleasure to have someone musical in the house. My husband is quite music-mad, as well as being an artist of no mean accomplishment. Those are his.' She pointed with some pride to a number of darkish oil-paintings depicting what appeared to be cupids going about their daily tasks against backgrounds of ruined buildings and glimmering Tuscan landscapes with goats. Emily admired them. The

254

cultural field being established, Lady Charlotte delicately approached the matter of the terms, which seemed to Emily very generous. They parted in mutual agreement, Peter Denys appearing briefly in the hall as they left, peering short-sightedly at Emily and Emma and giving them a guttural greeting.

Emma professed herself very happy with the arrangement. 'They are good people, and so well connected. She will be very glad to have you with her, for though she's so amiable she has frequent fits of melancholy, I believe.'

Emily was surprised to hear it.

'Oh, something handed down from her mother, I was told; not madness or anything so disagreeable. And as to your saying the money is too much, they are almost next-door to Richmond, and you'll be hard put to it to save your money there, my dear – it's almost as fashionable as t'other Richmond in Surrey. Oh, the whole thing is quite perfect.' To prove which, Emma burst into tears. Emily embraced and comforted her.

'Oh, hush, hush. I hate leaving you, too. But I must be independent, and give you a chance to economise and get your affairs in order. I dare say I shall come to London often with them, and see you.'

Emma shook her head, sobbing. 'I would rather – it were anyone but you. Sarah Reynolds or any of them. Even Horatia, may God forgive me for saying so.'

'Yes, well He may. Think of it, you have Nelson's child to bring up. Is not that a charge worth having? She will do you and him justice, I'm sure. Look, I've made a little purse for her, with her name on in beads.'

But it was hard to be sensible and cheerful when the time came for Emily to take the night coach for Yorkshire. As they said their last farewells she was desperate enough to say what she had never dared to before.

'Have you nothing else to say to me? Nothing else to call me?'

Emma's eyes met hers – wonderful eyes, limpid and pleading as the eyes of a deer with the knife at its throat. But she said nothing, only gave the smallest headshake, and a last embrace.

And, after all, it was very pleasant at Draycott Hall. It lay west of Richmond, in lovely Swaledale, between the village of Grinton, with its bridges over the Swale and its little Norman church of St Andrew where the Denys family worshipped, and busy Reeth humming with the life of the farms and the lead-mines that brought so much money to Peter Denys's pockets. On a Saturday night its inns sent forth a noise that could sometimes be heard at Draycott; from the Black Bull, the Burgoyne Arms, the Shoulder of Mutton, the King's Arms, and the Red Lion came the sounds of farmworkers and miners enjoying themselves before the strictures of Sunday. The gentry of the district met at Reeth for balls and soirées, rather than in Richmond which was a place for shopping – a sophisticated, handsome little town whose castle was begun by the hands of the first Normans to reach Yorkshire, and whose Chapel of the Holy Trinity in the cobbled market-place still rang the Norman curfew.

Emily was attracted by the picturesque ruins which here and there basked by the river; places of pointed arch and skeleton lancet window, with sheep roaming among their fallen stones.

'Nunneries,' Peter Denys told her, pointing with his whip from the curricle he drove himself on the roads of the Dale. 'Marrick, there – Benedictine nuns in black. Ellerton, there – Cistercians in white. All gone now – finished off by old Henry. A great Catholic place, Swaledale, in the ancient times. Jacobites, many of them about Grinton, no more than fifty years ago. Went out and buried their crucifixes after Cumberland beat Charlie. They say he was an ancestor of my wife's.'

'Who, sir?'

'Oh, Peter!' Lady Charlotte remonstrated from the back of the vehicle. 'Pray don't bring up that old story. You know it isn't true.'

'Don't know anything of the kind, my love. Your father told me himself. Said the Butcher Cumberland sired your mother.'

'Well, I should hate to think so. Don't believe a word he says, Miss Carew.'

But, looking askance at Lady Charlotte's features, it did seem to Emily that a faint look of the House of Hanover lay upon them. Perhaps it was the explanation for the fits of melancholy Emma had mentioned, which were certainly no legend. After weeks of placid amiability, Lady Charlotte would withdraw into herself and retire to her room, seen only by her maid. Sometimes her muffled weeping could be heard; at others all was silence.

'She lies on her bed, just looking at nothing, miss,' confided Kitty Rucroft, the maid. 'Seems like a different person. Won't speak nor smile, even to the little girls. I'm that glad you've come, miss. Mebbe she'll cheer up a bit now.'

Emily smiled sardonically to herself. It seemed a major irony that she, nameless, bereaved, penniless but for her wages and Emma's charity, should be supposed an enlivening influence on this still young woman who had everything – a husband, children, three homes and boundless riches. Certainly Mr Denys was no Adonis, but the two girls were charming little creatures, the easiest pupils Emily had ever had, docile and intelligent, and the house was elegant and comfortable.

She had felt at home in it from the moment she had first gone through the front door, embellished with a stained-glass panel of Old Time, into the wide hall with its tessellated floor. The drawing-room was stately in the best Mayfair traditions, high-ceilinged, panelled in green and gold, with long mirrors set round its walls, and a shocking number of candles in the crystal chandelier below the great gilt ceiling-rose. The only thing she found disagreeable was the garden at the back of the house. It had been very oddly designed to slope steeply up from ground-level, forming a kind of hill which terminated in a stone folly, battlemented as were the garden walls. It darkened the drawing-room and all the other rooms at the back, giving a shut-in feeling. It resembled, when one came to look at it, one of those ancient barrows in which the bones of Saxon princes were found; poor Sir William would not have been able to resist excavating it.

Perhaps it was responsible for Lady Charlotte's black glooms. At any rate Emily was glad that little Charlotte and Anna-Maria

257

were allowed to run free in her company in the fields and among the fells, rather than staying cooped up in the garden. It made her smile to see their bright red heads bobbing along in front of her, and their long legs twinkling beneath comfortably short skirts, shrieking happily at each other before turning to bound back to her like puppies.

Of their elder brother, George, she saw little; he spent most of his time in London in Parliamentary circles, and was, his mother said, always in love. 'I only hope he will choose right in the end. He sees far too much of Eliza Lind, and heaven knows we want no alliance *there*.'

'Why not, ma'am?'

Lady Charlotte looked shocked. 'You mean Lady Hamilton has not told you? That dreadful woman, the one who was at Merton when we first met, *she* was a Lind.'

'Mrs Denis?'

Lady Charlotte closed her eyes with a pained expression. 'It makes me wince to hear her called that, though of course it is her name. People *will* say that she must be related to us, but her husband is Flemish, and Mr Denys, of course, was born in Geneva. There is no relationship at all; it is simply unfortunate that she is an acquaintance of Lady Hamilton's.'

The mention of Elena Denis sent Emily's thoughts back to the last time she had seen her, in Ann Connor's company. What a curious friendship that was – not, surely, a good one. It hurt her to think much of Clarges Street or Merton, and of all the unhappy events. It hurt much more to think of Francis. There was no question now that he had deserted her, and when she had most needed him. The thought that he might have been her assailant never entered her mind, and even Ann Connor had not ventured to put it there. It seemed as though a door had been closed and locked on the whole episode. And, as is the way of locked-up rooms, the compartment in her mind which held the knowledge of that day in Arundel Street grew airless and unsavoury, a place of dust and shadows.

When the Denyses went to London she stayed in Yorkshire

with the children. It seemed better to keep out of Emma's way altogether until she had composed herself after the catastrophe of Nelson's death – if that day ever came – enough to weigh her need for her daughter against her dread of scandal.

News came from time to time: an incoherent, almost unintelligible scrawl from Emma, with no punctuation or capital letters except in the wrong places, bemoaning the defection of her greatest friend, the wife of the new Earl, who had refused an invitation on the grounds of not wishing to meet company not proper.

I need not assure you my dear Emy I am so very particular about my company that it is a favour to be admitted to Merton for alltho I am not grown proudish yet I am *very very* severe about the Choice of my acquaintance the Revd Lancaster dined yesterday with me and told me I was an Example for the neighbourhood.

One letter contained news which disturbed Emily.

You will scarce believe this but that bad wicked girl Ann Connor goes about telling people she is called Carew and is my *daughter* I have turned her out of door and she may be at her Mothers home or in Hell for all I care but the damage is done and I can but write to all our friends to take no notice their is Madness in that family as you will know having lived with them the Brother Charles that our glorious Nelson took under his wing and granted a Commission ad to be took out of the Victory and put in the Portsmouth hospital with his hands bound violently insane.

Emily sighed. Only her devious, naïve parent could have written such a letter to the person most affected by Ann Connor's delusion. With considerable forbearance she wrote back to Emma, commiserating, and added:

I am glad to hear Ann is no longer a member of your household, however. I never thought her to be a good influence, as I told you at the time; and I have besides a curious impression that she is in some way my bad angel. I beg you, therefore, to have no more to do with her. There are plenty of persons genuinely affectionate towards you and thoughtful of your welfare without your encouraging the company of those who only desire to batten upon you. I know your kind heart, which might well tempt you to forgive Ann.

She sealed the letter firmly. 'Never let it be said I was vindictive,' she told it, 'but the enemy is the enemy, and no battle was ever won by obliging him.'

Over the months more bulletins came. Ann Connor was not mentioned, but Emily was told that Emma and Horatia spent their days in visits to one or another relation. The Matchams had moved to Sussex; they had all been to the new Worthing theatre to see *The Stranger*; Princess Charlotte was staying at Warwick House, but nobody had any eyes except for Horatia, Nelson's angel. Clarges Street was given up, Merton up for sale. Emily, reading between the lines, knew that Emma's life was a gradual descent into chaos and despair, disguised by a pathetic pretence of success.

She laid the letter down on the grass where she sat beside a stone wall on a hillside, looking across green and gold slopes dotted with sheep that seemed as tiny as a child's toy lambs towards the river. Cloud-shadows floated across the fells, followed by bursts of brilliant sunshine. Emily leant back and sighed with contentment. Charlotte and Anna-Maria were playing out of sight, their voices ringing on the still air. She should by rights call to them not to shout so; but why should they not shout, in their youth and freedom? The sadness roused in her by Emma's letter fell away, succeeded by utter peace. Safe, secure, among the hills that shut off the past.

Anna-Maria appeared over the crest of the hill, a bunch of wild flowers in her hand. 'For you,' she said, laying them ceremoniously in Emily's lap.

'For me? Thank you.' Anna-Maria was wearing her appealing expression, head on one side and right foot twisted behind the left ankle.

'When you look like that I know you want something. Come, what is it?'

'Only please may we take our stockings off?'

'Oh dear. Your mamma might not be pleased – but perhaps you may, just for a little, as it's so warm.' Before she had finished, Anna-Maria was off and away, and in a moment Emily heard her joyful shrieks mingling with her sister's. She got up and strolled towards them. They were paddling in the stream, their skirts hitched high, giggling and squealing as the cold mountain water lapped against their plump white legs. Anna-Maria tired first and bounded out to fling herself down beside Emily, who had settled against the trunk of a hawthorn. Charlotte followed her, flopping like a puppy on the grass, her eyes screwed up against the sun, red-head freckles gathering on her small snub nose. A lamb wandered close to them, eyed them suspiciously, and bounded back to its mother.

'Have you got any little girls?' asked Charlotte suddenly.

'Why, no, Charlotte – I am not married.'

'Oh. Will you have, one day?'

'How can I tell? That's as God wills.'

'Should you like some children?'

'Very much. But since I have you, I can't complain, can I?'

What would it have been, the child lost on that day she could not remember? A brown-eyed boy to break the chain of ill-luck that bound her and Emma and the blue-eyed women who had gone before them? She pushed the dream from her and began to gather daisies to make crowns for the children's hair.

In the Java Sea, off the coast of Batavia, the *Culloden* was in action against a French privateer. In the main battery men were dying from the enemy's broadside fire, those who lived slipping in their blood. Francis Carew was one of these, the 'after-men' despised by true sailors for being landsmen, pressed men, unskilled in seamanship, 'silk-stockinged gentlemen'. Francis looking anything but silk-stockinged, half naked as he was, streaming with smoke-blackened sweat, dashing to and from the after-magazine with supplies of powder for the guns. The crash and thunder of the cannon and the screams of the wounded mingled with the whistling of the round-shot and the shattering of timbers as a shot went home. Francis had never believed in hell, but he did now, and there was no need to die to experience it. He felt neither fear nor the exaltation of battle; he was one among other blackened devils choking and coughing in sulphurous heat and stench.

22

It was late on a May evening that Emily first saw the nun.

Young George Denys's birthday fell within a period when the family were out of town; a fact for which his mother thanked Providence. To entertain the flock of London beaux and belles who were George's friends would have involved festivities on a far more lavish scale than a modest ball in Yorkshire. Money was of very little object, but Lady Charlotte did not share her friend Emma Hamilton's passion for large assemblies. George might grumble at the rustic nature of the occasion, but his mother was firm.

'You know the Pavilion house is being decorated, and I cannot possibly interrupt that after all the trouble it has been. And this is not even your twenty-first birthday. Next year, when you reach your majority, it will be a very different matter.'

'Very well, Mamma.' George sighed. 'I suppose I may ask Caroline and her brother? At least they talk about something other than lambing and lead.'

'By all means. Your father detests the Hills but I've nothing against them myself.' His mother settled herself to making a list of desirable guests. As it happened, nobody on it proved obnoxious to George, particularly as a number of pretty girls had been invited, to the annoyance of Miss Caroline Hills, who had marked George down for herself.

Emily, much to her own surprise, was invited to join the festivities. Lady Charlotte had so far kept her firmly pigeon-holed as an employee from the 'poor relation' class; it did not do to ask too keenly the exact status of these young people, of whom most good families had one or two. They were to be treated as ladies, of course, but not as family equals, and Emily had lived so since she came to Draycott. But some quirk of Lady Charlotte's resulted in her finding herself in her best gown, dancing quadrilles with George and his friends and attracting more than a few admiring glances. Peter Denys raised his lorgnette to his short-sighted eyes to follow the slight figure in the simple dress of green and white stripes in the graceful movements of the dance.

'A pretty girl, dat,' he said to his wife. 'Strange how gover-nesses merge into their backgrounds; one thinks of dem as young persons. You'd better watch out for George's heart, my love. I believe it's disengaged at present.'

Indeed, George was whispering quite extravagant compliments into Emily's ear and pressing her hand in a marked manner. He was in duty bound to take Caroline Hills down to supper, but managed to separate himself from her for long enough to get to Emily's side with a large glass of claret cup, and to remain with her while she drank it thirstily, hot from the energetic dancing. It seemed to go instantaneously to her head; the room began to tilt round her, and faces blurred and dazzled in the head of the candles. She rose, with a slight stagger.

'I am so sorry, Mr George, but I think I feel just a little faint. Will you forgive me if I take the air?' George began eagerly to offer to accompany her, but she was gone, unwilling to make a fool of herself before her employers.

It was blissfully cool in the garden, and light enough for her to see her way up the path that led to the terraced walk. She strolled leisurely along it, feeling her head become steady again and her cheeks cool. The shape that glimmered by the stone archway she thought at first to be a bush in blossom, picked out by the starlight. Something about it drew her nearer, and as her eyes became used to the dusk it resolved itself from an amorphous mass into the form of a woman. The figure, which stood motionless, seemed to be wearing filmy light-coloured draperies. The face was invisible, but there was a veil over the head, coming low down on the brow.

In the space of a moment Emily took it to be a servant trespassing into the garden to keep a rendezvous, and she was about to retreat when it occurred to her that the woman might be a sleepwalker, in danger of falling down the precipitous garden steps. The thought had hardly entered her mind when a curious, cold sensation began to creep up her spine; a feeling unknown from experience, yet familiar from far back in the past, her own or her ancestors'. Her mouth went dry and her scalp began to prickle. As if in a nightmare, she felt rooted to the spot, unable to stir. With a tremendous effort she forced her feet to move, back towards the path to the house, keeping her eyes on the figure all the time. Then, as a sharp stone jabbed her foot through the thin sole of her dancing-sandal, she looked down to kick it away. When she lifted her eyes the shape was gone.

She began to shake uncontrollably, hurrying down to the safety of the bright windows and the music. Reaching the door, she stopped to steady herself. It was nonsense, of course. The figure might have been an illusion of the half-light. It had looked uncommonly like someone in the dress of a nun – not that Emily had ever seen one, but popular novels were full of them, and Emma was fond of posing for Attitudes in a nun's habit. In that case the visitant might be some local eccentric, one of those pathetic elderly women who wander the roads in strange clothing, talking to themselves; there was one in Wimbledon who dressed entirely in white and was given to stopping people to exhort them to follow her to her Master in Heaven. It would be easy enough for someone to get into the garden of Draycott Hall from the road, or even from the fells above.

Emily drew a long breath. That was the explanation. The horrid sensation of chill could be put down to a night breeze striking through her flimsy dress, though the air had seemed perfectly still: unusually still.

But it did not account for a heaviness that had come over her, a feeling of spiritual blackness, of mindless despair. She was reluctant to enter the lighted room, but there was no other way of getting into the house. As she appeared in the supper-room, where some dancers were still refreshing themselves, George, gnawing a chicken-leg, saw her and left his companions to greet her.

'Where the dickens have you been, Miss Emily? I've been

waiting to take you up for the cotillion. Are you over your faintness?'

Emily shook her head and went past him, leaving him open-mouthed, disappointed. Regaining her room, she flung herself on the bed, uncaring about the creasing of her dress or the earth on her sandals, and lay staring into the dark.

It was the beginning of a nightmare. The terrible depression lay over her for two days, bringing with it the nebulous feeling of guilt she remembered from childhood, when she had wondered what wrong she had done to be banished by her family to the Blackburns. The agony of the day she had broken Greville's statue came back as sharply as though it had just happened, followed in quick dreadful succession by other memories of sins or faults unremarkable at the time, now seeming enormous, and at last the worst sin of all, when she had lived with Francis outside marriage and had conceived a child who was to die before its birth. She was beyond reason, bowed down with guilt. Giving the excuse of a headache she kept to her room, visited anxiously by Lady Charlotte who provided her with her own vinaigrette and a flask of eau-de-Cologne.

The immense relief, as the black cloud passed, sent her into an extreme of happiness. The little girls had missed her, George had missed her; it was like a return from a great distance to the warmth and light of home. For three weeks her life was normal; then, going to her room to change her dress before supper one evening, she opened the door to be confronted by the figure she had seen in the garden. It was standing, tall and still, beside the fireplace, almost blending into the wallpaper of striped gold and white, but unmistakably a woman's form in a long robe drawn in at the waist with a cord from which a crucifix hung. Emily, breathlessly staring, was aware of neither colour nor features in the thing, only of a projection of intent regard and menace. Then, before she could back away, the apparition was gone. There was nothing where it had stood, only the wall, and a bell-pull which Emily realised she had been able to see through the figure's outline.

Just as in the garden, after the fear came the awful melancholy, this time lasting for three days. Again she stayed in her room, unable to face company, unable to weep or to pray. The pattern was repeated once more before Lady Charlotte spoke to her husband.

'This is growing quite impossible. The girl seems half mad when she gets into this state. Oh, you see little of it, away at your mines and up and down to London, but I have to stay here and see the children losing their lesson-times and growing wild, and the servants grumbling because they can never get into her room to clean it, and cook fussing because the food goes to waste. I never bargained for this when I obliged Lady Hamilton by taking her in.'

Peter, who was deep in the financial columns of *The Times*, emerged from them sufficiently to suggest that Emily might have taken to drink. His wife snorted.

'Rubbish! One can always tell – there is the smell if nothing else. Besides, she hardly touches wine. No, it is some sort of tiresome illness. When I was a girl there was a great deal of talk about greensickness in young women, but I put *that* down to tight corseting. Now they're all wearing dresses with no waists it don't apply any longer. In any case, the girl is in her twenties.'

'Well, my love,' said Peter mildly, removing his spectacles and laying down his *Times*, 'you do have very similar attacks yourself, remember. And Dr Bradberry has never found a satisfactory explanation for them.'

Lady Charlotte paused, with her mouth open to speak, and stared at him. 'It's a most extraordinary thing when one comes to think of it, but I have not had one for months. They have quite ceased – touch wood.'

'That's true.' Peter meditated. 'Your spells of melancholy have always taken place here, if I remember, never in Chelsea. Can there be something deleterious in the well water? Or the climate?'

'I am still drinking the water and breathing the air, and I am no longer subject to the attacks. No, we must send for Dr Bradberry.'

The doctor examined Emily thoroughly, and pronounced her healthy though naturally frail of constitution. He was a little puzzled by certain marks on her body which suggested that it had been subjected to violence at some recent date, but tactfully forbore to enquire into them, or into others which implied that she was less than virginal. 'There seems nothing to explain Miss Carew's symptoms but a tendency to migraine. It has usually manifested itself by the twentieth year, but . . .' He pulled his beard. 'A course of the Harrogate waters can do nothing but good.' He scribbled in a notebook. 'If you will send a servant to my surgery, milady, some medicine will await him.'

Harrogate was an entire success. The family had taken off for London to attend George's wedding to Miss Eliza Lind, for whom he had abandoned Miss Hills. Emily and the children put up in comfortable lodgings with a maid in attendance, and enjoyed the air and amenities of the pleasant little spa, the children pretending extreme revulsion for the waters of John's Well and the saline springs of Low Harrogate. 'Ugh! How can you take such stuff, Miss Carew?' But they romped happily on the grass of the Stray, and enjoyed outings by carriage to the romantic ruins of Fountains and Bolton Abbeys – Emily's enjoyment being slightly modified by the fear that the apparition might loom up in such appropriate surroundings. But it kept away, and for a blissful fortnight she was at peace, herself, untroubled by mad thoughts. It had gone, then, and she was free. She travelled back to Draycott Hall with colour in her cheeks and a smile for everybody.

The nun was waiting. This time in the stable courtyard, in a dusky corner by the old servants' quarters, still as ever, and as menacing. Emily had seen the set face of her employer during her last spell of melancholy; this time she forced herself to stay out of her room, behave as nearly normally as possible, and present a cheerful face to the household. It deceived nobody, but at least she was fighting the evil, regardless of Lady Charlotte's tight lips and the sad wondering faces of the children. The time came when she could pretend no longer; the time had come to give way. Whatever the apparition wanted of her, she could no longer bear the stress of fear and mental misery. The night before she resolved to speak to Lady Charlotte there appeared before her in a dream the image of Mother Demdike, as vividly as when she and Maria had stood before her in the little room above the green door. The witch held a bunch of green herbs in her arm, and behind her red flowers bloomed on the narrow sill of the latticed window. Her lined face was sorrowful, her voice clear and kind.

'Ye forgot to summon me, lass. Earlier I might have helped, but now the other's spell's too powerful. Pray every night, and keep a branch of rowan in thy room, and when time offers go from this place.'

The voice was still ringing in Emily's ears when she woke. After breakfast she went to Lady Charlotte's parlour.

Her ladyship's face paled from its normal bright colour as Emily told her story. Then, 'Nonsense,' she said. 'What a ridiculous, superstitious tale. Who has been filling your head with notions about ghostly nuns and such? The servants, I warrant.'

'No, ma'am,' said Emily earnestly. 'Nobody has said a word to me. I know nothing of the history of Draycott or of spirits, but I swear to you I saw it as clearly as I see you, and I think if I see it again I shall go mad.'

Lady Charlotte's cheeks blazed again with the colour of affronted pride. 'Very well,' she said, 'pray leave at once. There is no need to work out your notice. Governesses are easy to find. I hope that in your next place you will be untroubled by figments from the novels of Monk Lewis, and that your unfortunate pupils will suffer less from the loss of teaching than my daughters have done.' She bent her head over her desk and wrote furiously. Emily turned and left the room, choking back tears. She might at least have listened, have asked questions, said something of her own attacks.

Lady Charlotte dashed into a letter to a confidential friend.

'Unfortunate girl! Why should her delusions be inflicted upon our family? I fancied that George's eyes lit on her somewhat, and tho the Hamilton connection wd. be no bad one, albeit rumour says *she* is fallen on hard times, I am only too glad my boy is married and out of danger of an alliance with such an hysterical creature. Eliza will make him a good wife, after all, I think.'

Emily, at the same time, was writing to Emma, asking if she might come to Clarges Street or Merton until she could obtain another situation. Days came and went, but the post brought no answer. In the end, worn down by Lady Charlotte's grim looks and the children's appealing faces and sad questions, Emily booked a passage on the coach from Richmond to London, and said farewell to Draycott Hall for ever, her baggage addressed to the Golden Cross Inn; for other address she had none.

Because she was not quite happy in her mind about Emily's dismissal, Lady Charlotte threw herself with more than usual briskness into the removal of all traces of her. The maids were sent upstairs with brushes and pails, a man sent for from Reeth to repaper the room in a more modern style. 'It will do very well for the girls when they are older,' she told her husband, 'a fine room with a good view. Meanwhile we must take them to Chelsea with us – or perhaps put them to school in Bath. This place is far too rustic for growing girls.'

Peter nodded without enthusiasm. He had been very sorry to see little Miss Carew go. In his youth he had known poverty, had earned his living as a schoolmaster, like his father, had seen his sister struggle to run a boarding-school in an unpromising neighbourhood. It was all very well to be an earl's child, like Charlotte. Others had to work. He hoped very much that Emily would fare well.

They were taking coffee in the morning-room when an agitated tap announced Kitty Rucroft and Maggie Garth, the two maids who had been sent to clear up Emily's room. Kitty sketched a curtsey.

'If you please, milady, there's summat queer upstairs. When we rolled back carpet to clean t'floor, brush-head went reight through boards.'

'Into an 'ole,' added Maggie.

Lady Charlotte looked from one to the other. 'You mean a mouse-hole?'

'Weren't no mouse, milady. Mice lives in skirtin'-boards; this were by t'fender, and it goes deep.'

Peter swallowed the last of his coffee. 'Very well, Kitty. I will come and see.'

With Dick Alderson, the only manservant to be found, they stood around the black hole in the old boards of the bedroom which had been Emily's. The wood had splintered under the impact of Kitty's brush, but not merely with the ravages of dry rot; there was a clear line where at some time the boards had been cut to make a square panel that could be lifted up. Dick put his hand inside and felt round the edges.

'There's a hinge, milady, seems like.' He exerted pressure and the panel reluctantly creaked upright, flakes of rotten wood breaking off where the brush had penetrated. A musty air came up to them, causing Lady Charlotte's nose to wrinkle. Dick knelt and peered down.

'Theer's a rope-ladder, or a bit of one,' he said. 'I reckon I'd best get a proper ladder from t'stable and see what's to be seen, before ony necks get broken.' He left, and returned swiftly with a sturdy ladder which he lowered down the hole, looking up triumphantly to say, 'It's touched bottom. Ah thought mebbe it were too short. S'll Ah go down an' see, sir?'

'I think you'd better, Dick,' Peter said. 'Take a candle with you. One of you girls light one for him. If it goes out we shall know the air is foul, and you must come up at once.' Other servants had silently collected, drawn to the spot by some mysterious message that spreads through a house at such times. Eagerly they watched Dick cautiously disappear, first body, then head, until he was gone altogether and the dark depths glowed with a faint flickering light.

271

'Keep away from the edge, all of you,' said Peter. 'De whole floor may be rotten.' Below them, Dick's voice was heard to utter what sounded like an oath.

'What is it, Dick?' Lady Charlotte called. After a moment Dick replied.

'Ah'll want a box – tea-chest, summat like that – or an owd sheet.'

Maggie went scurrying up to the attics, returning with a deal box which had held household goods when the Denyses had moved into Draycott Hall. 'This big enough?' she asked, holding it where Dick could see it.

'Aye, that'll do.' They heard him cough, then give a cataclysmic sneeze. The light was still burning clearly.

'No leak from the sewers, evidently,' said Peter. 'But what the devil was this place made for?'

Dick emerged in stages from the darkness, the box held above him. He was black with dust and veiled in cobwebs, 'Ah con tell you, sir,' he said. 'It were a priest's hole.'

Amid gasps and shrieks from his audience, he unpacked the box of its gruesome contents: a jumbled heap of bones, yellow-white with age, the upper part of a skull, some rags that were all that remained of the clothing. Intact was a dulled metal chain with an ivory crucifix suspended from it, and among the bones some mouse-nibbled leaves of paper bore still legible Latin printing. The Denyses and their servants stared transfixed at the remains.

'He were an owd priest, he were,' Dick said, pleased at his own scholarship. 'When owd King Harry booted t'monks out, he came here to hide. They must have forgot him, so he clemmed to death.'

'No!' said Lady Charlotte strongly. 'Not a priest – a nun !' Very gracefully she subsided on to the floor in a dead faint.

Emily had no idea that a footman from the Denyses' Chelsea house was scouring London for her. She sat uncomfortably in the smallest and most uncomfortable of the Golden Cross's rooms, counting her money and wondering what she should do if she could not trace Emma. Clarges Street was let to another tenant, who knew nothing of Lady Hamilton's whereabouts. Sacrificing two shillings of her small hoard, Emily took a coach to Merton. Dismounting, she walked up to the familiar gates. They were unlocked, and there were no curtains at the windows of the little gatehouse. Within the gates the lawns grew ragged, weeds and dandelions coming up where there had once been only smooth velvet grass. The bushes were ragged, the roses going back to bramble, the Little Nile's waters scummy with the growth the children called Jinny Greenteeth. As for the house, it had the unmistakable look of a place abandoned. The windows were still curtained, but some were broken. Emily stepped up on to the balcony where she had once sunned herself, at peace with the world. Through the dirty windowpanes she could see shrouded furniture, chandeliers muffled with cloths like giant puddings, thick dust everywhere. Over the drawing-room mantelpiece a life-size portrait of Emma smiled towards one of Nelson on the side wall. A mouse scurried across the floor, disappearing under Emma's shrouded harp.

Emily shivered, and retraced her steps to the village. In the pastry-cook's she asked if she might have a cup of tea, and was given one by plump Mrs Perry, who failed to remember her.

'Lady Hamilton? Why, we hear nothing of her these days. Must be all of two years since she was at Merton Place. Poor old Mrs Cadogan ran it for a bit, then Mr Goldsmid bought it off her ladyship, and – do you mean you've not heard, miss? I thought everyone knew.'

Emily shook her head. 'I've been in the North.'

'Why, poor man, he shot himself through the head there, in the shrubberies, not a fortnight since. They say he went mad through money troubles, something to do with the City. Such a kind gentleman, so generous to the tradespeople, we miss him sorely. I'm sure I could have cried my eyes out when I heard. They say there was blood everywhere . . .'

Emily's attention wandered from Mrs Perry's laments. It was

as hard to believe that genial Abraham Goldsmid was dead by his own hand as to believe that Merton Place was as dead as a house could be that was not pulled down. She made herself listen to what Mrs Perry was saying; the other Goldsmid family, the brother's, had come to be with the widow and her children. Their grief had been terrible, their mourning above all that was ever seen, even for Jews – the house shut up for a week, nobody speaking or eating, then the grandest funeral, six plumed black horses and a train of mutes, a ton of beautiful flowers covering the coffin in the glass coach as it made its way up to the Jewish cemetery in London. Mrs Perry wiped her eye at the remembrance.

Emily stood up. 'I must go and see Mrs Goldsmid,' she said. 'Poor lady. I used to teach Rachel.'

'Did you, miss? Ah, poor little Rachel, her daddy's favourite. I doubt if they'll see you, miss.'

Mrs Perry was right. The front door of Morden Hall opened only after Emily had jangled the bell several times, and the impassive dark-faced butler who answered it informed Emily that Mrs Goldsmid was still prostrated and not receiving. He appeared not to recognise Emily, though she had so often visited the house in the old days.

'Please give her my sincere condolences,' Emily said. 'Joseph – have you heard anything of Lady Hamilton lately?'

'I couldn't say, miss, I'm sure. I believe there was a wreath. Good day, miss.'

The door was shut, even banged, in her face. Slowly she walked away, scuffing through the September leaves as she had done as a child, towards the London coach.

23

There is no isolation quite like being friendless in a great city. In spite of having lived for a time at 11 Clarges Street, Emily knew nobody in London outside Emma's circle, and pride kept her from approaching anybody within it. She had a shrewd idea that those who had treated her as an equal when she was in Emma's household would not be at all anxious to recognise her away from it; so she discarded any thought of calling on Georgiana Devonshire or Lady Bess Foster. There were the musical set, of course, but she had no idea where to find Mrs Billington, the Storaces, or Mrs Bianchi.

The only possibility for her was to get work. But what kind of work? A domestic agency might find a post for her as companion, governess, even nursemaid. She had seen such an agency somewhere in Fleet Street, and determined to call there the morning after her melancholy visit to Merton. She dressed as quietly and neatly as she could (which was not difficult, as she had very few clothes), but at the last minute discovered a hole in one of her gloves. She cursed it silently. One might apply for work looking far from prosperous, but to appear slovenly was unthinkable. Once more she opened the little box in which she kept her little store of guineas – savings from her wages and the extra money Lady Charlotte had pressed her to take.

The box was empty.

Hardly able to believe her eyes, she searched frantically in the drawer where it had been, in case she had absent-mindedly put the money back between the folds of a garment or a scarf. But it was not there, or anywhere else in the room. Emily began to weep helplessly. There was no need to count the money in her purse; exactly one shilling and twopence were left in it from the fare from Merton. 'Idiot! Ninny! Numskull!' she said aloud, 'to leave money in an unlocked box in an unlocked room. This is

London honesty, then. Well, we shall see.' A wave of hot anger dried her tears. The box in her hand, she went swiftly downstairs to the coffee-room where a gloomy-looking waiter was clearing up tables after the departure of a coach. 'I want to see the landlord,' she said imperiously. The man jerked his thumb over his shoulder towards the next room, a small office in which bills were made out and accounts kept. Emily tapped and entered, to find the landlord, Mr Busby, seated at a table engaged in adding up aloud.

'. . . and ninepence ha'penny,' he concluded. 'Well, young woman, come to pay me? I've your bill here somewhere. Yes, here we are.'

'I can't pay you. I have been robbed, by one of your servants or a guest. Look.' She showed the box. 'All the money I had was in here, and now it is gone.'

He sneered. 'A likely story !'

'It's true ! I had twelve guineas in that box. I am not a liar, sir.'

He looked her up and down insultingly. 'And where did you get twelve guineas, my fine gal? Out of your mistress's pocket or your master's strong-box? I know your sort, well-spoken ladies' maids cut and run to better 'emselves. See this?' He pointed to a whistle on the table. 'I keeps this to whistle up the Runners when a customer like you comes along singing the old song to me. Shall I blow it? Eh?'

'You may do what you like. It would be more sensible to question your staff and find the thief.'

'My staff is honest, miss, I'll have you know, which is more than can be said for you, most like. I thought it was a rum thing, a gal on her own staying at an inn.'

'I have greatly disliked staying at your inn. It is noisy, uncomfortable and dirty. I have only stayed here because I – I have left my situation and am looking for another. As soon as I have my money back I shall go, have no fear !'

He grinned. 'You'll get no money back from me, my lady. Nor you won't leave till my bill's paid.'

Like a bright light, a name flashed into her head. 'I can

276

borrow some money from – an acquaintance. If you distrust me so much, keep my clothes and belongings until I come back.'

The landlord put his head out of the door and shouted to the waiter. 'Simmy! Here a minute. Keep an eye on this young piece while I'm upstairs.'

Emily waited, flushed, humiliated and furious, as the old man kept watch over her with the air of one who had done the same thing many times, his arms folded across his dirty apron. In the coffee-room new arrivals were banging on the tables and shouting for him, summonses which he ignored completely.

In a few minutes the landlord returned. 'Well, your odds and ends will do, I suppose.' In fact, he had been agreeably surprised at the silver-backed brush and comb, the good quality of the clothes, and the modest little necklet of pearls he had discovered by ransacking the drawers. If the girl didn't come back he would be more than satisfied with the value of them.

Emily left him without a word, walking swiftly and purposefully past the old Royal Mews and the district known as Pudding Island, from which came a tantalising smell of coffee and hot pies. She was very hungry, but there was no time to stop; she had a long way to go.

The name which had come into her mind was Greville. She had not seen him since she was too young to remember. After Sir William's death he had paid Emma out in harassment for her old offence of having married his uncle. He had not been a caller at Clarges Street, and on the one occasion when he had been invited to Merton he had cried off under pretence of having the influenza. So it would be possible to ask him for a loan of money without the embarrassment of asking one of Emma's friends and being refused. 'Besides,' Emily thought, 'I believe he owes me something, if not money.' She remembered Emma saying that he still lived at Paddington Green, though not in the same house in which Emily had been born.

It was a long walk to the village of Paddington, and she had to ask the way several times, but at last she reached the Green and stood hesitating, looking for someone to ask. A maid with a shopping-basket merely stared at her and shook her head at Greville's name. His house might be any of the handsome houses surrounding the Green. Then she thought of the church. They had attended it, Emma had told her, though that must have been another building, for this one looked very new. She went in, and was glad to see a man who must be the vicar laying out orders of service in the choir. He looked up at her approach, and smiled.

'Can I help you?'

'If you please, sir. I am looking for Mr Charles Greville's house, and I am not sure—' His expression halted her.

'My dear young lady, Mr Greville died over a year ago.'

Wearily she returned to the Golden Cross. The landlord was standing in the entrance lobby; and she thought he looked a shade disappointed to see her.

'My friends have gone away,' she said. 'I cannot pay you.'

He nodded. His course of action was already decided. 'Then you'll have to work, won't you, till your debt's paid off.'

'Work?'

'Kitchen work – housemaid's work if you like that better. Can you peel spuds, make beds, clean up the taproom, wash glasses, or are you going to tell me your fingers are too fine for scrubbing?' He eyed the small pretty hands with admiration, and then transferred his gaze meaningly to the whistle.

So it was back to scullery-maiding, which she thought had been left behind when she quitted the Blackburns'. And why not, since if she refused she would be not only penniless but without a roof over her head.

'I can do any honest work,' she said with pretended indifference.

It had not been pleasant staying at the Golden Cross as a guest, but working there as a servant was acutely unpleasant. She was banished from the stuffy little room to a long dark attic which she had to share with five other women, maids and cleaners. They resented her presence and made her life as uncomfortable as they could by jeers, rude remarks, practical jokes

278

and anything else that occurred to them. The washing-water in the morning was thrown out of the window before she could get to it, so that she had to go downstairs unwashed, and earn a reproof from Cook. The worst of the kitchen jobs were given to her: the plucking of chickens and cleaning of fish, things that made her feel sick. On the fourth day of her employment the head of the female domestics ordered her to go up and empty the guests' chamber-pots.

It was the last straw. She refused, and the woman struck her across the face.

'Stuck-up bitch! Think you're too good for us, don't you?'

Emily went straight up to the landlord's office and marched in without knocking, to his manifest surprise.

'I have been asked to do a most humiliating task,' she said. 'I have refused to do it, and been struck. Your people are persecuting me and making my life a misery, through no fault of my own. I would rather beg in the streets than stay here, and I will.' She tore off her apron and threw it at him. 'I would like my own clothes back, please.'

He regarded her with something like respectful admiration; he liked a girl of spirit.

'Hoity-toity! What a little shrew. Now sit down, and we'll talk it over.'

Reluctantly Emily sat down.

But the gratifying result of her mutiny was that she was taken off kitchen duties and given only reasonable tasks such as the mending of linen and the counting of sheets and towels. She won Cook's heart by volunteering to help at rush-hours when famished, clamouring travellers arrived in hordes; and to her immense relief she was allowed to have a room to herself, a tiny room, under the rafters, with no carpet, a mere slit of a window, and mice, but to her a palace after the dormitory.

It was not long before she discovered the main reason for this change. The landlord had taken more than a slight fancy to her, having decided that after all she was a lady, no doubt the well-connected daughter of parents from whom she had run away rather than marry an unwelcome bridegroom. There was a trying scene when, going up to her attic late, she found him sitting hopefully on her bed. With her new-found ability to stand up for herself she told him tersely that if he persisted in remaining, she would inform his wife. Furious but routed, he left.

After ten days he sent for her, still hopeful of winning her favour, to tell her that she had paid off her debt to him in work and was free to leave.

But, she asked herself, where would she go? Surely it was better to stay at the inn, with a roof of sorts over her head and food provided, than to cast herself on a world which was uninterested in unprotected females.

'I would prefer to remain, sir,' she said. 'At least for the moment, until I can either find my friends or obtain some more suitable employment. You see, I am being quite forthright with you.' She gave him a smile which ensured her the answer she wanted.

'Stay if you like. We can do with plenty of help till winter sets in and fewer folk are travelling. I'll pay you what the chambermaids get.' Baffled, yet still hopeful, he eyed the slender waist which an apron emphasised, and the pretty auburn ringlets set off becomingly by the little cap with white ribbons. Damn it, he thought, if the wench ain't staying on purpose to torment me.

On a day in late October, Emily was taking an off-duty walk round Covent Garden, savouring the fresh fragrances of flowers, fruit and vegetables after the horsy and tobacco-heavy air of the Golden Cross. She paused outside the newly-built Theatre, which had arisen in its glories of marble and porphyry from the ashes of the old one destroyed two years earlier in the fire which also wrecked the fortunes of the Kembles. On the playbills outside their names appeared, for they had struggled back to popularity by putting on shows which would attract audiences large enough to fill the vast spaces of Robert Smirke's huge temple. And there was the honoured name of their sister, Sarah Siddons, never to be forgotten from those evenings in the Theatre Royal,

Manchester. But no friend of Emma's seemed to be playing at the Garden. Emily turned away, and ran straight into the arms of Elena Denis.

When the cries of astonishment and pleasure had died down and warm kisses and embraces had been exchanged, to the delight of the market porters who witnessed them with salty comment, Elena whisked Emily into a coffee-shop and overwhelmed her with raptures.

'That I should find you – and here – when everybody has been looking for you high and low, and even an advertisement put in the *Morning Chronicle*, and my Lady Denys all but having the river dragged for your body, and poor Emma quite frantic – my dear child, where *have* you been?'

Emily took a deep breath and began her explanation, interrupted not much more than four times a sentence. But when she came to the story of the ghostly nun, Elena swelled and crimsoned so with portent that Emily was forced to let her have her head.

'But that is just *it*! After you had gone they found the bones and relics which proved there truly had been a nun at Draycott Hall, or at any rate in the old part of it where your bedroom was, and that she must have starved to death during the persecutions' – she crossed herself hastily – 'and Lady Charlotte believes now that you were not simply having tiresome fits of vapours, and that her own *crises des nerfs* were caused by the same thing. Oh, she is quite converted and all remorse, and you are to go and see her and all will be forgiven, that is if *you* will forgive *her*.'

Emily shook her head. 'I could never go there. A place where one had known such fear – no, it would be impossible, though Lady Charlotte is kind to think of it.'

'But *chérie*, consider, the ghost is laid!'

'How do we know?' countered Emily. 'In the romances such spirits prefer their remains to be buried with proper rites, I believe, and I can scarcely imagine Mr Edmondson consenting to hold a Roman Mass at Grinton. Now please do let us talk

about something else, for the mere mention of those times gives
me horrors. Where is Lady Hamilton? Have you seen her? I've
tried so hard to find her, but Clarges Street is let and Merton
quite deserted. I am all anxiety to hear of her.'

'Alas, poor creature, her fortunes have declined sadly. She
lived in Richmond for a time, in a house Old Q lent her, but
since then she has gone from Boltons to Matchams and back
again, always with that very pert Horatia in tow, and now she
has taken a lodging in Dover Street, number sixteen. Sarah
Connor is with her, the only Connor she can still bear about her;
all the others have offended her past bearing.'

'What became of Ann?'

'Ah, *quel scandale*! She behaved worse and worse after you
went to Yorkshire, then ran away and got into the grounds of
Buckingham House, where the guards found her beating on the
door and insisting that she was the rightful Queen of England.
After that she was committed to Bedlam for a time.'

'Bedlam! How dreadful.'

'Oh, it was not for long. She was released, God knows why,
and got taken up by – well, I really must not say the gentleman's
name, but he is a cadet of a very noble family. It seems he has
set her up in the country, near – well, if you must know, near
Burghley House in Lincolnshire.' She flickered a wink at Emily.

'Oh – a Cecil.'

'Exactly. How taken in I was by that girl, my dear, nobody
will ever know. I placed such faith in her, poured so many con-
fidences into her ear. It was only after that terrible business of
the attack on you—'

Emily hastily changed the subject.

'And the other Connors – how is Eliza?'

'Emma has cut her off with a shilling, but I happen to know
she is married to a very respectable person, a Norfolk man called
Thomas Seaman – is that not an odd coincidence, when one
thinks of our glorious Nelson?'

'Are they living in Cheshire?'

'No, here in London, in the Paragon at Blackheath, a pleasant enough neighbourhood.'

Emily hesitated over the next question. 'Have they any children?'

Elena laughed. 'Why, how curious you are, my dear. They have one, a little boy, I believe Sarah said. But tell me all about yourself and where you are staying.'

Her horror at hearing about the Golden Cross was genuine.

'Of course it's impossible for you to remain there. We must find you somewhere else at once. But first let us take a coach to Dover Street. I can hardly wait to see the reunion. Oh, how Emma has talked of you and lamented that you and she were parted. I think she was fonder of you than of any of them. Poor love, she has never had a penny from this wretched Government or from that beast of an Earl, and she with all the expense of educating Horatia and keeping up a position in society . . . As you went to Merton I suppose you heard about poor dear Goldsmid?'

'Yes. I was deeply sorry. It surprises me that Lady Hamilton did not write to tell me. I have heard nothing from her for over two years.'

Elena sighed. 'I suppose like most of us she prefers to tell good news, and there has been so little. Poor Mrs Cadogan—'

Emily started. 'What?'

'Dead. Last February. Her third stroke. Emma was quite, quite heartbroken. I think it aged her by ten years. Such a devoted mother and daughter, the old lady a favourite with everybody. Emma had her buried at Paddington, where they used to worship together. She says that now the greatest happiness she has to look forward to is to join her mother in the grave.'

Elena chattered on as their coach rolled towards Mayfair, but Emily made only mechanical replies. She was thinking of her visit to Paddington Church, unaware that all that was left of her grandmother lay beneath the earth she walked on. This was no moment to weep for the woman who had known her in her worst days in Manchester, had loved her so much. Elena knew quite enough already; Emily was determined not to let her know any more, whatever she might guess.

And poor little Charley, where was she? Not with Eliza and her husband, unless she had become a 'relative', not worthy of mention by Sarah. As they drew near Dover Street, Emily's heart began to beat wildly and she had to twist her hands tightly together to stop them trembling.

After all, there was no reunion. The door of number sixteen was answered by a small woman with a suspicious expression and snapping black eyes. No, she told them, Lady Hamilton was not there—gone into the country somewhere, and the little girl and Miss Connor too. They'd only stayed in their apartments for a few days, a lot of coming and going what with furniture-man and a carter trying to deliver coal, 'which I've no place for and not surprising, seeing as her ladyship's filled up my cellar with a lot of wine-bottles that'll take a good few months to get drunk unless there's more entertaining done that I bargained for when I let the rooms . . .'

'Yes, yes,' broke in Elena, 'but we are particularly anxious to get in touch with Lady Hamilton, Mrs —'

'Daumier.'

'Mrs Daumier, and I should be vastly obliged if you would send to me as soon as you hear from her.' She produced from her reticule a visiting-card and put it into Mrs Daumier's dirty hand.

'Mean, sly and dishonest,' she pronounced as they returned to the coach which she had prudently kept waiting. 'Just the sort of harpy to get our poor Emma into her clutches. I'll wager she fleeces her. And now, my dear, what are we to do with you? You can't go back to that dreadful place. I forbid it.'

Emily insisted gently but firmly that she must go back. 'I have nowhere else as yet, and I am well respected there.'

'If only I had a decent lodging to offer you; but I have only one small room in Henrietta Street with barely space to swing a cat. I keep it because I have been engaged for the Theatre – did

I not tell you? Kemble is presenting a musical extravaganza and naturally thought of me when casting, as I both sing and act.' She refrained from mentioning the hours she had waited to see the great man, or the nature of the extravaganza, which was not very far removed from pantomime. 'It is quite unthinkable to travel from Staines to London and back every day: I should be entirely *fatiguée*. But you, child, we must look out for something better for you, after all your misfortunes. Have you ever heard any news of that wretched man Carew? I shall never forgive myself for introducing you, or rather encouraging you in that *affaire*.'

'No, I've heard nothing,' Emily replied in a tone which did not invite further questioning. Elena shot her an enquiring look; some bitterness there. Perhaps what Ann Connor had hinted was true, and the man had both ruined and assaulted the poor girl.

They parted affectionately, and Emily was scolded for returning to the Golden Cross an hour late; but she hardly heard the reproof, or cared that a shilling would be stopped out of her wages.

The trade winds were blowing, the sails bellying out as though forcing the ship on to some distant and desirable bourne. Willingly she scudded through waters of sapphire and emerald, the waters of the Indian Ocean, shoals of flying fish attending her, dolphins leaping and twisting about her bow. It was the time of evening when the crew also disported themselves below, with grog and the extra provisions they had bought at their last port of call: figs, melons, and dates, over-ripe to rottenness but more than prized by men accustomed to meat hard enough to be carved into toys, oatmeal skilly too repulsive for eating without molasses and butter, and weevil-breeding biscuits. They liked their music of an evening, too, dancing and clowning to the music of the ship's fiddler.

Francis Carew was playing the tune of 'Packet Ship',·a ballad of the mutiny of the *Bounty*, his shipmates joining in the chorus.

'*Bounty* was a packet ship,
Pump ship, packet ship,
Cruising on a trading trip,
In the South Pacific.'

He had grown able to play this and other grog-time favourites mechanically, his mind on other things. From time to time he took a sup of his drink ration, the rough red wine despised by most of them. He was neither happy nor unhappy. Life at sea had become second nature. Until Bonaparte was finally beaten he saw no future for himself other than cruising round the oceans in a King's ship whose work was to guard Britain's merchant vessels. At first it had occurred to him to desert, but now he had no wish to risk it and the awful punishment recapture would bring. What would be his fortune ashore? Even if he regained England his wife would still be living – her kind was indestructible. And sweet pretty Emily, whose face was growing dimmer and dimmer in his memory, she would be married long ago, with her great connections – even though saddled with their child. He had been frantic at first, the press-gang prisoner, desperate to get news to her or of her. He had thought he would go mad. Once on board he had fought his way into the presence of the captain, narrowly escaping a shot through the head from the marine sentry's musket, and had begged him to send a message to his friend Lady Hamilton; at which the captain roared with genial laughter and ordered him a flogging that almost killed him.

At first the enemy encounters seemed like foretastes of hell. Then he had begun to comprehend that they were the merest dog-fights compared with real warfare, almost enjoyable when you got used to them. In a tedious degrading existence they provided excitement and an outlet for the violence so sternly repressed by ship's discipline. Francis was faintly disgusted with himself for having become almost indifferent to the blood, noise and destruction, and for being sorry when a French or Dutch vessel turned tail and scuttled away.

He had learnt to drink, to smoke rank tobacco, to take a woman when one offered herself, white, brown, yellow or black – and some had been remarkably educative. His shipmates had ceased to jeer at him as a nancy, a silk-stockinged gentleman. He was one of them now, no worse and no better but for a sweet voice to sing the songs of home, wife, and sweetheart which drew tears from the eyes of sentimental tars. He was aware that the conditions of his life and lack of practice had utterly destroyed the hopes he had once entertained of being more than a music-teacher to schoolgirls and spoilt children. He had seen himself becoming as famous as John Braham, but with a repertoire independent of the cheap ballads with which Braham had prostituted his gifts. He had dreamed of Covent Garden Opera as something better than meretricious music sung by women who lived on their charms as well as their salaries, and men to match them. He was not quite sure what it would be like; perhaps a revival of ancient and beautiful works, unsung for a century or more, perhaps a completely new school of *il bel canto* for which he, Francis Carew, would be remembered.

It was only a dream now. He scraped out the last note of the tune, and began another.

The dolphins had ceased their dance. Great bright stars began to come out in the dark blue sky.

24

The days passed, and still Emma did not return. She might be in Sussex with the Matchams, in Norfolk with the Boltons or the Piersons, almost anywhere except with the estranged Earl and Countess Nelson, who had not even invited Emma to the funeral of poor young Horace when he died of typhus at nineteen. Emily was determined to do nothing about changing her situation until she could see Emma and force her to confess at last their true relationship. In the meantime she begged a half-day off from her duties to travel to Blackheath.

The address Elena had given her was in an elegant terrace in the centre of that little town with the wonderful expanse of common land, the spot where Kent met London and the air was exhilaratingly fresh. A small slavey admitted Emily and led her up to the first floor, where the Seamans were to be found. As the maid tapped at the door the babbling of a child could be heard within, and Emily's heart jumped.

Somebody who was undoubtedly Eliza sat by the fire knitting; an Eliza twice as plump and plain, and heavily pregnant. A baby of about two crawled on the floor, dragging a toy cart on a string.

'My God! Emily!' exclaimed Eliza, hurrying so far as her bulk would allow to throw her arms round her cousin. They hugged each other joyfully before Eliza stepped back to view her.

'My, how you've filled out. You was as thin as a lath before. Whatever's happened to you?'

'Nothing, dear Eliza, but good Yorkshire air and food.'

'Well, well, come and sit down. How did you get my direction?'

Emily told her of meeting with Elena Denis, but nothing of the Golden Cross; then she admired the infant.

'My young Nelson,' Eliza said fondly. 'The next,' patting her apron, 'if a boy, will be Collingwood.'

'So your husband's a seaman by trade as well as name?'

'That's it. I came to know him through Tom Allen, his lordship's servant – you'll remember him, no doubt. It's a long story, all to do with Lady Hamilton's Norfolk people and Cecilia meeting them in Chester, but the end of it was I met and married my Tom, and got away from the cockling business once and for all.'

'You look very happy,' Emily said.

'I am that. Tom's a good man to me, none the worse for being away a fair bit. In the merchant service, thank God. I pray every night those press-gang villains won't catch him when he comes into port. And how's Cousin Emma? Still under our Sarah's wing?'

Emily told her as much as she knew of Emma's affairs, putting off the moment when she would ask the question that burdened her mind.

'Eliza, what of little Charley?'

Her cousin's broad, good-natured face changed. 'Poor mite. She lived only two years or so after you left Cheshire. Tom and I brought her down here with us – Tom was employed in Greenwich then – and whether it was the change of climate or not, she lasted but a few months.'

Emily was silent for a moment. Then she asked 'Did she grow any brighter?'

'Not to say like a normal child. But there was something about her, Emily, I can't put it into words; it was as if she knew something we didn't. She smiled so much more than other infants do, and she seemed to want nothing but to play by herself. There was a tale got about, at Ferry, that she could cure sick folk who came to her . . . I don't know. One woman brought her boy with the consumption for Charley to touch, and his cough went that day. It seems against Nature such things should be true. The vicar said she was one of the Holy Innocents, too good for this world. I was afraid at first the

289

other children would poke fun at her when I took her out with me; but they never did.'

Emily remembered Doctor Nelson, the gentle old man who had been torn between loyalty to his son and to that son's wife. Better for Holy Innocents if they were like Charley, unburdened with intellects.

They said no more of the dead baby, but talked of Connor family matters, of Tom Seaman and of the precocity of young Nel, never still and the image of his father, always wanting to go down through Greenwich Park and look at the ships. Emily put a shilling in his hand, getting a flirtatious grin in return. Soon afterwards she left, strangely relieved in her mind. 'Is it well with the child? It is well.'

On a cold blustery day in late October, Emily was summoned from the linen-room by Jane, one of the maids. 'Gemman wants you in the coffee-room.'

'What kind of gentleman?' A bright vision flashed into her mind, to be instantly dismissed.

'Dunno. Young. Flash. Just your sort.'

A straight back presented itself to Emily's gaze; the gentleman concerned was looking out of the window at the uninviting inn-yard. He turned at her entrance to reveal the face of George Denys.

'My dear Emily. At last. What a chase we've had.' Cordially he shook her hand. 'My mamma has been posting all over town for you since she found you were not with Lady Hamilton.'

'How did you find me in the end, Mr George?'

'My revered cousin-in-law – I suppose one would call her that – or should it be aunt-in-law? – happened to call at Bruton Street and revealed your whereabouts.'

Emily remembered with an effort that Elena Denis had been Elena (or probably Helen) Lind, sister of Frederick Lind whose daughter George had married. 'It was very kind of her,' she said.

'My own suspicion is that the lady thoroughly enjoys interfering. But that's beside the point. Why the devil, if you'll forgive me, did you not come to Hans Place when you found Lady Hamilton not in town?'

'I thought I should be unwelcome. And I felt I had been enough trouble to Lady Charlotte already.'

'And so you decided to work in this place. Very independent of you, Miss Emily. I'm surprised you didn't choose to walk from Yorkshire rather than be dependent on the coach. But that ain't important. Mama says I am to take coach at once and convey you to Hans Place.'

'I don't think—' Emily began. A large, red, choleric face rose like a surly sun from behind the bunker-seat alcove in which they were sitting. Mr Busby had been enjoying a cup of his kitchen's brew on the other side of them.

'You needn't trouble yourself to think, miss,' he growled. 'I'm sick to death of you and your airs and your gaddings. You can take your things and get out, and good riddance to you. This comes of taking folk in out of charity.'

'Charity!' Emily faced him like an irate kitten. 'You took me in because I was penniless after one of your honest, respectable staff had robbed me of all I had. If any charity was bestowed it was on my part, in consenting to work for you.'

Busby drew a deep breath which imparted an even richer crimson to his face, but before he could speak George broke in. 'Get your things, Miss Emily, as the gentleman says. I fancy he and I can pass the time in pleasant chat till you return.'

But Busby, muttering under his breath, stumped away and shut himself into his office. Emily was soon back with her small valise of belongings, to be escorted to a cabriolet and driven through the wind-raked streets to Hans Place.

Once again, after more than four years, she stood in the opulent drawing-room which made a handsome setting for Lady Charlotte's brilliant colouring and the inevitable black dress, today enriched by a fur tippet. Embracing Emily warmly, she repeated George's sentiments at length and with force. 'You bad, naughty girl, to hide yourself away. You knew you would be welcome here!'

'I rather doubted it, Lady Charlotte, in view of our parting.'

Lady Charlotte looked discomfited. 'That was entirely my fault. I was much too hasty. I suppose George has told you of the discoveries after you had left?'

'No, ma'am. But Mrs Denis told me something of them.'

Lady Charlotte rang for tea, then launched into a vivid account of the gruesome find at Draycott. 'We have no notion what the poor creature was doing there – indeed, we were astonished that such an old part of the house even existed. I imagine that it was left untouched when previous owners rebuilt round the Tudor chimney-breast. We think she was a nun from Ellerton Priory, perhaps threatened by the troops of that *dreadful* Henry. What was left of her robe was light-coloured, so she would be a Cistercian.'

'They say monks and nuns often "walk",' said Emily, 'especially those who have been persecuted or walled up.'

'This one had certainly been walled up, in a manner of speaking. Of course it was very wrong of them to wish to live such an unnatural life, but one can't help feeling sorry for them, being turned out into the world. However, my dear, there is the whole explanation for your strange experiences and mine – though I thank heaven I saw no apparitions. We must both be creatures of excessive sensibility.'

'Yes,' said Emily, 'and much though I should like to have remained with you, I really shuddered at the idea of returning.'

'Oh, never fear, the Hall is entirely free of hauntings now. Mr Edmondson stepped in and said a few prayers, and he was kind enough to have the remains buried at Grinton with a pretty stone cross saying *Requiescat*, not Roman-looking at all. Let us hope that is that. But speaking of your returning to us, I fear that is impossible. The girls are both at school in Bath, so you would have nothing to do. But – do take another cup of tea – tell me, would you entertain any objections to going abroad?'

'Abroad? I had not thought of it, Lady Charlotte.'

'I ask because – do get down, Bruno—'

'No, no, he remembers me.' Emily stroked the miniature spaniel who had climbed on to her lap and was licking her hand. Lady Charlotte was looking faintly embarrassed, twisting a ring round and round her finger.

'I really hesitate to broach this subject, in case it may recall unpleasant sensations to you; but I have just heard from a friend in France that she has formed a kind of educational establishment in her house at Villefranche. The extraordinary thing is that my friend, Madame Saint-Cyr, is a Roman Catholic – not extraordinary in itself, of course, as that is the religion of France, but that the ladies who teach in her household are nuns driven from their convents by the Revolution.' She paused to see the effect of this upon Emily, who was visibly taken aback.

'It seems she is very anxious,' Lady Charlotte went on, 'to have somebody in her community who can teach English. Now, don't you think it would be valuable experience for you to go to her for a time, gain a knowledge of the world, and – and so forth?'

Emily caressed Bruno's satiny ears, her expression troubled. 'I am not drawn towards the religious life, Lady Charlotte, I fear. The – the apparition at Draycott Hall filled me with a great horror partly because of what it was, I think. I mean that if it had been the ghost, or whatever we may call it, of an ordinary person, perhaps I should not have been so afraid.'

Lady Charlotte patted her hand. 'You've been reading too many of those shocking novels by Monk Lewis and Mrs Radcliffe. I met Madame Saint-Cyr many years ago when my parents were travelling, and I can assure you she is a highly sensible lady, with nothing eerie about her.'

Emily stared into the fire, as though the flames and falling coals could conjure up meaningful pictures. The prospect of living in a house full of holy women sounded most unattractive. On the other hand, what was to be her future in England, poor, nameless and dependent?

'I had hoped,' she said at last, 'to join Lady Hamilton's

293

household again, and to be of some use to her if I can. I think I must try to see her very soon. What she decides will make up my mind for me.'

Lady Charlotte sighed. 'I'm afraid, my dear Emily, you will find she *has* no household to speak of. She has fallen upon very evil times. I have not seen her lately – not since George's wedding, in fact, when she sent him a handsome present I'm sure she could not afford – but I hear she has heavy debts. If only she would consent to live permanently with one of Lord Nelson's sisters, it would be so much better. I know Kitty Matcham has begged her to join them in Sussex, but her heart is all set on educating Horatia and bringing her out in London society. The poor child is only eight, but so spoilt and bad-tempered. Emma dresses her like a fashion-plate and has her taught dancing and music and all sorts of fancy arts.'

'Is she a pretty child?' Emily enquired, remembering the stolid toddler of Merton and Clarges Street.

'Well – I suppose I should not say so, but since we are alone – she is exactly like poor Nelson, which hardly makes for prettiness – just his long nose, and the mouth, but without his sweet expression. I believe Sarah Connor has a terrible time with her.'

I could manage Horatia, Emily thought. I could manage both of them. I have learnt to be strong for myself; now I can be strong for my mother and my sister. Cheerfulness returned to her. 'I am so grateful, Lady Charlotte, for suggesting a position for me. May I see Lady Hamilton first, before deciding?'

'Of course you may. And meanwhile you'll stay with us, won't you? Pray don't make your stubborn face at me, for we have all had enough of your independence. If you really cannot exist without mending linen, as George tells me, then I will happily provide you with some.'

Emily laughed, and accepted. The Pavilion made a most welcome change from the Golden Cross.

Lady Charlotte looked after her affectionately. Poor thing, as though it were not perfectly obvious to everybody what was her kinship to Emma, particularly now that she had filled out a little in face and form: the big blue eyes in the heart-shaped face, the small full-lipped mouth which could widen into an unexpectedly jolly laugh, and the curls that had darkened almost to Emma's colour. How could anybody be such a lackwit as to think her one of the dark-haired, high-nosed Connors? She was twenty-eight now, though looking such a child. Villefranche might not prove exactly gay, but she would undoubtedly flutter the hearts of many Frenchmen, and perhaps find a husband who would not care about an ambiguous pedigree.

She thought with gratitude of the happier lot of her own daughters, secure in their school at Bath, wealthy, each with a handsome dowry to ensure her a good match; and of her son, settled down at last with his beautiful dark Eliza, to whom Lady Charlotte had rapidly become reconciled. He was dabbling very successfully in politics and was a favourite in the Duke of Sussex's circle – so much more substantial than the fribbling court of the Prince of Wales.

Lady Charlotte sighed; the Fates had been very kind to her.

Mrs Daumier was no more communicative when Emily called at 16 Dover Street than she had been before. 'Yes, 'er ladyship's back from the country. But she's out visiting; went out 'smorning. I don't know when she'll be back, I'm sure.'

Emily arrested the half-closing door with her hand. 'Did you give her my friend Mrs Denis's card, as she asked you to?'

'I may have. There's plenty comes calling, most with bills. If it was for that, likely she'll have taken no notice.'

'Mrs Denis was not presenting a bill.' Emily felt her temper rising. 'I am most anxious to get in touch with Lady Hamilton. Perhaps I may come in and write a note for her?'

The landlady looked her up and down as if weighing her capacity for stowing away spoons and other small items. 'Well, if you must, but I can't have persons bothering me day and night . . .' Muttering, she led the way upstairs and preceded Emily into a small double drawing-room which could only have been furnished by one lady. There was the elegant Tomkinson pianoforte, the mahogany secretaire which had belonged to Sir William, and his portrait by Beechey; a glass-fronted corner cupboard contained the dinner-service Nelson had had specially painted, each piece with a different portrait of Emma. Everything Emily's eye lighted on was recognisable, either from Merton or from Clarges Street.

She sat down at the secretaire and wrote a brief note saying she had called, and would call again as soon as she heard it was convenient, giving her address as Hans Place. Mrs Daumier, arms akimbo, watched with impatient suspicion, and all but bundled her off the premises.

The days that followed were some of the longest Emily had ever known. No answer came from Dover Street. Perhaps Emma had changed her mind and no longer wanted to see her. Sorrow, suspense, indecision chased each other round and round her brain; all her old feelings of being unwanted returned, battering down the independence she had learnt. On Sunday morning she could wait no longer. She sat down and wrote a letter. It was a stiff, formal letter, the sort of copybook letter Mrs Blackburn had long ago taught her to write. She had reached a stage when she was afraid to give utterance to emotion, for fear of being rebuffed.

My dear Lady Hamilton

Mrs Denis's mention of your name and the conversation she had with you have revived ideas in my mind which an absence of four years has not been able to efface. It might have been happy for me to have forgotten the past, and to have begun a new life with new ideas; but for my misfortune, my memory traces back circumstances which have taught me too much, yet not quite all I could have wished to have known – with you *that* resides, and ample reasons, no doubt, you have for not imparting them to me. Had you felt yourself at liberty so to have done, I might have become reconciled to my former situation and have been relieved from the painful employment I now pursue. It was necessary as I then stood, for I had nothing to support me but the affection I bore you; on the other hand, doubts and fears by turns oppressed me, and I determined to rely on my own efforts rather than submit to abject dependence, without a permanent name or acknowledged parents. That I should have taken such a step shews, at least, that I have a mind misfortune has not subdued. That I should persevere in it is what I owe to myself and to you, for it shall never be said that I avail myself of your partiality or my own inclination, unless I learn my claim on you is greater than you have hitherto acknowledged. But the time may come when the same reasons may cease to operate, and then, with a heart filled with tenderness and affection, will I shew you both my duty and attachment.

In the meantime, should Mrs Denis's zeal and kindness not have over-rated your expressions respecting me, and that you should really wish to see me, I may be believed in saying that such a meeting would be one of the happiest moments of my life, but for the reflection that it may also be the last, as I leave England in a few days, and may, perhaps, never return to it again.

I remain, with every affectionate wish,

E. CAREW

She read it through with distaste. It was too long and too pedantic. Too cold-sounding, perhaps. On impulse she dashed off a postscript on a separate sheet.

Will you not at least let me if only once call you by the name of Mother, and hear you call me Daughter? Believe me this is my dearest wish. I have visited your lodging twice but found you from home, each time leaving word where you could send to me.

Two days passed without an answer. At the end of the second Emily told Lady Charlotte that she might write to Madame Saint-Cyr telling her to expect her. Up to the very moment of departure there was hope; a ring at the lodge-gate, the entrance of a servant, a messenger in the drive, all these might mean Emily was saved. Or perhaps a carriage would turn in at the gates, and a beautiful face would be at the window, looking for her. 'If only she would come! I should not mind even if it were to reproach me, to tell me I am presumptuous in asking to be acknowledged. If only she would tell me I am loved by her, the only one I have to love me.'

But there came neither letter nor carriage. Kind Elena Denis, shedding real tears at Emily's departure, offered to travel with her as far as Canterbury, where a particular friend of hers was appearing, and reduced Emily in turn to tears by her rendering of 'Mary Stuart's Farewell'. Lady Charlotte gave her a beautiful shawl as a parting present, and Peter Denys solemnly presented her with a fine Swiss watch, engraved with her initials in a garland of flowers.

The sun was bright and the November air frosty when the Dover coach left the White Bear in Piccadilly next morning. Emily, seated next to the window, breathed on the misty glass and rubbed it vigorously with a handkerchief until the passing scenes were clearly visible. She had choked down her disappointment and sorrow at Emma's abandonment of her. This journey to France was to be the beginning of the 'new life with new ideas', and she would undertake it with all the courage of a mind misfortune had not subdued.

As they turned into Cockspur Street she looked across at Carlton House. 'The flags are flying,' she said to Elena. 'That means the King is still alive, poor man. I read that his life was despaired of when Princess Amelia died. If only—' She broke off with a gasping cry which turned all eyes towards her.

'What is it, child?' Elena asked. 'Why, you've gone pale as ashes.'

Emily was trembling almost too much to speak. Then, 'That woman,' she said. 'It was the same – I remember now – O God!' She put her hands to her face to stop the shaking of her jaw. Elena leaned across her. 'Where? What woman? What is she like?'

Emily began to tell her, in a spate of words, of the memories the sight of that coarse dark face under a purple bonnet had brought her, and Elena's eyes widened in horror as she heard the tale.

Sleepy from a late-night party at Betty Billington's, Emma shuffled through a pile of letters with London postmarks, most of them, she knew without the trouble of opening them, demands for money. They came in by almost every post, to be put aside until the moment when she should be able to bring herself to face them. Sometimes, as now, they lay for a week or more. Almost at the bottom was one addressed in a delicately beautiful copperplate hand that struck a chord of familiarity. Turning it over, she saw the little seal, the dog-lion they had joked about when she gave it to Emily, calling it the Beast in Revelations. She tore it open and read it rapidly, exclaiming under her breath, then crossed to the fireplace and tugged the bellrope violently. After a long pause, during which she paced about with wild impatience, Mrs Daumier appeared, wiping her hands on her apron.

'You take your time,' said Emma. 'When I ring a bell I expect it to be answered.'

'I've my work to do, haven't I? If some paid me reg'lar I might be able to hafford a butler and a hunder 'ouseparlourmaid.'

'Why did you not tell me a young lady had called? This letter says she has been here more than once.'

Mrs Daumier shrugged. 'Slipped my mind. Beside, she lef' a note last time – wrote it at the desk while I waited, not knowing if she was to be trusted. I put it there, with the letters.'

Emma exploded in one of those rages which had in their time driven Sir William to his club and Nelson to tears. Sarah Connor, arriving with Horatia in the middle of it, gently pushed the child out of the room again.

Five

A Veiled Face

25

Like sequences in a nightmare the stages of Emily's journey
followed one another in relentless succession. After a flea-ridden
night at the Lord Warden hotel in Dover came a rough sea-
journey across the Channel. Emily had not known that it was
possible to be so sick for so long. She had not the slightest concern whether the ship went down or reached Calais in safety; it
was unfortunate that Emma's often-told story of their Neapolitan
Majesties' stormy voyage to Sicily occurred to her over and over
again, in ghastly detail.

But reach Calais they did, and a shabby, unfriendly place it
looked in the murk of a November afternoon. Nobody understood a word Emily said, the French of a Manchester schoolroom
being very unlike that spoken by the natives. The people at the
inn where she boarded the diligence that was to take her south
seemed to take a positive delight in misunderstanding her
simplest requests, staring at her with blank, closed faces as she
tried to order food. '*Café*' alone they found impossible to mis-
interpret, so that a large cracked cup of strong, almost undrink-
able coffee was all she got in the way of refreshment.

Then began the journey. If stage-coach travel in England was
unpleasant, that of France was execrable. Her fellow travellers
smelt strangely horrible, as did the cage of hens one woman
insisted on taking with her and putting under the seat, after a
fearful quarrel with the guard. Emily was shocked by the cruel
treatment of the horses, poor bony nags lashed unmercifully by
the postboys on their backs so that they arrived at each stage
sweating and trembling. Nobody spoke to Emily, but everyone
looked at her, from bonnet to slipper and back again, with
stares of withering contempt or insulting interest, depending on
the sex of the starer. At the inn at Abbeville a roughly-dressed
man seized her and pulled her into a corner, attempting to kiss

and fumble her while making a proposition whose meaning was quite clear to her. She struggled free, leaving one of the clasps of her pelisse in his hand, and ran back to the coach, with not even a cup of rank coffee to restore her. The incident had, however, been remarked by the woman with the hens, who, after taking her place, leant forward and tapped Emily on the knee.

'*Tu n'a pas mangé, p'tite?*'

'*Non, madame,*' Emily managed to say, as much surprised to hear herself uttering a comprehensible word of French as to see a kindly expression on the woman's face. Her benefactor rummaged in a basket and with a toothless beam produced a slab of something that seemed to be egg and bacon pie in a crust, heavily laced with the garlic which, it seemed to Emily, pervaded everything in France, from the air to the bed-linen. From then onwards they conversed as best they could, and Emily was sorry to see the hen-wife leave the coach at Amiens.

The flat Pas de Calais was behind them; Beauvais, Compiègne; there was Senlis named on a road-sign, names from childhood history books, and then they were approaching Paris. She had looked forward to seeing it, but when they arrived it was nightfall, and she was too weary to do anything but retire to the narrow-plank bed which was all the overcrowded inn had to offer, and saw nothing the next morning but the shimmer of the Seine and the towers of Notre Dame.

Orléans, Melun: the names were becoming meaningless, the sights repetitious, even the changes of landscape hardly worth remarking. She tried to concentrate on the conversation of the other passengers, picking up increasingly the rhythm of their speech. They were talking of Bonaparte facing Wellington in Portugal, this accursed Wellington who had no pity for civilian or soldier, even for his own men, whom he would hang for looting as calmly as he would a deserter. But someone's sister had been told that not all the English had hearts of steel, for they were tossing biscuits on the points of bayonets to the starving French sentries posted before Wellington's lines, and had smuggled food and tobacco to them. More fools they, growled a countryman, then turned his wrath on Bonaparte for the heavy taxes which were weighing down 'our poor France', and the conscription which was tearing boys of sixteen from their families to die by the Tagus.

It was a relief to be able to understand what people were saying, even though Emily knew herself to be silently reviled as a member of the race which had won Trafalgar. It kept at bay the image which seemed etched on her mind like the impression of an object in bright sun : the face of the woman seen near Carlton House, and the memory of the scene in Arundel Street. There was no doubt, of course, as to the woman's identity; the face was unforgettable, the words she had spoken still sounding in Emily's mind. It was a double shock to remember, after so long, and to know that such a violent enemy still lived. Yet, along with the fear, a tiny ray of happiness shone. Emily had sensed, even though no one had breathed it to her, that Francis had somehow been blamed for the assault on her, and now she knew that unthinkable idea to be untrue. From that thought grew another – had Katina's hatred been enough to seek him out and kill him as she had tried to kill Emily? Something had happened to him on his way back to Arundel Street. But what? She determined to write to Elena and ask that active lady to follow up every clue to his disappearance. As the diligence rumbled between rows of neat poplars, bare winter fields, past struggling untidy farms where wandering pigs and hens drew colourful addresses of abuse from the coachman, she imagined Francis assassinated, knocked on the head by some bully paid by his wife, or imprisoned on a false charge.

But surely he would have got word to her, even from the Fleet or the Marshalsea? He had had some money in his pocket, enough to pay a messenger. Even if he had been taken suddenly ill, or met with an accident, he carried letters with him, being of that nature which automatically pockets pencils, papers, or any small objects lying about for which no immediate place is obvious. Emily had even tracked down the thread-waxer and needle-case from her work-basket to one of Francis's overladen pockets. No, it was a complete mystery which might never be solved in this world.

She had heard that those women whose men had not returned from the wars swore they would rather know for certain they were dead than wait, day after weary day, for news. But to believe Francis dead would be the end of hope, and hope was life. She did not feel he was dead. But she had not sensed whatever calamity befell him four years ago; why should she expect to be conscious of the moment of his death? They had lived such a short time together. If it had been longer perhaps their spirits would have been in complete accord, reaching each other across space and time. Their wild impulsive mating had fettered her to him more strongly than any marriage ceremony, yet not strongly enough for his spirit to visit her if he were dead, or to come to her in sleep, as those parted from their loves in life are said to do. As the carriage trundled over the rough roads of France she tried to will herself to see him, as he now was, in her mind's eye; but only confused pictures appeared, faces and objects in a bewildering jumble. Uneasily she slept.

They had reached the mountains and rich valleys of the Auvergne, one beautiful scene following another until the eyes were tired of looking and it was a relief when white morning mist hid the view. Emily slept more and more, used now to the grinding and rocking of the vehicle and the aching of her bones. She was asleep when a sharp finger prodded her and a loud voice shouted in her ear: '*Villefranche! C'est Villefranche! Éveillez-vous, m'selle!*'

The carriage had stopped in a square of inns and ancient, leaning houses. Three outside passengers were climbing down, inn-servants were swarming about with baggage, hens and begging children and dogs getting under everybody's feet, valises being hurled about to the danger of the public; one might have been back at the Golden Cross but for the babel of French voices. Emily climbed stiffly out, nobody offering to assist her, and managed to find her own valise among the heap which had been pulled out of the boot. She stood there helplessly, pushed and shoved without apology, wondering what to do. Then she remembered that she had Madame Saint-Cyr's address written on a piece of paper. She caught a passing groom by the arm and showed it to him, but he turned away with an incomprehensible word.

Emily lost her temper. 'The French!' she said loudly to whomever it might concern. 'A mannerless pack of beasts!'

A hand pulled at her sleeve. Beside her was a small boy, dirty, dark-eyed, and ragged to the point of indecency, but smiling. He said something which meant nothing to her, but with a skill born of long practice managed to convey that he was prepared to take her wherever she wanted to go. Shown the written address, he shook his head. 'Madame Saint-Cyr, Rue Moissac,' she said slowly and distinctly. This time he nodded like a Chinese ornament, smiling all the time, and taking her arm propelled her towards the north side of the square. Possibly he was leading her to a thieves' den, to be robbed and murdered, she reflected, yet it could be no worse than standing in a crowd of foreigners as unnoticed as if she were a ghost.

But after a short, steep walk up a few cobbled streets the boy paused before a large house separated from its neighbours by a strip of courtyard. It was built in a completely un-English style, with shutters, white stone facings, and a gabled roof, and looked very unwelcoming.

'Madame Saint-Cyr,' said the boy, holding out a filthy hand into which Emily put some small coins from the French money she had obtained at Calais. Her guide seemed pleased with it, and retreated, blowing her a backward kiss.

When the door finally opened after she had jangled the bell for what seemed like minutes, it was to reveal a tall elderly servant wearing a starched cap and a kind of pinafore. Emily began to explain her identity and her errand in words which obviously meant nothing to the woman. With insulting deliberation she shut the door, leaving Emily, still stammering, on the step.

She was about to turn and go back to the coaching inn ▴

307

anywhere – when the door was opened again. Another woman stood there, tall, stout, dressed as befitted a lady though with extreme plainness. With a faint smile she said, 'Miss Carew. Please enter. I am Madame Saint-Cyr.'

So furious was Emily by this time that she omitted any curtsey or greeting and said, 'Your servant has very strange manners, madame. I thought I had been turned from the door.'

'Agathe is well trained. Come this way.' Emily followed her up a narrow staircase of uncarpeted wood to what was obviously her hostess's sitting-room. It was high-ceilinged and small-windowed, with stiff-backed furniture and a general air of discomfort. A very small fire flickered in the grate, in spite of the cold outside. Emily began to wish she had obeyed instinct and gone back to the inn.

Madame Saint-Cyr turned to face her, neither inviting her to sit down nor seating herself. Everything about her seemed to be grey: her dress, unpatterned, long in the sleeves and high in the neck; her hair, drawn backwards from her brow and coiled in neat plaits on top of her head; even her complexion had a whitish-grey tinge, as though, Emily thought, she lived on chalk. After a moment's steady survey she indicated a chair. Emily sat on the edge of it, still with a lump of fury in her throat, ready for argument or battle. She looked very like her mother.

Madame, however, launched into conventional small-talk. Had the journey been pleasant? What was the climate like in England? How was Lady Charlotte Denys? Had Emily admired the scenery around the Dordogne, reputedly among the finest in France? And, finally, would Emily like a cup of coffee? A little calmer, Emily said that she would, perfectly aware that she had been put through a smoothing-down process.

The coffee appeared, brought by a young servant. It proved to be literally one cup, not the pot Emily had been hoping for; it was well made but not sufficiently hot. When she had finished it Madame Saint-Cyr said, 'Now, to business. In the first place I shall require you to speak French at all times, until you are sufficiently fluent in it to teach English. If you find yourself in any great difficulty you may consult me. As you can hear, I speak English well enough.'

'I will do my best.'

'You are of a very mutinous disposition, Miss Carew. I am sure you will find that residing here will correct that. Kindly take your bonnet off.'

Speechless, Emily loosened the strings of her black bonnet.

'I see. Do you curl your hair artificially?'

'No, indeed. It curls by nature.'

'A pity. You will feel out of place, I am sure, among our other young ladies, who cultivate the plainest possible styles of hair-dressing and costume. Your dress, for instance.'

Emily glanced down at her best winter dress, of a pretty dark blue; high-waisted, as was the fashion, it had a tiny ruff at the throat which she knew to be becoming, but nobody could have called it ostentatious.

'What is the matter with my dress?'

'It is not quite suitable for this household.'

Emily rose swiftly to her feet. 'It is the only good winter dress I have, and I am sorry, Madame, but I feel that you and I are not going to be compatible. I resent criticism of my appearance when it is unwarranted, as yours is. Perhaps your servant will bring me my valise, and I will leave at once.'

'Sit down, sit down.' Madame Saint-Cyr was smiling her tight smile. 'You have considerable spirit; one can tell you have not been used to the discipline to which our other young ladies are accustomed.'

'I am very glad I have not, if it springs from the life of a convent.'

Madame actually laughed. 'You English! How belligerent you are. We will talk of this later. Now come with me and you shall meet my children and their teachers.'

On the same floor, built out at the back of the house, was a large room with desks, bookshelves, and a blackboard. Several young people were seated at the desks. To Emily's surprise none of them looked up until Madame spoke to them, at which they rose to their feet with an almost simultaneous movement. Madame immediately put Emily at a disadvantage by introducing her in very rapid French, so that she only gathered roughly who the various girls were – two Saint-Cyr daughters, Angèle and Céleste, and one or two others from different families. Three older women, she learnt later, were Ursule Delbreil, Marie Boutaric and Eléonore Dutriac. All wore black or grey dresses and had their hair parted in the middle and drawn back. Such a set of frights I never saw, thought Emily, and if they expect me to look like that, don't they wish they may get it.

The introductions over, Madame rang a bell for the small servant, who with an impassive face conducted Emily to her room. It was a little apartment containing a table, a chair, a wash-stand with ewer and basin, a fireplace in which obviously no fire had burnt for a long time, and a small narrow bed with a crucifix over it.

Left alone, Emily burst into tears. They were as much of anger as anything else: anger with Lady Charlotte for sending her to such a wretched place, with Madame Saint-Cyr for her abominable rudeness, with Emma for abandoning her. When she had had her cry out, and had washed her hot face, she sat on the side of the bed and considered what her future actions were to be.

It would be useless to return to the inn. She had scarcely enough money for a night's lodging, let alone for the fare back to England. Until she could speak French well enough to be understood it would be impossible for her to find another situation locally. She was caught in a web from which release would not be easy. But they shan't break my spirit, she resolved. I'm English and I shall behave like an Englishwoman. On which she applied the last of her eau-de-Cologne to her neck, hair and hands, and sailed downstairs with her head held high, and scarlet flags flying in her cheeks.

Madame Saint-Cyr was on the landing below, in conversation with a young woman who had not been in the schoolroom.

'Ah,' she said blandly, *'Mademoiselle Carew, permettez-moi à présenter une autre Emilie.'*

For the first time, Emily looked into the dark burning eyes of Emilie de Rodat.

26

Elena Denis put her feet up luxuriously on a footstool before the fire of the parlour above the bar of the inn. It was most agreeable to be so warm while the world outside was so cold, snow lying heavy on the Windsor road, the Thames swollen and surly, hungry ducks and swans applying at the kitchen door for food. It was also most agreeable to have a letter to read, particularly as she was almost out of gossip these winter days, with her engagement at Covent Garden finished on a note of acrimony and no prospects of social chit-chat in town until the weather mended.

18 Rue Moissac,
Villefranche-de-Rouergue,
Aveyron,
France

December 28 1810.

My dear Mrs Denis,

I expect you will be surprised to hear from me so soon after my departure for France; but to tell truth I am so satiated with the continuous speaking of French that I must fly to writing English as a relief to my feelings.

You will probably like to know something of the town in which I find myself . . . [Here followed an account of medieval houses, the imposing Collegiate Church with a street running beneath its tower, the three ancient bridges over the river, and so forth, which Elena hastily skipped.] . . . As to this establishment, it is of a most unusual, and, to me, uncongenial nature. I have no quarrel with the practice of religion; indeed, I have often thought more freedom of worship in England would be desirable, while the banishment of God from the councils of the French Revolution can only have encouraged Anarchy.

This household, however, carries piety a good deal too far. No comfort or ornament is permitted, either of dress or furniture, and the régime is virtually that of the nunnery from which my fellow-teachers have been driven by Bonaparte. Continual services are held in the private chapel which Mme Saint-Cyr has added to this already large house, bells summon us at all hours of the night, and our diet is of the poorest, meat allowed not more than once a week. Madame has a private chaplain, M. Marty, who regards me, I am well aware, as a heretic fit for the burning, and loses no occasion to put me in a poor light.

I expect you will say, Emily must be rendered quite wretched in such an environment. Indeed, I am far from happy, but, my dear Friend, I am also far from conquered. I have steadfastly refused to take part in services which are not those of my own church, to listen to pious precepts from persons who I am sure are no more virtuous than myself (for what that is worth) or to wear the vastly unbecoming clothes which are affected by the unfortunate females of the house. Often, when circumstances are particularly trying, I ask myself, What would Lady Hamilton do in my place? and I am invariably supported by the knowledge that she would declare 'Britons never shall be slaves!' and act correspondingly.

I do not suppose Madame Saint-Cyr wishes to keep me here any more than I wish to stay, but she would find it so difficult to fill my place that she dare not dismiss me, while I find I am gaining a most useful knowledge of French which I propose to improve even more before I leave this place for ever; and besides, I find myself increasingly able to be amused by the foibles and eccentricities of this remarkable community, in which I only have one friend, a young woman named Emilie de Rodat, who is pious to yawning-point but has a kind heart and I believe seriously wishes to help me in my state of dis-grace.

And now I will come to one of the purposes of my letter. The deep impression made upon my mind by the sight of

313

Mrs Carew, recalling my vanished memory of the attack upon me in 1806, leads me to ask you of your kindness, to endeavour to discover something, even so long afterwards, of my Francis's fate. Now that he can no longer be blamed in any way for the harm done to me, I am most anxious for him to be found, if he still lives, as I pray he does. I leave the means to your ingenuity.

I wish you and M. Denis all Christmas happiness; there has been little rejoicing here, as you may guess, but a great deal of chanting and bell-ringing, rendering the holiest night of the year absolutely hideous.

Believe me, I send you every kind wish, from my heart.

EMILY CAREW

Elena folded up the letter and proceeded to the studio upstairs, where her husband, in freezing conditions, was working on a large landscape-painting of a Thames Valley scene with an impressive if improbable waterfall in the background and some Flemish-looking cows cropping the grass.

'All it needs is Vesuvius,' she observed, looking over his shoulder. 'Simon, I have the most delightful commission. As soon as this horrid snow stops I shall go to town and see *everybody*, from the Prince downwards.'

'Pray don't trouble him too much, *cara*,' said her husband, stepping back to admire the finished cattle. 'By the time you reach town he may well have become Regent.'

'That's true. Very well, I shall go to him first.'

And indeed, when Elena did return to London, it was to find that the Prince of Wales was for once unapproachable, involved in the acrimony surrounding the passage of the Regency Bill which on 6 February 1811 transferred the authority of the Crown from his mad father to himself. But his social circle, in which Elena had always moved freely, was there as usual, wasps round a honey-pot, and from their buzzing she had every hope of learning something about Kate Carew. She was unlucky. Someone thought Kate had been living with an Irish half-pay

314

captain a few months before, but no name or address was forthcoming. Another said that when last seen she had been lifting the elbow rather more than became a lady, and had quite lost her looks in consequence.

Enquiries among the less exalted characters of Hungerford Market, the sleazy district hard by Charing Cross, produced no more information. Elena pondered whether her reputation could stand a discreet visit to a few of the better-class brothels, and decided that it could. Here again there was no news of recent date, only a report that a fight between Kate and an equally hot-tempered whore had led to them both being brought up before a magistrate; but that had been a year or two ago.

There remained only the theatre world to explore, and here too Elena drew a blank for Emily, but a happy turn of fortune for herself. A chance encounter with an actor who had once been a particular friend of hers led to the offer of an engagement, not in town but in the theatre at Stamford, Lincolnshire, where a new musical spectacle required the services of an experienced actress and singer. Elena's friend gave her an introduction to the manager, who was recruiting his players in London, and who surveyed her with a look she recognised. She met the critical appraisal with a bold smile.

'I can look fifteen years younger on the stage,' she said.

'Ah believe thee,' replied the gentleman, bestowing a sharp pinch upon her fashionably ample bottom.

Stamford proved an agreeable change from the discomforts of London, being small, rustic, and apparently populated by folk honest in the main, if the landlady was any criterion. Elena approved of the pretty theatre, some forty years old, and the wealth of old churches and hospitable inns. Here one was Somebody, an actress-lady to be stared at and bowed or curtsied to by the sweet Stamfordians. Elena thought Shakespeare would have enjoyed Stamford.

The first night of *Cherry and Fair Star* was the rare variety on which nothing major went wrong. Nobody in the orchestra or cast turned up drunk or speechless with influenza, the HOUSE

315

FULL notices were up, there was no London fog to invade the theatre and the players' throats, and Elena herself had a charming pink gauze dress with silver spangles, and looked, as she had promised the manager, not a day over forty.

One of the pleasures of her part was that she remained on the stage for long minutes, decoratively posed but silent, which gave her time to survey and sum up the audience, its quality, dress, and reaction to herself. There might be a Benefit Night towards the end of the season, when she would be grateful for every seat filled by an admirer. Some actors considered short-sightedness a mercy, protecting them as it did from seeing clearly the expressions on the faces of the audience; but Elena had no such inhibitions, and a pair of very bright sharp eyes. During the second act she almost missed her cue in surprise at seeing in the third row a face once familiar, unseen for years.

'Ann Connor. Good God!' she said to herself, and spent her inactive moments during the remainder of the evening recalling what had happened to Ann. Something about Bedlam, and a nobleman, one of the Cecils of Burghley House, the stately pile on the edge of the town.

It was too good to miss. Taking her call at the end of the performance she rose from a deep curtsey with her most dazzling smile directed towards Ann. She was rewarded, leaving the stage door, by the sight of that lady waiting in the gathering of worshippers at various shrines.

'My dear Miss Connor!'

'My dear Mrs Denis!'

They embraced, both talking at once. Ann was easily persuaded to accompany Elena to her lodging in one of the gracious houses of grey-gold stone that lined St George's Square, round the corner from the Theatre. 'Some coffee, Mrs Lamb, if you please!' shouted Elena as they passed the landlady's living-room on their way upstairs to her own apartment; and coffee there was, with a hearty cold meal on a tray for Elena.

'Do the people of the house not object to serving you so late?' asked Ann, covertly watching Elena tucking into half a Melton

Mowbray pie with cucumber, cheese and pickles, and a quantity of bread and butter.

'Bless you, no. They know us theatre people and our ways. 'Twould be death to eat before the play, but afterwards – ah !' She kissed her hand to the remains of the pie. Enjoyment of her supper had not kept her attention off her guest, who sat sipping coffee, little finger rather too elegantly cocked. Ann had aged – women of that horsy type always did – too many lines for her years, which Elena guessed to be about thirty-five, a lot of grey in the black hair under that elaborate head-dress, and a distinct redness about the haughty nose. Too much hot tea, or drink? She was dressed very stylishly – though the style was several years too young for her – and in good materials. Her long hands were covered with rings, among which Elena thought she detected some jewels that would have passed muster on the stage but not, decidedly, off it.

'Tell me,' she asked when her mouth was not inconveniently full, 'have you seen anything of your family – your sisters, Lady Hamilton?'

Ann tossed her head. 'Not for years. I hope I am above such people now.'

'Oh?' Elena's eyes were all round innocence. 'I did hear you had a rise in fortune, though not the details. Pray tell.'

Ann smiled, a tight-lipped haughty smile, royalty all condescension. 'You had not heard? I am *Lady* Ann now. Lady Ann Cecil.'

This time Elena's astonishment was real. '*Mon Dieu!* Why, whom have you married? Not the Marquess – the Earl – whoever he is?'

The other fanned herself languidly. 'No, no. A close relation.'

'But his name? Don't be so confoundedly tantalising, woman. Bless me, if I had a title I'd put it up on the hoardings and have it cried through town, for everyone to know.'

'There are – reasons – why our union cannot be made public just yet. Policy in high places, you know – difficulty with a certain personage.'

'I see.' Elena, who did not see at all, thoughtfully lit and puffed a segar, disregarding Ann's ladylike coughs and waftings. 'And where do you live, then?'

'In Burghley House. Where else? It is the most magnificent residence, I assure you, built for Queen Elizabeth's Lord High Treasurer, crammed with every possible richness. Oh, such furniture, such pictures, such hangings! Do you know, I have a bed in which the Queen herself slept, hung with drapes of gold and peacock blue, the very same *she* used, and tapestries on the wall, the finest from France . . .' She babbled on of the glories of Burghley while Elena half listened, glancing now and then at the clock and suppressing small token yawns. She had not heard her own voice for quite five minutes, and was bursting to tell Ann about Simon's latest picture and what had been offered for it, about his failing health and their possible return to Naples, together with the stirring drama of her interview with Kemble before she swept out of his theatre, and her impressions of the Stamford company. It was getting late; the streets were almost silent. Desperate to have her say, she suddenly interrupted the flow with a completely irrelevant question.

'By the bye, have you seen anything of Kate Carew?'

Ann stopped in her tracks, bridling. A curious sly expression came over her face. 'Why should I?'

'Only that you were so interested in her when we used to have those delicious long talks of ours. I believe I even introduced you, though God knows I had no inclination to consort with the creature. As it happens, I have been searching for her in town.'

'You will not find her,' said Ann. 'She is dead.'

'Dead! How?'

'Of a dropsy, I believe. She grew quite enormous. I heard it from Captain O'Kelly, who had her in keeping for a time. He said she cost as much to feed as Cluny the elephant.'

'Are you quite sure of this? Utterly sure?'

Ann's eyebrows arched. 'Of course. She is buried at St Anne's, Dean Street. Go and see if you doubt my word.'

'Oh, not for a moment. I'll tell you why I ask.' Elena launched into a detailed account of Emily's career since the Clarges Street days, the disappearance of Francis Carew, and her own determination to discover his fate. So wrapped up was she in her story that she failed to notice the growing look of triumph on her guest's face, or the occasional prompt which drew from her more and more details, including Emily's present address. But the moment she had given it she was conscious of a sharp rebuke from that sixth sense which dictates what should be said and what should not. Hastily she tried to retract it.

'But since she wrote to me she may well have taken some other post,' she said. 'I will find out.'

'Pray do. I should like to write to her, poor girl.'

Soon after this Ann declared that she must be going, and gathered up her wraps. 'How is it, my dear friend, that you don't have an attendant?' Elena asked, helping her on with them. 'In your position I should have thought you would have had at least a carriage waiting.'

'Oh, I love to walk. It keeps my figure in trim. Pray look after yourself, dearest Mrs Denis, and we must meet again while you are here.' She bestowed a chilly kiss on each cheek, and departed.

Instead of shutting the house door at once, Elena watched her go. To her surprise, the tall hooded figure was walking not down St Mary's Street, the obvious way to Burghley House, but in the opposite direction. Sudden impulse made her set off, uncloaked, for the night was mild, in pursuit; she could not bear to go to bed with at least one puzzle unresolved. Hugging the wall, and walking silently in her heel-less sandals, she proceeded catlike as Ann stepped briskly north-west, and suddenly disappeared out of sight round a corner. Elena hurried her own steps, and was just in time to see her quarry stop in front of a small, ancient cottage a few doors past the Half Moon, produce a key, and let herself in.

'Well!' said Elena to herself, walking thoughtfully back. 'Burghley House, forsooth. *Quelle blague!* The great humbug!'

27

For Emily, time was passing quickly, busy as she was from morning to night. The French custom of rising and going to bed very early, and the limited hours for recreation, ensured that she had little leisure to brood on her circumstances. She began to enjoy her silent duel with Madame Saint-Cyr, who in turn was ironically amused by the Englishwoman who was brave enough to stand up to her. Penances imposed by Madame on Emily's pupils and considered by Emily to be unfair had a curious way of being minimised or cancelled altogether. Attempts to compel Emily to attend divine service in the Chapel met with a blank refusal. And when, on the advice of Monsieur Marty, Madame's chaplain, a personage whom Emily cordially detested, her food was deliberately rationed and became of even lower quality than that of the other teachers and the resident pupils, she neatly counter-attacked this move to render her less aggressive and more likely to yield to the voice of authority.

At the communal breakfast-table one morning her allowance of thin porridge was smaller than the others', and served without milk. Politely she requested some. Madame raised her eyebrows.

'The milk has gone bad overnight. What is drinkable I have allotted to Mademoiselle Dutriac, whose health is poor at present.'

'Why, then, do you not keep it in ice, Madame? In good houses in England we always do so.'

'This is not England, mademoiselle,' replied Madame in a voice chilly enough to preserve milk for several days. At the mid-day meal Emily found herself looking at a bowl of watery soup in which a few peas and beans weltered. Her neighbours' bowls contained meat as well. This time she was unable to protest aloud, as the meal was taken in silence to the accompaniment of a religious reading by Monsieur Marty. She ate the soup, not without casting a meaning glance at Madame, who was watching her. That afternoon she went into the town during her half-hour of leisure; and when the usual frugal supper of black bread and a sliver of hard cheese was served, Emily produced from her apron pocket a crisp roll of bread, a slab of butter, a piece of cheese of golden richness, and a large apple. Amid stares and gasps from the rest of the table, Madame put down her knife.

'Mademoiselle Carew, what are you eating?'

'My supper, Madame.'

'That is not the supper provided for you.'

'No, madame. I have not had enough to eat today, and the supper with which you have provided me would hardly nourish a mouse.'

'Where did you obtain that food?'

'From the shops, Madame.'

'You have been into the town alone? You know very well my young ladies are not permitted to walk unchaperoned.'

'I do not consider my virtue in any danger, Madame. Perhaps theirs is more fragile.'

A dark flush overspread Madame's normally pale face. She struck the table with her fist.

'Go to your room at once. I shall order your door to be locked so that solitary confinement may render you sensible of your wicked, rebellious ways. And you, Mademoiselle Fermier, will also retire, since you seem unable to control your idiotic giggling.'

Very slowly Emily finished her roll and cheese, chewing every mouthful. Then, pocketing the apple, she strolled to the door, turning there to bestow a sweet smile on Madame. In her room was a further store of food, purchased from the salary she hoarded for the day when she might use it to journey home. She spent a pleasant, relaxing evening with another apple and *The Adventures of Tom Jones*, which she had brought with her along with other novels which Monsieur Marty would undoubtedly have burnt publicly if he could have laid hands on them.

'Put her out into the street,' he was advising Madame downstairs. 'Leave her to the fate she deserves. She is an evil influence here, a force for corruption.'

'On the contrary, Father, if I may presume to differ from you, she is an example to her pupils of the shocking aspect disobedience wears. In time they will profit by it. Besides,' folding her plump white hands complacently, 'I am firm in the belief that such behaviour will be rewarded as it deserves. And she is, as it happens, an excellent teacher.'

Emily had learned to speak French fluently with a speed which had astonished her. Partly she had acquired it in self-defence and to allow herself to teach efficiently; but, unknown to her, the language was in her heritage, for her paternal grandmother had been the lovely Sarah Lethieullier, who came of a Brabant family and had instilled into her son Harry Fetherstonhaugh an early knowledge of French and a love of it which never left him. With the occasional aid of a French-English dictionary she taught English as well as if she had taught it all her life, taking a detached pleasure in the knowledge that Madame wished it taught because one day the anti-Christ Bonaparte would be defeated, and then it would be an advantage to all Europeans to speak the language of the victorious nation. She also, voluntarily, took on the teaching of music, though her pupils took to it only poorly and were exasperatingly slow.

She was sadly aware that she lacked friends. The other teachers regarded her with horror, her pupils with shocked awe; but nobody became a companion to her, someone to chat and laugh with. For the first time she was completely alone. Except for Emilie de Rodat.

Five years younger than Emily, a girl of a good and deeply religious family, Emilie had all the makings of a saint and martyr. Several times she had tried to take the veil, prevented always by a terrible melancholia which came upon her and which she regarded as God's sign that He did not wish her at that time to enter a convent, and deterred by her confessors who feared that such devotion as hers could not last. In the house at Villefranche she was, oddly enough, regarded as some kind of freak in her excessive practice of humility and self-denial. Others might live on poor fare and wear frumpish clothes because it pleased Madame and Monsieur Marty and the ex-nuns who taught them, but Emily discerned that beneath their conformity they were perfectly ordinary young women. Emilie de Rodat, with her passionate asceticism, was a welcome target for mockery.

'Sœur Emilie has a boil which prevents her from sitting down, but she will not let the doctor lance it for fear of immodesty.'

'Madame has offered her a fire in her room because of her cough, but she refuses to have it lit.'

'My grandmamma met her in the street and greeted her, but Sœur Emilie wouldn't even look up in case she saw something worldly.'

Yet her severities were only towards herself. She taught with affection and patience, using rewards instead of punishments, never correcting a pupil before the others, only in private, trying to show by example how to be good. The English Emily admired her, and in return received from the French girl a gentle pity, the nearest thing to friendship she had in the establishment, though Emilie could not allow herself to become truly fond of her namesake, for that would be a sin; one should love only God and His Mother.

She tried bravely to save this brand from the burning, this arrogant, flighty, frivolous, disobedient young woman who was going straight to hell. Emily Carew, at table, with her eyes on the young trees outside the window and her mind on anything but the sacred reading which was in progress, often caught the dark eyes of her namesake resting on her with a tender, divine regret. They talked, so far as they could with their sharply different natures and viewpoints, with mutual reproaching. Emilie de Rodat had persuaded Madame to let her take on the teaching of some forty poor children from the town, on condition that she kept them to her tiny room, that bare cell in which she slept with only a cotton counterpane to cover her. She taught them geography, among other subjects, bringing a religious light to bear on it, and begged scraps of material from other pupils in order to teach them to sew clothes for themselves. After one such lesson she appeared in the common-room, her face shining with the inner light which always burned brightest after giving a lesson or making an act of devotion. Emily thought how beautiful she looked, even with her excessive thinness and ugly dress. Then she noticed unusual activity in the short, rough dark hair, and gave an uncontrollable shriek.

'Emilie! There are lice in your hair!'

The girl put her hand to her head, and nodded slowly with a smile. 'My poor scholars have them. It is to be expected they should come to me as well.'

'Then for mercy's sake get rid of them before they spread to all of us. *I* had poor scholars with bugs once, but I never allowed the filthy things to spread.'

'Why should I kill them? They are God's creatures.'

Emily exploded. 'You are quite, quite mad. I shall go at once to find some turpentine, and then I shall take you into the yard and wash your head. You may kick and scream if you like but I shall do it. Do you realise you might infect the whole house?'

Emilie smiled her beautiful smile. 'I shall not kick *or* scream, little sister, if you wish to do so. I see I have been selfish in wishing to endure this mortification. Thank you for opening my eyes to my own vanity.'

Emily turned on her heel and went for the turpentine. It was only one of many battles as she tried to bring the French girl to understand that in order to be good one need not be cold, ugly, infectious, ill, deprived or humiliated. In turn Emilie used all her gentle force to the task of explaining to this stubborn Englishwoman how vain are the pleasures of this world, how fallible its inhabitants, how endless the joys of the spirit. Only once did her message penetrate. They had had a long argument which ended in deadlock, as ever, until Emilie asked softly of her opponent who had lost her temper yet again, 'Little sister, for all that you have of this world, are you happier than I?'

And Emily, startled, said after a pause, 'No.'

Something like happiness, however, came to her twice, each time by post from England. The first letter was from Emma, an almost incoherent scrawl.

My dearest E, here I am still in the land of the living, as you see, tho' very ill, I fear my broken heart will not mend in this life I cannot wait to join my beloved Nelson and my dear Mother for there is no one but you that ever cared for me else Horatia that I will never part with for she is His child is grown so disobedient I cannot deal with her. I have had to give up my lodgins as debters are pressing me every day, we are now living in the Rules of King's Bench were at least they cannot touch us. My dear E I long for you, why did you not stay with me insted of going among those Beasts of French-men as my Nelson called them . . .

Emily sighed. Not a word of answer to the request she had made in her farewell letter. If only this had been signed Your Loving Mother, not merely God Bless You, then indeed she would have returned to England by hook or by crook. But what could I do for her now? she wondered. I have no money, no home, no influence in England. Yet, poor hapless lady, she loves me still, and that is something in this nest of cold-hearted foreigners.

The second letter was from Elena, a typical outpouring of that lady's dramatic (in every sense) experiences, performances, tribulations and encounters, which made Emily laugh out loud for the first time in many months. Among all the frippery one passage leapt out at her.

I have tried in vain to get news of your Francis, but the matter remains as much in the dark as ever. The nearest I have come to it is meeting with Ann Connor when I played at Stamford, and she told me that wife of his is *dead* of a dropsy, so at least she can never plague you again, the monster. I must tell you that Ann is turned quite lunatic; she actually tried to bamboozle me that she is *married* to a Cecil . . .

So, if Francis still lived, one barrier between them was down. Perhaps it was a sign of changing fortunes. Suddenly she was aware of the light of summer on the mountains that surrounded Villefranche, of the nestling, romantic châteaux, the ripening vineyards, the clear waters of the Aveyron; and in the town itself the clustered medieval buildings now had a charm for her, the sweet market smells drew her as she had once been drawn to the stalls of the Market Cross in Manchester. She felt a new charity towards her colleagues, even towards Madame. In the mirror she had bought (for none was provided) she saw her face transformed back to youthful softness instead of being set in tight lines of mutiny and indifference; the strands of grey she had noticed in her curls seemed to have vanished.

'Heureux qui, comme Ulysse, a fait un beau voyage . . .', or even a bad one, if the voyager might reach port at last.

The third letter came on a day of early autumn. Ann Connor had delayed many months before writing it, savouring her coming blow at the woman she had hated and envied so long – at Emily, who held the place she coveted in the affections of Emma. A strange, perverted passion for that lovely face had lodged with Ann since she first saw her cousin Emma, long ago at Merton, and it had worked on the seed of madness in her, driving her to imagine other exalted positions for herself, since she could not occupy the one she craved, that of being Emma's beloved favourite.

The letter she had so much enjoyed writing was quite short.

My dear Cousin Emily : I was pleased to have intelligence of you from Mrs Denis, and had intended writing before now, but my engagements as you may imagine are many and demand so much of my time, and my Correspondence has suffered sorely. We are very social here in Stamford, tho' such a small place; nothing but comings and goings, balls and routs. 'Tis said the Regent himself will visit before long; my Lord has ordered me a diamond necklace and earrings for the occasion.

Alas, Cousin, I have melancholy news to convey to you; I wish it were better. The strange business of your Lover's disappearance is a mystery no more. My friends in town have written to me that some workmen, pulling down an old warehouse by Hungerford Stairs, recently came upon the remains of a man who by property found upon him was proved to be Francis Carew. The verdict of the Coroner's Court pronounced that he had met his death by means of stabbing with a knife. No relatives being traced, the remains have been buried in the same graveyard as those of his wife, who as I think Mrs Denis has written to you is also deceased. I trust this sad news will put your mind at rest after so long a period of ignorance of his fate. Truly this is a wicked World.

The room went black round Emily. She slid from the window-seat where she had read the letter on to the floor, and lay there until she came back to sick, dizzy consciousness. She was alone. Staggering to her feet, she clawed her way out of the room, clinging to furniture so that she should not fall again, slowly, slowly into the passage and up the stairs, meeting at the next landing a surprised Madame.

'But what is the matter, mademoiselle? You are ill?'

Emily managed to nod. Madame watched her as she propelled herself by the banisters towards her own room. Then she shrugged and returned to her duties.

When she did not come down for supper Emilie de Rodat asked leave to go up and see to her. The door was unlocked. Inside, the room was dark. The light of Emilie's candle flickered over the body of the English girl, prone on the ground, face downwards, unmoving. Emilie knelt and gently touched her shoulder.

'*Va-t'en*,' Emily said. '*J'ai besoin de personne.*'

'Yes, you are in need – in great need. Let me help you, little sister.' Her thin arms were round Emily, turning her over and lifting her into a sitting position, holding her so that she could not slump down again, resting her back against the side of the bed. Emily sat there like a doll from which a child has ripped the stuffing, her eyes shut.

'You are not ill, *ma sœur*. You have suffered a great grief, I think. Will you not let me help you? Come, lie on your bed, and I will fetch you a little wine.'

Emily's eyes opened. She spoke, tonelessly, in English.

'He is dead, after all. Francis is dead. Nothing is left of him but bones in the earth. They found things in his pockets. He was always putting things in his pockets, even little clothes I was making for our child. That was how they knew who he was, you see. I wish they had not known. I wish she had not told me. I keep seeing him all the time, as he is now, as he must be now, and I can't bear it, I can't bear it, I shall go mad!' She put her hand to her mouth and bit it till the blood came; and Emilie de Rodat, who shunned all contact with others lest it endanger her chastity, rocked the stiff body of the English girl gently in her arms until Emily suddenly began to weep, her face buried in the thin shoulder, and continued until she could weep no more. Emilie managed to lift her and lay her on the bed, kneeling beside it.

'*Venez, petite sœur,*' she said. '*Venez au Bon Dieu.* He will heal you, and bring you to His peace.'

Emily's swollen eyes opened, and met the tender dark ones.

'Will you show me the way?' she said.

28

To the inhabitants of the house in the Rue Moissac it was the greatest wonder of their lives. A veritable miracle had taken place. The cold, haughty, heretical Englishwoman had suddenly become meek, obedient, a changed being. She attended divine service with every appearance of devotion, wore the crucifix that was given to her, received instruction from Monsieur Marty, who was disinclined to believe that a real conversion had taken place, particularly when he heard her first confession, which sincerely shocked him. But when her way of life followed exactly the pattern of Emilie de Rodat's, even he became convinced. The comfortable warm dresses were given to the poor; all Emily begged for herself were cast-off gowns too shabby for Ursula Delbreil, the former nun, who was about her size. The little pearl necklace she presented to Madame to sell for the poor; *Tom Jones* and his wicked brotherhood were meekly handed over to Monsieur Marty. Shivering she lay at night under a thin coverlet as Emilie did, and no longer took any care of her appearance. Her pretty almond-shaped nails were neglected, broken; her hair, uncombed, was hidden by a cap. Truly our Sainte Emilie has made a convert, said they all.

But Madame Saint-Cyr, for all her piety and discipline, was in her way a worldly-wise woman. When Emily came to her asking that in future her salary be given to the poor, so that she might work only for her board, Madame shook her head.

'I cannot make you take the money, mademoiselle, but I insist on putting it aside for the day when you emerge from your present state. It is my firm opinion – and I have some experience – that you are suffering from a shock which has deranged you for the time. One day you will come to yourself and wish to resume your former life.'

'What life is there for me? I wish only for seclusion.'

'That is not the reply of a true *dévote*. I do not see the joy in your face that I see in Mademoiselle de Rodat's. I pray you will find consolation in your practice of our religion, and give thanks that you have adopted it; but I doubt if your present state of sanctity will last.'

On her knees in the Chapel, Emily fixed her eyes on the statue of Our Lady with the Child in her arms. At first it had been difficult to kneel there and look at it without her thoughts straying. The face of Mary was a little like Emma's; the Child made her feel the emptiness of her own arms, empty now for ever. She made herself kneel there, hour after hour, as Emilie advised her, until her knees and back ached almost unendurably and the colours of the statue were only a dazzle before her eyes. Then, with perseverance, she became able gradually to fix her mind on the statue itself and its meaning; then on the Cross, without the dreadful picture of Francis, dead by the knife, rising before her. The austerity of her dress and the diet she enforced on herself had been sore trials at first, but as time went on she found that, just as Emilie said, she began to find a new exaltation in being light-headed from hunger and stiff with cold. It helped her to shut off the past. Emma, Elena, all the other figures in her former life became unreal. Emilie was quietly joyful.

'It has been so with all the blessed saints. Through great trials they have come to Him. You have done well, little sister.' Together they went into the slums of the town and mixed with the diseased, the miserably poor, even a woman who appeared to be leprous. Emily saw her companion flinch at the sight of dreadful sores, then advance, smiling, to bathe them. She tried to do the same, and succeeded, though it sickened her. Unlike the rapt Emilie, she took care to wash thoroughly when they returned to the house, and in time came to enjoy, within limits, the feeling of doing good to those for whom nobody else cared. In this, perhaps, lay her salvation, when she was able to face it.

When she made her confession to Monsieur Marty he was harsh with her.

'You are full of spiritual pride, my daughter. I shall not

administer the Sacraments to you until I am certain that you truly feel the presence of God. You think that now you lead a life of self-abnegation you are perfect; but you are far from perfect. Go away and reflect on your own sins.'

It was not within Emily's compass to climb higher by spiritual means. Urged on by her guide and friend, she resorted to more and more privations. As winter came on they told on her health. Her old chest trouble came back, bringing with it continued coughs and colds. The doctor whom Madame called in pronounced that she must rest in bed until her latest illness subsided, be fed on nourishing food, and take wine and broths. She tried to resist, but weakness forced her in the end to accept what was brought to her. 'We cannot afford to lose a good teacher through excess of saintliness,' commented Madame with a grim smile.

In that far-away room where the letter had been written that had changed Emily's life, Ann Connor was reading a book. The room was the same one Elena had seen her enter, the tiny cramped front parlour of the little house in St Paul's Street. Ann had grown tired of being 'Lady Burghley'. It meant too much expenditure on finery, and as the member of the Cecil family whose mistress she had been for a time had now returned to London and could no longer be annoyed by her presence in Stamford, she sought for other amusement.

In her childhood, anxious to escape the menial tasks that fell to her sisters, Ann had taken to wandering away into the countryside, picking flowers to make crowns for herself to wear when she explored the ruins of Flint Castle and Basingwerk Abbey, pretending that she was a princess of old Wales, directing her troops against the forces of English Edward, or being wooed and won by some brave and handsome prince. She had an infinite capacity for making up stories of which she was the heroine, and believing in them. At first she had told some of them to her family, who soon made fun of them as 'Ann's romances'; all but her father, who would sit her on his knee and listen to every word, sometimes picking up his fiddle and playing a few accompanying phrases. He had been the only one she had truly loved, of all of them, and he had gone so soon.

One day, straying into the hamlet of Pentre Halkyn, between the mountains and the river, she had knocked at a cottage door to ask for a drink of water. The woman who had come to the door and taken the child in, offering her milk instead of water, was called Nesta ap Huw. She and her husband owned and herded a few cows on the lower mountain slopes. They had no children, only a number of cats, admiring their proud impassivity and aristocratic air, very unlike that of their mistress, who was short and dumpy, with a bosom almost touching her chin and greying fair hair scraped back into a knot.

But Ann admired Nesta too, for she could tell tales even better than her own, real tales of history and faery legend, and could sing, in a high sweet voice, the old songs of Wales. She spoke Welsh far more fluently than English, her accent lending charm to every word she spoke in the 'foreign tongue' in which she told her stories to Ann.

She made simples, too, from herbs, to cure her cows and her cats of their ailments, and knew verses that would take away warts and blains, and charms for the megrim.

'Are you a witch?' Ann had asked her.

'No, indeed, you must not call me that. Do you not know what ignorant people still do to witches? Only let a neighbour know that you cast spells, and the first time you offend her, up will go the cry "A witch!"' She shut her eyes and made a sign with her fingers, muttering something. 'But I have the power,' she said. 'And you have it too, bach, for there is the Irish in you beside the Welsh.'

'Could you teach me to cast spells?'

'No indeed.'

'Why?'

'It would put you in danger. I would not teach them to Huw ap Huw himself.'

'Are they bad?'

Nesta made the sign again. 'Mine are only good. But there

332

are bad ones that will bring madness or death on the hated one. There is hate in you, cariad. Beware it.'

And so Ann had learnt nothing from Nesta ap Huw but songs and legends; but she never forgot what had been told to her. 'I have the power,' she repeated to herself when anyone crossed or rebuked her. 'I have the power to send you mad or kill you, if I choose.' But she knew it was not true, because the spell was not in her possession.

The woman Ann had found the spell at last; or one very like it. There was in Stamford a little shop kept by a very dirty old man, who sat in his back room taking snuff and boiling kettles for tea, apparently uninterested in the sale of the hundreds of books which lay in dusty disorder in the shop, uncatalogued and unpriced. If you found a book there you wanted you took it to him, and he opened it, pronounced on a price and accepted your money with a grunt. Ann, with time on her hands, had spent hours ferreting among the books in search of she knew not what before she came upon the special one.

It was in manuscript, roughly bound by an amateur, the boards held together by a pair of metal clasps which had once had a key.

It seemed at first to be a book of recipes, and Ann was about to reject it when her eye was caught by a heading : 'A Charm to cure Fitts'. She sat down by the window and began to read, flushed with excitement. Someone, probably a man from the strong clear hand, and not more than fifty years or so before to go by the spelling, had written down the very magic Nesta had practised, in clear language and much detail. Ann skipped through impatiently until she found the section she wanted : 'To parry a Curse. To cause Barrenness or Impotence. To make your Enemy mad.'

Hardly believing her luck, she took the volume in to the old man, who with barely a look at it said 'Ninepence.' The book was hers, and at last the power to use it.

She had been very disappointed that her long-savoured letter to Emily had brought no visible results. It is very unsatisfactory to perpetrate a practical joke or a malicious attack if the victim cannot be seen to writhe. Ann had been to town and sought out Emma, who, bothered and distrait, said there had been no word of Emily. The same reply was made by Elena, now in the throes of selling up her inn so that Simon could go back to Naples before the winter. Thwarted, Ann returned to Stamford. Not until the discovery of the book did she see a delightful, an undreamed-of way to make sure that her rival suffered, even if the news Ann had sent her had not struck home. It was always possible that Emily had long forgotten the man who had been briefly her lover, and had formed a new attachment or settled for spinsterhood. But the spell would not fail to strike.

At first she practised it on minor subjects: a neighbour who had been nosey, a boy who had thrown a stone at her. The results were disappointing. She tried again, and this time had the most satisfactory evidence that she did indeed possess the power and the instrument.

Emily woke one day from a heavy sleep to hear a voice saying in English 'Come now, that's better.' She struggled up from a half-dream and saw a man's face bending over her, a young, pinkly healthy face with a crest of cheerful red hair above it. She pondered on this pleasant apparition for a moment, then saw that Mademoiselle Boutaric, one of the ex-nuns, was sitting in a corner knitting, her eyes never raised from her work. Emily addressed herself to the young man.

'You spoke in English.'

'Hardly surprising, mademoiselle, as I *am* English – or rather Scottish. Don't you remember me?'

She shook her head. 'I am your doctor,' he said. 'Colin Macdonald. I think you were too ill to know anybody when I first attended you. Do you not remember being told to drink your broth?'

She smiled. 'No. Did I?'

'Will you not drink some now?' He held the bowl towards her. It smelt delicious, of meat and aromatic herbs. She took

334

some, spoonful by spoonful. It seemed so long since she had enjoyed anything. Somehow the bowl was empty.

'Well done!' said Doctor Macdonald. He felt her pulse and touched her brow. 'You are well on the way to recovery, I congratulate myself. I think now you may sit up, and m'selle here may pass you a mirror.' Mademoiselle Boutaric expressionlessly did so. Emily gave a cry of horror. 'That is not *me*? What has happened to me?'

'Merely a serious illness,' said the doctor, 'and a certain degree of rather foolish fasting before it. Come now, confess.'

'I don't remember. But I have often been ill like that. Once they cut off my hair.' She felt it. 'Oh. It is still long.'

'And very pretty.' Doctor Macdonald had a smile that would have melted an iceberg. Emily gave him one in return. Mademoiselle Boutaric made a tight mouth over her knitting. Only the strict rule of obedience and self-effacement prevented her from joining in with an adverse comment. The doctor and his patient were talking freely, too freely. He was telling her how his great-grandfather had left Scotland after the '45 to follow his chief, and had eventually settled here and taken to growing vines and small-farming. 'We had lost our Highland lands. Why should we go back? My grandfather had taken a medical degree at Edinburgh, and I followed in his footsteps. So here you have a red-headed Presbyterian man of medicine, Miss Carew.'

'Presbyterian?'

'Yes. Does that shock you? I hear you are a great *dévote*.'

Emily thought. She could remember nothing about being a great *dévote*, or about anything else. Once upon a time she had felt just so, when a great gentleman – Good God, it had been Sir William Hamilton – had brought her grapes and champagne. She gave a sudden laugh, joyfully echoed by her medico. He was a good enough doctor to know that she needed normality above all things. He talked to her of his ancestor's flight to France, of the strangeness of growing up bilingual, of his mother's wonderful cock-a-leekie soup and of his own discovery of the songs of a poet called Robert Burns, who had died only a few years ago,

335

young and unregarded by the world. He quoted to his entranced patient.

> 'A fig for those by law protected;
> Liberty's a glorious feast;
> Courts for cowards were erected,
> Churches built to please the priest.'

Mademoiselle Boutaric silently slipped away, to report to Madame that the foreign doctor was preaching heresy to Mademoiselle Carew. Madame waved her away. '*Il connait son métier.*'

From that moment Emily began to get better. And Doctor Macdonald fell deeper and deeper in love.

Emily went out into the bare yard at the back, where a few plants grew in pots, and sat with the sun on her face. She was still very weak, but gaining strength daily. Very soon she was able to be taken in a chair to the house where Colin Macdonald lived with his parents, a house of uncompromising French exterior which inwardly displayed all the insignia of British comfort. There were cosy patchwork cushions, glittering decanters of whisky, family portraits by Ramsay, a fat tabby on the hearthrug and a brace of water-spaniels always at the ready to burst in and overwhelm the entire company with ingratiating licks. The meat was superb, the vegetables fresh and lavish, the sweets irresistible. Colin's father was a gentleman farmer, big, expansive, sandy like his son, a man in whom one could not but trust; his mother a remote cousin, Scots-born, small and neat, with a withering sense of humour and enough charm to empty all the trees of Villefranche of their birds. It seemed to Emily, as they all sat at ease after the meal, Mrs Macdonald at the pianoforte singing one of the sweet old songs of false lovers and roses' thorns, that the house in Rue Moissac had never existed, though she knew that she must go back to it that night, and that Emilie de Rodat's great sad eyes would meet hers in the morning. 'Little sister! Where have you gone?'

Then, without warning, the dreams began.

She woke from the first one in a cold sweat, shivering with fear. Well enough now to carry out her teaching, she went through the day with an uneasy consciousness of it leering over her shoulder, laying a cold hand over her heart. At night she asked leave to go over to the Macdonalds' house, and it was granted.

'I felt,' she told Colin and his parents, 'as though it were not quite I, but someone in my place, who had strayed into a deserted building. A cellar, I think – at least it was cold and tomb-like. There were two witches in it.'

'Witches?'

'I don't know . . . evil people. They were wishing bad things on me – or the person I was – showing me ways out of the place, stairs and slopes by which I could get free. But I held a sprig of rosemary in my hand, knowing it would keep me safe from enchantments, and I knew somehow that if I did what they told me I would have to drop the rosemary to do it, and so would be open to their spells. I got out – I can't recall how – and they followed me, legions of them, and beset me like hounds on a fox; and I knew that I must keep uttering the Holy Names and making the sign of the Cross, which I did, and was given strength to hold on to my rosemary. And then I awoke.'

Three pairs of blue Macdonald eyes were consulting each other. Colin reached out and took her hand. 'It was your illness. It has strange effects.'

'In my young days it was elder that held the magic properties,' said his father. 'I mind that folk grew it at the end of their gardens to keep off witches.'

'Rosemary, too,' said Mrs Macdonald. 'You dreamed right, Miss Emily. It is like parsley, flourishes where the mistress is master, and blossoms at midnight on Twelfth Night. It got its name from the spikes the flower grows in, Mary's rose among her Son's crown of thorns.'

'I never heard that,' Emily said. 'It means nothing to me now. But then it did. I knew it would keep me safe.'

337

Colin gave her a draught that would make her sleep deeply that night – as it did.

But again the dreams came. Now she was in a house that seemed to be her own, suddenly invaded by a terrible horde of demons who destroyed her belongings and put her to torture. Sometimes a way out would appear, then close up. Shrieking, she beat on the walls, tried to prise out bricks and open windows, while the creatures dragged her back. Once she got as far as the path outside the back door, only to find the garden wall grown into a huge cliff, and the demons swarming in the garden, mocking her.

That morning she was too bemused to teach properly, forgetting the French for ordinary words, losing the thread of her sentences. Madame strolled in to listen, advised by one of her spies.

'You had better retire to your room, mademoiselle. It seems you are not yet recovered.'

One after another they came, the nightmares, if such they were. She had had bad dreams before, troublous and frightening, but never such terrible ones as these. She told Emilie about them.

'They are the visitations of the Evil One. You have neglected your devotions since your illness, sister. Return to them, and the visions will cease. Meanwhile put the crucifix under your pillow.'

Emily visited the Chapel at night and prayed before the altar; alas, with nothing like the passionate fervour she had once displayed. Still they came, the wicked mocking faces, the threats and hollow voices. Once she was herself an enchanter, pleased to find she could raise spirits at will, then increasingly daunted as they came, more and more of them, crowding upon her, clamouring to be restored to their bodies, stifling her with the sulphurous fumes they exhaled. A cock crowed at the first light of dawn, and her heart leaped, as even in the dream the opening of *Hamlet* sprang into her mind: 'It faded on the crowing of the cock.' But these creatures took no heed of the bird of dawning, as they scraped at her clothing, plucked her hair and her flesh. She raised her hand to make the sign of the Cross, but it

338

was leaden, the fingers would not move; and a great gale of devilish laughter swept round her, louder and louder, until she awoke screaming.

'Mademoiselle, what is the matter with you? Are you out of your mind?'

Out of her mind. She began to think she was. Every night the dreams came, and lingered over the day, so that she dreaded the coming of the night. The hideous faces of her visions obscured those of her pupils; she could no longer find any pleasure in visiting the Macdonalds and seeing their concern for her, and Colin's more than concern. He spoke to her alone one day.

'Leave Madame Saint-Cyr and come to us. My mother would have you gladly. Away from this place you'll be better. Emily, please come. I am afraid for you, and I can't afford to let anxiety for one patient ruin my care of others, yet that is how it is at present.'

She looked away. 'No, Colin. There is something more to it. I believe I am being punished. I took the vows in my heart, and I have betrayed them by returning to a worldly life.'

'That is Mademoiselle de Rodat speaking!' he burst out. 'I know the arguments. Why do you let yourself be bammed by such nonsense? You've already surmounted so many trials – from what you've told me, which I suspect is not all. Will you admit yourself vanquished by a lot of superstition?'

The most terrible dream of all overtook her. She was crazed with anger, maddened by a hatred that she had never felt, that was taken over from another. Infuriated by the cries of her child, a tiny naked infant, she flung it into a cauldron of boiling water and watched it die, horrified yet fascinated. A reasonable voice said within her 'This is only a dream', yet she could feel, hear, see as clearly as in the day. Faces loomed up at her, spoke. They were likenesses of those she knew to be dead: Thetis Blackburn, Sir William, her grandmother. The black servant, Fatima, swam out of the dark at her. 'Remember me, missee? I went mad and died, like you do some day.' Indeed, she remembered, Fatima's weak wits had given way while Emma still owned Merton, and the poor creature had been taken away to Bedlam, where she had lasted only a few weeks. Again Emily struggled to make the Holy Sign, but now her hand would not even stir.

'It is a clear case of possession,' Monsieur Marty said to Madame. 'I would be prepared to carry out an exorcism, if you permit, Madame.'

'You may exorcise the girl and her devil out of the house to-gether, for all I care. In any case, I shall be rid of her soon. The poor mad de Rodat has the intention of founding her own order and taking Delbreil, Boutaric and Dutriac with her, besides la Carew. They are searching for some ramshackle building in the town which they can turn into a convent.'

'But then you will lose all our teachers, Madame. How will you carry on this establishment?'

'I shall not carry it on.' Madame had the pleasure of seeing her chaplain's haughty face pale, even to the tip of his large retroussé nose. 'I am heartily tired of Villefranche, and now that there is peace, the monster Bonaparte chained up at Elba, our King back on his throne, and His Holiness once again in the Vatican, God be praised – why, I see no reason for remaining here. I shall make a pilgrimage to Rome, with Céleste and Angèle, then we will join my sister in her château.'

Monsieur Marty, whose chaplainship of Madame's household had been not merely comfortable but profitable, appeared about to reply with some violence; but, thinking better of it, turned away.

Emilie de Rodat's habitual gentleness of manner could in a good cause become transformed into an irresistible force. Every day she worked on Emily Carew, weakened and perpetually tired from her nocturnal experiences.

'Can you not hear God calling you through my humble voice, little sister? Come with us, take the beautiful vows of poverty and chastity, and all these visions will cease to plague you. Mademoiselle Alric has promised to rent us part of her house, and to help us. We could be there tomorrow, think of it.'

'Then go,' said Emily wearily. 'I am no use to you, sister. I have no true vocation. I know that now; it has come to me since my illness. I should only shame you. Leave me to myself, I beg you.'

But it was so hard to argue, always with the same negative reasons, against Emilie's passionate, urgent pleadings. Her burning eyes were hypnotic, her voice persuasive. Perhaps it would be easier to give in. She went to bed that night with a crucifix beneath her pillow, praying to be guided rightly.

The dream which came to her was very different from the former ones. Against the darkness a circle of light began to form, spreading into a great blending of colours of an unearthly beauty, sunrise and sunset, rainbow and the ocean's blue, rose, gold and violet, trembling and shimmering with life; and within it there became visible the figure of Mrs Demdike, just as she had been when Emily saw her. Even the brooch that clasped her shawl was the same, a black gem set in seed-pearls. But her face was young, calm and happy. In her arms was a grey cat, cradled like a child, patting her cheek softly with its paw, and round her feet swarmed small creatures of every kind: cats black, white, orange and tabby, toads, mice, dogs, goats, hares, and little birds; and in the glorious light above them bats danced and flittered.

Emily, staring entranced, felt rather than heard the words that were spoken. 'I'm a spirit now, young lady, as you see, and my job's to care for these, all the little ones that have suffered for being the friends of them that were called witches. We can help you better now, the little ones and I, since you're yourself bewitched. Look here, who I've browt you.'

It did not seem at all strange that a spirit should have a Lancashire accent, nor that the figure which Mrs Demdike led forward by the hand should be that of a nun, very young and pretty, with eyes of a transcendent beauty. Again the words were felt, not heard. The voice was soft and sweet, with a strange cadence, a little like Irish, or perhaps West Country. Emily recognised it by instinct, not knowledge, as the speech of Tudor England.

341

'I tried to warn you, lady, at Draycott. But then I could only come to you in an ugly likeness, for my poor bones were unburied. Oh, I pray you, hear me now! Take not the veil, sweet madam, or 'twill be your ruin as 'twas mine. Hear me, and be saved.'

'I hear,' Emily heard herself saying, 'and I will be saved.'

She stretched out her arms to the two visions; but their smiles were fading, with their outlines, and the small creatures were dissolving in the radiant cloud; then even that was gone, leaving the dreamer with a sense of disappointment more acute than any she had known.

Yet, wakening into ordinary daylight, she was happy, restored to herself. She knew in her heart that the nightmares would not come back, that she was protected by forces stronger than evil. She went down to breakfast hungry and cheerful, stared at in astonishment by Madame and the others. When Emilie de Rodat approached her with a question in her eyes, she shook her head.

'No, Emilie. I cannot come with you. I am not meant for a religious. Please do not ask me again.'

The French girl uttered no reproach; only her deep sad eyes spoke it. Then, '*Dieu vous bénisse,*' she said, and turned away.

There was no need to tell Colin Macdonald that his patient was recovered. In the garden of his father's house he took her hand and kissed it.

'Now I can ask you what I could not while you were my patient. Dearest Emily, will you marry me?'

29

For long moments they stood, their hands still clasped. The birds were silent. A puff of smoke drifted over the garden from a neighbour's pyre of dead leaves. Then Emily spoke.

'Dear Colin, believe me, I would like to answer as you wish. I am very sensible of your worth—'

'Sensible! Worth! Those words ring my knell, I fear.'

'No, no. But – what can I say? I have been too disturbed in my mind, until today, even to consider whether you admired me, or I you.'

'Consider now.'

'Well, then – I do admire you, what I know of you. And I admire your parents, and like them. It would be very pleasant to belong to such a family. But, oh, why does my life repeat the same pattern, always the same? When I was very young there was a man, much older than I, who offered me what you do; and, just as now, I had been unhappy for a long time. I accepted him, and if death had not come between us I would have married him. Yet I knew later that I would have been wrong to do so, when I – when I found the man I truly loved.'

'But you have lost him. The pattern is changing, surely.'

She sighed. 'How can I tell? Colin, I must have time. Give me time.'

'Of course. What a rash, headlong fellow I am! Always was. Come now, sit under the tree and tell me what has done you so much more good than any of my medicines.'

In halting words she tried to describe the dream, the colours, the apparitions, and the strange ecstatic quality of it all. 'It sounds so – unbelievable. I'm sure you will think me crazier than ever.'

Colin's face was serious. 'Do you think I have centuries of

Highland blood in me for nothing? I know when I hear the truth.' He mused.

'Whither is fled the visionary gleam?
Where is it now, the glory and the dream?'

'Yes, that is exactly how I felt,' she said. 'Who wrote it?'
'An English poet – William Wordsworth. A very great man.'
'How long it is since I read any poetry. Anything at all, indeed, except missals. I wonder what Monsieur Marty did with *Tom Jones?*'
'With *whom?*'
'I gave him my books – *Tom Jones* and *Joseph Andrews* and *Paul et Virginie* and the others – when I thought myself converted. I wish I had them back. Do you think he still has them?'
'He probably sits up half the night reading them. Emily, you are a dear, sweet, ridiculous little idiot, and I shall have to marry you if only to stop you getting into such sorry scrapes. Now let us go in before you catch cold.'
Her arm in his, they strolled towards the house.

Just as she had said, the pattern was repeating itself. Within a few weeks of Colin's proposal of marriage a letter was to change her life. It lay there on the gloomy coffer outside the teacher's common-room, addressed to her in a hand she could not mistake. Her own hands shaking, she opened it, breaking the seal which was an intaglio of the young Emma's profile.

Common of St Peter's, 2 miles
from Calais.
October 12 1814.

My dearest E, you will be happy to know I am free of my debts, one or two kind persons having paid them for me but I felt it best to leave England and live quiet here for a time. Horatia and I take the air every day and live very cheap on good fare but I have been very ill my Dear and am still not

344

recovered I would like so *very very* much to see you has we are now in the same Country it seems redeculous we should not meet I have very much to communicate to you

Horatia is well grown and speaks French like a French girl and is everywhere admired

Pray do come to me my dear E God bless you

your—

The next word had been scratched out so thoroughly that there was no possibility of reading it. Emily could only hope it was the word she longed to see. The signature was a sprawling EMMA.

Madame did not seem surprised to hear Emily's request that she might leave at once, or as soon as a coach could be found, to take her to the side of her sick relative. Emily had already told her that she proposed to leave in any case. She opened a small drawer in her desk and produced a packet containing what looked to Emily like an enormous amount of French money.

'Your earnings,' she said with the merest twitch of a smile. 'Are you not grateful now that I did not give them to the poor?'

'Yes, Madame. I was very foolish. I do thank you.' There was enough money in the packet to pay for her journey to Calais and on to England if she wished; and to pay for the comforts she suspected her sick mother sorely needed.

When, at the end of the week, she said farewell to Madame, that lady enquired whether she expected to return to Villefranche.

'I am not sure, Madame. It may be so.'

'*Eh bien,* in any case I shall not be here. At Christmas my household will disperse. I bid you goodbye, Mademoiselle Carew.'

The farewell to Colin was of a different order. Harassed as he was by an epidemic which had spread through the town from the slum quarter, he drove her in his gig to the Market Square by the Collegiate Church, which had been the first thing she saw in Villefranche, and would be the last.

Standing by the coach as it prepared to depart he looked up at

345

her pale, sad face, framed in the black bonnet, and clasped the hand she reached down to him.

'You will come back?'

'I will try. I promise you I will try.' Her voice trembled on the edge of tears. 'It is not easy to leave my only friend.'

'I wish to God I could have kissed you. But I daren't for fear of this confounded plague. Take care of yourself, my dear girl.'

She tried to smile as the coach began to move, leaving the tall familiar figure in the plaid cloak and tall hat growing ever smaller in the distance. But it was impossible not to cry instead.

That winter would always be remembered as the most terrible for years. Hurricanes swept Europe, driving the West India fleet back into harbour, tearing anchors and cables, blowing great casks and bales of merchandise from the safety of the quay into the sea. Factory chimneys crumbled like piecrust, crashing and killing the workers beneath. In Dublin trees of a hundred years' growth were torn up by the roots. A daring packet ship, the *Dart*, fought her way out of Dover harbour in an attempt to reach Calais, and was ignominiously blown northward into Ramsgate. The Seine swelled to the level of her banks with the torrential rains. In the Western Ocean the *Amphitrite*, sailing from Quebec to London, managed to unload her passengers and crew on to another vessel before their lives might be lost in the waves.

A violent storm of wind and hail, thunder and lightning beset the neighbourhood of Stamford, smashing window-panes, ripping off roofs and blinding one unfortunate boy. Ann Connor had spent a frustrating hour at her latest piece of magic, 'A Charm to see another Person at a Distance.' It involved the use of a mirror, a rhymed verse, and some herbs which had been hard to find. Perhaps they were not quite the right ones, for the charm had not worked at first try some weeks before the night of the storm. Then, slowly and dimly, had come an image of Emily, haggard-faced, all in black, kneeling in some building whose detail Ann could not quite discern. Good. Then clearly the other spell had taken and the victim was suffering. At another time

346

Ann saw her lying on a narrow bed, asleep, frowning and tossing under the persecutions inflicted on her in a nightmare.

But after that, nothing. Each time she tried, the best result she could get was a milky blank. Someone or something was blocking her view; powerful white magic was being used against her. She cursed the unseen person – or persons; there seemed to be more than one, very strong and potent. Time and again she mixed the potion, spoke the words, polished the mirror, the steel spectacles she now wore half-way down her nose giving her just the look of a witch in a story-book – all in vain. She had hardly noticed the rumbles of approaching thunder or the increasing patter of rain turning to the gunfire of hail. In the street people were running for cover, shrieking. She went to the window – the round mirror in one hand, a knife for chopping the herbs in the other – just as a vivid electric shaft of forked lightning struck, smashing the mirror into fragments, running up the steel of the knife into her nerves and veins, turning her blood to fire.

It was many days before they found her on the floor among her books. The discovery caused a stir in the sleepy little town such as it had not had for some time. When the remains had been taken to the George Inn for the coroner's consideration the vicar dropped in at the cottage, interested in neighbours' tales of strange books and objects. He was a man strongly opposed to superstitious practices, though learned in them; and what he found, combined with his knowledge of the Cecil affair, decided him in refusing the body Christian burial. Generously the Cecil family, who alone in the town had known the dead woman, offered her coffin a refuge within the grounds of Burghley House.

The coach in which Emily was travelling came off the road on a hilly pass, blown over by savage gales, only two days after it had left Villefranche. Nobody was seriously hurt and by degrees the travellers were got to the nearest village and put up at inns and in lodgings. There was nothing to be done but look out of the window at the tossing trees and the wild wind-light in the sky. Emily had to possess her soul in patience. In a few

347

days the coach was repaired, and the journey continued, very slowly, until, just through Aubusson, the driver declared that he would take the vehicle no further. A man had his duty to his wife and children. He would go back with the horses to the last stage and hope to find transport to his home.

After the hurricanes the snows came. It was 10 January 1815 when Emily at last, by many different transports, arrived at the village of Saint-Pierre. The day was lowering and bitterly cold, the ground a morass of icy mud under the wheels of the rickety chaise she had hired at Ardres. It was almost too good to believe that she was within a few yards of Emma.

But nothing in this journey was to be easy, it seemed. Emma's letter had furnished only the vaguest of addresses. Emily knocked at the doors of six or seven cottages before finding one person who could help her; some preferred not even to risk opening the door after glimpsing through the window an unknown female in a travel-worn pelisse and a tired bonnet, who might well be a beggar of evil intent. At last she was directed to a farmhouse some quarter of a mile away, as being that of two sisters who took in lodgers. Grumbling, her driver consented to take her there, 'But not an inch further without extra money, mademoiselle.'

The farm was a solid old house right on the common, surrounded by a high creeper-covered wall. Her knock was answered immediately by a pleasant-faced woman. 'Lady Hamilton? Alas, mademoiselle, she has been gone from here almost a month. She was very ill, poor lady, and the cold winds here were too much for her.'

Emily felt as if her heart had turned to lead and plummeted down into her soaked boots. She sat down suddenly on the seat in the porch. 'Is she – dead, then?'

'Dead? God forbid, mademoiselle, though she had suffered greatly for many months. They have gone back to Calais, she and the little girl.'

'Do you know where in Calais, madame?'

Madame did not, but she guessed it would be to the Hotel

Dessin, where they had stayed before moving to Saint-Pierre. Moved by Emily's defeated look, she urged upon her a glass of wine, and invited the driver to step in and warm himself by the kitchen fire, with a similar glass. As they drank, she told Emily how Emma had been stricken just after her arrival by jaundice, a recurrence of an earlier illness. Such pains, such sickness, such fever, and as yellow as a leaf of autumn. For weeks she had hardly eaten, though so large of build; it seemed that only wine brought her any relief. Then in September she had become better, able to ride in the little cart they had found for her, while Horatia rode an ass of kindly disposition. They were even able to go on Wednesday evenings to the *bals champêtres* given by the actor Plante at his house near the church of Saint-Pierre, which, as mademoiselle would of course know, miledi attended most devoutly. She was also able to resume her instruction of her daughter, which she faithfully carried out every morning, having, figure it to yourself, learnt German and Spanish in order to teach them to the young one as well as French and Italian.

'Did they appear affectionate?' asked Emily, with an envious pang.

'Alas, one was very often sorrowful to hear sounds of quarrelling. The child was pert and high-spirited, as they are by nature, and the poor mother made irritable as one must be by an affection of the spleen, which, mademoiselle would agree being herself French, was considered in our country to be the organ most affecting the passions, and not, as some believe, the heart. And there were also troubles because they had very little money, Madame approached confidentially. On one occasion miledi was very, very angry because she discovered that the young Horatia had written to her uncle requesting money, and had received some. She would not like to repeat what miledi had said of this uncle, who, it appeared, was an English milor.

Emily could have sat for hours listening, but the afternoon was darkening and she must leave for Calais. She asked madame if the driver might be persuaded, in her opinion, to take her there.

'No, indeed, the poor man, he must return to Ardres before dark. His horse is old and too feeble for these icy roads. But my Jean-Louis will take you, mademoiselle, if you can but wait until he has finished feeding the beasts.'

Jean-Louis proved to be a young giant of few words but amiable character. Smilingly he lifted Emily into the seat beside him, under the overhanging canopy of a covered cart drawn by a sturdy, imperturbable animal who could not have been described as feeble. Madame showered blessings as they departed, informing Emily in a jovial shout that Jean-Louis had cost her two and twenty thousand francs a year by his refusal to serve the ogre Bonaparte.

Monsieur Dessin regretted that Lady Hamilton and her suite were not staying under his roof but promised to find out within a few hours where she was. He also regretted that his house was so full with English travellers who had been detained by the bad weather that he could not accommodate mademoiselle; but his partner, at the Hotel Quillac down the street, would be happy to oblige her. Monsieur Quillac triumphantly produced a small vacant room, in which mademoiselle, weary, dirty, and suffering from dashed hopes and growing anxiety, glady stripped off her clothes and saw them borne away to be laundered immediately by a trim maid with streamers on her cap. The same maid shortly returned with a hip-bath and relays of hot water more than welcome to the exhausted traveller. It seemed very important to be fresh, comfortable and strong before setting out to rescue Emma.

With breakfast came news from Monsieur Dessin: Lady Hamilton was at the house of Monsieur Damy in the Rue Française, just round the corner. It was not a cheerful-looking house, the six shuttered windows giving it an eyeless, secret look. It was on the north side of the narrow street, unlikely to catch any sun even on the brightest day, and overshadowed by the house opposite. Emily pulled the bell at the side of the entrance to the mews, a large door obviously locked. In a few moments a small slip door opened cautiously, and the long face of an elderly man peered out at Emily.

'Monsieur Damy?'

'Yes.'

'I believe Lady Hamilton is staying with you. I am a relative of hers from – from England, and I would like to see her.'

Monsieur Damy, in whom communicativeness was not a strong point, murmured that the lady was ill. Emily discovered later that he was an ex-monk, dismissed from his vicarage at Notre Dame at the Revolution. After knowing Monsieur Marty, she recognised the type.

'Will you ask her please, if she is well enough to see me?'

Silently he turned on his heel, shutting the door and leaving her standing in the street, stared at by passers-by. A few moments later the door reopened and he beckoned her in. Standing in the bare, gloomy hallway, pervaded by a smell of damp and onions, she looked about her with distaste. Surely Emma could not tolerate such a place?

As Monsieur Damy disappeared into another room a young girl came down the uncarpeted staircase. Emily gasped almost audibly. She had last seen Horatia as a plump, stolid child of four, rosy-cheeked and chubby. This girl was tall and thin to gauntness as though she had grown far too quickly, an appearance emphasised by a frock that was too short. She must be about fourteen, Emily reckoned. At the first glance she caught a fleeting likeness to herself in the hair that curled all over the head and the large eyes; then it was gone, banished by the long, wandering Nelson nose that made the child superficially the image of her father. There was no look of Emma at all.

Horatia's expression was not welcoming. 'What do you want?' she asked in French. Emily replied in English.

'I would like to see Lady Hamilton, Horatia. Do you not remember me? I am Emily Carew, your – relative. We knew each other well when you were little.'

'I don't remember you. We have so many relatives. And my lady is not well enough to be visited.'

'May I not merely come up for a moment? I—'

'Does she owe you money?' Horatia broke in rudely.

'No, of course not.'

'A lot of them say that and then push bills into my hand when I let them in.' She looked Emily up and down disparagingly. 'You don't look very prosperous. If you want to beg some relic of my father from her before she dies, there are none left. Everything's gone to the pawnshop. *Everything!*' There were tears in her voice. 'Our best dresses and my watch, and the little chair . . .' She turned away abruptly, her hands covering her face.

'Horatia!' Emily put her arms round the thin body. 'My poor dear. I knew nothing of this. Believe me, I only came to help you and my lady. Look!' She unfastened the purse that was secured to her belt for travelling. 'I have plenty of money, see, and more at the hotel. I can buy my lady anything she needs. Horatia, I've come so far to see her. She wrote to me, begged me to come. Won't you let me upstairs!'

Horatia's hands had come down from her wet face. Sniffing, she looked at the healthily full purse, then at Emily's pleading face, and nodded. Emily followed her up the shabby staircase, its stone striking cold to the feet. The room she was taken to was on the first floor, at the back of the house. It was small, dark, and completely cheerless. The ceiling was low, the window dirty. There was no fire in the grate and the floor-boards were bare. A few pieces of cheap furniture had been put in, doubtless to justify Monsieur Damy's asking money for it at all, but the bed was in a wall alcove, a cramped, narrow affair with a wooden canopy over it but without curtains. The room smelt of illness and of brandy.

Emily hurried to the bed. The woman who lay in it was all but unrecognisable. She had put on many pounds of weight. Fat blurred the once perfect features; a flush of fever overlaid the yellow stain of jaundice. The nightcap could not hide the grey streaks in the auburn hair. From time to time she coughed painfully, and moaned.

'Good God! Is a doctor attending her?'

'He was angry last time because I had no money to pay him.'

'And what are all those bottles?' They were piled up in a corner, twenty or thirty empty bottles, the final touch of squalor to the room.

'All she can take is wine, or brandy,' said Horatia. 'It kills the pain and makes her go to sleep. But sometimes she's so wild and angry after drinking, and thinks I am somebody else – someone called Fanny.'

'But the last thing she should have is wine. With a complaint of the liver it should never be taken. It only inflames the trouble. No wonder she has come to this.'

'How do you know?'

'I have done a lot of nursing among the poor. A very wise nun who had nursed all her life told me this. For jaundice a patient should be given thin soups, plenty of fruit, nothing rich. Horatia, take this money and buy what I tell you and I will prepare it. Has Monsieur Damy a kitchen? Good. Then fetch the doctor, and tell him I will see he is paid.'

Horatia, staring, took the francs and went. Emily set about making the room as presentable as possible, having discovered Monsieur Damy in his remote stony kitchen and obtained from him a bucket of water, cloths, an apron and everything else she needed for the moment. Emma slept uneasily through it all. Then, as Emily was putting the last of the bottles outside, she heard a soft, still-sweet voice behind her.

'*Qui est là?*'

She went to the bedside. 'It is I, my dearest lady. Emily.'

'Emily?' The sick woman seemed to drag her wits back from some far distant place, but Emily could see that she was not recognised.

'Don't worry your head. I've come to help you.' She took off the disfiguring night-cap, propped Emma up so that she could breathe more easily, then washed the hot, perspiring face. It was alarmingly obvious to her, from her experiences in Villefranche, that not merely jaundice but pneumonia was the matter.

The doctor, when he arrived, proved very unhelpful. He was

quite uninterested in his poor patient, and only too glad to be dismissed with a token fee. Emily would dearly have liked to move Emma, but she feared things had gone too far for that. For four days she spent all her time by Emma's side, or taking turns with Horatia to do the shopping. There was a fire in the grate now, and clean sheets on the bed; the stink of wine had gone. Emma was hardly conscious at all, knowing neither of them, only now and then speaking in a rambling murmur. On the fifth morning, when Emily arrived from the hotel, a change had taken place. The flush on Emma's face had faded and the swelling had gone down. Her eyes were open and as Emily entered she was met with an attempt at a smile.

'She has been talking to me,' said Horatia. 'I think she is better.'

'Nelson,' said Emma. 'He must be very cold out there in the Downs. I have told Allen to put a fire in his cabin.'

She rambled on at intervals, talking of Merton and Naples, of Nelson's sisters and of people and things unknown to Emily. Horatia was getting more and more quietly distressed, Emily could see.

'Go out for a walk, my dear,' she said. 'Go to the Jardin Richelieu and feed the birds. Poor things, they must be starved in this weather. And then why not go to the hotel and ask Madame Quillac if you may have some dinner?'

Horatia nodded. At the door she turned and gave a last, long look at the bed.

About midday Emma's breathing became slower, and the rambling ceased. 'Please hold me,' she said suddenly. Emily put an arm round her shoulders, and stroked her brow with Cologne-water.

Emma's eyes closed; she seemed asleep. Then she said 'Emily.'

'Yes, my dear? Oh, I thought you would never know me.'

'I know you – very well. Has it been you – all the time?'

'Horatia and me. Don't talk.'

'Yes – must. The chair at the pawnshop – for Lady Charlotte. She was – so kind to you.'

354

'Of course.'

'The little box. For you. Something for you!' She pointed to a small inlaid box on the window-sill. A smile of extraordinary sweetness came over her face, restoring all its old beauty and a quality of radiance Emily had never seen on it before. She seemed to be looking past Emily, at someone standing near. Then she drew Emily's face down to hers and kissed her. 'Thank you – Emily – my dearest daughter.'

30

It had been cold in wind-raked Calais. It was colder in England, with the chilly damps of February. Emily reached out from her bed in the tiny room of the Golden Cross and pulled her cloak over her as an extra coverlet. She was worn out with the coach journey from Dover – she had travelled outside for cheapness – and so cold that even the thin bedclothes provided were a luxury to her stiff limbs and numbed hands and feet. Yet, in spite of her longing for sleep, sleep would not come.

Pictures flowed into her mind, blending into one another. Horatia's grief and her own after Emma's death; her vigil the night before the funeral, beside the body, and the awesome beauty that had come back to her mother's face since the spirit had been released. So beautiful it was that the undertaker's men, who by tradition shared the vigil, had stared and talked in whispers of Saint Clare, whose coffin, being opened after many centuries, had revealed her as young and lovely as when she had come to Francis of Assisi, dressed as a bride with her gold hair flowing. And, they whispered to Emily, the saint had been some sixty years old when she died, ten years older than the lady over whom they watched.

The little inlaid box which Emma had said was to be hers contained only one thing : a small unframed painting, a rough, vivid sketch on ivory by a master's hand. It showed a very young, almost childish mother with a naked baby on her lap. The heart-shaped face under its cloudy crown of chestnut hair was bent tenderly over the child, one graceful arm was raised above it, dangling a toy for its amusement. On the back was written : 'For dearest E. This was done by Sir Joshua of me and you when you was newly-born.'

Friends unknown to Emily had come forward. Mr Henry Cadogan, British Consul and Lloyd's agent – from whose family,

Emily gathered, her grandmother had 'adopted' her surname – had stepped in to make the funeral arrangements and pay for everything. His sister-in-law, Mrs Rothery, whose husband was Counsellor of the Admiralty, living near Boulogne, had arrived full of distress because she had not been summoned before to the aid of Lady Hamilton. Both families had come to know her in her early days at Calais, had been charmed by her. 'Why did she not tell us she had returned from Saint-Pierre?' Mrs Rothery demanded of Horatia, who merely shook her head, saying, 'She would not let me.'

'Pride, of course. Ah dear! What a cruel thing it is to be so proud. Well, all we can do now is to settle the poor thing's debts and see to your return to England, Miss Nelson.'

Kind Mrs Henry Cadogan brought Horatia a set of onyx jewellery: a necklet, bracelets and earrings. 'Your poor mother gave me these; they were a present to her from the Queen of Naples. I value them greatly but I should like you to have them back. I know how little is left to you.'

Horatia refused. She too had pride. Emily tried to talk to her but found her withdrawn in the extreme. She mourned Emma, yet would not admit to having loved her. Once she burst out, 'She would never say I was her daughter, only the adopted daughter of Lord Nelson and herself. I know, I'm sure that Lord Nelson was my father. But she – it would have been different if I had known for sure. As it was – things were not right between us.'

Emily nodded. She knew all too well how Horatia had felt. In the circumstances, to spare the child's feelings and to carry out the spirit of Emma's wishes in life, she introduced herself to the Cadogans, the Rotherys and the priest from Saint-Pierre as a distant cousin of Miss Nelson's. And when Mr Cadogan sailed back to England to convey Horatia to her Uncle Matcham, Emily remained behind to catch the next packet.

Now she was back at the Golden Cross; how strange was life. When she had first entered the inn the landlord was standing at the door, welcoming travellers who looked in any way important. As Emily passed him he stared at her and through her, not insultingly, but with obvious non-recognition. Looking about for a vacant seat in the coffee-room, she caught sight of herself in a mirror over the fireplace, and was shocked. For a second she seemed to be looking into the face of her grandmother, as she first remembered her. The pale, grimy face, weary with travel, had fallen into lines of sadness. She looked what she felt and was, a woman of thirty-three.

Lying in the dark, brooding, was a useless pastime. She lit her bedroom candle, got out of bed, and stared into the fly-spotted mirror on the dressing-stand. The image she saw was a little more cheering than that reflected in the coffee-room. Her face was not lined, only unrefreshed after months of winter and care; her eyes were still large, her chin still piquantly pointed; and though it had been years since her hair had been near the hands of a coiffeur, it had not ceased to curl.

'Well, Emily, my dear,' she said to herself, sitting back on the counterpane of woollen patchwork, 'it has come to this, then. You are all but thirty-three, which makes you a middle-aged lady ready for the cap and shawl. To all intents and purposes you are a spinster, your past folly having failed to ruin you completely. You have neither the vocation of a nun nor the domestic leanings which by now would have drawn you to some good man's hearth. (Poor Colin. How ghost-like he now seems to me in England.) You have seen the sad example of a mother brought to her death by foolish pride and obstinacy. Very well, then, profit by it. Tomorrow you will seek out anyone who may put you in the way of an honest situation, from Lady Charlotte to Signora Storace, and there is to be no more sallying abroad or playing at devotions. You have a certain gift for instructing others – then use it. And so repay life for what it has given you; for penniless, nameless, and growing every day older, there is no other fortune left to you.'

Communing thus solemnly with herself made her laugh involuntarily, hoping there was nobody in the next room to hear her. Then, relieved by having taken a firm decision, she slept.

The next morning brought the faint daffodil sunshine which pretends to be a herald of spring. Dull grey London walls brightened, sparrows twittered on the roofs. As Emily emerged from the inn a woman perched by the edge of the pavement pulled at her skirt.

'Buy a flower, dearie. Buy a pretty flower from the country.'

A bunch of wilting snowdrops was being thrust on her. She pulled out her thin purse and gave the gipsy a penny for the flowers, receiving a shouted blessing, then she reproached herself for being so spendthrift with what little she had. How should one in her situation make use of a bunch of flowers? Yet she buried her nose in their coolness, touched the wilting white heads, and it came to her what she must do with them. She set off up Whitcomb Street, through Leicester Square and north again, into the district where savoury smells of foreign food hung on the wintry air. Shutters were being opened, pavements swept, people were beginning to move between the shops selling cheese and wine, sausages and strings of onions, booksellers were laying out their cheapest volumes on stalls outside the shops. Emily turned off Compton Street into Dean Street. There was the tower of St Anne's with its four-faced clock, and weather-vane; the hour of nine was about to strike. She walked slowly up the churchyard path, putting off the moment when she must turn aside among the graves and read on the tower wall the epitaph of that poor King of Corsica who, like Emma, had died in debt.

> *The grave, great teacher, to a level brings*
> *Heroes and beggars, galley slaves and kings.*

And lovers too, my Francis. Here was one grave she sought, on the edge of the older ones, near the churchyard wall, a new, light-coloured stone.

Katina, daughter of Georgiou and Maria Papoulas, born November 9 1780, died in London February 26 1812.

Then followed an inscription in Greek. Emily felt cold and sick. What had been so far only a reported happening was true and real. She turned reluctantly towards the stone that should mark Francis's grave, beside his wife's.

It was not there.

There was not even a mound. No new burials were visible near Katina's stone. The grave was undisturbed, had been for many years. Ann Connor had evidently made a mistake; he was not buried next to Katina. Emily looked wildly round, the snowdrops falling unheeded from her hand, to be pecked at by a questing sparrow. An old man was unlocking the church door. Emily hurried up to him. Yes, he said, he was the verger, had been these many years.

'Francis Carew? Don't remember no such name, not three years ago, nor five, nor ten. Are you sure this is the church, missy?'

'I was told so. There is no other St Anne's in Soho, is there?'

'Nay. St Giles's, St Martin's, and there be a Roman mission chapel corner of the square. St Mary's, St Andrew's, maybe?' He peered at her, his head on one side like an enquiring robin.

'No, I don't think so. I have destroyed the letter, but I am sure it was St Anne's. Have you a book – a register of burials?'

'Aye, in the vestry. But vicar wouldn't like it, me showing church-papers to a stranger.' The robin's eye had in it a gleam of cunning. Emily put a shilling in his hand, and was conducted into the icy church and the dark vestry, where the verger produced a volume filled with beautiful copper-plate entries. Emily read all those for recent years. Katina was there, under the name of Carew, but no Francis.

'Thank you,' she said, 'I must have been mistaken.' The old man watched her curiously as she went out, then began his daily dusting and laying-out of service-books.

She was shaking so much that she had to sit down on a table tomb. She had had no proper breakfast, only some coffee and a roll. The thin grass and lichened stones began to spin round her, and she clasped her hands together until they hurt to stop herself fainting. At last she felt able to stand. But where to go? Ann Connor might be anywhere. Elena Denis had left England. Covent Garden was nearby, but there would be nobody at the Theatre to ask at that hour of the morning.

Suddenly she rose and went back into the church, to the surprise of the verger, and dropped upon her knees in a rear pew. She had not prayed consciously since the early days of her false vocation at Villefranche, when she had tried so hard to reach a heaven which was not for her. At once she knew that she was not beating at a closed door. *'Voce mea ad Dominum,'* she whispered into her hands; 'I will cry unto God with my voice, and he shall hearken unto me.'

Was it wholly wrong, irreverent and blasphemous, to remember the words of Mary in the Garden? 'They have taken away my Lord, and I know not where they have laid him.' She hoped she would be forgiven for recalling them. Then, calmer, she made her way back to the Golden Cross. About to enter the inn door, something made her turn away up the Strand, to the place where she had been so happy and so unfortunate, where she might be able to think of Francis as he had been.

The house was unchanged, tall and shabby, the varying curtains at its windows advertising that it was still let out in lodgings. Gulls were crying, circling round something on the river at the foot of the street. In front of the house opposite, a tabby cat which Emily was sure she remembered was washing itself. But for the winter air, all was much as it had been nine years before. On an impulse she pulled the bell of the rooms where their landlady had lived, but though she heard it jangling inside the house nobody answered. The door yielded to a push. Emily went in. A child was crying somewhere, but otherwise all was quiet. Feeling foolish, she began to climb the stairs up to what had been, so briefly, her home. Since she could not find his grave, she would see again the place where she had last seen him alive.

At the door of the room she paused, then knocked timidly, prepared to make some excuse if the tenant proved too formidable. 'I lived here once; I left something behind, a trinket. I wondered if it had been found . . . I am sorry to disturb you.'

There was a pause before a key turned in the lock, and Francis opened the door.

For a year, nine years, an eternity, they stood staring at each other, white-faced and aghast. Then Emily reeled and fell into the arms of her dead lover – arms that were living, warm and strong, that lifted her and carried her to the bed, where she lay gasping and sobbing, saying his name over and over, while he kissed her and wept too, and they talked incoherently between kisses.

'I thought you were dead. I was told so.'

'I lost you. I was away so long, and when I came back Lady Hamilton was gone. Nobody knew anything.'

'I went to see – oh, I went to see your grave. I can't believe you're alive. Francis. Francis!' Over and over again she touched his face, very brown and much thinner, and the greying hair, longer than it had been. There were deep lines of experience on his brow and around his mouth, a livid scar from the right ear to the cheekbone; only the beautiful eyes of dark amber were unchanged. It was a long time before either of them was calm enough to talk coherently. Then he gently raised her, put cushions at her back, took off her pelisse and bonnet, poured a glass of wine and put it to her lips. As she drank it her eyes never left his face. 'Where have you been?' she asked. 'I came here – just to look at the place again. I never thought – never expected . . .'

'A miracle must have brought you. I only came back to London a week ago from Cheshire. My father is dead and I've had to help my brother settle his affairs. They were in a terrible muddle because of my absence, though Jack did his best. I came up to see a London lawyer who was handling part of the estate, and something drew me back here. God's hand has brought us together again.'

She was still stroking his face, kissing him, persuading herself by touch that she was not dreaming. 'What is this on your hair?'

'Is the stuff not off yet? It's grease, grease and flour. You would scarcely have known me with a pigtail, my love.' He began to tell her his story, from the day of the press-gang arrest up to the summer of 1814 when he and his shipmates were paid off after the capture of Bonaparte. 'It was to save taxes, not from any kind feelings towards us poor fellows. Otherwise I might have found myself sailing round the world for ever, like Vanderdecken. Now, don't ask me to relate all my adventures, for I assure you they were much the same as any ordinary seaman's, and consisted mostly of endless tedium at sea, waiting for the enemy that never came, or squandering our pay in port.'

'That scar. Did you get *that* in port?'

'A bit of flying shot, no more. We had the occasional skirmish. I believe that one was in a dogfight with the Yankees. I am not in the least a hero, Emy, and I suspect you have more to tell me than I you.'

Leaning back against his shoulder, she began. He heard the account of her attack in silence, then broke out. 'God! That evil woman. I wish I'd killed her before she could do such a thing. Who in the devil's name told her about you, and where to find you?'

'I don't know. I have tried not to think of it. But now – Francis, I believe it must have been Ann Connor.'

'Ann Connor. There were so many Connors. Was she that haughty creature who was at Clarges Street with you and her ladyship? I always fancied she had an eye for me.'

'I believe now that she was bitterly jealous. Of me, of you – who knows? Because it was she who wrote me the letter saying you were dead.' She told him the rest of her story. When she had finished it he passed his hand across his brow, and Emily saw that it was damp with sweat.

'So you might have become a nun, all because of that lying bitch. But why did you not write to Elena? She had told you of that – of my wife's death. You would have learned from her that it was all a pack of wicked lies. I could almost be angry with you.'

'It sounded so convincing, I had no choice but to believe it, and I think I must have gone a little out of my mind, for the thought of joining a sisterhood fills me now with absolute horror.'

'So I should hope. But at least it kept you from marrying.'

'Yes.' She said nothing of Colin; that was something to be dealt with later. Francis took her hands and held her at arm's length. 'How pretty you are! Prettier than ever, I do believe.' She laughed up at him.

'Nonsense. I am getting old, and quite plain. I decided only last night that I ought to take to a cap and shawl.'

'Pray don't let me see you in them, then. Have you looked in the glass lately? You are more like your mother than ever you were.' He kissed her. 'Now I am going to be serious, Emy. I have not been faithful to you.' He felt her tremble. 'It may seem cruel to tell you this, but there must be no deceit between us two, and I know you're no missish prude. I have known many women in these last years, the kind of women you could not even begin to imagine. I dare say I have left a child or two in Port of Spain or Leghorn. No, you must listen to me. I have done many things, but there are two things I have not done. One, I have never offered marriage. Two, I have never caught the pox. The second was good luck, the first was deliberate, for I could have had a sea-wife in every port in spite of being – God help me – a married man in England. Do you understand me, Emy?'

Shaken, she nodded.

'I tell you this to prove to you that although I never thought to set eyes on you again – for all I knew you were married or even dead – I held you in my heart, kept a kind of faith with you, just as you did with me.

'So you see, you fell in love with a romantic young parlour performer who has become a man. I shall never sing pretty ballads to duchesses in drawing-rooms again. I've seen things too

364

ugly for your eyes, and heard things I can never repeat to you, and spoken things I hope I may never say in my sleep. I used to be bitter, at first, because I thought my life was ruined, but now I know I would never have become God's great gift to music. John Braham may hold the palm, and good luck to him. At least I've come back to you, unlike poor Nelson, with all my limbs and both my eyes. Do you mind me as I am?' He tilted her chin and made her look at him.

For answer she began to unfasten his shirt. He stopped her hand. 'What are you doing?'

'I want you to love me. Now.'

'Why? No, be still. Why?'

Her head was bent. 'To prove – that I don't mind.'

He kissed the top of her head and gently disengaged her fingers. 'No. It's not necessary. All in good time. Emily, will you marry me?'

'Yes, oh yes. But please let it be very soon, for I think it would kill me to lose you again.'

She lay in his arms that night, happy beyond belief. 'Am I a disappointment to you, after all those others?' she whispered.

'Do you need to ask? There was one thing none of them could give me.'

'What was that?' But she knew the answer.

'Love.'

Tightening her arms round him, she felt him wince and draw a sharp breath. 'What is it, dearest? Have I hurt you?'

'It's nothing.' Her fingers were exploring his shoulders, and she gasped at what she found. 'Turn over to the light,' she said. 'I want to see. You know I shall have to know, now or another time.' He sighed, and rolled over so that the candlelight showed her his back, from waist to hairline, criss-crossed with white weals, the scars of deep cuts that would never fade.

'Francis! What in the name of God are these?'

'My dear one, very few sailors escape a flogging now and then.' His voice was deliberately light. 'I was remarkably incompetent in my duties at first, and so I incurred quite a few.

There's nothing to cry for, love. It was so long ago, and really I have forgotten it.' Forgotten it, indeed! What an expert liar one had to become where women were concerned. Never until the day he died would he forget.

Emily was weeping, her cheek damp against his shoulder. 'How cruel life has been to you and me!'

'So it is to everyone. We are no different. Try to forget now. The bad times are over – think of what has to come. No more governessing for you and no more sailoring for me. Jack, God bless him, has managed my father's mill so well that he and I and our workpeople will be as prosperous as parsons if the peace lasts; and when my father's estate is settled there will be a fair bit of capital. Jack and Father started a model village for the workers, in the valley where the mill stands, and I intend to complete it. There's no reason for them to live like pigs, as the poor hands in Manchester do. I'll have no women and child slaves working in my mill, I can tell you.'

'I shall teach the children,' Emily said happily. 'Music and French and housewifery—'

'And algebra and the use of the globes. Pray do, if you have any time left from teaching your own children,' he said. 'Now stop chattering and go to sleep, because tomorrow I intend to take you home.'

They were married in the tiny, beautiful Norman church which looked across a reedy mere where swans floated towards their home, a manor-house of Elizabeth's time, serene in its glory of black timbers and snowy plasterwork, its many diamond-paned windows flashing back light to the sun: a madrigal of a house. Together they walked, hand in hand, from the church. Emily wore a new dress of a blue that matched her eyes, and a white bonnet; Francis said that she looked like an exotic kitten from the Indies. In the cobbled courtyard he lifted his bride and carried her over the threshold into the cool high-arched hall, where Carew portraits watched them from the walls in quiet greeting.

366

But upstairs, in the great chamber which was theirs, Emily shook her head at the Tudor lady who stared stiffly from the panel above the fireplace. 'I'm afraid she will have to come down, love,' she said.

'I knew you would think so,' said Francis. 'I have already taken care of it. From a chest by the bed he took a picture, small in itself but surrounded and glorified by a new frame of gilded wood carved with flowers of every kind, and among them tiny wild creatures, mice, rabbits, birds – bringing back to Emily's mind her vision. 'Forgive me, madam,' he said to his ancestress, and taking her down he put the Reynolds sketch in her place. It was only fitting that his children should come into the world and grow up under the tender eyes of Emma, holding for ever in her lap the baby who had been Emily.

POSTSCRIPT

Readers interested in the factual aspects of this story might care to know that Horatia Nelson married the Reverend Philip Ward, vicar of Tenterden, and died in 1881, at Pinner, Middlesex, where she is buried in Paine's Lane Cemetery. (The phrase 'Adopted daughter of Lord Nelson' was much later altered to 'Beloved daughter' : the only acknowledgment of her parentage that Horatia ever received.)

'Little Emma', or Charley, is buried in the churchyard of St Margaret's, Blackheath, together with Eliza and Thomas Seaman and the Bunn family.

Simon Denis, husband of Elena, died in Naples in 1813, in circumstances suggesting poison.

Emilie de Rodat founded the Congregation of the Holy Child soon after her parting from Emily, and became the founder of over two hundred religious houses all over the world.

And Emily herself is said to have died in Bath in 1877.